Workplace Romance:

A Christmas
Date

TAWNY WEBER

TINA BECKETT

SHARON KENDRICK

MILLS & BOON

First Published in Great Britain 2024
by Mills & Boon, an imprint of HarperCollins*Publishers* Ltd,
1 London Bridge Street, London, SE1 9GF

www.harpercollins.co.uk

HarperCollins*Publishers*
Macken House, 39/40 Mayor Street Upper,
Dublin 1, D01 C9W8, Ireland

Workplace Romance: A Christmas Date © 2024 Harlequin Enterprises ULC.

Naughty Christmas Nights © 2013 Tawny Weber
The Nurse's Christmas Gift © 2016 Harlequin Books S.A.
The Sheikh's Christmas Conquest © 2015 Sharon Kendrick

Special thanks and acknowledgement are given to Tina Beckett for her contribution to the *Christmas Miracles in Maternity* series.

ISBN: 978-0-263-39667-6

Printed and Bound in the UK using 100% Renewable Electricity
at CPI Group (UK) Ltd, Croydon, CR0 4YY

NAUGHTY CHRISTMAS NIGHTS

TAWNY WEBER

To my awesome brothers, Ron and Kevin!

I love you guys.

Prologue

HOLIDAYS SUCKED.

Gage Milano had no issue with the *idea* of a holiday. Celebrations were great. Kinda like parties, which he rocked. Or remembering and commemorating events, which showed respect. Gage was all for respect.

But holidays?

Holidays meant family.

Obligation.

That freaking heritage crap.

Gage looked up from his plate. Crystal glinted, china gleamed. Ornate flower arrangements in fall tones lined the center of the rosewood table big enough to seat two dozen people. Which was twenty-one more than were sitting here now.

Stupid.

There was a perfectly sized, comfortable table in the breakfast room. But no. Couldn't eat Thanksgiving dinner in the breakfast room. Not because it wasn't fancy enough. Nope. Gage figured it was because his father was still trying to drive home the fact that in the Milano dynasty, he still had the biggest…table.

Marcus Milano was all about who was biggest. Best. Holding the most control. Something he loved, probably more than his sons. He'd taught Gage and Devon to be fierce competitors. From playing T-ball to pitching deals, he'd set the bar high and dared both his sons to accept nothing but a win. Unfortunately, with two of them, that meant one of them was always losing. Something Marcus always found a way to capitalize on.

As if hearing Gage's thoughts and ready to prove them right, Marcus looked up from his perfectly sliced turkey and portion-controlled serving of carbs to bellow down the table.

"Gage. New venture for you to take on."

Ahh, dinnertime demands. The Milano version of conversation.

"No room." Gage scooped up a forkful of chestnut dressing and shot his father a cool smile. "I'm in meetings with my own clients next week, then I'm on vacation."

"Make room," Marcus barked. "I want this account."

Ahh, the joys of being under the cozy family umbrella. Gage might be thirty years old, have a rep as a marketing genius, be the VP of a Fortune 500 company and own his own marketing start-up, which was quickly racking up enough success that he'd be forced to make some decisions soon.

But in his father's mind he was still at the old man's beck and call. There to do the guy's bidding.

It wasn't that Gage didn't appreciate the opportunities Milano had afforded him. But dammit, the company's success was as much because of him as anyone else. When he and Devon had come on board six years previous, it'd been sinking under the economic collapse. Between Devon's restructuring and Gage's marketing, they'd turned it around.

The old guy didn't see it that way, though. To him, he was Milano and his sons simply adjuncts.

Gage glared down the table. Pointless, since his father was nearsighted and too far away to notice. Not that he'd care if he could. Marcus Milano had built his rep on not giving a damn. So Gage shifted his anger across the table at his brother.

Devon, his black hair and blue eyes the spitting image of their father, only grinned.

"You're the king of the sales pitch, little brother. You know how we depend on you for these special projects."

Devon was also the king of bullshit.

"I don't have time," Gage repeated, his words delivered through the teeth of his own smile. "I've been going full speed ahead for six quarters with no break. When I signed that multimillion-dollar deal last month for the electronics division, we all agreed I was off the books until the end of the year."

Five weeks away from Milano. Time to chill, to relax. Hightail it to the Caribbean, where he could lie on the beach, chug the booze and check out the babes. And think.

Think about his future.

Think about leaving Milano.

Weigh the risks of going out on his own.

The old man had built a multipronged business with its fingers in various consumer pies. Milano made everything from tech to textiles. Devon was R & D, Research & Development. He came up with the ideas, put together whatever new product he thought would reel in more coin for the very full Milano coffers.

Gage was marketing. He could sell anything. Water to a drowning man. Silicone to a centerfold. Reality to the paranoid.

He knew people. What made them tick, what turned them on.

A trait that served him well, in business and in pleasure.

A trait that told him that getting away from this dinnertime trap was going to be one helluva feat.

"Off the books except in an emergency," Marcus said

around his mouthful of oyster stuffing. "This is an emergency."

"An emergency is pictures of Devon doing a donkey being displayed on the cover of *People* magazine. An emergency is the accounting department being caught using our computer system to embezzle from a foreign government or your last wife showing up pregnant, claiming the baby is yours. Whatever new product you want to peddle isn't a marketing emergency."

"I say it is."

Gage ground his teeth. Before he could snap, his brother caught his eye.

"Look, it's an easy deal," Devon said quietly, forking up a slice of turkey and swirling it through his buttery puddle of potatoes. "We're launching that lingerie line. The merchandise is ready. We just need a platform. Marketing came up with a great idea."

"Then why do you need me?"

"You know Rudolph department stores?"

"Dirty old man with the Midas touch and a handful of elite stores in California and New York?"

"That's the one. His spring fashion launch is an exclusive deal guaranteed to put any line he includes on the map. He's never missed. Whether it's because he has a keen eye or because the fashion industry is a bunch of lemmings, waiting for him to call the next trend, I don't know. But if we get that lingerie contract, Milano is gold in the fashion field."

Gage shook his head. He was a marketing consultant. He specialized in consumer branding, digital management and online strategic development. Nothing in that description said anything about talking to eccentric billionaires about women's underwear.

"Seriously, it's not going to take up more than a few days of your time. Rudolph is announcing his choices next weekend, and the contract will be signed and delivered before Christmas. You go in, make the deal and leave." Before Gage could point out that anyone could go in and pitch this, Devon dropped his voice even lower and added, "You can even add the time you lose on this to the New Year. You'll still get your five weeks off."

"This isn't about the time off." Even though that was a part of it. "It's about respecting our agreement."

"Look, I've had to set aside my projects to take on this new online store the old man wants to launch. It's not going to kill you to hit the beach a few days—or even a week— later than you'd planned."

So that was it. Lifting his pilsner glass, Gage gave his brother a dark look. Someday, one of them was going to be at the helm of Milano. The question was, which one? Marcus had made it clear that to run the company, his sons had to do three things: Be absolutely loyal. Prove they were more worthy than the other. And not piss him off.

Gage and Devon had realized a few years back that it was going to take building their own business success separate from Milano to prove their worth. The trick, of course, was doing that while not jeopardizing rules one and three. And more important, doing it faster and better than the other brother.

Or in Devon's case, while sabotaging the other brother's chances of doing it first.

"You're playing dirty," Gage said decidedly.

"I'm playing to win."

"What're you two muttering about down there?"

"We're talking about our tradition of breaking the wish-bone," Gage shot back, not taking his eyes off Devon. "I'm thinking we should sweeten the pot. In addition to the 10K for the winner, I think the loser can take on this new project of yours."

Devon's grin slipped. He couldn't talk his way around a

wishbone bet. There were no cards to slip out of his cuffs. It was a straight-on deal with lady luck. And of the two of them, Gage always had better luck with the ladies.

"Fine. You win, I take the deal. But if I win, I get to pick your costume for the Christmas party this deal requires you to attend."

Gage grimaced.

A Christmas costume party? What the hell kind of joke was this?

Appetite gone, he shoved his plate away.

Yeah. He hated the holidays.

1

HAILEY NORTH LOVED the holidays.

All the glitter and fun. Smiling faces glowing with joy, the secrets and excitement. And the gifts. Gifts and surprises always rocked. Especially hard-earned ones, presented at a fancy dress-up ball. Or, in this case, a ballroom packed with the rich and influential of the Northern California fashion scene all dressed up like holiday cartoons.

She should be ecstatic. Over-the-moon excited.

Tonight she'd finally be sure that her lingerie company wouldn't be joining Father Time in waving goodbye at the end of the year.

Instead, she was afraid the past couple of months of financial worries and stress over keeping her company had sent her over the edge into Crazyville.

Here she was surrounded by male models and wealthy designers, many of the most gorgeous specimens of the opposite sex to be found in the Bay Area. And it was the six-and-a-half feet of green fur, snowshoes and a bowling-pin shaped body across the room that was making her hot.

Hailey squinted just to be sure.

Nope. There was absolutely nothing enticing about the costumed guy at the bar. But sex appeal radiated off him like a tractor beam, pulling her in. Turning her on.

Green fur, for crying out loud.

Wow. Month after month of no sex really did a number on a healthy woman's libido.

Or maybe it was a year dedicated to the objective of making romance sexy. Of studying romantic fantasies, and finding ways to tastefully re-create them in lingerie form and show women that as long as they felt sexy, they were sexy.

Or, possibly, it might have something to do with the glass of champagne she'd knocked back for a little social courage when she'd walked into a ballroom filled with high-powered movers and shakers, most of whom had more money in their wallets than she had in her bank account. And all of them here to impress Rudy Rudolph, a department-store tycoon with a wicked sense of fun and prized openings in his new spring fashion lineup.

She glanced at her empty champagne flute, then at the bar. She should trade this in for something nonalcoholic. Something that didn't make her go tingly over green, grouchy holiday figures.

Then the Grinch pushed back his fur to check the time. When the hairs on his fingers caught on his leather watchband, he yanked off the gloves in an impatient move, tossing them on the bar.

Thirst forgotten, Hailey stared at his hand as he reached for his own drink. Long and lean, with tapered fingers. Even from across the room, his palm looked broad. Her mind played through every hand-to-penis-size euphemism she'd ever heard and came up with the only conclusion possible.

The Grinch was hung.

The only question was, did he go for cute elves? Or was he strictly a man-and-his-dog kind of guy? Maybe she should have dressed up like a Who?

She'd taken two steps toward him, her body desperate to find out, before she caught herself.

No. She was here for business.

She peered at the baggy, saggy, furry back and grimaced. Not for fun. No matter how big the fun's hands were.

"Hailey, darling."

Relieved, both at the distraction from lusting after the Grinch and at there actually being someone here who knew her name, Hailey turned.

Her social smile shifted to genuine delight at the sight of the man who'd made this night possible for her. Jared Jones, assistant to the wealthiest—and most eccentric—tycoon in the department-store business.

Jared had taken her under his wing last summer when they'd met in an elevator. Hailey had been on her way to pitch her lingerie designs to the sales team and Jared had been bemoaning a rip in his shirt. Before they'd reached the sixth floor, she'd pulled out some fabric tape for a temporary mend, earning his gratitude and his endless devotion.

Apparently, a fashion faux pas was, to some, the end of the world.

"Jared," she greeted, leaning in for a hug but careful not to let him bump her head. It'd taken her twenty minutes to get the bell-festooned elf hat pinned to her curls in a way that didn't make her hair look like fluffy poodle ears.

"I love your gingerbread-man costume. Is that your favorite holiday character?" she asked, flicking her finger on one of his cheerful, oversize buttons. Her eyes widened before she laughed aloud as she noted the words *Eat Me* etched on the red plastic.

"Edible goodness, that's me," he said with a wink. Then he shifted his head to the left and gave a little wag of his chin. "And if all goes well, that drummer boy over there will be having a taste before the night is out."

Used to Jared's aggressive sexuality by now, Hailey

gave the drummer an obligatory once-over before sharing an impressed look with her horny gingerbread friend.

"But look at you," he gushed, his loud enthusiasm aimed as much at getting the drummer's attention as it was appreciation for Hailey's costume. "You know, I've seen at least a dozen elves tonight, but you're the best by far. You look fabulous. Is everything you're wearing straight from your lingerie line?"

"Everything but the skirt," Hailey confirmed, arms wide as she gave a slow turn to show off the goods. Her candy-cane-striped bustier with its red satin trim and white laces paired nicely with her red stockings and their white seams up the back that ended in clever bows just below the hem of her green tulle ballerina skirt. She was proof positive that the right lingerie could make any woman feel sexy.

Nothing like a year in the gym, a carb-elimination diet and a great tan to make a girl look damned hot in lingerie.

Too bad she'd only hit the gym maybe four times in the past twelve months, loved carbs like she loved her momma and was closer to winter-white than sun-kissed tan.

But that was the beauty of Merry Widow lingerie. A girl didn't have to have a supermodel body to look—and feel—fabulous in it.

"Oh, darling," Jared breathed in admiration as he completed his inspection.

Hailey didn't have to follow his gaze to know where he was staring. After all, the guy might not be interested in what her lingerie was covering, but he was all about fashion.

And her boots were pure fashion candy.

The white Manolo booties were an early Christmas present from her father. Well, not really *from* him, since he never knew what to get her. But she'd bought them last month with the holiday check he'd sent, so that made them his gift to her.

"Hailey, you have the best taste in footwear," he sighed. "Those boots are perfect. And such a great touch to bring the outfit from cute to couture."

"Thanks. Will Mr. Rudolph be arriving soon?" she asked, shifting from one foot to the other. She wiggled her toes in her most excellent boots as a reminder that a girl could handle anything if she was wearing fabulous footwear. "Since he's announcing his choices for the spring exclusives, shouldn't he do it before all the designers are drunk?"

While she was still tipsy enough to use getting one of those prized exclusives as an excuse to seduce the Grinch.

"Drunk designers only add to Rudy's sense of fun," Jared told her with a sly grin. He didn't say a word about the contracts, though. She knew he knew who'd been chosen. And he knew she knew. But they both knew she wouldn't ask.

"Quit obsessing," Jared said, giving her a nudge with his shoulder and leaving a streak of glitter on her arm.

"Maybe you should see if the drummer boy's sticks are worth checking out." She tilted her head toward the guy he'd been scoping. "I can't clear my head enough to be fun company."

"Darling, I'm here to enjoy the party with my favorite designer. If there was anything I could do to set your mind at ease so you could give the party the appreciation it deserves, I would. But you know me—I don't kiss and tell."

Giving in to her nerves, and reminding herself that she'd taken a cab here, Hailey traded her empty champagne glass for a full one, then arched one brow at Jared.

"Okay. So I don't spill company secrets." He hesitated, then wrinkled his nose and leaned closer. "At least not the ones that could get me fired."

Then he looked past her again. This time when his face

shifted, it wasn't into lustfully suggestive lines. Instead, he came to attention.

"I don't think the news will be secret for long, though," he told her, twirling his finger to indicate she turn herself around.

"Welcome, welcome."

Hailey, along with the rest of the ballroom, turned around and came to the same subtle attention that Jared had as a skinny Santa took the stage with two helpers dressed in swaths of white fur and a whole lot of skin.

She leaned forward, peering at the trio. The nerves in her stomach stopped jumping for a few seconds as she stared in shock. "Wow. Mr. Rudolph sure looks different without his tie."

Or maybe it was the fact that the pervy old guy was shirtless under his plush red jacket. Wasn't he in his seventies? Now, that wasn't a pretty sight. Afraid to look at it too long, in case it rendered her blind, Hailey glanced at the rest of the crowd. Nobody else seemed surprised.

"Thank you, everyone," he said, "for joining the Rudolph-department-store annual holiday costume party. As you can see, my favorite character is Santa Claus. Appropriate since I'm the man giving out the gifts tonight."

Fingernails digging into the soft flesh of her palms, Hailey puffed out a breath, trying to diffuse the nerves that'd suddenly clamped onto her intestines.

This was it. The big announcement.

She felt like throwing up.

"This year, instead of simply awarding spring women's-line contracts, I've decided to make things fun. I've chosen two favorite designers in each department. Women's wear, shoes and lingerie. Those designers will compete through the holiday season for the top spot."

Hailey's stomach fell. Competing? That didn't sound good. She wasn't the only one who thought so, either, if the muttering and hisses circling the room were anything to go by.

She gave Jared a puzzled look, trying to shrug off the sudden despair that gripped her. The contracts weren't being awarded tonight? But she needed to know. Without that contract, she was going to lose her business.

Jared ignored her stare, tilting his head pointedly to get her to pay attention.

She dragged her gaze to the stage with a frown. Instead of looking abashed, the old man seemed delighted by the angry buzz. His grin shifted from wicked to a visual cackle as he held up one hand for silence.

It took all of three seconds for him to be obeyed.

"So without further ado, here are the finalists in women's wear," he announced. A model featuring an outfit from each line crossed the stage behind him as he named the designer.

Hailey swallowed hard, trying to get past the tight worry in her throat. It wasn't as if she'd irresponsibly put all of her hopes on this deal. It was more a matter of everything else falling apart until this deal was all that was left to hope for.

She shifted from one foot to the other, trying to appreciate the gorgeous shoes as Rudolph announced the designer finalists for footwear. But not even the studded black leather stilettos could distract her worry.

Then he got to lingerie.

She didn't even listen to the names.

She just watched the models, her eyes locked with desperate hope on the curtain they entered from.

One strutted out in a wickedly sexual invitation in leather. It was the complete opposite of the Merry Widow's style, a look that screamed sex. Hot, kinky sex.

Hailey frowned. It wasn't her style, of course. But it was appealing. *If you like hot, kinky sex.*

Did she like hot, kinky sex? She'd never had the opportunity to find out. For a second, she wondered if the Grinch was into leather. Before she could imagine that, worry crowded the sexy thoughts right back out of her brain. She held her breath.

"And last but not least, Merry Widow Lingerie." Echoing the announcement was a model in a white satin chemise trimmed in tiny pink rosebuds, a design Hailey had labeled Sweet Seduction.

Fireworks exploded in her head, all bright lights, loud booms and overwhelming excitement.

"Ohmygod, ohmygod, ohmygod," she chanted, hopping up and down in her gorgeous booties. She spun around to grab Jared in a tight hug, then did another little dance. "That's me. That's me. I made it."

She made it. She had a chance.

An hour later, she was still giddy. It wasn't a contract, but it wasn't a rejection, either. And she'd learned young to take what she could get.

"This is so cool." Ever since Santa Rudolph's announcement, people kept coming up to congratulate her. That part was great. What was even better, though, were the compliments about her designs, which were displayed all around the room.

She felt like a rock star.

"I'm excited for you, darling. I am sorry it's not a definitive answer, though," Jared said quietly, his face taking on a rare seriousness. "I know how bad you need this deal, and I've been pitching hard for you. But Rudy got this wild notion that a contest would bring in more publicity and make it more fun. He'll decide before the New Year, though. He has to for marketing purposes."

"What kind of publicity?" Big publicity? Good publicity? Could it net her some new clients, maybe a few features in the fashion rags? Hailey's stomach danced again.

"Well…" Jared drew out, wrinkling his glittery nose. "I

honestly don't think he has a lot of publicity lined up. We were all under the impression that he was simply choosing a single designer for each line. But Friday he talked to some marketing guru who convinced him that it'd bring in great promotion if he made it a competition of some sort instead of a straight-up announcement."

"Who makes the final decision?" she wondered.

Jared pulled another face and shrugged. Clearly he didn't like not being in the know any more than she didn't like not having a clue.

But before Hailey could ask more questions, they were joined by a dapper-looking guy dressed like a festive reindeer with his green-and-red-plaid bow tie.

"Congratulations, Ms. North. I'm Trent Lane, the photographer for Rudolph department stores. I was happy to see your designs in the running. I've taken test shots of each submission and yours is my favorite."

"Really?"

"Really. It seems to epitomize romance. But sexy romance. The boudoir-photo kind, not the *Hustler*-spread kind."

Hailey giggled, wondering if the leather getups were *Hustler* material.

"It's my favorite, too," Jared agreed. "I told you when I first saw the line. It's perfect. Next season is all about nostalgia with overtones of passion. Bridal fresh but womanly confident."

Hailey wrinkled her nose, wondering if he realized he'd just described her gorgeous designs in the same terms used for feminine-hygiene products.

"Baby's breath and air ferns lining the runway. Satin backdrops. Maybe one of those long couch things, like Cleopatra would lounge on," Trent mused, falling into what she immediately saw was a creative brainstorming habit between him and Jared.

"A chaise. Perfect," Jared agreed. Tapping his chin, he added, "Maybe carried down the runway by four muscle-bound sex slaves?"

"That's not romantic," Trent dismissed. "You know Rudy really wants to lead the trend this season. If you suggest sex slaves, he might seriously consider Cassia Carver's mesh love sleeves for a part of the women's-wear line."

Hailey barely kept from shuddering. Avant-garde minis and maxis made up most of Cassia's line, and while they were edgy and fun, they would hardly compliment Merry Widow's lingerie. They would, she realized with a frown, go great with Milano's leather.

Suddenly the simple contract she'd thought she'd have was now even more complicated. All of the choices were going to have to flow together into a single, cohesive spring debut.

"Even if Rudy wants mesh and love slaves, there's no way marketing will go for it," Jared dismissed. "They'd bury him in the horrible sales data from the last time mesh hit the runway."

Oh, yay. A point in her favor. She just had to make sure she racked enough to win this baby. Hailey held her breath, willing herself to look invisible. Maybe if the two men forgot she was there, they'd spill some insider info that she could mop up and use.

"Well, Rudy wants Cherry Bella to model the entire spring line, and Merry Widow will look perfect on her."

Hailey couldn't contain her little *eep* of excitement.

Her designs? Perfect? Cherry Bella?

Oh, man. That shooting star was getting close enough that she could almost feel the heat.

"She'd look great in Merry Widow or Milano's," Trent agreed. "It's really going to come down to whichever line Cherry wants to wear. She'll be the final judge of all the lines, I'm guessing."

"Rudy has to get her signed first. And so far, she's not interested."

Trent looked to the left. Jared and Hailey looked, too. Then he looked to the right. They obediently followed his gaze. Forgetting that she was supposed to be invisible, Hailey leaned in just as close as Jared did to listen.

"I hear Rudy's pulling out all the stops. He's crazy to get Cherry signed. He's tried everything. Promised her the moon. So far, no go. He's shifted all his promises to her agent now." Trent gave them both a wide-eyed look, then nodded sagely, his reindeer ears bobbing in emphasis. "Whoever gets him Cherry Bella? They're golden."

Excitement ran so fast through Hailey's body, she shivered with it. Her lingerie was perfect for Cherry. The statuesque redhead had started as a soulful torch singer, but lately had branched into modeling and a few minor acting gigs, as well. Merry Widow's flowing, feminine designs would suit her as though they'd been custom made.

All Hailey had to do was cinch the deal.

She'd find Cherry's agent, charm him or her into listening to a personal pitch on how perfect Merry Widow designs would look on the retro singer.

"Do the other designers know?" she wondered aloud. Seeing the guys' arch expressions, she scrunched her nose and gave a shrug. What? They all knew she wasn't really invisible. "Just wondering."

"It's pretty hush-hush since a lot of competitors are always big to get a jump on Rudolph's spring debuts. So unless the other designers are chatting up Rudy's staff, I doubt they have a clue."

Jared's snort of laughter was more sarcastic than amused.

"Which means no," he explained at Hailey's questioning look, a little of the sugary glitter flaking off his face as he sneered. "Your competitors are all well established, with top-of-the-line reps, darling. They, unlike you, have huge egos. None of them see the need to fraternize with the help. They talk to Rudy, or they don't talk at all."

She peered through the costumed crowd, looking for any of the lingerie-clad models circling the room. She sighed as one lithe blonde floated by in a Merry Widow nightie. Cotton flowed. Lace rippled. The pearl buttons down the front caught the light, even as the delicate fabric molded to the woman's perfect body.

So romantic.

And so perfect for the Rudolph account, especially if he got Cherry as his spokesmodel.

She didn't want to jinx it but the little voice in her head was already planning the victory-dance moves.

"I'm surprised Cherry's agent isn't all over this deal," Hailey mused, wondering what they were holding out for. "A contract with Rudolph department stores would rocket her from national to international exposure, wouldn't it?"

"Oh, yeah," Jared agreed, looking like a dejected gingerbread boy with his furrowed brow. "We can't figure out what the problem is. Rudy'd be tearing his hair out if he wasn't already bald."

"Best we can figure, it's because the agency is one of those co-op places. The agents all work together on every client. Make decisions by consensus. We don't even know which agent is at the party. Guy, gal, nobody's got a clue," Trent complained, looking like a very grumpy reindeer whose gossip rations were being withheld. "Like I said, whoever reels her in is going to be golden."

Then a passing model dressed in a fishnet candy cane and spangles shaped like question marks caught his eye. He straightened his bow tie, gave Jared and Hailey an absent smile, then tilted his head. "Well, I think I'll go talk up the models and see if any of them are repped by the same agency as Cherry."

With that, and a leering sort of grin, he was gone.

"So what do you think? Do I have a shot?" Hailey asked as soon as he left. Her gaze flew around the room as if the infamous agent might have hung a neon sign around his or her neck, just for fun. If she could find the agent, she could pitch her own designs for Cherry. If she could get the agent enthused, she'd have an inside track. Maybe even a guaranteed deal.

Excitement bubbling, Hailey gave the room another searching look. Her gaze landed on Trent, who'd apparently given up on seducing the woman in mesh and was now talking to the sexy Grinch.

Her excitement took on a totally different edge at the sight of that Grinchy butt. The hood of the costume now pushed back, she could see his hair, so black it reflected the blue and white Christmas lights of the tree next to him, wave into the green fur of his collar.

Her nipples tingled against the tight satin layers of her bustier. Her thighs turned to mush, only the sheer red silk of her stockings holding them together.

Oh, yeah. He was definitely the hot, kinky, sexy type of guy.

All she had to do was look at him and she was more excited than she'd been with any of the lovers she'd ever had. Or even all of them, combined.

And all she was gazing at was the back of his head. That was better than being turned on by his furry back, wasn't it?

Her breath a little on the shallow side, she sighed and wondered how great it'd be to strip that ugly fur off and see what kind of body was beneath the costume. Could it be as sexy as she was imagining? Long and lean, with strong thighs and washboard abs? Shoulders she could cling to as she rode him like a wild stallion?

She'd just flown a few miles closer to catching her

shooting star. Didn't she deserve a treat? Could she do it? Go talk to him? Ask his opinions on hot, kinky sex. Leather or lace. Roses or studs.

Her face, throat and chest all on fire now, either with lust or embarrassment, Hailey quickly drank the rest of her champagne and exchanged the glass with a passing waiter, hoping the bubbles would cool the fire blazing in her belly.

"Hailey, darling? Where'd you go? I've been filling you in on all of the Rudolph stores' holiday plans and you haven't said a word. What's got you so distracted?"

Unwilling to admit the horrifying truth, that she was all hot and horny for a guy whom she'd only seen from the side and back, both of which were covered in puke-green fur, Hailey tore her gaze away and gave Jared an apologetic look.

"Nothing. Just, you know, wondering if that guy Trent's talking to might be Cherry's agent," she improvised.

Almost on tiptoes to see around the crowd, Jared peered in the direction of the bar. Then he gave a shrug.

"No clue." He looked again, this time giving a little hum of appreciation. His eyes were as wide as the buttons on the front of his gingerbread suit as he fanned one hand in front of his face. "I'll be happy to go find out, though."

She looked over again herself, wondering what had got his attention.

And almost fell to the floor, thanks to her weak knees.

Oh, baby.

The Grinch was gorgeous.

Her lust cells stood up and did a victory dance, vindicated in their attraction.

Her brain couldn't argue.

Because the man was definitely lust-worthy.

Raven-black hair swept back from his forehead in soft waves, framing a face that would make Michelangelo weep. Sharp planes, strong lines and intense brows were balanced by full lips and wide eyes. Even though she couldn't tell the color, she was sure those were the most gorgeous eyes she'd ever seen.

For the first time in forever, Hailey didn't know what she wanted more.

Success? Or the man across the room.

2

"THIS IS THE most ridiculous idiocy I've ever seen," Gage said decidedly, his glare spread equally across the ball-room at his cousin and at those butt-ugly green fur gloves he'd been forced to wear to this stupid party. "And what's with the babysitting duty, Trent? You lose a bet yourself?"

"More like blackmail," Trent muttered, watching yet an-other leggy blonde slink by with a regretful sigh. "Believe me, if I had a choice, I'd be long gone by now."

"Yeah? Well, so would I."

Once, a party like this would have appealed to Gage.

A bachelor's playground, complete with booze, babes and enough variety in the guest list to stave off boredom.

The requirement to dress like your favorite holiday character, though? That was where it all tipped right on over to idiocy.

Yet, here he was. Smothered in freaking fur. Didn't mat-ter that it was almost December. San Francisco didn't get cold enough to make this costume anything but miserable.

"How'd they con you into this?" Trent asked, craning his head to one side to watch a woman's leather-clad ass as she worked the crowd. Gage vaguely recognized it. The leather, not the ass. It was one of the new Milano designs. Sexy Biker Babe, Devon had called it. Stupid, really. It looked hot, and definitely sent a strong sexual message. But who wore leather lingerie?

He gave an absent scan of the room, measuring the crowd, the reactions. There were enough people eyeing the leather with an appreciative look, as opposed to the ones peering in confusion at the mesh dresses some models were suffering in.

The most admiration seemed to be for the lacy getups floating through the room, though. The kind of lace you'd see on a forties pinup model, rather than the kind you'd see on a favorite internet porn site. Classy, he supposed it'd be called.

Noticing his attention, a tall brunette in a tasteful teddy and floor-length robe in white satin with fluffy trim gave him an inviting look before she stopped to exchange comments with a guest. The model moved on.

But Gage's gaze was locked on the woman she'd spoken with.

Helloo.

Interest stirred for the first time since he'd heard of this party, Gage straightened.

She was blonde and cute, with an air of sweetness surrounding her like a holiday promise. The women he usually went for were dark, sultry and cynical. So what was it about her that made him want to sit up and beg?

Sure, she was sexy. But even though her costume was obviously lingerie inspired, she was still stepping pretty close to the sedate line. His type usually danced on the edge of the slutty line.

Yet he wanted nothing more than to cross the room, toss her over his shoulder and haul her off to someplace where he could lick her wild. Obviously this work overload and insane costume were taking a toll on his sanity.

"Gage?"

"Huh?" With one last look to assure himself that she

wasn't his type, he yanked his attention back to his cousin. "What?"

"I said, how'd you get stuck with this gig? I thought you were on vacation."

"The old man played the emergency card, deeming getting the Rudolph contract to launch this new project top priority." He wasn't about to admit that he'd pulled the short end of a wishbone. A guy could only take so much humiliation at a time.

Used to his uncle's games, Trent didn't seem surprised.

"You do well enough on your own. And you hate working for your father. Why don't you just resign?"

Good question.

"It's not that easy. Nor is it something I want to talk about at a party full of people in their underwear and me in green fur."

Or anywhere else, for that matter.

Not because he was so private.

But because he really didn't know himself.

Money was a major factor. He'd seen plenty of successful people sink under the weight of running their own show.

Loyalty was another. He might hate the dictatorial way Marcus Milano ran things, but it was still a family company founded by his grandfather. As far back as he could remember, his father had claimed that Milano was run by Milanos. And Milanos were expected to make it a success. So much so that if one left, he was out. Out of the company, off the board and in the case of Gage's uncle when he'd quit, disinherited and ostracized by the family.

And there was always the competition between him and Devon. Gage glared at the furry gloves again, damned if he'd lose to his brother in an even bigger way. When he went out on his own his start-up would be bigger, stronger, more successful than any and all of Devon's put together.

None of which were thoughts he was particularly proud of.

The perfect distraction, the pretty blonde elf caught his eye again. Her eyes were huge, so big they dominated her face. A cross between adorable and arousing, with full lips and round cheekbones both a glossy red to match her stockings. Gage's gaze dropped again to those legs. They were very excellent legs, long and lean. The sheer red hose and sexy little boots reminded him of a candy cane. An image echoed by the striped bustier hugging breasts so sweet they almost overflowed the tight fabric.

Gage rocked back on his heels, humming in appreciation.

She didn't belong here.

Her costume might.

Her party partner might.

And the holiday theme might.

But she looked too sweet to be interested in something as lame as this event.

So sweet he wanted to invite her to a private party. One where he could taste her, just there where the satin met that soft flesh, and see if she was as tasty as she looked. Like a delicious Christmas treat.

"So, hey, I've got instructions from Devon I've gotta follow." Trent's uncomfortably muttered words pulled Gage's attention away from the sexy blonde.

"You babysat, you probably took pictures to share on Facebook, and you verified that I stayed until the announcement." Gage was still irritated that the best he'd been able to get out of this deal was to be in the competition for the contract. Despite his best pitch, Rudolph hadn't been willing to set aside his initial favorites. "I've done my part. I'm done. Showing up in this stupid costume was the end of my assignment."

"Yeah, sure. But, well, my instructions were to wait until after the announcement, and if Milano was in the running for the contract, to issue a new bet." Trent looked a little ill at this point.

Gage laughed so loud, half the room glanced their way.

"Is that reindeer headgear pressing too tight into your brain? You really think I'm going to take another one of Devon's bets?"

"C'mon. You know he'll make my life hell if I don't follow through," Trent beseeched, looking so pitiful even his antlers drooped. "It's not a big deal. I just have to mention that there's a bet on the table, and give you this."

This, Gage found out when Trent pulled it from the inner pocket of his Fruit-Stripe-gum-colored jacket, was an envelope. "That's it?" Gage asked, gesturing with his gloves to the paper. The envelope was thick and black, and he figured his brother had been trying for ominous. The guy was a little too dramatic.

"This is it," Trent agreed, holding the envelope closer. When Gage didn't take it, he set it on the bar with a shrug. "My instructions were simply to make sure you knew there was a bet and to make it available if you were interested."

"You did, and I'm not."

"No skin off my nose," Trent dismissed. Now that he was free, he was more focused on catching the eye of one of the mostly naked women than trying to change Gage's mind. "I'll let Devon know you met the terms of the bet. Oh, and can you tell him I did offer you the insider info? He promised to burn the pictures of… Well, it won't matter what they are of after tonight."

If Trent's grin was anything to go by, the evidence Devon had used to blackmail him was probably wearing a wedding ring. And just for handing over an envelope, that evidence was getting burned?

Gage frowned at the heavy black paper. His brother wasn't the type to let go of blackmail material that easily.

Always resourceful, Devon figured good dirt was worth using at least twice.

So whatever plan Devon was playing, it was big.

"Hold on," he said through his teeth, snatching up the envelope and ripping the heavy paper aside. He read the thick, purple papers quickly, shock seeping through his irritation. Then he read through them once more to be sure the itchy green fur hadn't impaired his comprehension.

No way in hell…

"He's willing to let me go?"

Trent leaned closer to read the letter, then gave a shrug. "Is that what it says? He told me to assure you that he's not bullshitting." Seeing Gage's doubtful look, Trent plastered on his most earnest expression. It went pretty well with the antlers and bow tie, actually. "He didn't give me details, just told me what to say if you opened the letter."

"What are you? His windup toy?"

"Funny you should mention toys. That's actually what those pictures…" Grimacing, Trent shook his head. "So, you gonna take the bet?"

Gage considered his options.

Being the trusting soul he was, Marcus Milano hadn't just used the threat that he'd cut them off if they ever left, he'd contractually tied his sons to Milano's.

But if Gage got this contract, his brother would arrange for an entire year of freedom. With full pay. Gage could do whatever he wanted, without losing his safety net or walking out on family obligations. In exchange, he just had to seal this lingerie deal.

"You gonna fill me in on what it'll take to win this Rudolph contract?"

"Why? You don't have any pictures of me, three blondes and a battery-operated rabbit."

All Gage did was shift. Just an inch. His shoulders back. His spine straighter. His chin lifted.

Then he arched one brow.

Trent's grin wilted.

"Look, I don't know anything. And what I do know is mostly rumor. But it's company rumor, so I can't tell. Your games with Devon aren't worth my job."

Unfazed, Gage nodded.

"I win this bet, I'll be gone for a year," he mused, taking a second to revel in that vision. A whole year, free of Milano. To travel without a tightly controlled, money-making itinerary. No board meetings, no R & D meetings, no personnel meetings. Just him and his own business.

He eyed his cousin. Yeah. He wanted that dream. Enough to take the bet and to bump the stakes.

"I'm gone a year," he repeated, "I got two choices. Garage my 'Vette. Or let someone play car-sitter."

"Your 'Vette?" Trent's eyes glazed over as if he was having a personal moment. Then he shook his head. "No way."

"Way."

It didn't take two seconds before his cousin grabbed his hand to seal the deal.

Everyone had a price.

Gage listened as Trent babbled on about a torch singer, a weird old man's trend obsession and secret agents.

"So whoever gets this singer to wear their line is gonna get the deal?" he confirmed.

Trent nodded. "If you get Cherry Bella to wear your lingerie line, you nail the contract."

And win the bet.

"And you're saying her agent is here, at the party, scoping it out to decide if any of the designs are worthy?"

"That's what I hear."

Gage's gaze shifted across the room again to the blonde.

There was only one person here who didn't belong.

One very sexy, very tasty-looking person who seemed

out of place among the eccentric designers and the nar-
cissistic models.

If he had to guess who the agent was, and apparently
he did, he'd pick her.

And now that he'd picked her, he just had to charm her
into choosing Milano for her client.

"Not a problem," he decided.

This was going to be quite the treat.

Beat his brother.

Win a year's freedom.

And make some time with a very sexy blonde.

Looked as if this party wasn't quite as idiotic as he'd
thought.

HAILEY GULPED.

He was coming her way.

She'd lost count of how many glasses of champagne
she'd had. Enough to make her head spin. But the tingling
swirls going on right now had nothing to do with alcohol
and everything to do with the Grinch.

The oh-so-deliciously-sexy Grinch.

"Trent looks like someone just gave him the keys to a
houseful of horny women. I'm going to talk to him," Jared
decided, clearly oblivious to Hailey's tingles, swirls or
even her overheated cheeks. "I'll bet he figured out who
the agent is."

"Go, go," Hailey encouraged with a little wave of her
hand. She wasn't really shooing him away, so much as
making room for the Grinch.

"Oh, baby," she sighed as he stopped next to her. He
was even yummier up close and personal. A faint shadow
darkened his chin, making her wonder if he was one of
those guys blessed with a luxurious pelt of chest hair. She'd
always wanted to get close enough to a guy like that so
she could bury her face in the silky warmth and snuggle.

Her fingers itched to tug the zipper of his costume down and see for herself.

"Hello." The greeting was accompanied by a smile that, for all its charm, edged just this side of wicked.

His eyes were dark, so dark they seemed black in the party lights, with thick lashes and slashing brows. And they were staring at her with an intensity that made her want to check herself to make sure nothing had fallen out.

"Hi," she said, giving him a bright smile. At a delicate five-one, which was why the elf costume had been so inspired, she had to tilt her head back a little to see his face. Bells jingled. At first she wondered if that was a sign from Cupid. Then she remembered that it was Christmas, not Valentine's. And that she was wearing bells on her hat.

"I'm Gage," he murmured, taking her hand.

"Hailey," she said on a sigh as her fingers were engulfed by his. He was warm. Strong and gentle at the same time, and his skin felt so good she didn't want to pull away.

Her usual nerves at meeting a gorgeous, sexy man were nowhere to be found. Probably doing the backstroke through a river of champagne. But she wasn't drunk enough to do anything stupid, like unzip his costume with her lips right here in the middle of the ballroom.

After all, she didn't want hair between her teeth.

"What do you think of the party?" he asked, not taking those intense eyes off her as he tilted his head to indicate the room. It was as if he were looking past her cheerful smile and holiday bells into her soul, where he could peek at all of the secrets she hid there. Like her dreams. Her darkest, sexiest fantasies. And every single one of her fears.

That was both sexy as hell and the scariest thing she'd ever imagined.

"The party's great," she said, nerves starting to poke through the champagne bubbles. "I thought it was a fun theme, coming as your favorite holiday character. At least I did until I saw the guy dressed as a pair of Christmas balls waving his candy cane around."

The words echoed in Hailey's head as she realized what she'd said. Eyes wide with horror, she slapped her hand over her mouth. Not that she could take the words back, but maybe it'd help slow down the next stupid thing she tried to blurt out.

Gorgeous Gage the Grinch just laughed, though. A deep, full-bodied sound that eased her fear and made her grin right back. His gaze changed, softened, with his amusement. He was still sexy as all get-out, but now he seemed real. Not quite so much like a sexual fantasy sent to rip away all her inhibitions. More like an intriguingly attractive man who made her want to toss them away on her own.

"I guess I don't have to ask if you've been entertained by the various displays here this evening."

A movement across the room caught her eye. Hailey shifted her gaze, noting Jared, flanked by Trent and Mr. Rudolph, heading toward the door. He looked frantic, doing a subtle wave of his hand behind his boss's back and jerking his head around. Either he was trying to give her a message, or he was being hauled off against his will.

She tilted her head, trying to figure out what he was saying. Then she realized he was pointing at Gage and mouthing something. She gave a helpless shrug, totally clueless. His disgusted sigh came across loud and clear, though, then he held his hand to his ear, thumb and pinkie outstretched.

Call him.

Then, just as he was swept out the door by a jolly old man, he jabbed his fingers toward Trent.

"Looking for that pair of Christmas balls?" Gage teased.

"Oh, sorry," she said with an abashed grimace. "It's just

so distracting here. Like a circus, but instead of performing animals, it's a bizarre fashion statement, all wrapped in holiday tinsel."

"And you're not into bizarre?"

Hailey arched her brow. Why did that sound as if he'd just passed judgment and she'd somehow failed?

"Should I be?"

"Hardly. *Bizarre* generally means weird and confusing. I'm not a fan of confusion."

"And the holidays?" she asked, gesturing to his costume. "Are they high on your list, or is your heart three sizes too small?"

He opened his mouth, then shook his head and shut it with a grin. "I'll skip over any size comparisons, if you don't mind."

Delighted at his sense of humor, Hailey laughed.

"How about we leave size issues to my imagination and skip right to the holiday question," she said with an impish smile.

"Just as long as you have a good imagination."

"It's amazing."

"A lot of dreams?"

"Big ones," she assured him. "Huge, even."

He gave an appreciative grin, then at her arch look, it faded to a deep, considering stare before he shifted his gaze to the decorated trees and holiday props around the room.

"I don't have a problem with the holidays, per se," he admitted. The way he said it, slow and careful, as if he were measuring each word, told her that he was a man who valued honesty. He might dance around the truth. He might refuse to answer. But whatever he did say, he expected to be held to it.

That kind of integrity was even sexier than his gorgeous

smile. Maybe not sexier than his body, but she couldn't say for sure since it was still covered in lumpy green fur.

"But there are parts you're not crazy about," she guessed, trying to stay on topic and quit undressing him with her mind. Especially now that her imagination was using the word *huge* in all its naked images.

"Sure. But you have to take the bad to get the good, right?"

No. She wanted to shake her head. The bad might show up from time to time, but the whole point was to avoid it if possible. To think positive and flow with the good.

But she wasn't sure her Pollyanna-esque argument was going to get very far with a guy who favored the Grinch.

"So which good parts are your favorite?"

"The food," he mused, gesturing to the Mrs. Claus walking by with a tray of sugar cookies. "Gotta love the desserts this time of year."

A man after her own heart.

"But as good as those cookies look, I'll bet you're sweeter. Like the candy cane your outfit reminds me of. But instead of peppermint, you'd be cherry flavored."

His words were low and flirtatious, his eyes dancing and hot as his gaze swept over her body as if he wanted to taste her and see.

Hailey swallowed hard. She knew she was totally out of her league. But she didn't care.

It was as if she were drowning in desire, passion burning low in her belly with a heat she didn't think anything could douse. She sure was ready to let him try, though.

Then his words washed over her like a lifeline, tugging at her attention.

What had he said?

Cherry?

A bright light went off in Hailey's head, clearing away the foggy fingers of passion. Ooh, she smiled as excitement pushed back—but didn't in any way extinguish—the hot desire in her belly.

Jared must have been trying to tell her that Gage was the agent. The man to persuade that her designs were perfect for his client.

Seriously?

Hailey almost laughed out loud.

First her designs were chosen as semifinalists.

Then the sexiest man she'd ever seen hit on her.

And now she had to do everything and anything in her power to make him crazy about her lingerie?

It was all Hailey could do to keep from clapping her hands together in delight.

This night rocked.

3

"So you don't seem like a designer or model," Hailey said, sliding a sideways glance at Gage. Not that all designers were, well, feminine. But the gorgeous man next to her was way too masculine, deliciously and temptingly masculine, for her to imagine him playing with ribbon and lace. Or even mesh and leather, unless they were exclusively in the bedroom.

His laugh echoed her assessment.

"Oh, no," he assured her. "I'm not a model. And I'm definitely not a designer."

And he didn't work for Rudolph's, or Jared would have told her. Which left, *dum da dum,* him being the agent.

Sweet. So sweet, she almost did her happy dance again.

"So you're clearly a fan of the holidays," he guessed, gesturing to her outfit. "And you look as if you're enjoying the party. Anything in particular impress you tonight?"

He had.

But she didn't think he was fishing for compliments.

Hailey tried to clear the champagne buzz from her head and pull together a strategy. She needed to pitch her heart out here. To make wow and impress him, not only with the designs themselves, but with her knowledge of the industry, of his client. And, because he was just so freaking yummy, maybe with herself.

It wasn't as if she was offering up her body in exchange for a good word to his client. More like she was willing to worship his body while never directly mentioning the client.

That wasn't stepping over any lines, was it?

"Hmm, there's so much to choose from," she mused as if her mind had retained anything other than impressions of him and the words *Get Cherry*. "I was really impressed with Rudolph's clever contest. The designs were all so diverse, weren't they?"

His eyes sharpened, as if she'd just triggered a switch. To what, she wasn't sure. But since he stepped closer, she hoped she could figure it out so she could trigger it at will.

"And your favorite?" he asked, so close she could feel his breath on her forehead. So close she could feel the warmth of his body wrapping around her.

She wanted to lean in and breathe deep. To snuggle in and nuzzle her nose in the curve of his shoulder. The tiny part of Hailey's brain that was still functioning at normal levels was trying to figure out what the hell was wrong with the rest of her. All she did was look at this guy and all of her senses were sucked into the lust cycle.

"Hailey?"

"Hmm?" She frowned, trying to remember what he'd asked.

"Do you have a favorite?"

"A favorite…?" Position? Flavor of body oil? Term for the male genitalia? "Oh, favorite designs?"

"Yeah. Are you drawn to any particular designer?"

There was that intense look again.

Hailey started to pitch her own line, then bit her lip. Maybe it was better to charm him first, before he realized she was one of the designers. That way, then she could gently lead him into the idea of Cherry and Merry Widow being the perfect match. She'd noticed one thing in this past year of trying to sell her wares—the minute someone thought you were pitching something, they went on the defensive.

Her gaze roamed over the masculine beauty of his face, making her sigh. Nope. She'd much rather he be receptive to anything she had to pitch.

So she shrugged instead and said, "There are a lot of great looks here tonight. I think it'd be fun to try to match each one to their perfect person." Hailey wanted to bounce in her Manolos, she was so proud of that subtle hint. Kinda like subliminal sales. She'd just lay a few bread crumbs here and there, and he could nibble his way to her line of thinking. "That's the key to a great design, isn't it? That it enhance the features, the personality, of the person wearing it."

"Do you really think there's someone that suits all of these, um, outfits?" he asked over the band, who'd turned their amps up louder now that people were hitting the dance floor. He gave a pair of sequined hot pants and a satin, cropped tee a doubtful look before arching a skeptical brow. Maybe because the outfit was the same nauseating green as his fur.

"I think everyone, and everything, has a perfect match," she said. Then she grimaced, worried her enthusiasm might be taken the wrong way—as if she were about to chase him down like a lovesick crazy woman who was looking for happy-ever-after forever promises. Instead of the right way, which was that they should get naked and see what happened when their bodies got sweaty together.

What'd happened to her? Hailey was almost as shocked at her body's reaction—instant horniness—as she was at her wild thoughts.

She rubbed one finger against her temple, as if she could reset her normal inhibition levels. She needed to stick with cheap champagne from now on. Clearly she couldn't handle the expensive stuff.

"What type of lingerie would match you perfectly?" he wondered aloud. His tone was teasing, but the look on his face made her stomach tumble as the lust spun fast, tangling with nerves.

To hell with resetting her inhibitions.

This was way more fun.

Her perfect match was a man who was there for her. Who wanted her for the long-term, not just for a convenient window of time. Perfect was fabulous sex, unquestioning support, faith in her abilities and enough love to want to actually dig in deep and be a part of her world, instead of flitting around the convenient edges.

But that was all someday thinking.

Tonight? Tonight perfect was dressed in green fur.

As if he heard her thoughts, the flirtatious heat faded from Gage's demeanor and his smile shifted from seductive to charmingly distant.

Hailey frowned as his look intensified, as if he were inspecting the far corners of her soul. The parts she kept hidden, even from herself.

Was he reading her mind when his eyes got all deep and penetrating like that? Did he know she was wondering if he was her match? Or was he the kind of guy who'd run, screaming with his furry tail between his legs, if he had a clue she was interested in more than business?

Before she could wonder too much about it, though, the floor show kicked off. All of the models hit the dance floor, "Gangnam Style." And Gage's attention shifted, so the heat in Hailey's belly had a chance to cool a little.

"Now, that's entertainment," he said with a laugh, wincing as more than one model had to grab her chest to keep it from flying out while dancing.

"It's getting wild," Hailey agreed, both amused and impressed at the same time. Wild or not, her designs looked great out there. Feminine and sexy. And it was nice to know her lingerie could dance horsey style.

"What do you say?" Gage asked, leaning in close so his words teased her ear. Hailey shivered, her nipples leaping to attention and her mind fogging again. "Want to get out of here?"

Despite her nipples' rapid agreement, Hailey hesitated.

She was willing to do a lot for her company. She was willing to do almost anything to get this contract. But while she was insanely attracted to Gage, she wasn't sure leaving with him was something she'd be proud of once the champagne cleared her system.

Correctly reading her hesitation, Gage gestured to the glass doors.

"How about a walk through the conservatory? It'll be quieter. We can talk, get away from the, um, dancing."

As if echoing his words, the music shifted to a raunchier beat. Hailey winced as the dancers shifted right along with it.

A walk. That was safe. They would still be in a fairly public arena and she'd be close enough to the party to remind herself that this was business. That should keep her from trying to rip that fur off Gage's body to see what was underneath.

"Sure," she agreed, accepting his invitation to tuck her arm into his. She tried to ignore the dance floor, where the hired help was doing a dance version of the upright doggy style. But she couldn't help blushing. Not because the moves were tacky. But because she wished she could do them, too. She couldn't, of course. Mostly because she was a lousy dancer.

She could—and should—get out of here before the dancers, and the champagne, gave her any more naughty ideas, though.

"A walk would be lovely."

GAGE WELCOMED THE cool night air like an alcoholic welcomed that first hit of gin. With greedy need and a silent groan of gratitude.

He'd been sweating like crazy in there.

Was it because of this god-awful hideous costume?

Or because of his body's reaction to the sweet, little elf next to him?

It had to be the costume.

Because he never sweated over women.

The lust wasn't a new thing. He'd spent most of his life surrounded by gorgeous women, so lust was as very familiar to him as breathing.

And it wasn't as if he had problems mixing business and pleasure. Gage worked with too many beautiful women to hamper himself with silly rules or false moral restrictions.

And while he wasn't a cocky ass, he'd had enough success with the ladies to feel both comfortable and confident that he could handle anything a woman had to offer.

Nope. He'd never had women problems.

So clearly, it must be the costume.

"Mr. Rudolph puts on quite a party," Hailey said as she wandered between marble columns wrapped in twinkling white lights. "Do you attend often?"

"This is my first," he admitted. "How about you?"

Gage didn't wander. Instead, he scoped the room, found a semisheltered wall and leaned against it. That way, she could come to him. She didn't, though. Instead, after an inscrutable look through those thick lashes, she shrugged and continued her slow meander through the conservatory.

"This is my first, too. I've talked to plenty of people who are involved behind the scenes, though. If the rumors are true, things are going to get pretty wild and naked in there soon."

Behind the scenes?

She must have a few models in there showing off the

wares. Theirs, and the designers. He debated how long to wait and steer the conversation toward some of her other clients. A minute or two, maybe. First he needed to figure her out. Usually by this point, fifteen minutes into their first meet, he'd completely pegged a person.

But Hailey the elf was a mystery.

"You don't sound disgusted by the idea of wild and naked," he observed.

Was she wilder than her sweet face and cute demeanor portrayed? His body stirred, very interested in finding out.

"Everyone has the right to enjoy the holidays in their own special way," she said, her laugh as light as the bells jingling on her hat. "And I like the idea that the lingerie samples might be so sexy, they inspire that kind of thinking."

"On the right woman, an elf hat and ballerina skirt inspires that kind of thinking," he murmured quietly.

Not so quietly that she didn't hear, if the pale pink washing over her cheeks was any indication. She didn't say anything, though. Just kept on wandering.

"So what did you find most interesting this evening?" she asked, trailing her fingers along the edge of a larger-than-life, white wicker sleigh filled with a tree, gifts and more lights. "Were you here for the shoes? There were some gorgeous new lines being shown. Or are you more a women's-wear kind of guy?"

Her arch smile was teasing and filled with as much light as the twinkling display around them. Gage had to wonder if she was always this cheerful or if she'd been hit with a little too much holiday cheer.

"I was only interested in the lingerie," he said, figuring it was time to start winding the conversation toward her coveted client. "At least I was until I saw you. Everything else sort of faded at that point."

"Uh-huh," she laughed. "Me versus a dozen perfect

women in lingerie. I can see how you were torn between the two views."

"Do you doubt me?"

At his mock offense, she stopped wandering and gave him a wide-eyed once-over. Then, finally, she joined him next to the nice, semiprivate wall.

"Doubt the Grinch? A figure known for his good cheer, holiday honesty and love of everything sweet and cuddly?"

Gage grinned. Damn, she was cute.

"Is that what he's for?" He looked down at the green fur monstrosity he was wearing and rolled his eyes. How appropriate. He had to hand it to his brother; the guy was clever with the inside jokes.

"You don't know? You're supposed to be portraying your favorite holiday character."

"I lost a bet."

"So you're not really all Grinchy about the holidays?" She tilted her head to one side as she asked the question, her bells tinkling as if to dare him to deny the joy of the season.

Gage hesitated. He never tried to hide his disdain for the holidays, nor was he worried about offending a potential business associate over differing views. But he couldn't quite bring himself to dim the sparkle in Hailey's eyes. Sharing his opinion of Christmas would be akin to telling a four-year-old that Santa was a sleighload of crap. Which was exactly what his stepmother-du-jour had done to him.

Instead, he did what he was best at. Sidestepped the question with a charming smile. "I promise you, I've never been called Grinchy in my life."

The speculation in her big eyes told him he might need to toss out a little more charming distraction. Otherwise, she seemed like the stubborn type. The kind who sweetly nagged at a person until they'd spilled their every secret, then thanked her for dragging them through the ugly memories.

"How about you?" he asked. "Why is an elf your favorite holiday character?"

"Elves are clever. They bring joy and create beauty, but they stay behind the scenes. They're the cute and cuddly part of the background." To emphasize her point, she offered a bright smile, tilted her chin toward her shoulder and twirled around so her skirt offered a tempting view of her stockings. Which, Gage's mouth watered to realize, were thigh-high and held up with garters.

"But elves don't have their own movie," he pointed out. "As grumpy as he is, even the Grinch gets top billing."

"*Elf* is a movie. And top billing usually comes with top headaches," she pointed out. "Expectations and demands of excellence. Appearances, groupies, haters. Is all of that really worth the spotlight?"

Gage frowned.

Hell, yeah, it was worth it. The other option sounded kind of...forgettable. Who aspired to that?

Maybe that was why she was an agent instead of striving to be the star, he guessed.

Still...

"Being on top is better than being on the bottom," he pointed out.

"Not always." Her words were low, teasing and lilting with innuendo. The look in her eyes was hot, sexy. And way more appreciative of the view than he figured his costume warranted. But who was he to dissuade a gorgeous woman from appreciating him?

His momma didn't raise no fools. Of course, she didn't raise her sons, either, but that was beside the point.

Right now, the point was seeing how hot this spark could flame between him and the deliciously naughty elf.

He stepped closer.

Amusement and desire both clear on her face, Hailey stepped back. With a quick glance over his shoulder, as if gauging their privacy, she wet her lips.

Gage almost groaned.

He probably could have walked away before.

Probably.

But now? Seeing that full mouth damp and inviting?

He wasn't leaving without a taste.

"Being on top has a few definite benefits," he decided quietly, now having completely switched places so her back was against the wall and his toward the ballroom.

"Does it? Like what?" Her eyes were huge, so big they were lost in the curls tumbling out from the white fur brim of her hat.

Need, stronger than any he'd felt over a simple flirtation, surged through Gage's body. He angled his body so Hailey was trapped between him and the wall.

For a second, one delicious second, he just stared.

Enjoyed the anticipation in her eyes.

The rapid pulse fluttering in her throat.

The tempting display of luscious flesh, mounded above the tight satin binding her breasts.

The need intensified. Took on a sharp, hungry edge.

"Like this," he said, giving in to its demand.

He took her mouth.

He'd intended to be gentle. Sweet, even.

But the kiss was carnal and raw and dancing on the edges of desperate. Tongues tangled. Lips slid, hot and wet.

She tasted as sweet as she looked.

But the sounds she made were sexual nirvana. Low, husky moans of approval as his hands skimmed over her waist to that tempting place just below her breasts. He didn't touch. He just tortured the both of them with the idea that he could.

Public, he forcibly reminded himself. They were practically in public, and if he did what he wanted, they'd be putting on a display for a ballroom full of people.

Knowing if he didn't stop now, that display was a very real possibility, Gage slowly, reluctantly, pulled his mouth from hers.

It was harder than he'd thought it'd be. And not just between his legs.

Unwilling to let go completely, his hands flat against the wall on either side of her head, Gage leaned closer. His body trapped hers as he pressed tiny kisses along her throat. Hailey's head fell back, her breath coming fast, filling the air with tiny bursts of white fog.

The move arched her back, so the long, delicious length of her throat was bare and those glorious breasts pressed higher against his chest. His hands burned with the need to cup her bounty. To weigh the soft flesh. To slide that candy-cane-striped fabric down and see if she was as tasty as he thought.

Public, Gage reminded himself again. *Keep it in control.*

Because while he wasn't averse to a little public display of passion himself, he had the feeling that Hailey would be. Especially if some of those models in there were hers.

Then her hands shifted, moving off his shoulders to press their way down his chest. Gage could feel their heat even through the thick fur of his costume.

He shuddered with need, taking in the flush of rosy color washing over Hailey's cheeks and pouring down her throat and chest to meet that tight satin.

One taste couldn't hurt, he decided.

Even as his mind listed all the ways it actually could, he moved closer, so his body was tight against hers. As Hailey's hum of pleasure filled the air, he pressed his mouth against the side of her throat, just under her ear, and gave in to the need to taste.

She was delicious.

Seriously worried for his sanity if she kept teasing him with those delicate fingers, Gage folded his hand over hers and pressed her palm flat against his chest. Then he grabbed the zipper tab and yanked.

It didn't move.

The grabby need clawing at Gage's libido slowed, even as the foggy desire tried to pull him back.

He yanked again.

Nothing.

"Hell," he muttered, pulling his mouth from Hailey's.

Unwilling to separate their bodies, he angled his head to peer at his chest. He got a better grip on the tab and pulled again.

The zipper was stuck.

"I can't get it down."

"Well, I guess I'd rather hear that than you can't get it up," she said, her eyes dancing with laughter. Clearly a smart woman, Hailey pressed those lush lips together to keep it contained, though.

Gage growled.

And yanked.

Nothing.

This was not happening.

His body straining against the thick fur of the costume from hell, he considered ripping it right off.

"I guess the moment's lost," he said with a reluctant smile when she couldn't hold back her laughter any longer. He figured that was better than acting like a spoiled, tantrum-throwing asshole.

Although he was reserving the right to throw the tantrum later in private.

"Maybe not lost," she said, her smile gentle now, her eyes bright with promise. "Maybe just delayed."

Gage considered the option of a delay over cancellation.

It had a lot more appeal. And while he wasn't so uptight that he had stupid rules about sex, clients and associates, he was also smart enough to know that women got funny about stuff. If Hailey thought he'd slept with her to get to her client, and to snag the deal, she'd go one of two ways. Give it to him because he was so damned good. Or withhold it out of spite.

He didn't see her as the spiteful type, but she didn't come across as the kind of woman who'd take kindly to ulterior motives, either.

Time for some careful maneuvering.

"Why don't I call you?" he offered. After a quick mental review of his calendar, he added, "I'm out of town for the next couple of days. Are you available for dinner on Wednesday? I'll pick you up at six."

Her eyes were huge as she gave him a long look.

It was the kind of look that'd usually make him nervous. A look filled with hope. With trust. With all those sweet, innocent emotions he'd never experienced in his life.

It was scary as hell.

His feet itched to run, even as his dick ached to stay.

"I have a meeting on Wednesday," she finally said. She reached up to trace her index finger over his lower lip, making Gage want to growl and nip at her soft flesh. Then, without warning, she ducked under his arm and shifted away.

Scowling at how lost his arms felt all of a sudden, he turned to watch her stop a couple of feet away. What? Did she think looking at her instead of touching was going to simmer down the need boiling through his system?

Impossible.

She was pure eye candy.

Still clinging with one hairpin, her hat was askew, dangling to one side. Blond curls, so soft when he'd tangled them in his fingers, were a bright halo around her face. And that face.

Gage wanted to groan.

He'd never gone for sweet. Sweet was dangerous. Sweet came with expectation, with demands. Sweet set off the run-don't-walk sirens in his head.

But he couldn't resist Hailey. He wanted all of the sweetness she had to offer.

But she was also the key to his winning this bet. And that, even more than the sirens, warned him to back off. At least until they'd settled their business.

"Well, if you have plans..." he started to say. Before he could excuse his way out of dinner and suggest a more businesslike meeting, she interrupted.

"Do you know Carinos?" she asked.

He gave a hesitant nod. Upscale and trendy, Carinos was the latest see-and-be-seen hot spot.

"How about I meet you there on Wednesday? We'll need to make it seven instead of six, though. I'm not sure how late my meeting will go."

This was it. His chance to back out.

But he couldn't make himself suggest alternate plans.

Gage tried to sort through his confused thoughts. Not an easy thing to do when he could barely stand, thanks to the throbbing hard-on he was sporting.

Before he could decide if he should accept or counter, she smiled.

That sweet, sexy smile that shut down his brain.

Looking like a naughty elf, Hailey wet her lips. He wanted to groan at the sight of her small, pink tongue.

And then, moving so fast she was a blur of blond, she kissed him. Hot, intense. A sweep of her tongue, a slide of her lips. Just enough hint of teeth to make him growl to keep from begging.

Then, before he could take control, or hell, even react

with more than a groan of appreciation for the hot spike of desire shooting through him, she moved back.

"See ya Wednesday," she said.

With that, a little finger wave and a smile that showed just a hint of nerves around the edges, she was gone.

Gage wanted to run after her. To grab her and insist she do something about the crazy desire she'd set to flames in his body.

Except for two things.

One, his dick was so hard, he couldn't walk for fear of something breaking.

And two, his mind was still reeling.

He'd tried to blame the costume. Because he didn't get stupid over women.

Ever.

But that cute little elf, with her candy-cane-sweet taste, had sent him so far into Stupidville, he might as well set up camp.

Until he'd figured it out, he needed to stay away from her.

Far, far away.

Because horny was all good and well.

And, he had to admit, stupid-horny was a pretty freaking awesome feeling.

But stupid-horny and business?

Not a good combination.

At least, not when his freedom was on the line.

4

"YOU'RE GRINNING LIKE a kid who just found a dancing pony under her Christmas tree. What's wrong with you?"

Wrong?

This was afterglow. Sexual anticipation. And a big ole dollop of nervous energy. It'd been three days since her kiss with Gage, and she was still floating.

Hailey inspected her image in the ornate standing mirror in the corner of her workroom-slash-office. Behind her were swaths of billowing silk, yards of lace and spilling bins of roses and romantic trim.

Only Doris would look at that and say it was wrong.

Hailey peered past her reflection to the woman behind her.

Doris Danson, or D.D. to her friends—which meant Hailey called her Doris—looked as if she were stuck in a time warp.

Rounded and a little droopy, her white hair was bundled in a messy bun reminiscent of a fifties showgirl. Bright blue eye shadow and false lashes added to the image. Doris's workday uniform consisted of polyester slacks, a T-shirt with a crude saying by a popular yellow bird and an appliqué holiday sweater complete with beribboned dogs, candy canes and sequin-covered trees.

The sweater and tee didn't bother Hailey. But as a designer, she was morally offended at the elastic-waisted polyester. Doris knew that. Hailey had a suspicion that the older woman haunted thrift stores and rummage sales to stock up on the ugly things.

"Nothing's wrong," Hailey said.

Not really. But she couldn't meet her secretary-slash-seamstress-slash-bookkeeper's gaze.

Despite her afterglow, she was kind of freaked out. She'd made out with a potential business associate. Now, granted, *associate* was a pretty loose term. But she was still walking a moral line here. Should Gage be off-limits? Maybe she shouldn't be obsessing over that kiss. Hailey bit her lip, chewing off the lip gloss she'd just slicked on five minutes ago.

"Might want to eat something besides your lipstick. Not like they feed you at these fancy meetings. Why you think it's a good idea to go talk to this guy after he burned you is a mystery, though."

"Mr. Rudolph didn't burn me. He'd never offered an actual contract. I'm sure I'll still get the exclusive. It's just going to be a little more interesting now." Jared and Trent wouldn't have praised her designs like they had if they didn't think she had the contract in the bag. And Hailey had a secret weapon now. A very sexy, very delicious one she was meeting for dinner.

"Interesting. Right. Instead of getting a solid deal you expected, you get to play some rich man's game." The wheels of her chair creaked as Doris shifted. The woman was barely visible behind the stacks of paper, catalogs and the tiny ceramic Christmas tree on her desk. Too bad she wasn't barely audible, too. "And where are you going to be when that other guy walks off with the contract? On the street, that's where."

Turning to give Doris a chiding look, Hailey insisted, "It's going to be fine. I'm going to get this deal."

Doris tut-tutted. "I'm telling you, Hailey, you are wasting your time. Better to accept reality than to keep dragging this out."

Hailey hated reality.

Especially when Doris dished it up with such bitter relish. It was as if she reveled in negativity. Hailey shifted her gaze from her own image to the woman behind her.

What a contrast.

Preparing for the meeting, Hailey was dressed in business chic. A black leather mini paired with leopard-print tights, a black silk turtleneck and a brushed cotton blazer with satin lapels. Along with her favorite boots and black knee-high schoolgirl socks, the look was savvy, sassy and modern. Just right for wowing a department-store tycoon and a fashion powerhouse.

And behind her was the elf of Christmas gloom.

An elf that knew the business inside and out, could finagle suppliers' fees down to pennies, worked magic with the books and, next to Hailey, was the best fill-in seamstress Merry Widow had ever seen. Which made her indispensable.

Indispensable gloom.

Not for the first time, she wished she were the kind of person who could tell Doris that her bad attitude wouldn't be tolerated and suggest the woman get her act together or clear out her desk.

But every time Hailey thought about doing it, she thought of everything the woman brought to the company. Then she remembered how lousy Doris's home life was, how Merry Widow was all she really had.

And whenever the older woman pissed her off so much that she forgot all that, the minute she got ready to get in her face, Hailey's tongue swelled up, her head buzzed with panic and she freaked out.

It wasn't that she was a wimp. She was a fierce negotiator in business, a savvy designer who insisted her company be run her way. She was smart. She was clever. She was strong.

She just sucked at confrontation.

Partially because her father had once told her that arguments always left scars. That even after making up, the memory of the conflict would forever change the relationship. Given that his advice had come on the heels of a hideous family drama that'd cost Hailey a whole year away from her new half brother, she'd taken the lesson to heart.

But mostly because she hated making people mad at her. Her mom had got mad and left her dad. Her dad got mad and refused to talk to Hailey. She'd seen plenty of mad in her life. Which was why she tried to avoid it like the plague.

"You want one of these cookies?" Doris asked, a frosted reindeer in hand. Doris shot Hailey a sour smile, bit the head off, then said around her mouthful, "Might as well eat up now, since things are gonna get tight after we go out of business."

"We're not going out of business," Hailey insisted, lifting a cream lace scarf to her shoulder to compare, then switching to one of vivid red cashmere.

"Right. Bet you still believe in Santa Claus, too."

"We're not going out of business," she said again. "Our sales are up ten percent over last year. Our projected first quarter should double that, easily."

"The Phillips kids are calling their daddy's note the first of the year," Doris reminded her like a persistently cheerful rain cloud.

Rotten kids. Or, really, greedy adults.

When Hailey had bought Merry Widow Lingerie from Eric Phillips three years ago, they'd agreed that he'd take a percentage of the profits for five years, with a final payment of the agreed-upon balance at the end of that time.

When he'd died in the fall, though, his kids had found a loophole in the contract, insisting that they could call the entire debt. They'd given Hailey until the end of the year, which was mighty big of them, in their opinion.

Without a significant contract the size of, oh, say Rudolph department stores, the bank wouldn't consider a loan in the sum the Phillipses were demanding.

Just thinking about it made Hailey's stomach churn, an inky panic coating the back of her throat.

No. She put the mental brakes to the freak-out. She wasn't going there. She'd found her answer; she just had to believe in it. She was going to snag this Rudolph-department-store contract.

Negative thinking, even the kind that had her second-guessing her date tonight, would only drag her down.

Giving her reflection a hard-eyed stare, Hailey vowed that she was going to rock this meeting and wow her date. As long as she didn't strip him naked and nibble on his body, she wasn't crossing any ethical work-relationship boundaries. Right?

Right.

Now she just had to get Doris off her back.

"When I pull in this department-store deal, we're golden. I can pay off the note, Merry Widow will be mine free and clear, and we'll be set," she assured the other woman.

"Do you bake special cookies to set out for Santa, or are you comfy settling for store bought? And those stars that fall from the sky, how many of those wishes actually come true for you?" Doris gave a pitying shake of her head. "You listen to me, miss. You keep going through life with your head in the clouds like you do, you're gonna fall in a big ole ditch one of these days."

What was it with the people in her life? Her mother was always warning that she'd get taken advantage of. Her friends worried that she was wearing rose-colored glasses. Even her father... Hailey bit her lip. Well, her father barely noticed what she was doing. But every once in a while, he did throw out a caution warning of his own. It wasn't as if she were Pollyanna with no clue. Hailey was a smart, perceptive woman. She'd made it to twenty-six without a major heartbreak, owned her own business and paid her bills on time. And unlike anyone else in her family, she hadn't had to resort to therapy and/or addictive substances along the way.

"I'm just saying, you might want to look at your alternatives. Me, I can retire anytime. But the rest of the team, don't they deserve a little heads-up so they can start looking for new jobs? It's all well and good to keep your hopes up," Doris said, her tone indicating the exact opposite. "But you can't let your Mary Sunshine attitude hurt other people, now, can you?"

"Everything is going to be fine. Why don't you focus on doing your job and let me do mine," Hailey snapped, her words so loud and insistent that the other woman dropped her cookie and stared.

She closed her eyes against Doris's shocked look. Hailey never snapped. In a life surrounded by simmering emotional volcanoes, she worked hard to be calm water. Mellow. Soothing, even. She'd grown up watching the devastation negativity and emotional turmoil caused, had spent her childhood trying to repair the damage.

And, of course, on the oh-so-rare occasions that she did respond to stress with a negative reaction, she always got that same horrified, might-as-well-have-kicked-a-puppy-and-cussed-out-a-nun look from people.

"I'm sorry," Hailey said with a grimace. "I'm just nervous about the meeting this afternoon. I want to make a good impression, to show Mr. Rudolph and his team that I'm the designer they want."

"You think the perfect scarf is going to make that dirty old man pick you as his lingerie designer?"

"I think the right look will show him my sense of style and savvy use of color and patterns," Hailey defended, lifting one scarf and then the other against her neckline again. "How a woman feels about her outfit affects her confidence, after all. If *I* think I look good, I'll project a strong image. And that might be all I need to get the deal."

"You might be a little overoptimistic about business stuff, but you've always had a firm handle on how well you put together fashion," Doris said with a frown. "Silly to start worrying about it now."

"I really want this contract." *Desperately needed it* was closer to the truth. But why put that fine a dot on the subject?

"An exclusive with the Rudolph department stores? It'll be so cool. The rich and famous shop there. They have a store on Rodeo Drive and everything. Can you imagine Gwyneth Paltrow in Sassy Class?" Hailey said in a dreamy tone, thinking of the pristine white satin chemise with delicate crocheted trim.

"Those highfalutin stars are the only ones who can afford to shop at snobby stores like Rudolph's." Doris's sniff made it perfectly clear what she thought of stars, snobs and all of their money.

"Well, unless you really do want to retire early and spend every day at home with your husband, you better cross your fingers that those snobs take to my designs," Hailey said, finally choosing the red scarf. It was sassier, she decided as she draped it elegantly around her neck. Frustrated, she wrinkled her nose. At least she was trying for elegant. It was hard when she'd knotted wrinkles into the scarf, so it looked like a soggy, deflated balloon around her neck.

Doris rolled her eyes, then hefted herself out from behind the desk to come over and adjust the scarf. A tug of fabric here, a tuck there, then she jerked her chin to indicate that Hailey turn back to the mirror.

While Doris fussed with the scarf, Hailey obsessed.

What if the other woman was right about it being impossible to come up with the funds to pay off the Phillips note?

What if Hailey's mother was right about Hailey shooting too high, wanting too much?

What if this was it, her last Christmas as the owner and head designer of Merry Widow Lingerie? What if it was the end of her dream?

"Not gonna happen," she muttered, lifting her chin to emphasize the promise.

"Whazzat?" Doris peered over her bifocals.

"Nothing," Hailey assured her in a cheery tone. With a smile to match, she patted the older woman's shoulder and promised, "Everything's great. Merry Widow is ready to fly, and this account is going to be our launchpad to make it happen."

The older woman harrumphed, but her usual grumpy look softened a little as she tucked one of Hailey's curls back into the faux chignon she'd fashioned at the base of her neck.

"Well, I will say this. If anyone deserves to make those dreams come true, you do." With that, and a stiff smile, Doris clomped back to her tin of cookies.

That was about the nicest thing Doris had ever said to her. It had to be a good omen, right?

Or the kiss of death.

AN HOUR LATER, Hailey stepped into the glass elevator in the center of the Rudolph Building and pushed the button for the top floor. Top floor, baby. Unable to resist, she watched the surrounding buildings of the Financial District as the elevator rose, sighing when the sun broke through the clouds, and off in the distance she could just make out the Golden Gate Bridge. That had to be some kind of sign. Any day that included a meeting with a powerhouse like Rudolph, a pat on the back from Doris and a date with a sexy guy like Gage couldn't go wrong. Hailey practically skipped out of the elevator.

Still, she paused outside the frosted-glass double doors. One hand pressed to her stomach to calm her nerves, she took a deep breath. A quick glance at her feet to peek at her Jeffrey Campbells worked as a reminder that everything went better when a girl wore great boots. Then, resisting the urge to fluff her curls into frizz and nibble at her lipstick, she called up her brightest smile and pulled open the door.

This was it.

Her first foray into fashion fabulousness and the beginning of the best day of her life. A prelude, maybe, to the best *night* of her life.

With that peppy chant playing in her head, she swept into Rudolph Headquarters.

"Hailey, darling." Jared greeted her as soon as she crossed the foyer. He hurried around the high counter where he'd been chatting with the receptionist to offer a hug.

Hailey shifted, suddenly nervous.

"Hi, Jared. What's up?" He looked normal enough. Metro chic in his electric-blue suit and skinny tie, his hair slicked to the side and quirky horn rims perched on the bridge of his nose. But he was all tense, as if someone had just told him shoulder pads and moon boots were about to make a comeback.

"Up? Nothing, nothing. C'mon, let me escort you to the meeting. Rudy isn't in yet, of course. But you can get settled. I'll fetch you a nice latte, shall I?"

Hailey's stomach sank. Now she knew something was

wrong. Jared didn't fetch for anybody. She slowed, all but digging the spikes on the heels of her boots into the plush carpet to make Jared slow, too.

"Seriously. If something's happened…" She swallowed hard, then forced herself to continue. "If I've lost the account, I'd rather know before I go in that meeting."

Quick as a flash, a grimace came and went. Not a small feat considering the amount of Botox injected in that pretty face. "It's nothing, really. Just, well, Rudy finally got hold of Cherry Bella. She's interested, but not committed."

That sounded familiar. Hailey didn't figure reveling in the turned tables would endear her to Rudy, though. She kept her lips still.

"She's in tentative agreement, with the caveat that she gets to be the final judge on the various lines for the spring show. She and Rudy are nailing down those details."

"So how is this any different than it was Saturday night when he announced that it was a competition?" she wondered.

"Well, before we were pretty sure he was going to go with Merry Widow since he had this whole soft spring theme in mind. But Rudy apparently left the party Saturday with Vivo, the shoe designer."

So? Hailey arched both brows. She wasn't competing for the shoe contract.

"Vivo is edgy, modern and quirky. Think eight-inch platforms shaped like dinosaurs."

Eww, tacky. Halfway through her cringe, it hit her why Jared was so upset.

"Rudy's going to want the line to be a cohesive message.…" Her words trailed off as it hit her.

Romantic sensuality didn't go with eight-inch platform dinosaurs. But snakeskin and black leather did.

And Rudy had a favor-wielding relationship with a designer who thought dinosaurs belonged on women's feet?

Anger ran, tense and jittery, along Hailey's spine. Fists clenched at her sides, she ground her teeth to keep from shouting that enough was enough. They kept changing the rules, shifting the playing field. Dammit, she deserved more respect than that. She'd worked hard for this deal, and until that stupid party, all indications were that she'd be awarded the contract.

She didn't say a word, though.

Yelling never helped anything. If she jumped all over Jared, it'd just make things uncomfortable, and might lose her whatever slim chance she had left.

Big picture, she reminded herself, taking deep breaths to try to push out the irritation. It was all about saving her company.

"I just found out a few minutes ago, or I'd have called to warn you. Cherry and Rudy are meeting with all of the designers together, listening to their pitches." Jared's words came at such a rush, they were spilling over themselves. Maybe because they'd reached the wide double doors of the meeting room.

"They're making the decision now?" she asked. Her fingers clutched her sassy messenger bag filled with marketing ideas and clever pitches aimed at the media. She'd come prepared to pitch the beauty of romantic lingerie that made women feel sexy. If she'd had more time, could she have found a way to work ugly shoes into her presentation? To show that even with the hideous footwear, a woman could still feel attractive?

His hand on the door, Jared closed his eyes for a second, as if he was fighting some inner battle. Then he leaned close and gave Hailey an intense look.

"Focus on Cherry. She's the key. Rudy will ignore his preferences in favor of whatever she likes, so chat her up. Make friends. She's on edge about something. Don't know if that's her typical personality or if she's having issues.

But she seems to be responding better to soft sells than hard pushes."

Before Hailey could process all of that, before she could do more than give Jared a grateful smile since she knew he was risking his job by showing preferential treatment, he'd pushed the door open and gestured her inside.

She wanted to grab his hand and drag him in with her. But she didn't.

Instead, she took a deep breath of her own, lifted her chin, pulled back her shoulders and plastered on her best soft-sell smile.

Then, with as much enthusiasm as if there were a bed of hissing vipers on the other side, she swept over the threshold.

And almost tripped over her gorgeous boots.

"Hi," she breathed, the word taking all the air from her lungs.

GAGE SHIFTED HIS glare from the window to the door, ready to get this damned meeting over with.

And, for one of the few times in his life, found himself speechless. He had to blink a couple of times to make sure he wasn't seeing things, then found his voice.

"Hailey?"

Damn, she was pretty.

Her hair, still a froth of blond curls, was tamer than it'd been at the party. Sleeker, as if she'd bribed the curls into behaving by tying them in a knot at the base of her neck. Her big, round eyes were subtly made up, her lips pale and glistening. She was definitely looking more nice than naughty today.

But even without a candy-cane-striped bustier and thigh-grazing ballerina skirt, her sweet curves were mouthwatering. Instead of skimpy holiday wear, today she was decked out in a simple black skirt a few inches short of her knees and another pair of sexy boots. Her scarf and turtleneck screamed class, while her leopard-print tights assured him she was all sass.

He'd never been a foot-fetish kind of guy, but he was starting to seriously wonder what other styles of footwear she had in her closet. And how she'd look riding his body wearing just a pair of boots in thigh-hugging black leather.

"Gage?" Frowning, she chewed on the full pillow of her bottom lip, making him want to offer to take over the task. Then, as if she'd realized something, her eyes cleared and she offered a smile. "I didn't expect to see you."

"I'm surprised you recognized me without the green fur," he said with a teasing smile, walking across the room. He met her wide-eyed look with a wink.

He swept his gaze down her body again, noting the edgy boots and knee socks paired with tights and black leather.

She was a study in contrasts.

"Your suit is a definite step up from that costume," she agreed. "I'm glad to see you finally got the zipper unstuck."

She gave him a once-over just as hot as the one he'd given her. Her gaze slowed when passing over his faulty-zipper zone, making him wonder if he'd be having issues with these slacks. The speed at which she inspired an erection was hell on his clothes.

"I didn't. I had to cut the costume off."

"Oh." Her eyes danced with amusement, but she pressed her lips together in an attempt to keep from laughing aloud.

She was so damned cute.

He wanted to lift her off her feet and pull that curvy body against his, to see if it fit as good as he'd spent the weekend imagining. Not for the first time, he cursed his brother, the bet and that damned Grinch costume. If it weren't for Saturday night's thick layer of green fur— and a faulty zipper—he'd already know what she felt like.

But this was a formal meeting.

In someone else's office.

Getting hot and heavy with a business associate was definitely on the stupid list. Especially since Rudolph was likely to walk in at any moment. If he caught Gage and Hailey making out, he'd probably grab a video recorder and put it up on the company's YouTube channel.

So reluctantly, Gage offered his hand instead. The delicate softness of her palm and her quick intake of breath reminded him that she was about as close to an innocent as he'd been since his teens.

Maybe this was a bad idea.

"I didn't realize you were going to be a part of the meeting," she said breathlessly, her hand still nestled in his.

Gage frowned.

Why wouldn't he be here? This meeting was supposed to be him, Rudy, that singer chick and the competing designer. He'd figured he'd play to Rudy's good-old-boy persona while pitching circles around the designer. Milano's leather designs already appealed to Rudy's misogynistic perverted side. All Gage had to do was play that up, maybe intimidate the other designer a little and snag the contract on his way out the door to meet Hailey for dinner.

A dinner he'd been of two minds about keeping.

Hailey was everything he liked in a woman.

Sexy, fun and sporting a body that'd starred in all his dreams since the party.

And Hailey was everything he avoided in a woman.

Sweet, trusting and sporting an emotional innocence that promised nothing but trouble down the road.

And she was a business associate. Distant, perhaps, but still close enough to this project for it to possibly get messy. If he were smart, he'd offer a clever excuse and get out of their date. He'd keep this business deal simple, and himself out of trouble.

Gage was damned smart.

And here he had a chance to pitch to the singer's agent, just him alone. Might as well use it. Maybe it'd help keep his mind off stripping Hailey bare of everything but those boots.

"Since Rudolph is late, why don't we get comfortable? You can fill me in on what you think Cherry Bella likes best. And, of course, tell me what you're wearing under that skirt."

So much for keeping his mind off her naked.

Eyes wide, Hailey's mouth rounded to a surprised O before she let out a gurgle of laughter. As he escorted her to one of the half dozen club chairs by the window, she slanted him a teasing look.

"Under this? What better under leather than lace? Merry Widow lace, of course."

Releasing her elbow, Gage frowned.

What the hell?

She wore the competition?

"I'm a little confused," she said before he could point out the blatant conflict of interest. "Wouldn't you know better than I what Cherry likes?"

Why would he?

Gage gave Hailey a hard look.

Before he could ask exactly what her connection to Cherry, and to Rudolph, was, the department-store mogul swanned in with all but bugles blaring a fanfare. The small, bald man apparently made up for his lack of stature by surrounding himself with as big an entourage as possible. Mostly made up of busty women in short skirts, Gage noted. Two carrying briefcases, one with coffee and another with a tray of tiny pastries.

The women paraded in, each setting her item on a wide, glass-topped table, then without a word, doing a snappy about-face and parading right back out.

Leaving Hailey to stare, wide-eyed, Gage frowning and Rudolph posing in the doorway. And Cherry Bella nowhere to be found.

Was that why Hailey was here? To rep her client?

"Darlings, I'm late. So let's not dawdle. Sit, sit." Rudolph waved his fingers at Gage, who, after a second's debate, sat. But opposite Hailey instead of next to her. He had a feeling he was going to get more out of watching her face than whatever the old coot spouted.

"It'll just be the three of us, I'm afraid." As if to emphasize his statement, he came over to sit with them, rat-a-tat-tatting his fingers on his knee and frowning. "I know you're both anxious to hear the decision of who'll be awarded the contract. I'd intended to give it today, with Cherry's help. But as she's ill, we'll have to reconvene tomorrow."

"Tomorrow?" Tension spiked Gage's system. And not the happy, sexual kind he'd been enjoying thanks to Hailey. This meeting was supposed to finish up his commitments to Milano for the year. He had his own clients to see, several projects in the works. He didn't have time to play babysitter to a leather lingerie line and a kooky, old guy.

"Unfortunately, Cherry felt ill after lunch," the old guy said, sounding more irritated than sorry. "She apologizes for missing the meeting, but insists on talking with the designers herself and having a say in the decision if she's to take the role of spokesmodel. I hate to inconvenience you, but we'll have to meet again tomorrow. Cherry feels the lingerie is the linchpin of her agreement to signing on as the face of Rudolph for next year."

Gage barely heard a thing after the words *talking with the designers.* His eyes shifted to Hailey. Her eyes were round, those full lips parted in a silent gasp. Not a gasp of pleasure, either.

Nope. She looked about as horrified as he felt.

"Inconvenient for the two of you, but as much as I'm sure you both want this contract, I'm sure you'll make adjustments." With that pronouncement of misperception, Rudy bounced up and scurried over to the tray-topped table. "So are you in the mood for cocoa? And a sweet, of course. What's Christmas without cookies? Then we'll take a quick look at the test shots my photographer took of Cherry in each of your designs. Consider it an early gift, since it gives you a chance to refine the pitch you'll need tomorrow."

Hailey closed her eyes, taking a deep breath, then shaking her head as if trying to shift the new facts into the old picture. If the pinched expression on her face was any indication, she wasn't liking the way it looked now.

Gage could relate.

Son of a bitch.

There went his Christmas treat.

5

WELL, THIS DAY had totally sucked.

Sinking deeper into the worn booth, Hailey looked around the retro diner and took a deep breath to keep from crying. Then wrinkled her nose as the acrid scent of burning burger filled the air. On opposite sides of the room, two babies screamed their dissatisfaction with dinner, their cries echoing off the curved glass window in stereo.

Carinos this wasn't.

Of course, there was nothing to celebrate, either. So a cheap diner was much more fitting than a four-star restaurant.

She wanted that account. She'd worked her ass off for it. She was damned good, her designs were high quality and on trend, yet unique and memorable. Her costs were reasonable, her profit margin solid. She'd put together a fabulous proposal.

She was perfect for Rudolph's spring line.

Her designs were perfect for Cherry Bella.

Now she was afraid perfect might not be enough. That this time, just like so many others, she'd get within touching distance to getting what she wanted, only to have it swept away.

She glared at the glass on the table in front of her.

Other than being made of melted sand, it in no way resembled the sexy, seductive wineglass she'd thought she'd be sipping from right now while flirting her way through a very promising date.

Nope, this glass was thick, with hot fudge sliding down one side and a puddle of melting, sprinkle-embedded whipped cream pooling on the stem.

She licked a smudge of chocolate off her knuckle, taking comfort from the bittersweet richness.

She was wearing her favorite lingerie under this chic outfit. A sweet, dove-gray demi bra with picot lace and tiny pink satin rosebuds. She'd imagined describing the matching thong and garter belt to Gage over candlelight and appetizers, letting that image set the tone for the rest of their evening.

Her garter belt pressed tight against her overfull tummy, a reminder of just how mistaken she'd been. No pleasant alcohol buzz and sexual zing happening here for her.

Instead, she had an ice-cream gut ache and felt as if she'd been beaten around by a bag full of gloom. Heck, she could give Doris a run for her money for the biggest downer award in this mood.

And it was all Gage Milano's fault.

As if her thoughts, or an ice-cream-inspired fantasy, had called him up, Gage suddenly appeared right there at her booth.

Sexy as hell, his black hair windswept from the chilly San Francisco weather and tumbling over his forehead in a way that made her fingers itch to tidy it. His eyes were intense, wicked and amused as he arched one brow. And his body. Yes, he was wearing a leather bomber jacket, so she didn't have full view of those delicious shoulders. But hey, she'd correctly pegged how gorgeous they were when he was draped in green fur. She could imagine them just fine covered in leather.

Leather.

Something he specialized in.

Hailey blinked a few times, sure he was just a sugar mirage. But he didn't disappear. Instead, he smiled.

Damn him. And he didn't even have the courtesy to look out of place. Instead, he was perfectly at ease. It was so irritating.

"What are you doing here?" she asked.

"I followed you."

She shook her head. No, he hadn't. She'd been here, stuffing her face and getting sick on ice cream, for almost three-quarters of an hour. Her body would have sent up horny signals if he was anywhere near her.

"I'd have been in sooner, but once I saw you were settling here for a bit, I had to make some phone calls."

Perfectly at ease and acting as if he had no doubt she'd be thrilled to see him, Gage shrugged out of his jacket and slipped into the seat opposite her. She was distracted from feasting her eyes on his shoulders when, with a grimace, he shifted to lift one hip, then slid back toward the seat's edge. Hailey smirked at the contrast of his sleek looks cozied up in an ice cream and burger booth. She hoped his hundred-dollar slacks had just got stuck in a chocolate smear.

Was that mean of her?

Sure.

But dammit, she'd really been looking forward to their date—and the sex she'd imagined they'd be having soon afterward.

Talk about disappointed.

It was like every Christmas she could remember.

She'd be promised something wonderful, be it that special gift from Santa or her parents not fighting for one blessed day. She'd spend the entire season winding herself up with excitement, hoping and imagining just how amazing it would be.

And, always, it'd been a huge disappointment.

Santa never brought her what she asked for.

Her family never kept their promises.

And her prettily imagined holiday never came true.

She knew it wasn't really Gage's fault. He hadn't known they were in competition for the contract, either. But she couldn't help but feel that the Grinch had, indeed, stolen her Christmas.

"Why'd you follow me?" For one tiny second she imagined maybe it was to beg her to go out with him still. To tell her how hot he was for her, that a silly thing like business shouldn't stand between what they'd felt for each other.

"I thought we should talk. Maybe work this out between us." His smile was pure charm, his look so potent that—despite her vow that he was now off-limits—she was tempted to start undressing right then and there.

"Really?" Her pulse joined the dance and Hailey shifted in her seat, her waistband a little snug from holding her breath—and all that ice cream.

"Really." He leaned forward and lifted her hand into his. His thumb rubbed along the center of her palm, heating and stirring. "I figure there's no reason we can't both have what we want, right?"

Her mouth was too dry for words, so she settled on a nod. He was so damned sexy. His eyes were hypnotic, as if he was trying to pull her in. She didn't think it'd take much for her to follow just about any suggestion he might offer up.

"I mean, who knows what kind of crazy things Rudolph might want in order to award the contract. Look at how he's dragged this out already. First he was supposed to announce the lineup on Saturday. Then it was today. Now it may be tomorrow. I know you're a busy lady, and I definitely have plenty on my schedule. So why don't we make this easy for him. What do you say?"

"What?"

Her pulse slowed to a thud, matching the feeling of anticipation deflating in her belly.

"How about I make you an offer? Hook you up with some other potential clients, some big names. A half dozen hot leads you could nail down before the weekend. And, probably, before Rudolph would get around to figuring out what he wants." Gage added a charming smile, as if he were plopping a fat, juicy cherry on top of his delicious proposition.

Delicious, that was, for him. She clenched her teeth against the rude words she wanted to spew, leaving a sick taste in her mouth.

When she didn't answer, he craned his head forward to check out her ice cream, then lifted a spoon from the place setting on his side and scooped up a bite.

"Not a bad chocolate," he commented. "I'd have pegged you as a more adventurous ice-cream connoisseur, though. Espresso, some exotic fruit or maybe bourbon flavored."

"But then, you don't know me very well, do you?"

Brows arched, he gave a slow nod and set the spoon down. He had a look of smug satisfaction on his face. As if he'd just been proved right about something.

"I know more about you than I did before," he offered, his smile so full of charm it was dripping in her ice cream. "You're an up-and-coming force to be reckoned with. Your designs are pure romance, created to make any woman and every woman feel sexy."

"How sweet." She reached forward with two fingers and slid her glass of leftover melted ice cream back toward her, out of his reach. "You memorized my promotional materials. Did you also notice that my designs are the perfect look for Cherry Bella?"

"Well, c'mon," he said, his smile teasing and light, even though his eyes were narrowed now, a little more watchful and a little less charming. "Cherry Bella's the kind of woman who can wear anything and make it look great. And she's going to be the total focus of the spring line. The clothes will barely be noticed."

"My designs always get noticed."

"Sure they do. I'm not saying they're not great. They are. But c'mon, we both know leather gets more looks than froth."

He was so sure he was going to win, he'd just given her the pity look. The oh-so-sorry-you're-a-distant-second look. She'd seen that look so often in her life, she'd have thought she was immune.

Except when it was on Gage's face.

Her jaw tight, Hailey had to work to keep her expression polite, when all she wanted to do was stick out her tongue, dump her melted ice cream in his lap and storm out.

She'd be damned if the sexiest man she'd ever met was going to think she wasn't good enough. Even if he was no longer in the running to find out just how good she *really* was.

"Are you trying to say my designs aren't good enough to get this deal when they're up against yours?"

"I didn't say that." His frown was a flash, gone in a blink. But she caught the surprise in it and realized he'd not only thought she wasn't good enough, he'd also thought she was a wimp-girl. As fluffy and frothy and fragile as her designs.

A lifetime of never being quite enough had, if nothing else, taught her to fight like hell for what she wanted. So before he could respond, she leaned forward and offered her sexiest smile. Her eyes locked on his, she trailed her fingers over the back of his hand in a soft, teasing gesture, then arched her brow.

"But that's what you meant." Hiding both her hurt and her frustration, she gave a pitying shake of her head. "A shame, really. Because if you'd played your cards differently, you'd have been able to find out firsthand just how fabulous my lingerie is."

VISIONS OF HAILEY'S curvy little body packaged in shimmering lace and delicate ribbons danced through Gage's brain like tempting sugarplums.

Visions he'd been damned close to seeing in real life.

He'd been so sure when he walked in here that he could charm her into stepping aside. He'd made a few phone calls, called in a couple of favors and lined up a handful of potential clients for her. Nothing as big as Rudolph in terms of prestige. But some solid deals that could keep her in sexy shoes for a while.

She had a good product, but she was still up-and-coming. Not quite in the same league as Milano. He'd figured she'd be so grateful, they'd not only keep their dinner date, but hurry right through so they could get to the dessert he'd been thinking about.

All he had to do was dish up a little charm, weave his marketing magic and ta-da. He'd be licking chocolate off her belly.

Instead, he'd barely warmed up when Hailey flashed those big green eyes at him and he'd totally forgotten his plan. That had never happened before. He'd had women flash their breasts in the middle of a sales pitch and he hadn't missed a beat.

But now, with his freedom on the line, he'd stepped all over his own tongue. Nothing like coming off as an arrogant ass to tip his hand and piss her off. He'd already lost his shot at seeing her naked. Time to table the idea of dinner, and dessert, and just get her to agree to give up the Rudolph deal. That way he could get the contracts nailed down before ole Rudy decided to add another twist or drag it out further. Then Gage could keep his own client appointments and maybe still get in a little holiday vacation.

Noting the chill in her eyes as she pulled out her wallet to pay for the ice cream, he figured he'd better do it before she walked out.

It was going to take some quick talking.

And some clever marketing.

Good thing he was good at both.

"I already know firsthand how great your lingerie is." He waited a beat, enjoying the way her eyes widened and a hint of pink touched her cheeks. Unable to resist, his gaze dropped to her chest. Completely covered to her chin in a black turtleneck, he could still imagine how she'd looked Saturday night. "You have a distinct sense of style, and now that I think about it, your elf outfit featured pieces of your lingerie line, didn't it?"

Like that bustier. The candy-cane-striped one that'd made his tongue ache to lick her.

"It did," she agreed slowly, as if not sure she wanted to trust him. Gage had to hand it to her; she looked like a china doll, but she was damned smart.

"I'm impressed. Most men don't notice what a girl's wearing, let alone remember and recognize pieces of it days later."

"You made quite an impression. Even if I'd known we were competitors, I'm sure I'd still have hit on you, but I might have been a little more aware that this could get awkward."

"Oh, I don't know," she said, her words as sweet as the hot fudge on the edge of the ice-cream glass. She reached out to touch her finger to the thick chocolate, then pressed it to her tongue. His brain shut down. Gage didn't know whether she'd done it because she was nervous or because she just knew it was the perfect way to torture him. Either way, the south side of his body took a quick leap north.

"You don't know?" he repeated, totally forgetting what they'd been discussing. Something about lingerie, probably.

"I don't know that this is awkward, really. More like a disappointment. I mean, we're both trying to win the same contract. That means our dinner date is off." As Gage was trying to find some appreciation for her practical acceptance of that, she gave a deep sigh that pressed her full chest against that lucky black fabric—and made the blood flow to his dick.

It was that rush of blood that inspired his next words.

"I don't think it has to be quite as cut-and-dried as that," he argued. "You can take my offer, reel in some big clients and everyone's happy. Then we can play the rest of the game just fine."

"You see this as a game?"

"The contract?" he asked. "Or our date?"

Her laugh was a soft puff of air, barely there and not enough to reach her eyes.

"Well, I guess that answers that."

"I'm just saying I don't think we need to let this contract business get in the way of any potential pleasure between us," he heard himself propositioning. This was the first time his dick had ever taken direct control of his brain and had him saying things he knew were insane. Gage wasn't sure if he should be impressed or terrified.

"Well, that does sound tempting," Hailey agreed, her look so warm and sexy that he decided terrified was the wisest choice.

"But I've got to ask," she continued, turning the ice-cream glass in slow circles, its tempting fudge and just a smidgen of whipped cream on the side making him crazy with hunger. "Are you comfortable in second place? Because I plan to win that contract."

It took him three whole seconds to rip his gaze off her full lips and realize what she'd said.

She thought she could beat him?

Hell, all she had to do was take a deep breath and he'd be so focused on her body, she just might have a shot at it.

"Babe, you might want to rethink your plan." Despite feeling as if he'd fallen off a very unfamiliar cliff, Gage gave her a cocky smile. "I never lose."

He knew that statement edged him over into total ass territory. But dammit, he was rattled.

Since this was a first, he clearly wasn't handling it well.

"Rethink my plan?" Her thick lashes fluttered over those big, round eyes, but she didn't look intimidated. Nope. If anything, Hailey appeared irritated. "In what way do you think it needs rethunk?"

Was that even a word? From the way she'd lifted her sharp chin, and arched one brow, Hailey looked as though she was challenging him to question it.

Gage shook his head, trying to bring his thoughts back in line. This wasn't about words, silly or otherwise. This was about her potential disappointment.

He might have had to kiss goodbye all of the prurient sexual plans he had for her body, but he wasn't the kind of guy who took his disappointment out on a lady.

He liked to think he was too chivalrous for that.

So he decided to warn her instead. Hopefully keep her from getting her hopes up too high.

"You're clearly the kind of gal who throws herself into things wholeheartedly," he observed. From the tiny furrow between her brows, he figured he'd hit the mark, and she wasn't exactly thrilled to be read that easily. No surprise. Most of his competitors weren't. "But in this case, you'd do better to have a backup plan."

"Because you're so sure you're going to win."

"I'm just saying I don't want to see you disappointed," he told her, his smile as soothing as the hand he gently glided over her arm.

Her green eyes chilled and she shifted her arm to one

side. Only a few inches, but enough to make it clear that touching her had just made the off-limits list.

"Ooh," she said, drawing the word out in a husky tone that made him think of bedtime moans and whispered words in the dark. She tilted her head to one side and nodded. "So you don't want me to be disappointed."

Never taking her eyes from his, she grabbed her jacket and purse from the seat beside her and slid from the booth. Her body moved with a grace that made it impossible for him to look away, even as manners automatically kicked in and sent him to his feet, as well.

Her lips flicked in a satisfied smile, as if she'd expected nothing less.

Then, in a move as deliberate as it was bold, her gaze slowly—oh, baby, so painfully slowly—drifted down his body. When she reached his zipper, and every wonderful thing contained therein, she gave a sad sort of shake of her head, then looked him in the eye.

"Since our date, and any other plans that it might have led to, are clearly canceled, I'm sure the odds of my being disappointed just plummeted."

With that perfect put-down, and a smile more wicked than a woman with a face as sweet as hers should be allowed, Hailey turned on one sexy heel and walked away.

Leaving Gage to stare at her very fine ass while trying to pull his jaw off the floor.

6

THE MAN WAS pond scum. Worse, he was sexy pond scum disguised as temptation. And he was so damned sure he was going to sweep in and snag the contract. Hailey ground her teeth, still pissed. A good night's sleep might have helped, but she'd spent the night having erotic dreams of Gage, covered in sexy pond scum that looked a lot like his Grinch fur.

Damn him.

There was no way she was letting him take this contract from her. No way in hell.

Hailey stepped into Rudy Rudolph's office riding high on a righteous anger, a double caramel latte and the feminine confidence only great lingerie and a new pair of shoes could offer.

The black leather of her double-strap Mary Janes was a perfect contrast to her red tights and purple knit slip dress. She'd offset the aggressive colors by pulling her hair back in a loose braid, letting tendrils curl around her face. As accents, she'd assured herself. Not for something to hide behind.

"Miss North, welcome."

"Call me Hailey," she told the bald little man for the tenth time. Her smile stiffened when she saw that Gage was already there.

Not only there, she noted, narrowing her eyes. But there, cozied up in the seating area by the window. Right next to a buxom redhead who looked as if she ate sexy guys for breakfast and snacked on the more adventurous ones for dessert.

Hailey's fashion eye took in the woman's expensive dress, a Zac Posen cloque in gunmetal, paired with a droolworthy pair of matching Louboutins. You couldn't begrudge the woman's excellent taste. In clothes, shoes or—Hailey noted as the redhead reached over to lay her hand on Gage's wrist—in men.

"Have a seat, Hailey. Can I get you a drink?"

Gage and the redhead still ignoring her, Hailey refused Rudy's offer, her fingers gripping her leather portfolio bag's handle so tight she was surprised the stitches didn't fall out.

"Cherry," Rudy called as he ushered Hailey across the room. "Here she is. The owner and designer of Merry Widow Lingerie, Hailey North. As you can see, she's just as fetching as her designs."

The redhead rose, a slow sinuous move that in the end had her towering over Hailey's petite frame. It was easy to see why Rudolph wanted her as the face of his spring campaign. She was the embodiment of smoldering sexuality.

"It's a pleasure to meet you, Miss Bella," Hailey said, her words stiffer than she'd like. Because Gage was giving her that smug look, she told herself. Not because the woman had just been touching a guy Hailey herself wanted to lick like a melting Popsicle.

"I love your designs," Cherry said, her trademark voice husky and low, more suited for a dim, smoky bar than a business meeting. But her smile was genuine, and her grasp warm and friendly as she took Hailey's hand. Not to shake. Just to hold for a second, as if making a connection while pulling her over and gesturing that Hailey take the seat next to her. "You create the most romantic celebration of femininity I've ever seen. I'm awed."

Oh.

Her throat tightened. It was enough to make a girl cry.

"And such a contrast to the raw power of Milano's designs," Cherry continued, sliding into her chair with a boneless sort of grace. "Also a celebration of the female form, but with a very different message."

And that was enough to make a girl want to throw things.

For once, just once, Hailey wanted to be the clear choice. The one someone wanted most. But hey, a lifetime of coming in second, third and fourth best taught a girl a few things about sticking with it.

So she kept her big smile in place and sat, not nearly as gracefully, beside Cherry.

"If you don't mind my asking, which do you think suits you best?" Hailey heard herself ask. She barely refrained from biting her lip to try to snap the words back. She'd planned to be charming, persuasive and subtle. Like her designs.

But Cherry didn't seem offended. Instead, she laughed and gave a noncommittal shrug. "I'm a multifaceted woman. Choosing isn't a simple thing. Much, always, depends on my mood."

Hailey almost pointed out that her designs suited a variety of moods, while Milano's only suited the kinkier ones. But this time she managed to keep her mouth closed.

Instead, she—finally—let herself look at Gage.

His dark eyes were aimed right at her, a small smile playing over those sexy lips. As if he were looking into her mind and poking through her plans and ideas, preparing to blow them all to teeny-tiny pieces.

Yet, she still wanted him.

If she closed her eyes, she could still taste that kiss.

Could still feel the touch of his fingers against her skin. Remember the scent of his cologne, the feel of his hair.

No, no, no. The man was a shark, she reminded herself. Not Prince Charming. He'd eat her up in one bite.

An idea which really shouldn't turn her on.

"Let's get started, shall we? Cherry's expressed her preferences between the other choices." Rudy went on to name the lines Cherry had chosen.

Hailey almost jumped out of her chair to do a happy dance when Vivo wasn't among them. They were all strong designers, but none so out there that her lingerie wouldn't complement them. Of course, none were so conservative that Milano's wouldn't work, either. But Hailey was going to ignore that for right now.

"Yours is the final line Cherry needs to review before we settle on the spring lineup," Rudy continued. Playing waiter with a dapper flair, he set a Plexiglas tray on the small table centered between their four chairs, motioned to the coffee, tea and juice as if encouraging everyone to help themselves.

When nobody did, he snagged a Christmas cookie shaped like a reindeer, bit its head off and gestured with its body. "I'd like the two of you to give a final pitch. Tell us why your design is perfect for Cherry Bella and Rudolph department stores."

"Ladies first," Gage said before Hailey could do more than take a nervous breath.

She gave him a look, intending to say something—anything—that'd put him in his place and let him know that he wasn't running this show.

But the second her eyes met his, her brain shut down. She hated that. But her body—oh, her body—it loved the results. Big-time.

Her heart did a little dance in perfect time with the nerves swirling around in her stomach. She could stare into his eyes for hours. Days, even. Nights would be even better. She wanted to see those eyes heat again, darken with desire and smolder with passion. Like they'd done when he'd kissed her.

She wet her lips, remembering his taste. The texture of his mouth. The sweep of his tongue.

"Hailey?"

"Hmm?" She blinked. Then she blinked again, her eyes widening in horror before she ripped them from Gage to focus on the man with the giant checkbook and the key to her future. "I'm sorry, what?"

"Why don't you go ahead and make your pitch."

She wanted to suggest that Gage go first instead. She wanted to ask for a bucket of ice. She could barely think straight with her brain locked in horny mode. But they were all gazing at her expectantly and she didn't want to make waves. Or worse, look as though she wasn't grateful for this opportunity.

Deep breaths and don't look at Gage, she instructed herself.

Okay, then…

She'd spent all night obsessing over this. Now that it was time to pitch it, she hoped like hell she'd obsessed in the right direction.

"Clearly you have two very strong lingerie lines to choose from," Hailey said, starting her pitch by offering Gage her first smile, then going right back to trying to pretend he wasn't there. "The question is, which one do you think is going to garner the best publicity and success for both Rudolph department stores and for Cherry Bella?

"Your theme for spring is A New You. Your strategy is to inspire makeovers, redos and taking chances. And where better to begin such a journey than with how a woman feels about herself. Lingerie goes beyond physical support. It provides emotional support. The right lingerie inspires a woman to believe in herself. It validates her femininity. Merry Widow Lingerie is more than a fashion statement. It's an empowerment statement."

Hailey paused, gauging their expressions. The interest in Rudy's combined with the agreement in Cherry's was great. But it was the concern on Gage's that rocked her. With that as encouragement, she continued her presentation. She pulled out graphs and sales figures, passed around a few samples of the merchandise in all its frothy lace beauty and put her entire heart into the pitch.

"It really comes down to messaging," she wound up. "What message do you want to send women, and what message do you think women will respond best to? I think you'll find that romance, with its empowering belief in love and happy results, will be a stronger selling point."

Pleased with her speech, and that she could sit back down and pretend she wasn't nervous enough to hurl, Hailey offered Rudy and Cherry a warm smile. Then, her body boneless, she slid into the chair next to Gage's. As soon as she did, he stood. Clearly he wanted to erase her impression as quickly as possible from the others' minds.

"Since it's just the four of us, let's be honest," Gage said in a persuasively amused tone. "We all know what sells. Especially when it comes to lingerie."

"And that is?" Cherry asked, clearly not willing to let him take the easy way through his pitch.

"Sex. Empowerment and emotions are all great between the pages of a book or at a self-help seminar. But nobody thinks that when they are buying lingerie. What women, and more importantly men, are thinking about when they look for lingerie is sex."

Hailey's mouth dropped open. It took her a solid five seconds to force it closed.

He'd thrown her under the bus. For the first time since she'd seen him all wrapped up in that green fur costume, she wanted to kick him. Gage wasn't the Grinch, she realized. He was a flat-out shark. A shark standing there in a very expensive suit, looking as though he owned the whole damned world.

"Now, as sweet and appealing as Merry Widow's lingerie is, let's face it…there's nothing that says sex like black leather." To emphasize his point, Gage lifted a presentation board from his portfolio and continued his pitch. Hailey barely heard him, though; she was too busy focusing on the photo of a leggy redheaded model swathed in leather and holding a microphone, a blatant play to Cherry.

To try to keep from hissing at being dismissed as sweet and appealing, as if those were stupid things, Hailey shifted her gaze toward Rudy and Cherry. Were they as disgusted by the hard sell as she was?

Her stomach sank.

Instead of disagreeing, Rudy was nodding away, his eyes on the leather-clad model's photos and his tongue practically draped over his tie.

And Cherry… Well, she was staring out the window, her expression as far away and morose as the gray clouds engulfing the bridge.

Gage just kept on pitching, reiterating and reframing the presentation he'd offered ten minutes before. He alternated between numbers that seemed to make Rudy drool and flattery that, thankfully, Cherry wasn't paying much attention to. Instead, the woman looked pensive as she stared out the window.

Her teeth clenched, Hailey wanted to yell *no*. They were smart business people, weren't they? Shouldn't this decision be based on an overall logic? On what fit best for the line? On the designs that'd appeal to the widest demographic?

As Gage finished his pitch, sliding the cover over his presentation board and taking a seat, Rudy's decision was clear on his face. Hailey's heart sank into her very cute shoes. He was clearly a man who'd made his fortune thinking a little south of logic.

"Well, thank you both. This was a very informative morning," the older man said. "Why don't we break for lunch now so Cherry and I can discuss this, and we'll notify you by this afternoon of our decision."

Her stomach plunged into her adorable shoes fast enough to make Hailey nauseous.

He was going to choose Milano. Despite the fact that Cherry had overruled his preference, Vivo's shoe designs, he was still going to pick the ugly leather.

And that would mean the end of Merry Widow Lingerie.

Oh, sure, she could eventually get a job doing design elsewhere. Maybe. But what about her employees? Her clients? Her dream?

She took a deep breath, trying to accept that she couldn't change the man's mind. She couldn't jump up, stomp her feet and insist he choose her. She'd tried that a few times over the course of her life, and had always been the one standing there alone with sore toes.

But…

She couldn't just let it go.

"Wait," Hailey cried, halting everyone midrise, their butts four inches from their chairs. Rudy and Gage frowned, but Cherry sat right back down, her expression warm and encouraging.

"I think he's wrong. Gage clearly has a strong grasp of basic marketing. And he's right. Sex Sells 101 is often an effective advertising ploy." She paused, letting the emphasis on the word ploy sink in. "But is that really what you want? A ploy? Gimmicks only go so far, don't they?"

She addressed that question to Cherry, who suddenly looked very tired. As if all this talking had sapped her energy.

"Gimmicks have their place," Cherry said, her shrug indicating that their place was nowhere near her.

At her words, the men settled back in their chairs. Gage's expression was guarded, but Rudy was watching his muse like a hawk.

That was her hook, Hailey knew. No matter how much Rudy might want to see women prancing down his runway come February wearing tiny strips of leather and stilettos, he'd defer to what Cherry wanted.

"Sex sells…. In this case, it'd sell to a very specific market. But you want to make this year's debut extraordinary, don't you, Mr. Rudolph? This is the first year you've ever built a line around a person rather than a theme."

"That's true. Although Miss Bella hasn't signed the agreement yet," Rudy said with a jovial sort of laugh that did nothing to disguise his concern over that detail.

"Once I know exactly what I'd be representing, I'll make my decision," Cherry said, her words friendly but firm, with just a hint of impatience. "My image, and my personal comfort levels, must be in sync with anything I do."

"Which is why Merry Widow is perfect for you," Hailey said, leaning forward and clasping both hands on her knees. "It's a line that focuses on the image of romance, of the ultimate in feminine empowerment, while ensuring you feel so real you can't be anything but comfortable."

Out of breath, Hailey forced herself not to grin. She was proud of herself. That'd sounded pretty awesome.

"I beg to differ," Gage broke in. His tone was smooth-as-silk friendly, but the look in his eyes was diamond hard. And, Hailey noted, just a little surprised. Obviously he really hadn't expected her to be any sort of competition. Just a bit of fluff, like her lingerie.

He turned to Cherry, charm oozing from every pore. Hailey wanted to hate that he could do that. But who could blame a man for being fabulous at what he did? She just wished he could be fabulous somewhere else.

Like in her bedroom.

"Miss Bella, you're a very sexy woman. Gorgeous, talented and not one to shy away from using both of those as a platform for your voice. Much like Milano Lingerie, you're distinctive, strong and bold. If anyone can showcase feminine appeal and edgy allure, you can."

Gage leaned closer to the torch singer, letting his smile widen, and laid a hand on the arm of her chair. He didn't touch her; he just suggested an intimacy, a connection.

Hailey had to actually clench her butt to the chair to keep herself seated. She wanted to leap out of her seat and smack his hand away.

You'd think her stomach would be too crowded already with nerves, panic and hurt to have room for one more nasty, balled-up emotion. But there it was, jealousy in all its hairy ugliness. "There is a lot to recommend both lines," Cherry said slowly, her gaze shifting back and forth between Gage and Hailey. "I'm not sure which I feel best fits my image."

"Isn't a better question, what message do you want to send by wearing the line?" Hailey asked before Gage could jump in with another one of those devastatingly effective innuendos. "Do your songs, does your image, equate to sex? Or to romance? Lingerie is about more than the physical act. It's about intimacy."

When the redhead's brows drew together as she considered that, Hailey took a deep breath and, ignoring her natural abhorrence for aggressive pushiness, plunged on.

"That's what it all comes down to, after all. Sex, which is strictly physical satisfaction. Or romance, which invokes the emotions, the mind and the imagination."

"There's plenty of imagination in sex," Gage said, finally dropping his charming facade to frown at Hailey.

"Sex sells for a very good reason. People like it. People want it. Sex, in leather lingerie, will appeal across the board to men and women alike. Fluff might get a few women's attention, but it won't get the men's."

"Women buy more lingerie," Hailey pointed out.

"To appeal to men," he countered.

"Romance sells much better than sex," she argued. "It sends a more empowering, desirable message and will bring in a wider customer base."

His hands loosely clasped between his knees, Gage leaned forward. He was still many feet away, but it was as if he'd moved right into her space. As if he were intimately pressing against her. Hailey's breath caught. Her body heated. She bit her lip, trying not to squirm and damning him for being able to trigger such intense sexual awareness in her body.

"Sex outsells romance. Just check the internet stats."

"Porn?" Hailey dismissed with a sniff.

"Pays well," he countered.

"Is that what Rudolph department stores is selling? Or are they focused on creating an exclusive image?"

"They're selling a trend." Gage's tone and expression were pure triumph. As if she'd just set him up to make the perfect point.

Hailey glared. She wanted to kick him for looking so smug over there, wearing his brilliant marketing-wizard face.

"Well, this has been a great meeting," Rudy interrupted before they could get to the eye-poking and name-calling portion of their argument. "The two of you have presented us with some very good reasons to consider either line. Both have great merit. But of course, we can only feature one."

Hailey ripped her gaze from Gage's smug, sexy grin to look at the man who could make or break her future. Suddenly she wanted to cry. She could see it, the decision on

Rudy's face. She'd got so close. She'd done her best and jumped way outside her comfort zone to argue for her designs. And he was still going to go with Milano?

She looked away, blinking fast to clear her burning eyes. The decorations lining the wall caught her eye. Awards. Trophies. Photo after photo of Rudy winning this or that. Many of them, she noted through narrowed eyes, at poker tournaments.

"Why don't we make a bet," she heard herself say.

"What?"

"I beg your pardon?"

"Ooh," Rudy intoned, rubbing his hands together and leaning forward. "What kind of bet?"

Hailey licked her lips, not having a clue what kind of bet. She tried to think over the roaring sound of panic rushing through her head. Taking calming breaths to try to overcome her horror at the temerity of challenging Rudolph. This man could break her. Wasn't leaving on good terms, with a possible order of future lingerie, enough? She'd made a good contact, and she'd garnered enough press and attention to possibly pull in more sales.

But a few sales and orders weren't going to be enough to get a loan the size she needed to save her business.

So stomach rock tight and nerves dancing, she wet her lips and forced herself to smile.

"Well, the question really comes down to which will be a stronger selling point for your spring line. Sex—" she bit off the word, letting it hang there for a second, then gave a deep sigh before adding "—or romance?"

Gage gave her an arch look as if to say, *didn't we already cover this?* Determined to get her point, whatever the hell it was, out before he interrupted and took over again, she sat up straighter and tilted her head toward Cherry.

"Miss Bella can sell either. But the true question is,

which one will have the widest appeal? Which one will send customers clamoring for the latest in Rudolph Exclusives? And," she added triumphantly, "which one will enhance Cherry's reputation and image in a way that benefits her career, as well?"

"I'm hearing the repeat of your sales pitch, but I'm not hearing a bet," Gage murmured.

"We each get two chances to prove our point. Sex or romance. Then Mr. Rudolph and Miss Bella decide which they think really offers the most to their prospective images."

"How do you propose we do that?"

She had no freaking clue.

But she wasn't going to let him know that.

Instead, Hailey fluttered her lashes and offered up a smug smile of her own.

"I have so many ideas, my challenge will be narrowing them down."

"We do have to get moving on this," Rudy started to say, his words drawn out and hesitant as he tried to read Cherry's reaction. "It can't go on for too long."

Trying not to let on how desperate she was, Hailey cast her mind around every idea, every argument, every possible persuasion she could offer that might get him to agree. She had nothing. Biting her lip, she looked at Cherry. The other woman didn't really want to parade around in a leather bikini, did she? It would probably chafe something horrible.

"I can give it a week," Cherry said, her eyes on Hailey. "At that point, I'll be able to let you know which lingerie line I prefer. And if I'm going to take your offered position as spokesmodel."

SON OF A BITCH.

Gage couldn't figure it out.

He'd been right there, in the winning position. They all knew Rudy was going to go with Milano.

That contract, and his freedom, had been in the palm of his hand. He'd felt bad, just a little, about playing to his strengths as hard as he had. Hailey was sweet, and clearly a talented designer. But she didn't have that killer edge that made the difference between success and luck.

Then, just when he was ready to pull out his pen and sign the contract, the pretty little blonde had outflanked him. Again. How the hell did she keep doing that? He didn't know if it was deliberate, or if Hailey was just lucky.

But now thanks to her, instead of heading up to Tahoe and mapping out the details of his brilliant kick-his-brother's-ass-and-prove-he-was-the-best business plan, he was going to be stuck pimping sex wrapped in leather for two weeks?

No way.

"I don't have another week available to negotiate this project," he said, shifting his body so he was facing Rudy. Not so much to cut the women out of the discussion as to keep Hailey from his line of sight. If he didn't see her, he wouldn't get distracted and she couldn't work her sweet magic. "And I thought you said you wanted your people moving on the advertising before Christmas. That means you don't have time to waste, either. It's not like they can whip up a brilliant campaign in a couple of days."

"You think this is a waste?"

Gage kept his grimace to a twitch, smoothing out his expression before he gave Cherry a warm smile. Her expression didn't budge. She was clearly a woman who expected to be catered to, which meant he'd just made a major misstep.

"I think your time is valuable, and that you must have more important things to do for the holidays than play..."
He paused, then hating himself but knowing it had to be

done, he gave Hailey an arch look. "What is it you wanted us to do again?"

She wet her lips, the move making the shell-pink flesh glisten. His own mouth watered.

He'd offered her an out yesterday. A chance to pick up a solid bevy of new clients, all ready to order. If she was as desperate as that look in her eyes indicated, she'd have grabbed his offer with both hands. She had to know her tiny company didn't stand much of a chance against an enterprise like Milano. He'd checked into her business this morning before the meeting and she wasn't heavily in debt or having obvious issues.

So it came down to one thing. There was only one reason she could have refused his offer and was pushing this silly bet idea.

Pure stubbornness.

"Maybe once we know how you think this bet will work, we can figure out the timeline," Rudy said, his tone pacifying. Not to Hailey, Gage knew. But to the lush, red-headed torch singer.

"Maybe we should just—"

"My thought is that Gage and I each take turns planning a scenario that we feel showcases the image our lingerie will offer. Mine would be to show you how romance would enhance both your reputation as a trendsetter and fashion icon, Mr. Rudolph, and the sensual image Miss Bella's built over the last few years, as well."

She tilted her head toward Gage, a lock of baby blond hair sliding over her cheek, reminding him of how soft it was. How it'd felt to tilt her face up to best receive his kisses.

Shake it off, man, Gage told himself, actually twitching his shoulders. *Don't let her get to you again.*

"And what do you suggest my scenario would be?"

"Whatever situation you think would best showcase the message your lingerie brings to the table, of course."

What message did leather panties suit?

A strip club? Bondage basement? Adult video store?

Hell, maybe she had a point.

From the look on her face, she knew it, too.

And so did Rudy and Cherry, Gage noted.

Crap.

"Not a problem," he lied smoothly.

"I like this idea. A lot, actually. And it'll only take a week," Cherry said with a languid wave of one hand, a walnut-sized diamond flashing in the morning light as she dismissed Gage's tight schedule. "But I've commitments, so my time is scarce. You'll have to plan these little tableaux for evenings when I'm not performing."

They all looked to Rudy, who ran one long-fingered hand over his bald head as he gauged Cherry's expression. When he saw her determined interest, he sighed and gave a shrug.

"Okay, then. Cherry performs four nights this week, if I remember correctly." At her nod, he continued. "That gives you three to choose among. Figure out the details and let us know by five this afternoon. If at any time either of you fails to create your scenario or in any way drops the ball, the contract goes to the other person."

He waited a beat, then stood, putting an end to the meeting.

Gage waited for the pleasantries to wind up and for the old man to escort Cherry from the room. The minute they hit the doorway, he turned on Hailey.

Damned if she wasn't adorable. Even through his irritation, all he could think of was how cute she was. And remember what she'd tasted like.

"Well, it looks like it's not quite over yet." Her voice was filled with bravado, but she'd chewed off her pretty pink lipstick and her eyes were wary. As if she wasn't quite sure what he was going to do now that they'd lost their buffer.

What he wanted to do was slide his hand up those smooth red tights, right under her skirt, and see if they were the kind that went to the waist or just to the top of the thighs. He wanted to touch her, to warm himself against her sweet little body again.

But mostly he wanted to tie her to his bed, where she couldn't cause him any further trouble. Except, he acknowledged as he shifted from one foot to the other, trouble to the fit of his slacks.

"You know what you've done, don't you?" he said, keeping his words quiet in hopes that the anger wouldn't come through. If the way her eyes widened as she leaned backward was any indication, he didn't succeed.

It didn't stop her from lifting her chin and giving him a so-what look, though. "I did exactly what I came here to do. I did my best to get this account."

Gage laughed. Couldn't fault her that.

"Sweetheart, you've got us double-dating."

7

How DID A girl dress for a date with her competition—the sexiest man on earth—a wealthy pervert with the power to make or break her future and a gorgeous woman who intimidated the hell out of her?

With killer lingerie, of course.

Hopefully, killer lingerie would make this evening magic. Parking her car, Hailey grimaced. Two days after she'd issued the bet challenge, and it was time to rock. She took a deep breath, the move pushing her lacy-edged breasts tight against the sheer fabric of her blouse. Tonight was all about romance. But that didn't mean romance wasn't sexy. To prove that point, she'd opted for exquisite lace and satin in a delicate shade of pink under a blouse the color of milk chocolate. Her full skirt, the same shade of brown, hit midthigh, the better to show off the delicate seams and bows climbing the backs of her sheer stockings.

That her thong and garter belt matched the pale pink bra visible through the filmy fabric of her blouse was Hailey's little secret. One that people might guess, which meant it'd titillate and intrigue. Not scream "do me because I wear sexy underwear"…like *some people's* lingerie.

"Miss North, you look amazing," the maître d' greeted as she swept into Carinos, where she'd set the scene for her special scenario pitch. It wasn't so much that she wanted to rub in Gage's face what he'd lost by choosing a contract over her. No. Carinos was her favorite restaurant. If he ate his heart out in addition to the delicious dinner she'd arranged, well, that was icing on the cake.

"Thanks, Paolo," she responded with a warm smile, following him to the private room she'd arranged, pleased at the ambience along the way. Soft music, flickering candles, the delicate scent of roses filling the air as they skirted the main dining room and stopped just short of the atrium, with its lush display of winter roses.

"The rest of the party should be along shortly," she told Paolo, slipping him a generous tip as he gestured to the door of their private room.

"One gentleman is already here, Miss North. I'll escort the others as soon as they arrive."

Figuring that gentleman was Gage trying to get the jump on her, and wanting to be sure Paolo was waiting for Rudy and Cherry, she told him she'd seat herself. Hailey took a deep breath, mentally going over her checklist for the evening, then plastered on her biggest smile as she entered the room.

Her breath stuck in her chest.

Oh, baby, Gage was gorgeous.

The navy suit fit him to perfection. And since his back was turned while he stared out the glass wall at the flower garden, she could see how well tailored the slacks were, cupping his butt in a way that made her jealous of the fabric.

Then he turned.

And the view from the front was even sexier.

Puffing out a little breath, she forced herself to lift her gaze to his face. It was like trying to heft a very reluctant elephant over her head. Her eyes wanted to slide right back down.

"Ahh, my date." His smile was wickedly teasing and

light. But his gaze turned hot fast as he took in her appearance. "You look lovely."

Uh-oh.

The first rule she'd set for this evening was to keep a distance between herself and Gage. To stay as far away as politely possible so she could maintain control. Of her thoughts. Of her body. And of the situation.

But as he crossed the room and took her hands in his, all she could do was sigh. After all, it'd be rude to pull away.

"Thank you." She gazed up at him, her fingers itching to touch his perfectly styled hair, to muss it just a little so it fell across his forehead like it had the first evening they'd met.

Then he raised one of her hands to his lips, brushing his mouth over her knuckles. Hailey's knees almost buckled. Talk about romantic. It was as if he had magic in those lips of his.

And if he could get her all weak in the knees with such a sweet move, what else could that mouth do? She knew his kisses were hot enough to melt her panties.

Suddenly she was desperate to know how much more power he had. To feel more of what he had to offer.

And he knew it.

The look in Gage's eyes was a combination of wicked amusement and sexual heat. A promise. One she had every faith he could keep, and one she was quickly becoming desperate to feel.

"Miss North…"

Hailey's eyes dropped to Gage's mouth. Those lips were curved. Soft. Full. She wanted to taste them. To feel them trailing down her body.

"Excuse me."

"Someone wants you," Gage said, his words low and amused.

Him?

"Miss North?"

Dammit.

Hailey pulled her hands, and her body, away from Gage and turned. Face on fire, she shook her head, trying to toss off the spell, then turned to give Paolo a shaky smile.

"Yes?"

"A message for you." As polite and circumspect as if he were totally oblivious to the sexual sparks flying around the room, he stepped forward and handed Hailey a slip of paper. Then, without a word, he turned smartly on one heel and exited. Leaving Hailey alone with Gage and all that sexual temptation.

Frowning, she opened the slip of paper and read it. Her frown turned into a scowl and she crushed the note in her fist.

"What's wrong?"

"Apparently Cherry can't make it. She's not feeling well this evening. She sent the message through Rudy, who said he'd meet us in an hour and to go ahead and start dinner without him."

Damn. Damn, damn, damn.

Hailey all but stomped her foot and shook her fist at the ceiling, she was so frustrated.

She'd planned this evening so carefully. The most romantic restaurant, a private room. She'd ordered the meal, the dessert, the champagne and even picked the music, all with the idea of impressing Cherry and Rudy.

Now, neither of them was here.

Her grand plan to prove she was the best pick for the contract, *poof.* Gone. She swallowed hard, trying to get past the lump of tears clogging her throat.

"Well, I guess we can get on with the evening," Gage said, his tone close to a shrug. "Rudy will get here when he gets here."

"What's the point? I'm not trying to convince *you* of the

merits of a romantic evening," she said, jerking one shoulder in a dismissive shrug. *Be nice,* a part of her chided. He might be her competition, but Gage was still a major player who knew a lot of people. If she angered him, he could easily spread the word that she was a bitch or a diva. Or just a pain in his butt.

But for once, she didn't care about that cautioning voice. She wasn't worried about upsetting anyone. Not when she was already this upset herself.

"Look, have a glass of wine and let's eat. We might as well," Gage persuaded. "There's no point in letting this ambience go to waste. The wine is chilled. The stomachs are growling. Let's enjoy it."

Hailey looked around the room.

Ambience, indeed. A cozy table for four covered in white linen, lit candles amid holiday greenery on the table and the sideboard. Instead of the Christmas tunes that were playing gently out in the restaurant, the speakers here played the bluesy romantic tones of Cherry's music. A bottle of wine waited, as did a tray of hors d'oeuvres and fruit.

And Gage.

Looking oh so sexy and sympathetic.

She might be able to resist the sexy—and that was a huge *might*—but the sympathy in his dark eyes? Her heart melted a little; it was so unused to anyone seeming to give two good damns about her.

"Maybe we should hold the meal until Rudy joins us," she murmured, sure an evening alone with Gage was a bad idea. One that'd feel amazingly good, but still… "Wouldn't it be better to wait for him?"

"No." Gage took her hand, led her to a seat with a perfect view of the garden and held out the chair. "He said to start without him. I'm starving, so let's eat."

Hailey hesitated, then sat. Because she was starving. Not because she wanted more time with Gage. She'd been so amped over this evening, so busy planning it all, that she hadn't eaten a thing since breakfast.

"This doesn't count as my pitch for the contract. Once we eat or drink, unless Rudy or Cherry are here, the pitch is void." Determined to settle that point, Hailey gave him an intent, narrow-eyed look. "Okay?"

"You sure?" Gage leaned back in his chair, giving her a considering look that made her shiver and wish she'd worn something that didn't actually show her underwear. When she nodded, he lifted his glass of ice water with a twist of lemon and drank. "I guess we'll just have to call this a date, then."

Her eyes rounding, Hailey gulped.

"No—"

"Hey, you said it," he interrupted. "It's not for business. Which means this is a date. Just you and me and what dates are all about. Pure pleasure."

GAGE LOVED WATCHING Hailey's face. She was an open book, every emotion, every thought playing across those pretty features. Right now, her slick berry lips pursed and her brows creased, he read irritation, dismay and—yes, oh yes, baby—a whole lot of interest and sexual heat.

He figured the heated interest was enough to overcome the other dismay. And he kinda liked the irritation. It meant he was keeping her on edge. And Hailey on edge was fun. Like watching a hissing, spitting kitten.

"This is not a date."

Gage grinned. She was so cute when she was stubborn.

"Sure it is. You. Me. Candlelight dinner, all the foofy romantic accompaniments. That says date."

"Foofy?" Her green eyes slitted and she spat the word, just like the hissing kitten he'd thought her. "You call romance *foofy?*"

"Sure. It's like frosting." When she frowned and shook

her head, he elaborated. "Frosting is sweet. It's fluffy and tasty and quite often decadent. But it's not the point. The point is the cake."

"And you think leather lingerie is cake?"

"No." He waited for the stiffness to drain from her shoulders and her face to relax again before adding, "The cake is sex."

He laughed when she almost fumbled her glass of water.

"You're awfully naive for a woman who designs sex clothes."

"I don't design sex clothes. I design lingerie. Underwear, sleepwear, apparel to make a woman feel confident and attractive and empowered."

As much as he was enjoying the view of her face, those round cheeks flushed and her eyes flashing, Gage let his gaze drop.

Her see-through blouse was ruffly and full, creating a hazy distraction from the delicious curve of her breasts, highlighted to perfection in a pink bra. He had to hand it to her. Lacy and dotted with pearly things, the bra was attractive. And if it made her feel confident and empowered, well, more power to that sweet satin.

But he was thinking sex when he looked at it.

A fact he knew was clear on his face when he met her eyes again. A fact that, if the way her gaze blurred and her breath hitched were any indication, got her a little excited.

Good. He still had hope of rescuing this evening. As irritated as he was to put off his departure to Tahoe until next week after he'd nailed down winning this contract, spending more time with Hailey was a pretty good consolation.

He'd be even happier if they could spend some of that time naked. Or at least—his gaze dropped again—seeing her lingerie in more detail.

"Then I guess I'm all for empowerment if it comes in

pink satin and—" He made a show of leaning closer. "Is that lace tan or brown?"

Pink, even darker than the last blush, washed her cheeks. Gage grinned. Teasing her was fun. Something he'd never actually experienced when it came to business. Missing was that sharp competitive edge, the driving need to win. Not that he had any doubt he'd triumph when it came to the contract. But for once, it was more about enjoying himself than proving himself.

Just then, the waiter stepped in with wine and a tray.

Gage leaned back, watching Hailey relax as she chatted with the man as he poured wine, letting him know it'd just be the two of them for dinner so to go ahead and serve. He waited until the man had left before arching a brow.

"We don't order for ourselves?"

She gave an impatient little sniff, then after an internal debate that had him wondering what she was hiding, she shrugged.

"The point of this dinner is romance. Which is more than just candles, wine and music."

"I might hate whatever you chose, though," he teased.

"If you do, then I'm not very good at relaying the message of romance, am I?"

She said it as if romance was real. As if it was more than a sales pitch. He knew she was sweet, bordering on naive. But to really believe in that fairy tale? She wasn't crazy.

"C'mon," Gage said with a laugh. "It's just us. Be honest. You're not really buying into this whole romance-versus-sex thing, are you? That's only a ploy to strengthen your pitch."

Her lower lip stuck out when she frowned. He wanted to reach over and trace the pad of his thumb against it, test its softness.

"You don't believe in romance?"

"It's a device. A sales pitch." He waved one hand to indicate the room, lifting his glass of wine with the other. "It's all imagery."

He sipped his wine, then gave an approving nod, pretending she wasn't staring at him as though he'd spouted a third head and started babbling about the coming of aliens to take over the world and dress everyone in little pink tutus.

"Imagery? Romance is emotions, not packaging."

"What's its purpose?" he challenged, leaning back to rest one arm on the back of his chair and giving her a curious look. "To sell something, right? Sex, maybe? Companionship? Accoutrements like candles and wine and lingerie?"

Instead of rising to the bait and defending the fluff and froth of romance as he'd expected, Hailey just stared. Her look was intense, searching. Gage shifted, wondering if she could suddenly see through him the way he could see through her blouse. If so, he was pretty sure she wasn't nearly as intrigued by what she saw.

"Is your lingerie just packaging?" she countered. "Is it just a way to make money?"

Yeah.

That was how his grandfather had built the company. On the concept of seeing what people thought they wanted and coming up with ideas to meet those wants.

That was how Devon developed new product offerings. He looked at the ideas people thought were so appealing and made them better. Bigger. More attractive, so they'd pay top dollar.

And that was how Gage sold it. By tapping into what people thought they needed and convincing them that his product was the only one that could perfectly meet that need.

It was Psychology 101, combined with Economics and Marketing 102.

But he didn't think telling her that was going to score him any points.

So he shrugged, then shot a smile at the waiter, who chose that perfect moment to bring their food.

"Imagery is imagination, yes. It's packaging and appeal. But romance is more than that," she said as their dishes were set in front of them. His favorite spinach salad, he noted with a frown. "Romance is emotions."

"Imagery taps into the emotions. Plays them," he said, still frowning at the salad and wondering how she knew exactly what he liked. He glanced up to ask her and winced at the look on her face. Clearly she didn't think the emotions were something to be played with.

He waited for her to chew him out.

Instead, she leaned closer, resting one hand on his forearm for support as she lifted her mouth toward his ear.

"And just so you know," she said, her words a whisper of heat against the side of his head, low enough so the waiter couldn't hear, "the lace is bittersweet chocolate. You know, like frosting."

Gage closed his eyes and bit back a groan.

Every time he thought he had the upper hand, she found a way to knock him off balance.

"Enjoy," the waiter said, breaking his thoughts.

Opening his eyes, Gage watched the guy leave. In the three seconds it took him to regain his equilibrium, Hailey dug into her own salad with a tiny moan of delight.

"I'm so glad you insisted we eat," she admitted with a sheepish smile. "I was starving."

"What's for dessert?" he asked, noting that her salad was slightly different from his. Spinach, yes, but hers had strawberries, which he was allergic to. Did she know that? "Something frosted, I hope."

She laughed, looking more relaxed than he'd seen her since they'd realized they were rivals.

"You don't really mean that about romance, do you? That you don't think it's real?" she asked after a few bites. "I didn't peg you as the kind of guy who didn't believe in the softer side of love."

Another one for the imagery books. Gage shoved a fork-ful of spinach in his mouth to keep that opinion to himself.

"I think we buy into what we want to believe," he finally said. "If you want to believe that love is romantic, you look for that. If someone else thinks that sex is about physical gratification, they find images to support that belief."

"And if I wanted to believe you're a grumpy sort of emotional curmudgeon who, after being exposed to a little romance, has his heart grow three times too large, will I see that, too?" she teased, her smile bright and her eyes dancing as she referenced his Grinch costume.

"I have no doubt you could make something grow three times larger…." It was difficult, but he managed to hold back his smile until he saw that pink on her cheeks. "But I doubt it'd involve my heart. Disappointed?"

Her lips pursed, as if she was debating.

"Well, I suppose it won't jeopardize my chances of winning the account to admit that I was disappointed to find out you were my competition," she said with a little shrug. The move did delicious things under that filmy shirt, the lush pillows of her breasts moving against the satin bra as if protesting their confinement. Gage's fingers ached to touch. To see if she was as soft as she looked.

"Disappointed because you are worried I'll win?" he asked, too distracted by the view to worry about nicing up his words.

"Disappointed that it meant we can't date," she denied, just a hint of irritation. "The man I met at the party was very appealing."

It wasn't her words, so much as the snap in her tone

that grabbed his attention. Gage noted the annoyance as it flashed in her eyes, then was gone.

"But now you're wondering if that man was real." Gage frowned, wondering that, too. And wondering why he cared so much.

"You're obviously real, seeing as you're sitting right next to me all but licking—" she hesitated, took a breath that made her breasts shift deliciously again, then said archly "—your plate. The only question I have is who you really are."

Marcus Milano's son.

Devon Milano's younger brother.

The last one consulted, the one who least fit the Milano mold.

And—definitely—a man who didn't need a pretty little blonde poking into who he *really* was.

Time to change the subject.

"Isn't the more important question how you're going to pitch this romantic fluff idea of yours?" he said with just a hint of disdain. As he'd hoped, her eyes flashed and she shifted her shoulders back into combat position.

Good.

The only time he wanted her focused on him was if it included naked skin, hot tongues and the buildup to incredible orgasms.

"You're very dismissive of something you don't understand." She arched one brow, poking a strawberry with her fork and lifting it to her mouth. She didn't bite it, though. Instead, she slid the juicy fruit over her lower lip. Gage's eyes narrowed and his body stiffened.

She smiled, her look pure triumph, as if her x-ray eyes saw through the table at his burgeoning boner.

"Don't you think you're proving my point?" Gage asked, shifting in his chair. He wasn't embarrassed at his physical reaction. But he wasn't sure where she was going with this, either. Hailey had a way of leading things along, all innocent-like, then just when he was sure he'd won, she'd bat those lashes and outmaneuver him.

He had to admire that about her.

"No." She touched the strawberry with the tip of her tongue, as if testing its taste. Gage's brain shut down and he suddenly didn't give a damn whether she won or not. Just as long as she did that same move on a particular part of his body.

"Your point was that it's just about sex. That the physical act and gratification are all that matters. My point is that the packaging is what makes that act so powerful. The buildup, the anticipation. The emotional journey."

She paused to let her words sink in, then bit that strawberry right in half. Gage almost groaned out loud as his dick did a happy leap to full attention.

"You know," she reminded him softly as she licked a tiny piece of strawberry off her lip. "The romance."

"Visuals," he countered after clearing his throat. Then, always ready to play to win, he leaned closer. Close enough to get in her space. Close enough that the delicate scent of her perfume wrapped around him. And close enough to see the rapid beat of her pulse against her throat.

"Imagery is powerful. I could describe to you exactly how I want to strip those clothes from your body, what I'd like to do once you're naked and beneath me, how I want to taste you and where I'll touch." He waited, letting those words sink in. And sink they did, as she dropped her fork next to her plate and blinked quickly, looking as if she was trying to fan away that image with her eyelashes. Gage grinned. "But that's sex. Which is my point."

As if he'd been waiting around the corner for just the right moment, the waiter came in again with their entrées. Gage vowed to give the guy an extra tip for perfect timing, since Hailey now had to sit quietly, looking shell-shocked and absorbing his words instead of skipping right past them while trying to prove her point.

A point, Gage had to admit as his dinner was slid in front of him, that was pretty solid. If she was basing romance on good food and ambience, she'd have nailed it. He looked closer at the plate, noting all his favorites, from the way the steak was cooked to the type of vegetables.

"So what'd you do? Hire an investigator to scope out what I eat? If Cherry and Rudy were here, would they be having the same?"

"If Cherry and Rudy were here, their meals would fit their tastes," she said primly, cutting a delicate sliver off her chicken.

Gage glanced at the place settings, trying to see how she'd designated it so the waiter knew who got what. They all looked the same. And he'd chosen his own seat, and hers, so that wasn't it.

"Clever, but I don't see what makes the meal choice romantic. Or what it has to do with lingerie," he added, needing to remember the real purpose of this evening.

"No?" She gave him one of those looks only women could pull off. The kind that made it clear she wondered where he kept his brains but didn't hold his lack of knowledge against him since he was so damned cute. "Romance is the effort to show you care about someone else's preferences. It's putting in a little extra time to make sure they feel appreciated. Special."

"My grandma does that. Is she romancing me?"

"Does she do it in a private room by candlelight, with your favorite music in the background?"

Well, there was an image. Gage grimaced as it filled his head. Damn. She kept winning those points.

Time to turn the tables.

"So tell me, what's the point of all this romance stuff

you're so hot on?" He disguised his shift closer to her chair by filling her wineglass. "Isn't the end result the same?"

"The result?"

"When a guy romances a girl, or vice versa, the hoped-for result is sex, isn't it? Same as a woman wearing lingerie. She wears it to get—" Gage winced before a very unromantic phrase slipped from his lips and corrected "—attention. The kind that will lead to sex."

"When you're hungry, do you prefer filet mignon or a burger from the convenience store?"

Ouch.

"Then I suppose Milano Lingerie's place in that scenario would be, what? The equivalent to hunting down your own meal in the jungle and roasting it over an open fire?"

Her lips twitched and delight danced in her eyes, but Hailey shook her head.

"Oh, no. Milano's not *that* adventurous. Maybe a gourmet-catered, rich-boy frat party," she mused, tapping her finger to her chin in a way that was both adorable and amusing.

Gage laughed. She was fun. Not just fun in a cute-to-tease-and-see-her-blush kind of way. But clever. Smart and talented. Add that to a hot body and a gorgeous face, and she was trouble.

A smart man took on trouble only when he had time to deal with it. Gage had no time right now. He had a goal, a plan for his life. He didn't have time to enjoy the kind of trouble Hailey represented.

But he had a point to prove.

With that in mind, he held her gaze with his and let his smile drop. His look became intense, hot. Sexual. He let her see how attracted he was. Clear on his face, he knew, was everything he wanted to do to her, with her and for her.

Hailey's smile faded. Her eyes widened and her breath quickened. Good. She was getting the message.

"Oh, I don't know. I think this Milano can be plenty adventurous," he said quietly as he leaned in closer.

He reached under the heavy cloth covering the table and touched her knee. The soft fabric of her skirt slid temptingly between his fingers and her skin. Her eyes softened, heated. Like green glass melting into passion.

He slipped his hand under her skirt, smoothing his palm up her thigh. Delighting in the silken texture of her stocking. When he reached the top of her thigh he found lace. A band of it, separating the smooth texture of her stockings and the warm silk of her skin.

"You shouldn't…" Her words trailed off into a soft, breathy sigh as he traced the lacy edge of her stockings, slipping one finger under the smooth satin garter, then skimming it between the stocking and her warm flesh.

She was so soft.

"I think I should." He pressed the flat of his palm to her thigh, his fingers now wedged between her legs. His eyes locked on hers, silently demanding she give him room.

Her lips parted, wet and glistening, and a tiny furrow creased her brow. But slowly, so slow he wanted to groan, she unclenched her thighs and let them slide apart. Just a little. So the fit was tight.

Good.

He liked tight.

8

GAGE WAS PRETTY sure he'd just found the gates of heaven. He pressed his hand higher, rubbed his thumb over the fabric covering Hailey's heated core. It was silk, like her skin.

"What color are your panties?" he asked, not bothering to clear the husky passion from his voice.

Her eyes darted to the doorway, then back to his. She bit her bottom lip. He wanted to soothe the soft pink flesh, but his hand was busy. Instead, he arched an insistent brow.

"Pink," she whispered. "Pink like my bra. The lace is chocolate."

"Yum."

He slipped his fingers beneath the hem of those pink-and-chocolate panties. He ran his index finger along the swollen flesh he found, then gently pinched.

Squirming, she gasped. But she didn't pull away.

He shifted, so to anyone walking in they simply looked as though they were in conversation. But the move put him at a better angle, so he could use his thumb to caress her clitoris while slipping one finger into her tight, sweet core.

She whimpered.

But didn't pull away.

"I can't see a thing," he murmured, his words husky thanks to the passion clogging his throat. He had to swallow before continuing. "But I can imagine what you look like under the table. Pale flesh, blond curls. I can feel how wet you are. The images are clear in my mind. Vivid. Mouthwatering."

She opened her mouth, whether to respond or not he didn't know, because all that she offered was a low, breathy moan.

He moved two fingers in, swirling and plunging in time with his thumb's rhythm on her clit.

"I can imagine what it looks like as I touch you. My mind is painting a picture of you, naked, beneath me. Of your body straining toward mine, opening wide. Welcoming."

Her breath was coming in gasps now, even as she bit her lip as if to hold back her cries.

"Now, that's an image," he said, forcing the words out as his eyes devoured her face.

She was so damned beautiful. The flush of passion washed over her delicate skin. Her eyes glazed, lids lowered but never moving from his. Her mouth.

Oh, God, her mouth.

He wanted those lips on him.

His fingers plunged deeper. He shifted angles, pressing tight along the front wall of her core.

She tightened around him. And then, one more swirling stab of his fingers, and she went over.

God, that felt good.

A satisfaction that had nothing to do with physical release poured through Gage.

He watched her explode. Her breath came in tiny pants as her body came in tiny tremors.

Unable to resist, he leaned in to take her mouth. To taste her gasps of delight. It was as if he was a part of her orgasm. As if he was deeply embedded in the passion that engulfed her. A part of her.

It was incredible.

Then all hell broke out.

Bursting their peaceful, romantic bubble was a clash of sounds. A braying laugh. A sibilant giggle. And the sound of someone asking directions to Hailey's private room. And footsteps, clomping and rat-a-tat-tatting across the atrium's cement floor.

It was like being doused with a vat of ice water while being awoken from a very hot, wet dream by a brass band. A grade-school band, at that; one that hadn't learned all the notes.

Trying to shake off the discordant horror spinning down his spine, Gage pulled his mouth off Hailey's.

The sound came closer, in all its irritating glory.

His fingers still buried in her warmth, Gage steeled himself, gritted his teeth, then looked toward the commotion just as Rudy Rudolph swept into the room. Hanging on him like a glittering party favor was a redheaded piece of fluff who, at first glance, bore a striking resemblance to Cherry.

Gage blinked away the haze of passion from his eyes and realized the only thing the woman had in common with the torch singer was their hair color and bust size.

And Rudy's interest.

"Sorry, sorry I'm late. Candy and I got caught up at a party. You know how that goes. But I'm here now."

Indeed, he was. Thank God for the man's noisy entrance and exquisite timing. A minute earlier, and Hailey would have been midorgasm. Three minutes later, and Gage was pretty sure he'd have been sliding into her hot, wet depths.

Still, it was hard to find an attitude of gratitude when his rock-hard dick was pressing painfully against his zipper.

He slid a sideways glance at Hailey. Horror was starting to replace shock on her face. Both of which had quickly chased away that glow of desire he'd enjoyed so much.

It was as much for that, as for the fact that he had to

surreptitiously move his hand back to his own lap now, that Gage cursed Rudy.

Not that the other guy cared.

His grin as oblivious as the vacant expression in his date's eyes, the old man plopped himself into the chair opposite Gage and Hailey and threw both hands wide.

"Well? Show me some romance."

HE'D GOT HER off over dinner.

In a restaurant.

With just his fingers. And his words.

Her face was still on fire. Hailey's breath caught in her chest and she had to close her eyes against the power of that memory. His murmured suggestions echoed in her mind, making her want to squirm.

Oh, yeah, those had been some powerful words.

And then, just as she'd been ready to throw off her clothes and ride him at the dinner table, her potential boss had come in.

And Gage, damn him, had acted as if nothing at all had happened. As if he hadn't had his fingers inside her as he greeted the other man. As if she hadn't been dripping wet, hot and horny beneath his hand while Rudy Rudolph introduced his bimbo du jour. Then, while Hailey was still reeling—she didn't even know if she'd said hello—he'd claimed they were finished with dinner and suggested they leave immediately for his sexy scenario.

And she'd been too busy trying to climb out of the orgasm haze to even protest.

It was enough to make a girl scream.

And not in a good way.

"Here we are," Gage said, his words just background noise to her whirlwind of thoughts. Throughout the car ride, she'd heard him chatting with Rudy and the redhead, who were in the backseat. But she hadn't taken in a word.

The most she'd been able to do was state that her pitch would take place at another time. Just as well, since she wasn't sure she'd even get her name right at this point, let alone be able to present her argument for romantic lingerie.

Still lost in thought, she absently took Gage's hand as he helped her from the passenger seat of his car. He'd insisted on driving her to *part two* of their evening. She'd tried to disagree, desperately wanting her own car—and some time to herself. But once Rudy and Candy had decided to ride along, she'd figured it was better to just go with the flow.

Now, staring up at the building in front of them while the valet took Gage's BMW, she desperately wished she'd stood up for her choice and had a car to escape with.

Pussy's Galore, the neon sign screamed in bright orange.

"Are you sure this is how you wanted to pitch your argument for Milano designs?" she asked as they approached the rough-stone building. The red light flashing over the door spelled out clearly what kind of entertainment the Pussy Cats would be providing.

And it wasn't anything Hailey wanted to see.

"I'm sure." Gage stopped, one hand on the brass door pull, and gave her an amused look. "You're not backing out, are you? Afraid of a little adventure?"

She figured her desire to hiss and scratch could be blamed on the club he was about to drag her into. But her reaction—a nervous knot in her stomach and a feeling of nausea clogged in her throat—was definitely fear.

She slid a sideways glance at Rudy, who was pretending to read the encased poster showcasing the evening's entertainment. From the smile playing over his thin lips, he thought she was afraid, too.

His date, Hailey noted, was busy checking her manicure and clearly didn't care.

Logically, Hailey knew she could object to visiting a club called Pussy's Galore. There was nothing wrong with that. It wasn't as if she was a prude or uptight in any way. Hell, she'd just had an orgasm with her chicken piccata.

She really didn't want to go into a place that screamed sex. If a romantic setting with Gage inspired an under-the-table orgasm, who knew what inhibitions she'd toss aside in a sex club.

But she didn't want to be the one who ruined the evening, either. Nor did she want to be the one going home alone by taxi while the others had fun, with Gage charming Rudy into the contract over naked bodies.

"You're paying my entry fee, I hope," she finally said, giving Gage a sassy look. "After all, I paid for dinner."

"You made this sweet girl pay for the meal?" Rudy interrupted, pulled out of his fake perusal to frown at Gage. "That's not right."

"Romance is genderless, Mr. Rudolph," Hailey said with a shrug that conveyed she didn't play to the double standard. "And it was my point for the bet, so it's only fair that I paid. Of course, that means Gage should pay for anything we encounter in here, too."

She sure hoped the going rate for hookers was a lot more than chicken.

Ten minutes later, her wrist stamped with a go-go boot and her butt perched on a magenta fur-covered chrome stool, Hailey gave Gage an arch look.

"You said it was a house of ill repute when we pulled up." At least, that was what she thought he'd said. She'd been too busy reveling in the memory of what his fingers had done between her thighs to be sure.

"Prostitution is illegal in San Francisco," he pointed out with a grin. "This is a Kitty Cat Club. More upscale and diverse than a standard strip club. There are strippers on three stages, but there's also pole dancing, a dance floor upstairs and, in case you get any ideas, a few rooms to rent by the hour in back."

She wanted to roll her eyes and blithely dismiss the innuendo. Except her thighs were still tingling from his fingers, her panties were damp from the orgasm and, thanks to the image he'd built in her head of licking her, she didn't think her nipples were ever going to lose their rock-hard perkiness.

So instead of being hypocritical, she opted to change the subject.

"Where did Rudy and Candy go?" She'd stepped into the bathroom after they'd entered the club and hadn't seen the odd couple since.

"I'm not sure. He said something about getting drinks, and that he'd catch up with us in a minute." Gage glanced toward the back with a frown. "But he headed in the opposite direction from the bar."

She followed his gaze toward the bank of doors along the back wall, all with lights over the top, a few lit bright red to show they were occupied.

"You don't think…"

"You don't not think…" he countered, his scowl deepening. Hailey didn't figure this was the moment to point out that since Rudy was here, this did count as one of Gage's scenarios. Then she frowned, too. What if Rudy's little private party was the kind of thing that proved Gage right, that it really was only sex that mattered?

Nope, she told herself. Not going to think about that. Rudy was the pervy, have-sex-anywhere-and-everywhere-while-he-could-still-get-it-up kind of guy. This was probably just business as usual for him.

Still… Her frown deepened. It did count as one of Gage's scenarios. And maybe a successful one, at that.

"So you come here often?" she asked, wanting to distract both of them from the image of that skinny, old, bald man and whatever he was doing in the room with the red light.

"Do I look like the kind of guy who spends a lot of time at a place called Pussy's Galore?" he asked, looking a little insulted.

"Well, you don't exactly seem like the kind of guy who had to do a lot of research to come up with what scenario you thought would best prove your point about sexy lingerie." As if to echo Hailey's words, a waitress wearing a tiny blue teddy, stockings and six-inch Lucite heels approached them with a pitcher and four glasses.

"Pussycat punch," she said, setting the tray on the table between them, then poured them each a glass of the neon-pink liquid. "Your tasty treats will be out in just a second, Gage."

"Thanks, Mona."

Mona? Hailey pressed her lips together but couldn't hold back her laugh. Eyes wide and trying to look innocent, she met Gage's glare with a shrug.

"What? It's not like the reserved sign meant that this is your very own special table or that the waitress, who knows you by name, asked about your family. I believe you when you say you don't come here all the time. I really do."

His scowl deepened.

"She just might ask that of everyone," he muttered. He looked so abashed, if he'd been standing he'd have his toe scuffing the floor. Hailey told herself not to melt, but man, he was so cute.

"She'd ask about your family?" she clarified.

When he nodded, the giggles escaped like champagne bubbles. She couldn't help it.

"Look, my brother is one of the investors in this club. He's big on keeping on top of his investments and I've come in with him from time to time to check up on things."

"Of course. That makes perfect sense." Her thoughts

putting an end to the laughter, Hailey put on a serious face and nodded. "I'm sure you only visit for the articles, view the women as hardworking employees and never, ever enjoy yourself."

He shrugged.

"I did try to pole dance once." He gave her a teasing look. "You do know what pole dancing is, right?"

He said it as if she were a complete innocent. What? Wasn't it enough that she designed lingerie—a product that by its very nature demanded an awareness of sex? How did that get her a ticket to the purity princess hall of fame?

Hell, she'd just let him feel her up, and bring her down, in a restaurant on what was questionably their first date.

And he still looked at her as if she were a sweet little thing who'd run screaming at the sight of a fully erect penis.

Hailey's shoulders stiffened and her chin lifted. Was it because she was a proponent of romance? Was that why he kept dismissing her sexual savvy?

She should ignore it. She didn't have anything to prove.

But dammit, the man made her think silk scarves, whipped cream and doing it doggy style. She'd be damned if he'd dismiss her as unworthy of those thoughts.

"Let's see, pole dancing," she mused, tapping one finger on her lower lip. "Crazy gymnastic moves that require an incredible amount of upper body and core strength in order to climb a hard, phallic-shaped dance partner."

She waited for that to sink in, then leaned closer. Close enough to breathe in the scent of his soap. Close enough to see his pupils dilate and his gaze fog as the image played through his mind.

"There's something so empowering about grabbing hold of that big, hard pole and sliding yourself up and down its length." Her gaze locked on his, she pulled her glass of pussycat punch toward her and wrapped her lips around the straw. She waited just a second, watching his pulse jump in his throat, then sucked. Hard.

And that's how it's done, she thought with a grin when Gage closed his eyes and gave a soft groan. That'd show him not to dismiss her as a naive good girl.

"You've pole danced?" he clarified when he opened his eyes again, looking at her as if he wanted to cement that visual in his brain. "In a skimpy outfit?"

Hailey's lips twitched and she took another sip of the surprisingly delicious punch.

"All the way to the top. In short shorts and a cropped T-shirt," she confirmed. He didn't need to know it'd been in a gym with fourteen other women during an exercise class. Why ruin the romance or, to use his term, the image.

"They have poles in the back for customer use. Let's go." He was off his stool, his fingers around her wrist before Hailey could swallow her punch.

Freaked, she started to shake her head. It was one thing to claim she'd danced the pole. It was another to do it in front of him.

"I don't think so," she started to say.

Before she could launch her full protest—or even come up with how to do it without making him look at her like a Pollyanna again—their waitress returned with a tray covered with snack bowls. Hailey squinted. Was that cat food?

Before she could use it as a distraction to keep Gage from trying to introduce her to a dancing pole, Rudy came strutting across the room, weaving between people like a happy rooster. Hailey didn't wonder at his smile, given that he was followed by a very disheveled Candy, who was hand in hand with another woman.

"Three of them?" she murmured, a little awed.

"Gotta hand it to the guy. He's not shy about having a good time," Gage muttered back, shaking his head.

Hailey wrinkled her nose.

"I'll bet you think this proves your point." It was all she could do not to slip right into a pout. Why couldn't Cherry have felt well tonight? If she'd been here, Rudy wouldn't have gone off to get off. He'd have stayed to woo his potential spokesmodel, giving Hailey plenty of opportunity to pitch charming point after charming point.

But *nooooo*. Instead, she'd said maybe a dozen words to the guy and paid a couple hundred dollars for dinner. With nothing to show for it but an orgasm.

Albeit a freaking awesome orgasm.

"I don't know if it proves my point," Gage mused. "But it definitely proves the old man has stamina."

Yeah. That was what he had. Stamina.

And a contract that Hailey wanted.

Which was why she kept to herself her irritation at Rudy's eccentric—which sounded better than *rude, inconsiderate* and *self-indulgent*—behavior and everything else about this evening all going to hell.

But now they could finally get to the business portion of the night, which was the actual point behind all this craziness. Hailey straightened her shoulders and put on her best smile. The one that didn't show how creeped out she was at imagining a skinny man in his seventies with two women who'd have to show ID to purchase alcohol, all doing sexual gymnastics in a room that looked about the size of Hailey's shoe closet.

"Rudy," she greeted when he drew closer. "Can I pour you some punch? It's delicious."

For the first time since she'd met him, the older man looked his age. Instead of bouncing on the balls of his feet, he was dragging them. His eyes were sleepy and his shoulders drooped. But his smile... Well, that was one satisfied smile.

"Gage, Hailey, this was great. Thanks to you both, I've

discovered a new restaurant and a club. But I'm tuckered out for the night, so we'll have to talk business later."

"But we're supposed to be pitching our points," she protested.

"Just one drink?" Gage suggested, who, unlike her, sounded perfectly content to write the evening off as a pitch-fail.

"No, no. It's my bedtime. We'll meet tomorrow, though. You both still have two shots to convince me. Sound fair?"

Not bothering to wait for a response, he wrapped one arm around Candy, offered his other to the blonde, gave them all a wink and headed for the door.

Hailey was pretty sure her mouth was hanging open.

So much for stamina.

BUSINESS-WISE, Gage was calling this evening a total bust.

He'd set out with the intention of intimidating Hailey, charming Cherry and tossing enough sexual entertainment at Rudy that the guy didn't give this whole stupid bet thing any attention.

He'd ended up fascinated by Hailey, Cherry was a no-show and Rudy had just walked out with way more entertainment than Gage had figured on. And not one single thing had been accomplished toward the goal of being in Tahoe by the weekend.

"Damn," he muttered, dropping back onto the fur-covered stool.

"I'm sorry."

He gave Hailey a skeptical look. "Yeah? Really?"

"Yeah, really," she said, sincerity clear in those huge eyes. "It's not fun making big plans and putting everything you've got into a pitch and then having it fall apart."

Right. Because her scenario had fallen apart, too. Even though this evening had been a bust, he supposed he'd got the better end of the deal in pitching. At least Rudy had shown up for his and had enjoyed it enough that he'd remember the next day.

Her frown ferocious, like a kitten showing its claws, Hailey glared at the exit, then huffed a heavy sigh. Lifting the punch pitcher, she gestured to his glass. When Gage shook his head, she shrugged and refilled her own.

He should probably warn her that the sweet drink was eighty proof under all that sugar. Before he could, though, she drained it. The whole thing, in one swallow.

His body stirred, sexual interest once again beat out his irritation.

"Look," she said, gesturing with both hands as if to indicate that he observe, like, everything around her head. "I want this done, too. Until it is, my future is on hold."

"I'd have thought you'd want to drag it out. Put off the end until you'd got a side deal or other options." He knew it was a rude assessment, but dammit, she was right. He wanted this over with.

"Why would I want to drag this out? I have a life of my own, a business to run and Christmas is only a couple weeks away. Believe it or not, I have other things to do than hang out with an old man, his treat du jour and a no-show torch singer."

He noticed she hadn't mentioned him on that list. Because she didn't have better things to do than spend time with him? Or because she didn't see him as a major factor in her life.

"You're really looking forward to the deal being struck? Once it is, the options are done for making side deals, you know."

And she'd have no reason to spend time with him. He couldn't imagine a woman wanting to date the guy who'd beat her out of a seven-figure contract.

Date? Where the hell had that come from? He wasn't a dating kind of guy. He was a fun-for-a-night guy. Maybe-a-weekend-if-the-woman-was-wild kind of guy. But his life was business, his focus success. Women, except on a very temporary basis, didn't factor in.

And now he was thinking dating? Gage eyed the punch, wondering if the alcohol fumes were getting to him. Because he didn't think these kind of thoughts about women. Ever.

"Well, sure I'm looking forward to it. Because I'm going to win the deal."

Gage laughed and shook his head in admiration. She never gave up, did she?

"You don't really believe that, do you?" He gestured to the rooms at the back where Rudy had had his fun. "You think you made a more persuasive argument than I did tonight?"

"Maybe not a more persuasive argument, given that neither of the judges was there to enjoy it. But I do think I'll win in the long run."

"You're quite the idealist."

She shrugged, either ignoring his sarcasm or floating on too much punch to recognize it.

"I figured out pretty young that things rarely turn out the way I want right away. But if I work at them, if I push and try my hardest, eventually it all comes together."

She was fascinating. A mix of naïveté, faith, sexual moxie and determination. Throw in a gorgeous smile, her hot little body and a hell of a lot of talent, and that was one potent package. Still…she wasn't going to win.

"Are you thinking that law-of-attraction mumbo jumbo is going to help you somehow?" he asked.

"Nope. Simple optimism. I just keep believing until what I believe is real."

"And that works?"

Her smile dimmed for a second, then Hailey shrugged. "Sometimes it has. I'm still waiting for the others."

"Like?"

If that wasn't a nosy question, he didn't know what was. But he'd had his hand up her skirt already tonight. Why balk at poking into her private life, too.

"Like, you know, business stuff. I have this secretary. She's aces at her job, she's loyal to the company and she works magic with numbers. But she wishes I'd disappear."

Gage could relate. Plenty of people wished he'd disappear. But none of them had the nerve to show it to his face.

"Why'd you hire her?"

"She came with the company." Hailey waved her hand again, as if dismissing question-and-answer period, clearly wanting to make her point. "But here's the thing. Every month, every week. Every. Day," she said with extra emphasis. "She's getting closer to accepting me. To liking me. Now, would I have liked that approval and being included? Yes. Did I want to be remembered, maybe treated like I mattered every once in a while? Sure. But does it stop me from believing that I belong? That I'm important and special? Hell, no."

She pounded her fist on the table in emphasis. Gage quickly grabbed the glasses that were in sudden danger of toppling to the floor.

Frowning, he peered at her. He didn't know who they were talking about now, but he was sure it wasn't her secretary.

Another man?

A vicious clawing sort of fury gripped his guts. It took him a few seconds to realize the feeling was jealousy.

He didn't like it.

"But hey, I figure someday, she's going to adore me. Because, you know, I'm adorable," Hailey added, giggling and looking just as adorable as she claimed. And, he noted, looking as though the punch was having its effect.

He should take her home.

But first…

"When do you give up?"

Her frown was the tiniest furrow between her brows, as if that wasn't a question she let herself consider.

"If it's important, you don't give up."

"Isn't it smarter to check your ROI, and if the return isn't worth the investment, simply walk away? Quit expending energy." Gage shook his head, unable to imagine trying over and over again without success. Or only eking a few inches of success out of any given deal. He was an everything-or-nothing kind of guy, though.

"Isn't it smarter to do what you love, and believe that it's going to work out exactly how you want, than to give up on a dream and settle for less?" she countered.

Gage wanted to rub his gut at that direct hit. One she probably didn't even realize she'd made. She couldn't know how much he wanted to leave Milano. How badly he wanted to make his own mark.

Feeling his face fold into a scowl, he tilted his head toward the door.

"Ready to call it quits? I'll drive you home."

"What about my car?"

"I don't think you should be driving tonight, do you?" He arched a brow at her empty punch glass.

"I don't feel like I've had that much to drink," she said, peering into the deep glass as if measuring her alcohol levels.

"It'll hit you in about ten minutes," he guessed. Through discussing it, he shifted off the stool and, his hand on her elbow, helped her slide off her seat.

The fur grabbed the fabric of her skirt, though, holding tight so as she slid off, he got a delicious view of her thighs. And those stockings.

Hello, baby.

Tiny roses, tempting lace.

Damn, but she did have a point about how enticing that romance look was.

He was so focused on watching her legs, even though she'd freed her skirt and that beckoning juncture was once again covered, that he forgot to move, throwing her off balance.

"Whoa," she said, falling against him, her hands splayed over his chest as she righted herself. Her curves were sweet and tempting, pressed against his for just a second. Just enough to tease. But not nearly long enough for his tastes.

"I guess you're right," she said, her voice husky. Still a little unsteady, she let go of his chest to push one hand through her hair. "You're going to need to take me."

9

Pussycats packed a wallop.

Hailey leaned her head against the leather seat of Gage's car and let herself float on the punch-inspired sea of relaxation.

She wasn't drunk.

She'd been drunk a few times. So she should know.

Nope. She was just relaxed.

Her body.

Her worries.

Her gaze shifted from the blur of taillights of the other cars on the freeway to the man driving.

Her inhibitions.

She wished she were drunk. It'd make it easier to do crazy things. The kind of crazy things that wouldn't be smart business decisions. The kind of crazy things that'd make the next week's competition with Gage much, much more difficult.

The kind of crazy things that'd feel oh so incredibly good. Things that followed up on the incredibly good feelings he'd given her earlier.

She'd like an orgasm where she didn't have to be quiet. She'd enjoy having one that included naked body parts. And it'd be even better if most of those naked parts belonged to Gage.

Squirming a little, she dropped her gaze to his lap, and even though it was impossible to enjoy the view since he was seated and driving, she still stared.

Because what she wanted was right there.

Barely aware of what she was doing, she reached her hand out. Maybe to touch it, she wasn't sure.

Before she could, Gage parked the car.

"Why'd you stop?"

"We're here." He tilted his head toward her apartment building. Eyes wide, she followed his gesture. They *were* here. How'd that happen so fast?

He gave her a curious look. "Are you okay?"

She took a quick inventory. Yep, still relaxed. But there was just enough horror coursing through her at the fact that she'd been about to pet his penis to assure her that, nope, she wasn't drunk.

"I'm fine." She offered him a bright smile, then gathered her purse, tucked her scarf tighter into her jacket to battle the chilly San Francisco air and reached for the door handle. "Thank you for the ride."

"I'll walk you up."

"You don't…" *Have to,* she thought, staring at the empty seat and closed door.

Well, then.

She turned to let herself out, but Gage was there, opening her door before she could fumble with the handle. He reached out to assist her from the car. Whether because he was a gentleman, or because he was afraid she'd faceplant it on the sidewalk, she wasn't sure.

"Thank you for the ride," she said, stepping onto the sidewalk with her feet, not her face. Not a hint of swaying, and only the tiniest desire to rub herself against his body. She was doing great.

"I'll see you up."

"It's a secure building." She pointed at the cameras and keypad by the glass entrance. "I'll be fine."

"I'll see you up," he repeated. Then he gave her a cute little shrug. "Hey, it's a guy thing. End of date, see lady to the door."

"This wasn't a date," she murmured. But hey, if he wanted to go inside, ride the elevator up, walk her the thirty feet, then ride the elevator back down, that was up to him.

She just wished he'd keep a little distance between them on the way. He was so close, she could smell his cologne. She could feel his warmth, tempting her to slide closer.

Suddenly nervous, she wet her lips and tried to think of something to say. But nothing came to mind.

Nope. Definitely not drunk.

And not even relaxed anymore.

In silence, she coded them into the building, then punched the button for the elevator. She gazed at the stainless doors as if her blurry reflection was no end to fascinating, trying to pretend she didn't feel the heat of Gage's stare on her face.

Suddenly, all she could think about was the treat he'd served up at dinner. That delicious, mouthwatering orgasm, brought to her by just the tips of his fingers.

It was enough to make a girl beg.

All the more reason to keep her mouth shut. Just in case.

Which she managed to do for the entire elevator ride.

When the doors slid open, she gave him a sidelong glance. Yep, he still looked determined to see her to her apartment. She didn't bother to suggest they say goodbye, and he followed her out of the elevator.

She silently led the way down five doors to her apartment.

"Well, here we are," she said in a cheery tone, pulling

her keys from her purse and giving him an *it's okay, go away now* look. "Thanks for the ride home."

"Thanks for the great double date," he shot back with a grin. Then, probably because he'd got the message from her expression, he leaned one shoulder against her door frame and got comfy.

She rolled her eyes.

"Quit saying that." She put her key in the lock and turned it, but didn't push the door open. "It wasn't a date. And if it was, it was a lousy one, given that half of our double didn't show and the other half spent his time in a room with two women whose ages, added together, still don't equal his."

"Maybe we should try it again, just the two of us," he suggested quietly. So quietly she had a feeling he was just as conflicted by all this crazy passion between them as she was.

The look he gave her was long and considering. Long enough to send the nerves in Hailey's stomach tumbling all over each other. She didn't have to wonder what he was considering. The passion in his eyes said it all.

Her chest hurt with the effort to breathe normally, to not give in to the need to whimper and beg. She stared into those dark, intense eyes, her fingers itching to touch his face. To give him back some of the same delight he'd given her earlier.

She forced herself to be practical. To think straight. In other words, to ignore the pounding desire that was screaming through her system.

"Don't you think that'd be a mistake? You know, since we're competing for this contract and all." She tried to soften her refusal with a smile, wishing like crazy she'd taken her chance with him back when he was still just the guy she'd met at the party.

Or that she was the kind of person who could separate

one thing from the other. Because she wanted him, badly. So badly, it made her ache.

"Yeah. Competitors," he confirmed, his smile falling away. The intensity in his gaze didn't. If anything, it got more powerful. As if he were through searching her mind and was ready to dive into her soul.

"Good night," he said. His words were a whisper over her skin. A soft caress echoed by his hand sweeping over her hair, cupping the back of her head.

She stared, her eyes huge, as he leaned in. Not touching, except his hand to her hair. His lips descended, his gaze never leaving hers. She sighed as he brushed her mouth with the gentle promise of a kiss.

So sweet.

Who knew he had it in him to be so damned sweet. He made her heart melt. And her resolve, dammit.

He shifted the angle, tilting his head to one side and rubbing his lips over her lower one, then taking it between his teeth to gently, oh so gently, tease.

It was as if he'd connected her to an electric wire. Sparks shot through her body, powering up every cell, sending the smoldering passion into flaming heat in an instant. Hailey gasped. Her nipples hardened and wet desire pooled between her thighs. Desire he knew just what to do with, she recalled.

She finally understood what he'd been looking for with those intense stares. The switch that'd turn off her ability to think and turn her body's need to desperate.

It worked, too.

Frantic for more, she shifted the kiss. Her mouth opened, enticing, tempting. Trying to tease him into taking more.

Gage groaned but didn't take the bait. It was as if he was forcing her to make the moves. Daring her to take the role of aggressor.

Okay, then…

Hailey swept her tongue over the seam of his lips, smiling when he opened, letting her in. She sipped, as if he were sweet nectar, until he went wild.

Then he took over.

His tongue plunged, taking hers in a wild, desperate dance.

His fingers tunneled through her hair, holding her captive to his mouth.

Yes.

Excitement pounded through her. On tiptoes, she pressed her body against his, loving that there was no give. Just a brick wall of hard, male flesh.

Releasing her hair, he swept one hand down her back, his fingers curling around the curve of her butt, pulling her closer. Hailey shifted her body so her legs were pressed against his, her core aching, needing more pressure. Needing his touch. His erection, so temptingly hard, pressed against her belly. She wanted to feel it. To see it. Oh, baby, to touch it.

She wrapped one foot behind his calf, then slid it higher, angling herself tighter against his thigh. When her foot skimmed the back of his thigh, he stiffened.

He pulled his mouth away.

Hailey frowned. Forcing her passion-heavy lids open, she gave him a confused look.

"We can't do this."

"Sure we can. If we're lying down, the height difference won't be a problem," she assured him breathlessly, releasing her grip on his shoulder to pat one hand on his cheek.

His lips twitched, but Gage still shook his head.

"We can't. You're drunk."

"No," she told him, giving her head a decisive shake. "I've already done a thorough inventory. I'm relaxed, but I'm not drunk."

"Relaxed?" His eye roll was more a suggestion than an actual move. As if he didn't want to insult her, but couldn't hold back the skepticism.

"I'm not drunk," she repeated. "I can prove it. Come inside. I'll do that sobriety-test thing."

"Why can't you do it here?"

Eyes wide with faux horror, Hailey looked up, then down the hallway.

"Here? Where the neighbors will see and start gossiping? Seriously?"

A silly argument, given that she'd just been wrapped around his body like one of those stripper poles they'd discussed. If the neighbors were the gossiping kind, that would have fueled them plenty. But Gage fell for it, nodding and then slowly—as if he were reluctant to let her go—stepping away.

Hailey turned quickly toward the door to hide her smile.

Dismiss her desire as alcohol-fueled stupidity?

She didn't think so.

This was pure determination. She wanted him, and for the first time in her life, she was grabbing what she wanted and reveling. If that reveling took place naked, so much the better. She wasn't going to worry about how it affected others; she wasn't going to let her fears stop her. She was going to enjoy every delicious second of Gage Milano tonight.

With that in mind, Hailey stepped across the threshold and tossed her purse in the general direction of the hall table. She didn't notice if the clatter meant she'd hit it, knocked everything over, or if her bag was flying across the floor.

She didn't care.

The second Gage crossed the doorway, she slapped the door shut and attacked.

With her body, wrapping it around his as tight and close as she could get with both of them in winter coats.

With her hands, skimming and skating them over his rock-hard form, reveling in the rounded muscles of his biceps under his coat, then across the granite planes of his chest.

With her mouth. Oh, baby, with her mouth. She tasted. She nibbled. She wanted to gobble him up.

For a second, a long enough second to inspire untold neurotic worries in her head, Gage was stone still. Other than the heart beating against her hand, he didn't move.

Shit.

Had she attacked too soon?

Had she misread his signals?

Had that been a pity orgasm over dinner?

Before she could do more than wonder at the depths to which her paranoid mind came up with things to worry about, Gage came to life.

He shoved at her clothes. Her hands pushing his away just as quickly, Hailey shrugged out of her coat and let it fall to the floor at their feet. She wasn't sure who pushed, shoved or pulled, but her scarf and gloves quickly fell, as well.

Their mouths slid, hot and wet, over each other. Tongues tangled in a wild dance, neither leading, both tempting.

He tasted so good.

He felt even better.

Finally, she was able to get her hands on that body. To scope out the hard planes of his chest, to feel the rounded strength of his biceps.

Hailey growled low in her throat, delighting in his shape. In the power of those muscles. He was built. He was hard. He was hers for the taking.

So took, she did.

She nipped at his lower lip, then soothed the flesh with

her tongue. Her fingers made quick work of the knot of his tie, tossing the fabric aside so she could get to his buttons. Then, oh baby, flesh.

She whimpered a little when her hands found bare skin. He felt so good.

She was so focused on his body, on discovering every little delicious bit of it, that she barely noticed how busy he was.

Not until cool air hit the naked skin of her thighs.

He'd unzipped her skirt, so it fell to the floor, billowing over her shoes. His hands skimmed already-familiar terrain, caressing her thighs there, just above the lacy tops of her stockings.

She shivered, even as heat gathered lower in her belly. Her thighs trembled a little, making it hard to balance on her high heels. To compensate, she wrapped one leg around the delicious hardness of Gage's, her heel anchored below his knee. Her core pressed, tight and damp, against his thigh.

"We should…"

"Now," she interrupted. "Here."

Her words were barely a breath, her mind a misty fog.

She was pure sensation.

All she could feel was delight.

Sexually charged, edgy, demanding delight.

She wanted more.

She needed more.

Even though she was reluctant to leave the amazing hard warmth of his chest, her quest for more demanded she head south. Her hands slid, fast and furious, down the light trail of hair of his belly, making quick work of his belt.

She wasn't a fashion diva for nothing, so fast did she unsnap, unzip and dispose of his slacks. His boxers went, too, everything hitting the floor with a satisfying thud.

"Babe…"

"No," she protested against his lips, even though she had no idea what he was going to say. She didn't care. This was her fantasy and she was going to lap up every delicious drop.

With that in mind, and grateful for all the fabric on the floor to ease the impact on her knees, she dropped down in front of him.

"Oh my God," he said, his words a low, guttural groan as he stared down at her.

Loving that look on his face, appreciation mixed with fascination, coated with a whole lot of lust, Hailey held his gaze with hers as she leaned forward to blow, gently, on the impressive length of his erection.

Like a lollipop, she ran her tongue from base to top.

Gage's eyes slitted, as though he wanted to close them but couldn't resist watching the show.

The audience adding even more heat to an already-incendiary delight, Hailey shifted higher on her knees so she could wrap her lips around the smooth, velvet head of his penis. Just the tip. She sipped, swirling her tongue in one direction, sucked, then swirled it in another.

Gage's fingers tunneled into her hair, whether for balance or to make sure she didn't stop, she didn't know. She didn't care.

Her mouth wide, she took him in. Slipped her lips down the length of his dick, then back up again. Each time, she tightened her lips, until she was sucking hard, and he was squirming.

Just when his body tensed so much she thought he was going to explode, she pulled back so she was only sipping at the tip again.

"Enough," he growled, swooping down to lift her high, spin her around and pin her against the wall.

His hands raced over her body, slipping down her curves, then back up again. With his lower half pressing deliciously tight against her belly, his erection a tempting reminder of the incredible promise to come, he cupped her breasts in his palms.

Even through the heavy satin of her bra, Hailey could feel the heat as his fingers flexed and squeezed. Needing more, too impatient for him to get there himself, she reached around behind to unsnap her bra, letting the cups fall over his hands.

Gage grunted his thanks, flinging the bra away then grasping her soft, full flesh in his fingers again. His look was intent, laser-focused. As if he was getting as much pleasure from watching the slide of his thumb over her nipple as he was feeling it.

Even if he was, Hailey decided, it wasn't nearly as good as she was feeling. Her head fell back against the wall, her eyes closing so she could focus every single atom of her being on the magic his fingers were working.

He pinched her aching nipple, rolling it around gently, then swiped his thumb over its hardness. Over and over, until she was ready to scream. Heat, tight and wet, pooled between her thighs.

When she squirmed, he shifted. But not, damn him, harder against her aching core. No, he slid down.

His mouth took one nipple in, sucking gently, laving his tongue over and around the aching bud. His hand continued to work the other. Pinching, teasing.

Driving her crazy.

Hailey's fingers slipped through the silk of his hair, holding his head in place as her other hand skimmed over his chest, giving his nipple the same treatment.

He growled.

As soon as he shifted, she did, too, wrapping her leg around him again, this time closer to his waist.

Taking a hint—bless him for being so perceptive—he

released her breast, his hand speeding down her body to cup the hot curls between her thighs.

Welcome back, she thought.

Right at home, his fingers slid along her clitoris in teasing little pinches before plunging into her core.

Hailey exploded.

The power of her orgasm made her whimper at first, then as it built, she cried out, both hands fisted in his hair.

"More," she demanded, greedy and needy.

"Oh, yeah." His words were somewhere between a pant and a growl against her breast.

For just a second, Gage let her go, moved away. Before she could ask, she heard the rip of foil, felt him move away just enough to sheathe himself.

She wanted to help, but by the time she pried her eyes open, he was back in position, his hands on her hips.

Using his support, she lifted one leg up to anchor her foot behind his back. Then the other. There was something wildly erotic about trusting him so much, in believing that he'd keep her from landing on her ass.

His mouth took hers in a voracious, biting kiss.

Hailey's body started the tight spiral toward climax once again with just the touch of his tongue.

He plunged.

She shattered in another miniorgasm.

Her back slammed against the wall at the impact.

Hailey wrapped her legs tighter, no longer worrying that the sharp heel of her stiletto might be cutting into his body.

She needed him to move harder.

Deeper.

And he did.

Plunging.

In and out.

Hard and fast.

Her breath came in gasps.

Her mind swirled in a rainbow of desire, thoughts decimated beneath the power of their passion.

His moves grew jerky. Short. He plunged hard. Paused. Plunged again.

She reached low, gripping the small of his back in her hands, her feet tight against his butt, as she tried to pull him in tighter.

"Baby," he growled, plunging again.

"Do it," she demanded.

As if he'd been waiting for permission, Gage exploded. His jerky thrust sent Hailey spiraling yet again, her body splintering into a million tiny pieces of heaven.

She thought she heard him cry out. She wasn't sure, though, because her mind shut down with the power of her orgasm.

It might have been five minutes, it might have been fifty, before she settled back into her body.

It was still trembling, held against the wall by the hard power of Gage's. Tiny orgasmic quakes still trembled through her.

His breath still came, fast and furious, against her throat.

"Wow," she whispered.

"I think you took advantage of me," he finally said, his words still breathless.

Her head cuddled against his chest now, Hailey smiled.

"Ooh, poor big, tough guy," she teased, her fingers swirling through the hairs on his chest. Finally, she pulled her head back to gaze up at him. "Should I apologize?"

He looked as though he was contemplating that. Then he shook his head.

"Nah. I'll take advantage of you now. Then we'll be even."

Her giggle was cut off to a squeak when he swept her into his arms. Grinning, Hailey wrapped her hands around his neck and crossed her feet at the ankle, loving the view of her stockings and sexy shoes from up here in his arms.

"Bedroom?"

"Down the hall and to the left."

In swift, sure strides, he went that way.

She loved a man who knew how to follow directions.

Now to see what other instructions he might like to follow.

HAILEY WOKE SLOWLY, her body a melting pot of sensations. It was morning, wasn't it? From the patches of light dancing over her closed eyes, it must be. She wanted to stretch, but at the same time didn't want to move because everything felt so good.

But what might feel better was a hot, tasty breakfast of French toast and fruit. A quick mental inventory assured her that she had the ingredients to make Gage a delicious morning-after treat. Then they could come back to bed and enjoy another sort of treat. The naked sort.

And then, riding on a wave of passion and delight, they'd be able to amiably settle this whole silly competition thing. They were two intelligent, clever adults. She was sure they could figure out a way to keep that contract from being an issue. Or, more important, from keeping them off each other's naked bodies.

Finally, more to feed the desperate need to see Gage's face than anything else, she forced her eyes open. A soft, dreamy smile on her lips, she turned her head to the pillow next to her.

Ready to ask him if he liked whipped cream with his French toast, or his other treats, the question froze on her lips.

The pillow was empty.

She shifted to one elbow, looking past the tumbled waterfall of blankets tangled with her clothing from the night before.

His clothes, though, were all gone.

And so was he.

10

THIS FEELING-LIKE-a-complete-prick thing was new to Gage. He sat quietly in the corner of the meeting room, resisting the urge to hunch his shoulders, and tried to shake it off. This was a business meeting.

With a man he'd watched leave the pussycat club in the arms of two women fifty years his junior because he knew sex would hook the guy's vote.

And a woman who refused to look at him. One who was presently pretending he didn't exist, even though she'd blown his mind, among other things, the previous night, who'd provided hour upon hour of the best sex of his life, and whom he'd left without a word that morning. Why? Because he'd got a text from his brother, letting him know their father had called yet another emergency meeting.

So instead of letting Hailey know he was leaving, he'd sneaked out with his shoes in his hands.

Yeah, he was a real prince of a prick, all right.

"As you both know, Cherry's schedule has been somewhat in conflict with this little project. She'd hoped to make it here this morning, but had an unexpected doctor appointment."

"Not that this hasn't been fun," Gage said, shaking off his odd hesitation and leaning forward to give Rudy a direct look. "But how long is this going to drag out? A decision was supposed to be made by today. I don't know about Hailey, but I do know that I have a lot of other things on my schedule that need attention."

Clearly not a fan of being pushed, even when it was to keep his own word, Rudy bristled.

"If you'd like to step out of the game, feel free. That'd make this entire decision much easier."

Gage was tempted.

Dancing to the tune of an eccentric businessman with more power and money than manners was getting old.

And if he stepped off, Hailey would win the contract. Something that obviously meant a lot to her.

But he flashed back to that morning's meeting. Just him, his brother, the old man and the board of directors. All fourteen of them. All wanting to take the New Year in a different direction. None of which Gage gave a damn about, and even more, none of which had required his input. He was marketing. But the old man wanted him there as another token Milano. A show of force. A pawn.

That was another game he'd like to step out of.

And he would. Just as soon as he could do it without giving up his shares in the company or his place at the family table. Although he was willing to negotiate the latter.

"I'm not stepping out," Gage said, reluctantly giving way to the always-present nagging pressure of family obligations. "I'm simply suggesting we finalize this as quickly as possible."

Rudy's glower faded a little and he slowly nodded.

"I agree. But my arrangement with Cherry guarantees her final say in the designs she wears. If I back out, she very well might, too."

Something Rudy looked to be very concerned about. Given that the woman had barely been present so far, he probably had reason to worry.

"As happy as I am to hear that Milano is still in the

competition," Hailey said in a tone that said the complete opposite, "I'd like to make sure you're judging each of the lines fairly. After all, last night wasn't a true test, seeing as you weren't able to experience my presentation."

For the first time since she'd walked in, Gage looked Hailey full in the face. Granted, he was staring in shock at her temerity.

But damn she looked good. Her dress was green, almost as vivid as her eyes. It wrapped around her curves like a lover, sweeping from shoulder to knee with deceptive modesty. He wanted to follow the flow of the fabric, to skim his fingers along the hem, then up under that skirt to touch her soft, warm flesh.

Of course, he'd probably get his hand chopped off if he tried. But that didn't ease the need.

"What you'd have seen if you'd been present at either of our events, Mr. Rudolph, was a sharp contrast between messaging. Romance, which is all about love and happiness, promises not only fabulous sex, but of having it over and over again. That means a variety of lingerie options for each romantic fantasy." She swept her hand through the air, as if waving to a dozen invisible fantasies dancing around their heads.

Gage frowned as Rudy's eyes blurred, obviously taken in by her spiel and focusing on all his own happy fantasies.

"In comparison to the message of sex. Which, let's face it, is impersonal and can be performed just as easily in the nude as in a six-hundred-dollar leather bustier." She gave a tiny shrug, as if saying it wasn't the cost that was a drawback, but the image. "Sex is a physical sensation. Love is an emotion. And while people might be satisfied with sex—they might even crave it—it's the idea of romance and having someone worship them in a physical way that will sell you the most lingerie."

She didn't look Gage's way as she finished, but instead, Hailey gave a sharp nod, all but clapping her hands together. Her smile oozed satisfaction. As it should. Gage was ready to toss aside the leather and go for lace himself.

Then he remembered what was at stake.

"Are you saying romance equals love? You're not really using that as your selling point, are you? Because we, and Rudolph's audience, are savvier than that."

Gage wasn't proud of bashing her argument that way. But dammit, he had to get loose of Milano. He was so sick of playing his father's puppet. He needed that year of freedom, and his chances of getting it were quickly slipping away.

Clearly as impressed with him as he was with himself, Hailey made a show of rolling her eyes.

"I'm saying romance makes people feel good. When they feel that good, they are much more willing to spend money—a lot of money—on keeping the feeling."

She shifted her gaze to Rudy and tilted her head to one side. "Isn't that the point? To not only present a strong visual that will create a trend, but to get people into your store to spend money?"

"Or is it to build an air of exclusivity, something that women will aspire toward and envy?"

Gage didn't go as far as to claim that people—women especially—would pay more for the exclusive designer aura than for the feel-good romantic image.

Because from Hailey's glare, and Rudy's nod, he didn't have to.

"The real question is, which line will better suit Cherry Bella's image and enhance the message Rudolph department stores is trying to send?" Hailey put in quickly.

Rudy heaved a sigh, then watched his fingers tap the desk for a few seconds before he offered them both a grimace.

"Okay, I'm going to be honest with you both. I'm inclined to go with Milano, simply because I think the look is more cutting edge, high-fashion oriented."

Yes! Other than a slight relaxing of his shoulders and tiny twitch of his lips, Gage managed to keep his triumph to himself. But in his mind, he was already packing his bags and heading for Tahoe.

His gaze slid to Hailey, wondering if she might be in the mood for a little snow for the holidays. He frowned. Her face was like porcelain. White, stiff and brittle-looking. Did she hate losing that much? How long would she hold a grudge? Maybe he should send a car for her next week instead.

"But," Rudy continued, drawing out the word in a way that grated up and down Gage's spine. "The decision isn't mine alone."

What? No. He was already on the highway, heading up the mountain. No buts, dammit.

"Of course it's your decision," Gage said quickly, adding a man-to-man smile. "Not that Cherry's input isn't important. But, let's face it, she hasn't been in attendance for much of these meetings. Her priorities are clearly elsewhere."

The old guy pursed his lips. Gage knew that look. It was the screw-everyone, I-want-to-get-my-way-and-be-done-with-this look. He'd seen it on his father's face a million times. Usually right before he waved away every reasonable, well-thought-out and time-intensively researched argument Gage waged.

Kinda like Rudy was about to do to Hailey.

Gage glanced over at her again. Her chin was high, her smile in place. But he could see the hurt and frustration in her eyes.

Crap.

Before Rudy could say anything, and before he could talk himself out of playing hero, Gage gestured to the six-foot mock-up of Cherry surrounded by items from the various lines already chosen.

"But you've put so much time and effort into building a launch around Cherry Bella, you don't want to rock the boat," he said quickly. "She said it herself—the lingerie line is her breaking point. Can't ride roughshod over a woman's choices. You know how that'll come out if you do."

Rudy's grimace made it clear he'd paid the price for doing that a few times in his life. Big surprise.

"Okay, fine," the older man finally said with a huff. "But no more of these clever scenarios. No more romance versus sex. The two of you put together a fashion show, pitch your best spring look. I guarantee, Cherry and I will both attend and the decision will be made within an hour. We need to get on with this."

"When?" Hailey cleared her throat, then started over. "When will we need to do the show? What are the parameters? I mean, how many pieces will you want to see? The designs I pitched were exclusive, intended for your spring debut. I don't have them on hand."

Good point. Gage pulled a face. He was sure that Milano was in the same boat, although he had a hunch Devon had probably already started producing the designs, figuring if Rudolph didn't take them, someone else would.

"I have to get this nailed down," Rudy said, his usually friendly face folding into a scowl. "I can wait a week, maximum. If we can't settle this by then, I'll simply run my spring show without lingerie."

"A week it is," Gage said, his tone quick and hearty. That was six days longer than he wanted, and probably a dozen less than Hailey preferred.

"Fine. The two of you hammer out the details and email

me by the end of the day. I'll green-light it then get hold of Cherry and see you in a week."

With that, a clap of his hands and a nod goodbye, Rudy rose and strode from the room.

Gage waited for the man's size sevens to cross the threshold before turning to offer Hailey a smile.

But purse in hand and black wool coat buttoned, she was already halfway to the door herself.

What the hell?

Wasn't she going to thank him? He'd just given her another chance. Hell, he'd even gift wrapped it.

"Hailey?"

She didn't slow down.

She didn't look back.

And she definitely didn't offer a thank-you.

Seriously?

"Hailey, wait." Gage had to run to catch up with her since she wasn't slowing one bit. How the hell did she move so fast in heels that high?

"Hold up," he said, catching her arm halfway down the hallway. "I thought we'd go out, get something to eat. You know, nail down those details Rudy wants by the end of business."

His charming smile and teasing tone earned him a chilly stare. Damn. He'd known she was one of those women who needed hand holding on the pillow the next morning.

"I've plans for the rest of the afternoon," she said, pulling her arm out of his grasp. "We'll have to settle the details separately."

Awww, she was so cute.

"C'mon," he said, leaning close with his most persuasive smile. "You're just upset that I left when it was three to one in the taking-advantage department and you wanted another shot at me to even it out."

Her eyes went wide, then narrowed in glass-green slivers of fury. Then, in a sweep of those lush lashes, her expression cleared to frosty disinterest.

"You think you were that good?" she asked, giving him an up-and-down look that indicated she was trying to see what he was so proud of.

Burying his irritation, telling himself she deserved to get in a couple of digs since she was hurt, he plastered on his most charming smile.

"Baby, I think *we* were that good."

Her laugh put his charm in the fail column.

"Actually, it has nothing to do with missing out on the various delights you seem to think you are so good at," she said. Her arch look was like a rock, pounding that dagger into his ego just a little deeper. "It has to do with basic manners. If you're a guest at a party, do you walk out or do you take the time to find your host and say thank you for the good time?"

Gage tried to keep his expression smooth, but didn't have much luck holding back the scowl. Was that all she saw it as? A good time? What the hell?

First off, it'd been great. Not good.

And second, she was pissed because he hadn't minded his manners? He wanted to call bullshit on that, figuring it as a face-saving excuse.

But the chilly disdain in her eyes didn't give way to any hint of hurt, no petulant rejection. Nope, just irritated dismissal.

He didn't know how to deal with that.

"I didn't want to wake you. If I did, I wouldn't have been able to resist more." He kept his voice low, but let all the heat he felt ring out, so his words were a little husky. Unable to resist, he risked losing a limb and reached out to trace one finger along the delicate curve of her cheek.

"I knew we'd see each other today at the meeting and fig-ured you'd appreciate some sleep."

Lame. As soon as the words were out he wanted to snatch them back. He didn't need to see her roll her eyes to know that was a suck-ass excuse.

What was it about Hailey that had him so off center? He'd never been this bad at talking to women, had never had any issue charming his way into or out of any situa-tion that involved a female. Then again, he'd never encoun-tered a business deal as weird and difficult to navigate as this one, either.

As the pretty little blonde glaring up at him was the common denominator, he had to figure it was her. Not him.

"Well, thank you so much for considering my needs. And now—" she shifted her arm out of his hold "—I've got an event to prepare for. I'll pull together my notes and email them to you. You can add or adjust as you see fit, then we can send them to Rudy."

In other words, she didn't want anything to do with him.

Pretty freaking insulting, considering she'd jumped his body and sexed him into an orgasmic puddle against her wall.

But if that was the way she wanted to play it?

Fine.

Without another word, not bothering to attempt an ar-gument or another lame excuse, Gage stepped back and let her go.

Just as well. They were business rivals. One way or an-other, one of them—her, specifically—was going to lose. Better to let it go now, chalk it up to lust and some sexy lingerie and get his life back on track.

Still, Gage had to wonder how many times he was going to watch the sweet sway of her ass as she stormed away from him. And ponder why he liked the idea of seeing it a few hundred more times.

"Hailey, how'd the meetings go?"

"Did you wow Rudolph with your vision of romance?"

"Of course she did. Merry Widow designs sell themselves. All our Hailey had to do was show the guy the lineup, sweet-talk a little and bat those eyelashes, and boom. We're in for a Christmas treat." To emphasize that, Jackie did a little happy dance through the warehouse that sent the jingle bells on her hat, shoes and necklace a dingling.

Hailey forced a big smile on her face, sidestepped the questions and tried to make it to her office. She was waylaid again to approve a new design change, then a third time to admire the Christmas tree made of coat hangers and decorated with bras one of the team had set up in the corner.

They were all so excited.

Every face in the warehouse glowed, not unheard of on a Friday afternoon. Or with excitement over the anticipated Rudolph deal.

She'd trained them well.

Shoo for the stars, and never doubt you'll have a happy landing.

What a bunch of crap.

"I've got some samples together for the spring-line photo shoot on Wednesday," Jackie said, finally through with her dance. "I know you want to hold off to decide which pieces we're offering until you know which ones Rudolph will make exclusive. But I figured it couldn't hurt to be prepared. I've been shopping for accessories and props to go with it all."

Jackie gestured to the variety of lingerie, jewelry, shoes and pretty accoutrements spread across a long, fabric-covered worktable. "I even picked up some little goodies that I thought would go well with our Christmas pieces, figuring maybe you might want to give Cherry a little gift for the holiday."

Hailey had to blink fast to keep from bursting into tears.

Everyone was so excited. So sure they'd get this account.

Just like she'd been.

Swallowing hard to clear her throat, Hailey tried to figure out when she'd lost her hope.

"That's a great idea," she managed to say, offering a shaky smile. "Thanks for putting in the extra time."

"Oh, believe me, it was my pleasure. This is going to be the best Christmas ever," the younger woman said, all but clapping her hands together. "Don't forget, you have to do the Secret Santa drawing today, too."

"Right." More Christmas cheer. Hailey kept her grin in place as the other woman danced away.

Ho, ho, freaking ho.

As soon as she hit the stairs leading to her office, Hailey let her cheery smile drop, along with her shoulders and her hopes.

"You're late." At the top of the stairs was a loft that spanned the length of the warehouse. Between the top step and Hailey's office was what she often referred to as the dragon-guarded moat. In other words, Doris's desk. Manned, as usual, by the beehive-haired dragon. "You were due here an hour ago."

"You knew I had a meeting," Hailey reminded her in a weary tone.

"You knew it was Friday. I work half days every Friday in December."

Seriously? Knots ripped through her shoulders. On top of everything else, she needed this crap from a woman whose paycheck she signed?

"So leave," Hailey snapped, waving her hand toward the steps and stomping past the huge desk to her own office.

She didn't get any farther than tossing her bag on the chair and her coat on the floor before the dragon stormed in after her.

"You're sure in a grump of a mood. I told you going to all that trouble to try and impress Rudolph was a stupid idea."

Hailey's glower covered Doris, the woman's dour words and the entire day in general.

"I thought you were leaving. Half-day December, remember?"

"I came in to give you your messages," the older woman said with a sniff, her sky-blue-tinted eyelids lowered in a sad puppy-dog look. "Thought they might be important. One from your date last night."

Her heart tumbled, then bounced around her chest in excitement.

"Gage?"

Had he left it before or after the meeting?

Was it an apology for leaving her, naked and wanting, in her own bed?

Or another nagging reminder that they had to figure out their final pitch?

And why did she care so much?

Sure, he'd acted as if he was trying to make nice after his toss-under-the-bus attempt in today's meeting. But she'd trusted him once. She'd got naked with him. And he'd left her.

"I don't want to talk to him," she announced. "If he calls back, tell him we'll handle it by email."

Doris's pout disappeared into a look of speculation. "No. Mr. Rudolph. Isn't that who you were out with? Him and the singer lady?"

Hardly.

But Hailey just shrugged and held out her hand for the messages.

Doris, of course, didn't hand them over. Instead, she kept right on looking as though she was trying to figure out all of Hailey's secrets.

What the hell was it with people inspecting her like this? Her face, her soul, her secrets, they were her business, dammit.

"Another call, too. This one from your mom."

Like a cement block, Hailey's hand dropped to her side. Disappointment settled deep and aching in her belly. She didn't need to hear the message to know what was coming. The same thing as always.

"She said she's sorry. She's not gonna be able to do Christmas with you, after all. Turns out she got a part in a traveling theater troupe and needs to be ready to hit the road on January one."

To her credit, Doris shared the news with a heavy dose of sympathy. Even her wrinkles seemed to empathize, all curving downward with her frown.

"Anything else?" Hailey asked, trying not to feel defeated by a morning determined to kick her ass.

Doris hesitated, then curled the messages into her fist and shook her head.

"Nope. That's it."

How was that for pathetic? The woman who regularly scorned Hailey's rose-colored-glasses-wearing optimism was hiding bad news from her.

"Doris?"

The older woman's sigh whooshed through the room and she gave a jerky shrug.

"Just those Phillips brats, checking to see if you've made arrangements to pay off the business."

Hailey pushed her hand through her hair, wishing she could as easily shove away all the stress tying knots in her scalp. She wasn't ready to throw in the towel, dammit. But, inch by inch, the towel was slipping out of her grasp.

"Maybe it's time to call a meeting," Doris murmured.

Clenching her jaw, Hailey stared at the workroom floor beneath her, clear through the plate-glass window that separated the loft-style office from the rest of the small warehouse.

Below, two desks were manned by her sales team, while her marketing guru was curled up in a beanbag in the corner, laptop in hand. She could see production just beyond the curtains, packaging up the smaller orders that were going out for the holidays.

Her tiny empire, a dozen people total including her and Doris. Wouldn't calling them together for a "we've failed" meeting be tantamount to giving up? Didn't she owe it to them, to herself, to see this through?

"Next week," she said quietly, turning away to meet Doris's oddly patient gaze. "Friday at our monthly meeting. I'll either give them their holiday bonuses or give them as much severance pay as I can pull together."

A week and a half to save her business. Hailey was damned if she'd give up before she had to. Chin high, she held the other woman's gaze, waiting for the slap down.

Instead, after a few long seconds, Doris gave a jerky nod.

"I'll take a look at the books, see what's what. For the bonuses. Or just in case."

Without another word, and with those vile messages still clutched in her talons, Doris clomped out of the room.

Just in case.

Hailey sighed, sinking into her chair and dropping her face to her desk.

Maybe everyone was right.

Maybe it was time she quit believing everything in life would work out if she just held on and had faith.

After all, what'd actually turned out that way for her?

Her father still didn't consider her a part of his *real* family. Her mother blew her off with more ease than a five-year-old making a wish on a dandelion. And now her business, the one thing she'd figured she could count on because she'd built it herself, was imploding.

Tears slid, silent and painful over her cheeks.

And she couldn't do a damned thing about any of it.

11

HER PALM DAMP, Hailey curled her fingers tight. Then with a grimace she shook her hands to air-dry them, curled one again and used it to knock at the heavy oak door.

Okay, maybe *knock* was an exaggeration.

Tap. Lightly.

Still, it counted.

She had to do this. Had to give it one last shot.

She'd wallowed in misery for an entire hour. She'd eaten Doris's entire stash of cookies. And she'd watched her employees, all buoyed up with holiday cheer.

As she'd realized that whether it made her a sucker or not, she had to keep trying. Giving up, it just wasn't her.

Of course, neither were uncomfortable confrontations.

So after another five seconds of silence, she figured she'd given it her best shot and, with a relieved sigh, turned to leave.

"Hailey?"

Crap.

Forcing herself to shift her grimace into a smile—of sorts—she sighed, then turned back around.

"Hi, Gage," she said in that fake, perky-door-to-door-saleswoman tone.

He looked gorgeous. More casually dressed than she'd ever seen him, he wore a plain black T-shirt and jeans with socks. She shifted from foot to foot in her Frye boots, rubbing her gloved finger over the smooth texture of her tights below her black wool miniskirt. Clearly she was overdressed.

As usual, whenever she was around Gage, Hailey had the urge to strip off a few layers of clothes and see what they could do together, naked.

Grateful for the cold night air against her suddenly hot cheeks, Hailey puffed out a breath.

Why was she here again?

Not for that, she reminded herself.

"I was hoping we could talk. Nail down those specifics Rudy wants."

"He wanted them by five." Gage made a show of checking his watch, then gave her an arch look. "That was an hour ago."

"I spoke with him. He's fine with having the information in the morning."

"Ahh, so that's why you've been ignoring my calls and emails." He paused, probably waiting for her to look ashamed. Hailey made sure to keep her smile in place, though. She was tired of other people calling the shots, dammit.

After a second, he shrugged and asked, "Did you send a hooker to his office to persuade him?"

Hailey's lips twitched. Too bad she hadn't thought of that herself. It'd probably have taken less time.

"No. But I did promise that I'd handle everything, including getting Cherry to show up."

"Good luck with that," Gage muttered, stepping away from the doorway to gesture her inside. "Come on in. I'll make coffee."

Hailey hesitated. This was what she'd come for, to talk to him on a casual—hopefully friendly—basis. Which meant going inside.

Still, her stomach did some tumbles as she did.

"Nervous?" he teased, his eyes intent on her face.

"Of what?"

"Good question."

Hailey lifted her chin and gave him a hard look. One she hoped made it clear that she was here for business. Not to see if the sex against his walls was as good as the sex against her walls had been.

Nope. That idea hadn't once entered her head.

Not once.

Because, she assured herself, a few dozen times didn't count as once.

Still, he didn't need to know that. A man who left the morning after without a word didn't deserve any ego strokes. Or to revisit the delights they'd shared.

Dammit.

"Let me take that," he said, gesturing to her purse. She handed it to him, then slipped off her leather gloves to give him those, too.

And, try as she might, she couldn't hide her little shiver as his fingers skimmed her shoulders when he helped her out of her coat.

"C'mon in," he said.

She met his grin with a glower. Yeah. He knew what that shiver had meant.

But once she moved out of the entry and into the living area, desire took a backseat to curiosity.

Wow.

She tried not to gawk.

She hadn't been raised poor by any means.

But Gage?

Clearly he'd been raised rich.

Art, not knickknacks or decorations, but signed-by-famous-people art hung on the walls, was tucked into cubbies, hung from a corner. The furnishings were simple, leather, sleek. But it wasn't cold or, well, fancy.

She noted the pair of tennis shoes kicked off by the couch, the newspaper tossed on the chair.

It was a home.

That shouldn't appeal to her so much.

But it did.

"Is coffee okay? Or would you prefer hot chocolate? Wine? Water?" he offered, playing happy host as he moved through an arched doorway to what, if the hints of stainless she could see were any indication, was surely the kitchen.

She followed, this time not able to hide her appreciative sigh.

"Wow," she murmured. Double oven, a stove and grill, hickory cabinets and granite countertops all screamed kitchen fabulousness.

"Yeah?" He followed her gaze, then shrugged. "I guess. But I mostly order out. Coffee and scrambled eggs are about the extent of my cooking expertise."

"But you offered me hot chocolate." Something she was suddenly craving like crazy, especially if it came with whipped cream.

He lifted a brown-and-white metal tin with a familiar logo. "Heat milk, stir in chocolate."

"No whipped cream?"

His gaze heated, then did a quick skim down her body, as if debating where in particular he'd like to dollop that cream before licking it up.

Hailey's nipples tightened in a silent scream of *here, put it here.*

Focus, she warned herself.

"I wanted to get this entire matter settled, and figured it'd be easier to discuss between just the two of us." She waved her hand between them. "No Rudy, no marketing gimmicks."

No sex.

She managed to keep that last part to herself. Not so much out of concern for saying it aloud. But because she still wasn't completely sure she could—or wanted to—follow that particular mandate.

After a long look, Gage nodded. He moved around the kitchen with ease, gathering a pot, milk, grinding coffee.

Happy to leave the discussion for a bit and just watch him, Hailey settled onto an oak stool cozied up to the work counter. He moved with an economic grace, totally comfortable in the kitchen and with himself.

When he added an extra scoop of chocolate shavings to her hot milk, she tried not to drool. Especially since her mouth wasn't watering over the drink, but the man stirring the spoon.

Maybe this was a stupid idea.

Maybe she should have called instead of seeing him face-to-face. It was much easier to control her urge to lick him over the phone than it was when he was within touching distance.

"So," he asked once they were both settled into the welcoming cushions, their mugs in hand and the fireplace crackling warmly behind them, "are you going to make me an offer I can't refuse?"

"I beg your pardon?" She glanced around the room, an ode to comfortable wealth, then shrugged. What could she offer that he couldn't walk away from?

He leaned closer, the rich scent of roasted coffee and his own cologne wrapping around her like a gentle net, pulling her tight. Making her want to close her eyes and simply breathe him in.

But she couldn't close her eyes, because his were holding her captive. The dark depths promised sensual delights. A promise, she knew from experience, he could meet.

Quite nicely, too.

Hailey's pulse sped up. Her body turned liquid.

Her brain filled with visions of the two of them, their naked bodies sliding together on this couch. On that wall. On any variety of whatever flat surfaces he had in the house.

Would she do him again?

Even though her ego screamed no, for crying out loud the guy didn't even say goodbye in the morning, her body was doing the *yes, please* happy dance.

Her body was much louder, and more enthusiastic than her ego. Her body wanted to touch the hard planes of his chest again. To feel him moving inside her, pounding, throbbing. Sending her spiraling higher and higher.

A little short of breath, Hailey had to pull her gaze away from the hypnotic depths of his.

As soon as she did, logic shouldered its way in, breaking up the fight between ego and desire.

"I don't think I have anything to offer that you'd find irresistible," she stated.

"Wanna bet?" he countered, reaching out to trace his fingers along the curve of her jaw, then down the long line of her throat. The move, so soft and gentle, made her shiver.

He wouldn't be able to refuse sex, between the two of them, in exchange for stepping off the Rudolph account?

"Yeah. Right." She laughed so hard she had to set the mug down for fear of spilling her chocolate. "You'd give up a seven-figure contract for a weekend with my body?"

His eyes were hot on said body, making it difficult for her not to wiggle in place to try to relieve some of the building heat.

"I asked if that's what you were offering."

Nice double speak. For a second, just one, she wanted to say sure. To stand up, strip naked and gesture that he come and get it.

But ego, the part that was afraid he'd laugh if she did, won out. So instead, pretending she wasn't hurt by that image—or by his leaving her—Hailey gave him a sardonic look, then made a show of tapping her fingernail against her lower lip.

"Let's see. Was it only last night that you had full access to my body? Yes, yes, I think it was. And you quite comfortably walked away from it this morning, without so much as a 'see ya, babe.'" She looked him up and down then met his eyes again and arched her brow. "Did something change between now and then?"

Gage set his coffee next to her chocolate before sliding a little closer, so his hard, warm thigh pressed against hers. He ranged his arm along the back of the couch, so close she could almost feel his pulse, but not quite touching her. As if he was crowding all around her, making sure she was very, very aware of his body. But not doing anything about that awareness.

Figured.

Hailey was so sick and tired of people making promises, getting her hooked and emotionally invested, then running out on her. Was there a flashing neon sign over her head, proclaiming her a disappointment junkie?

So instead of giving in to the desire, and the heat Gage was trying to tease her with, she leaned in closer herself.

His eyes flickered, desire flaring before he banked it.

She watched his pulse jump and smiled.

Then, for good measure, she shifted again so her breath wafted over his skin, close enough to leave a haze of chocolate.

"You want to make me an offer, Gage, you go right ahead. But make sure it's one you can keep. I'm tired of being teased."

It was on the tip of his tongue to offer her anything.

Everything.

In exchange for just one more taste. One more touch. One more wild ride between her thighs.

As if magnetically pulled forward, Gage found himself bending down, his mouth ready to take hers.

And to accept any deal she wanted.

A quick flash of triumph in those green eyes served as a kick-in-the-ass wake-up.

He froze.

What the hell was he doing?

Would he give up his bid for the contract for a weekend with her body?

If the stakes had been only the contract, the answer wouldn't just be yes, it'd be *hell, yes.*

But this was his freedom, a shot at breaking away from Milano, and doing so in a way that didn't destroy his questionable family relationships.

Maybe the better question was, would she give it up for his?

"Why is this so important to you? It's just an account. Albeit a fat one, but it's not like you can't scoop up another dozen fat accounts. You've got a stellar product, a smart sales pitch, and the kudos from being considered for this are enough to parlay into a dozen open doors." Yes, he'd tried this argument once before. But he wanted an answer this time. He'd gone up against some fierce competition in the past, but never one with so much heart, so much determination to win.

Hailey's gaze held his, her eyes more serious than he'd ever seen them. It was as though someone had squeezed all of the bubble out of her personality, leaving her flat. Still sweet, still beautiful, but without the effervescence that was so natural to her.

"I need this contract," she said with a quiet shrug. The kind that said *let it go, just move on.*

But Gage didn't want to.

He wanted to know her. To know what was pushing her so hard. He wanted to know what she had to lose when he won.

"So do I," he countered. Giving in to temptation, he brushed his fingers over the tips of her hair, watching the pale blond strands slide like a silken waterfall back to her shoulder. "What else ya got?"

Her lips twitched, and after a long, considering look, she pulled away and leaned over to get her mug of chocolate again. She didn't sip, just stared into it as if searching for the right words.

"If I don't get this, I'll lose my business."

"How?" Gage frowned. "I did a check on you when I heard we were competitors. You're solid."

"On paper, with the bank, sure." Her shrug was jerkier this time, irritated. "I bought Merry Widow from my mentor three years ago. We had what you'd call a friendly agreement. We both knew the business was worth a lot more if I built it up, kept it going. So we agreed that I'd pay him a set amount each year, and at the end of five years, if I'd doubled the net worth, my debt was paid. Otherwise we'd negotiate fair-market value."

Gage's frown didn't ease, even as he shook his head.

"I don't get it. I mean, it's a crazy agreement, definitely not like anything I've ever heard before. But it hasn't been five years. You're close to doubling your net worth from four years ago so you should be fine." He ignored her look of surprised irritation that he knew so much about her. "So what's the problem?"

"I know it's unorthodox, but it was Eric's way of pushing me. Of motivating me to do my best." She smiled, as if just that memory gave her joy. Then her lips drooped. "Then he died early this fall."

"I'm sorry," Gage murmured.

She nodded, taking a sip of her chocolate. More as a

way to get hold of herself, he figured, than any desire for cooling milk laced with cocoa.

"His kids are calling the loan. Full market value, without credit for previous payments."

"They can't do that."

"Sure they can. Eric and I didn't have a contract. We had a verbal agreement because he didn't want to deal with the drama his kids would put up if they found out what a deal he was offering me."

Pissed now, Gage shook his head. She had to have a good lawyer. Someone who could put an end to the bullshit claim.

"That's crap. I'll get my attorney to look into it," he offered.

For the first time since he'd pushed her on the topic, Hailey's lips curved into a real smile and her eyes danced.

"You are so sweet. But no, it's been looked at. They're within their rights."

"That's crap," he repeated.

"Sure it is. But if I get the Rudolph contract, it'll show a solid enough income that the bank will loan me what I need to pay off the Phillips kids." She sipped the chocolate again, wrinkled her nose and returned the mug to the table. "So there you go. My reason for needing the contract."

It was pure crap. Gage didn't bother to say it a third time, though. Instead, he silently fumed. Not because her needs put him in a difficult position, although they did.

But because she'd been screwed over, royally. Because some lame ass was too worried about upsetting his kids, Hailey was in danger of either losing her business or going deep into debt. A debt that, if he'd written up the agreement as promised, she'd never have had to take on.

Damn.

Suddenly, all he wanted was to make her smile. To show her how important, how special, she was.

He didn't have words, though. And even if he did, he'd feel like a complete idiot spouting off that kind of thing.

So he offered what he had.

A soft, sweet kiss.

A promise.

To worship her.

To take care of her.

To make sure her needs, her satisfaction, were primary.

Hailey's eyes were huge as bright green saucers as she pulled her mouth away from his.

"What's that for?"

"Because you deserve to feel good about yourself."

She gave a little laugh, as though she thought he was kidding.

Then, seeing that he was 100 percent serious, her smile faded. Desire, hope and something deeper washed over her face.

"You think so?" she asked, hesitating before running her fingers, just the tips of them, along his jaw.

Gage leaned into her hand, loving the feel of her.

"Spend the weekend with me."

Her gasp was sharp. Her pulse jumped in her throat. And those glorious eyes of hers filled with questions. He didn't know the answer to most of them, though. So he lifted her hand in his and brushed a kiss along her knuckles.

"Spend the weekend with me. Let me show you how special I think you are."

She pressed her lips together, then sighed and gave him a tentative smile.

"And how were you planning to do that?"

"Like this," he promised, grabbing the invitation and opportunity fast, before she changed her mind.

Just like he took her mouth.

Fast.

Hard.

Intense.

With every bit of passion and need and desire he had for her.

Her body melted into his as he pulled her onto his lap. Her lips gave way to his tongue, welcoming him into her warmth.

And suddenly, the only thing Gage wasn't sure of was if a weekend was enough time to show her how amazing she was.

12

"THIS IS RIDICULOUS. I can't believe I let you talk me into it."
Gage huffed, giving the woman responsible a hard look.
Difficult, since she was so adorable wrapped only in one
of his dress shirts and a layer of body lotion.

Lotion he'd slicked on himself after their shower that
morning.

The memory of that soft, smooth skin under his hands,
of the slide of the thick lubricant beneath his fingers,
stirred an interest in Gage's body. One that had nothing
to do with the crazy ideas Hailey was trying to get him
hooked into.

"C'mon. It'll be fun. I can't believe you've never done
this before."

"It's not like we're talking exotic sexual positions or
kinky toys, Hailey." He hunched his shoulders, really wishing they were. In those, he had experience in spades.

"No. As fun, exciting and important as those all are—"
she paused to give him an eye roll and a teasing smile
"—this is all of that, too."

Gage sighed.

Then, showing every bit of the reluctance he felt, he
approached the corner of the room with trepidation and,
giving her a grumpy look, took the thread she'd filled with
popcorn and tried to figure out what to do with it.

"I'm supposed to, what? Throw this over the branches?"

Hailey gave him a look that said she couldn't quite believe his professed cluelessness.

"Here, do it like this," she said, showing him how to drape the popcorn-covered string.

He really should be worried, because he was starting to think she could talk him into anything.

He'd figured the fact that he had no tree was a good enough excuse when she'd asked why he hadn't decorated. But no. She'd hauled on a pair of his sweatpants, pulled on her boots and swaddled herself in one of his sweaters before hauling him down to the corner lot to choose a tree.

He'd been so entertained by the seriousness with which she studied each specimen, rounding every tree and staring at it as if coded somewhere inside was the key to Santa's nice list. Finally, when he'd tried to grope her behind the wreath display, she'd settled on a tall, skinny one, claiming it'd be easiest for them to carry back.

Carry. He'd trotted down the San Francisco streets with a woman wearing his sweats and five-hundred-dollar boots, carting a pine tree.

What else could he do once they got it inside but strip her naked and make love to her?

Now, three hours and a handful of orgasms later, she was standing there, arms akimbo, giving him the hurry-up look.

"Isn't it enough to have the tree? Why does it need crap hung from it?"

"Because it's Christmas. Hanging crap from a tree is part of the holiday fun." She finished wrapping the string of lights they'd bought along with the tree, then bent low to plug it in.

Gage tilted his head sideways, grinning. He had to admit, the decorating view was definitely fun.

"Haven't you ever had a tree before? Ever?" she asked, pausing from her study of the perfect placement of lights to give him a puzzled look. "Does your family not celebrate Christmas?"

"Sure, we celebrate. But the tree always just sort of showed up in the lounge—lights, balls and presents."

Depending on which stepmother was ruling the roost at the time, it might be glinting with crystals or wrapped in yarn. One year, it'd had tiny porcelain dolls hanging from the boughs. That'd seriously freaked him out.

"I guess that's part of your fancy upbringing, huh?" she teased.

"I never thought it was fancy," he said honestly, trying to hang the popcorn strands the way she had, so they draped instead of tangled to look like something a bird puked up. "I mean, the house was huge and there might be a lot of social stuff going on, depending on the stepmom du jour. My brother and I were in boarding school most of the year, so when we'd come home for winter break, the tree was there. Done. If we ever decorated when I was little, I don't remember it."

Hailey paused in her adjusting and tweaking of the lights to glance at him, those big eyes of hers filled with tears.

"You were sent away."

"More like allowed to run away," he said with a laugh. "Don't feel sorry for me. I loved boarding school. Anything was better than the revolving circus that was that house's inhabitants."

She straightened, moving closer and giving him a look so deep with compassion that Gage actually felt his heart melt a little.

"Were you hurt there?"

His freak-out over the deep emotions she was inspiring gave way to shock. "What? Hurt? Nah. It was just crazy. My old man was a womanizer. Think Rudy, with less money and more to prove. We used to joke that he should lease wives instead of marrying them, since he traded them in as often as his cars."

"And that didn't bother you?"

"Why? None of them stuck around long enough to matter, so it wasn't like I missed them when they were gone."

It was only after a few seconds of silence, and his irritation with the strings of popcorn tangling together, that Gage glanced over.

Mouth open, eyes wide with sympathy, Hailey was staring at him as though she wanted to wrap him in her arms, pull his head to her shoulder and hug away all his hurts.

He figured he didn't have any, but he'd be willing to let her try, anyway.

"Don't make it into a big deal. It really isn't," he said honestly.

"What about your mom? Were you really young when she left?"

"Four and a half," he said with a shrug. "She came around a few times, I think, before she was killed in a car accident. But it's not like I grew up thinking there was a big hole in my life. It's just what it was, you know? One way or another, it was my dad, my brother and me. And a predecorated Christmas tree."

She didn't laugh.

"I'm done with the threaded popcorn," he said, tossing on the last bit in hopes of changing the subject. "Are we done or do you want more crap on the tree?"

"More crap," she said absently, handing him a stack of intricate snowflake shapes—cut from paper stolen from his office—that she'd cut out and hung on the same string she'd used for the popcorn.

"You must be really close to your brother, then."

So much for a subject change.

"At the moment, I'm almost tied. But by next year, I'll be ahead," he murmured absently.

Damned right he would. Devon had used his two-year advantage most of their life to stay in the lead, but a year off with no Milano emergency demands, and Gage was sure he was gonna sprint into first place.

"What?" Hailey shook her head. "What do you mean? Ahead?"

"You know, ahead. As in, which one of us is winning. Devon and I compete. Best grades, higher SATs, board support, bigger piece of the wishbone." He grinned, remembering. "That Grinch costume? I lost the wishbone bet at Thanksgiving and that's the price I paid. That's the kind of thing we do."

She squinted, as if trying to see through his words to the truth beneath. Why? He didn't understand her confusion.

"You're trying to tell me that the entire basis for your relationship with your brother is competition?"

Gage frowned. She made it sound so unhealthy.

"Sure."

"C'mon. No fraternal bond? No shared interests? Not even sibling rivalry?" She shook her head as if that were impossible to believe.

"Isn't sibling rivalry basically the same thing as competition?" After she gave a slow, considering nod, he shrugged and said, "Sure, we've got that. And we've got plenty of mutual interests. I check out his investments, advise him on marketing. He checks out mine, advises me on expansion options."

"That's it?" she asked.

He didn't know why she looked so horrified. Since it made him feel a little defensive, he racked his brain trying to find other examples for her.

"We aren't friends, like the kind who hang out together, but we respect each other. Family loyalty goes a long way, too. Shared life experiences, heritage, that kind of thing. But the bottom line is, we both want success. We both want to be a part of the family business, but we want it on our own, too. We both want to win."

He could see she wasn't buying his assurance that he wasn't emotionally scarred or harboring some hidden resentment of family-centered holidays. Rather than trying to convince her that, yes, he really was that shallow, he turned the tables.

"What about you? Now, granted, I was mostly focused on other things at your apartment the other night. Like your naked body and how incredible you felt under my fingers." He waited, then gave a satisfied smile when she blushed. "But I didn't see that you had a tree up."

Her expression changed, the frown seeming to turn inward before she slipped on a smile.

"I was waiting for my mom. It used to be our special tradition, and since she was visiting this holiday, I wanted to do it together. When I was little, we always decorated together as a family the weekend after Thanksgiving. After my parents divorced, I spent Thanksgiving with my father, so my mom waited until I was home and we did the tree together."

He tried to imagine her as a little girl, those flaxen curls in pigtails and some cute footsie pajamas on while she hung candy canes from the low-hanging boughs. He'd bet she'd been adorable.

"So you got to do two trees? No wonder you love this kind of thing."

"No. Just the one tree. My dad married the same year as the divorce, and Gina, my stepmom, liked to wait until closer to the holiday."

Leave it to the stepmom to shove the kid out. Gage had seen enough of it growing up to recognize the signs. He didn't even need Hailey's stiff upper lip, lifted chin or downcast eyes. And while he'd learned by seven to shrug it off, she was still carrying it around.

Time to quit bitching about the decorations, he decided. If a tree made her happy, they'd decorate. Hell, he'd take her to his father's place and she could decorate there, too.

"When's your mom arriving so you can do your tree?" I.e., how long was she available for freewheeling, wild and constant sex before family nabbed a portion of her attention?

On tiptoes, trying to wrap a thread around a high branch, Hailey went board stiff, dropping back to the flats of her feet. The snowflake was still in her hand, though. Its ripping sound was like fingernails on a chalkboard. Loud, invasive and painful. She grimaced, then crumpled the ruined decoration in her fist before shrugging.

"No mom this year. She called Friday and left a message. Something came up and she can't make it."

Did everyone let her down?

Underneath the hurt in her eyes, Gage could see acceptance. As though this kind of thing happened all the time.

"Well, hey, we'll go decorate your tree after this, okay? Just you and me. I'll bet you have actual decorations and stuff, right? So we can eat the popcorn instead of tossing it on the branches?"

As soon as the words were out, he realized he'd just volunteered to step in and play family. That was a serious thing. A way past *let's get naked and slide all over each other* thing. For a second, he wanted to grab the words back. Or change the subject. Then, as he watched her face melt into a beautiful smile, he realized he kinda liked it. Liked her trusting him. Believing in him.

"So what do you think?" he asked, gesturing to the tree. "Am I assistant material?"

"You're a great assistant." Her words were a little husky and her smile a little shaky, but—thank God—she didn't do anything crazy, like cry.

Whether because she wasn't a teary kind of gal, or because she could see how uncomfortable he was, she put on a bright face instead and looked at the tree.

"It still needs something," she decided, tilting her head to the side, as if she were critiquing an outfit about to hit the runway. Gage figured it must be a girl thing, since the tree looked fine to him. "Do you have anything shiny? Old jewelry, CDs, anything foil?"

Seriously?

He gave her a look, then glanced at the tree, then back at her. She had that stubborn tilt to her chin again, and her eyes were all soft and sweet.

Dammit.

"Let me see what I can find."

THAT WAS ABOUT the weirdest tree she'd ever seen. And given that there was one in her warehouse right now made of coat hangers and bras, that was saying something.

Gage's arms loose around her waist, Hailey leaned back against his chest and sighed.

"It's perfect," she decided.

"Okay."

"It is." Laughing, she turned in his arms, cupping her hands behind his neck and giving him a quick, smacking kiss. "You done good."

He cast a doubtful eye over her shoulder, clearly seeing the actual tree and not the sentiment hanging from its boughs.

"Okay," he said again.

Then, as if there was nothing else to say about a tree covered in foil condom wrappers, popcorn and paper snowflakes, he laughed, shook his head, then took her mouth.

Hailey let the power of his kiss take her over, pull her down, permeate her being.

Being with Gage was like being wrapped in warmth.

Not just the fiery heat of passion, although that was a constant and definitely keeping her excited.

But the laughter. The kisses. The gentle teasing and constant interest in her.

Her views. Her ideas. Her past and her present. What she wanted in the future, even. She'd never had anyone so focused on her. Just…her.

As though he really cared about her.

Breathing in deep, she pushed away the sudden tears that thought brought and focused on the kiss.

Her lips danced over his, her hands sliding gently, oh so gently, over his naked skin. Satin over steel.

They fell into the lovemaking with a gentle sigh.

Every move was a whisper. A breath of skin against skin. A tease of a kiss, a wash of warm air, wrapping them together in a sweet, dreamy sort of passion.

As Gage's body ranged over hers, Hailey stared up into the endless depths of his eyes and opened herself, welcoming him in.

As he moved, slowly sliding in and out, she held his gaze. She let everything she felt shine in her own.

The delight.

The desire.

The deep, intense emotions that she couldn't even put a name to herself.

He never looked away.

Even as she tightened, as passion caught her in its needy web, her body demanding total focus, complete attention, he still watched.

And when she went over, the desire pounding and swirling through her in deliciously hypnotic waves, he smiled.

A slow, satisfied smile.

And then with a low moan, he joined her.

Two hours later, wrapped together in front of the fire,

Hailey was still trying to come to grips with the power of their lovemaking.

Her eyes fixed on the flickering flames, the lights of the Christmas tree a soft glow against the wall, she tried to identify the feelings inside her.

Peace. Joy. Love.

Scary.

"Look," Gage finally said, shifting onto his elbow. "Next year, I'll have a lot going on. I'm going to be really pushing to get my own business solid fast. It's going to take focus and time."

Hailey froze, body and heart.

Well, at least he was being honest, she told herself, wrapping the sheet closer, trying to stave off the shivers. Still, she'd never been blown off while naked before.

"I'm going to take care of this whole thing with Rudolph, with saving your company. I don't want you to worry about it anymore," he said, his words quiet, measured. Her heart thumped a few extra beats before Hailey could catch her breath and turn in Gage's arms to face him. "I'll fix everything, okay?"

For a brief second, Hailey wanted to protest. She didn't need favors. She could win the contract on her own, without him stepping aside for her. But Rudy had already made it clear that if it were only up to him, he'd go with Milano. And she couldn't afford to put all her faith in Cherry, or to let pride stand in the way of saving her business.

"Are you sure?"

"Yeah. Totally sure."

"And the presentation on Tuesday? Should we cancel?"

His frown flashed for a second. "Nah, it's more professional to keep it. I'm sure I'll have everything taken care of, but it's a good fallback just in case, too."

Just in case.

Her heart melted, the entire world taking on a rosy glow.

He really was taking care of her.

"And us?" she asked, feeling as if it were Christmas morning and Santa had not only brought her entire list, but had doubled up on the things she hadn't even thought to ask for.

"After this deal with Rudolph is done, I want to make us a priority," he said, brushing the hair off her cheek and giving her a tender look. "It's going to be hard, but I want to make sure we get time together. It might take some juggling, maybe a few cancellations or rescheduled dates here and there. Are you okay with that?"

Hailey blinked.

"What?"

"I want us to be together. I want to build on this, to see where we go," he said, gesturing between their bodies before sliding his hand into her hair to caress the back of her head. "I want to give us a chance."

A chance.

He wanted her. Them.

Without any prodding or girlie manipulation, he'd straight-up claimed them a couple.

Hailey's smile started slow, tremulous, since she refused to cry. But then the giggles took over and she pressed her free hand to his cheek, pulling his face close for a kiss.

Then another.

And yet another, this one turning hot.

Sweet passion poured over them. She shifted, pressing his body down against the floor, the warmth of the fire flickering over their entwined forms.

Gentle kisses, soft caresses gave way to heat.

Grateful for his resourcefulness, she stretched over, tugging one of the glinting foil condom packages from the tree. She quickly sheathed him, then before he could do more than moan, she slid onto the hard length of his erection.

Together, with her taking the lead, they made slow,

sweet love again. This time, he came first. The feeling of him, throbbing and pulsing inside her, sent Hailey over, too. She collapsed, breathless, onto his chest and gave a purr of satisfaction.

"I take it that's a yes?" he murmured against her hair as they were shivering with orgasmic aftershocks.

He didn't elaborate. He didn't have to. She knew he was asking if she wanted to give them a chance.

Hailey's laugh was a whisper, nuzzled close against his throat.

"Yes. Definitely yes," she agreed.

With just the flickering warmth of the fire, and Gage's body, covering hers, Hailey drifted off to sleep. Her last thought before sliding under was to wonder if she should be happy that the contract was hers. Or terrified that she'd had to fall in love to get it.

HAILEY WAS ALMOST skipping as she made her way up the steps of the Rudolph building.

This was it. The last presentation.

She and Gage had told Rudy Friday night, before their delicious weekend together, that they'd meet on Tuesday for one final time.

Each would bring the designs they felt most represented the line, a marketing plan they planned to implement to support the Rudolph debut, and their final pitch. Even though it wasn't going to be necessary, since Gage was backing out of the contract, Hailey had still prepared as if this was the most important day of her life. And, she thought, bubbling over with optimism, it just might be.

As she exited the elevator and headed for the board-room where they were to meet, Gage came hurrying toward her. She melted a little at the sight of him and that gorgeous smile.

"Hey, you," she said, brushing her fingers over his

cheek as if it'd been weeks since they'd been together instead of that morning. "I missed you."

"Ditto," he said with a grin. Then he tilted his head toward the double doors at the end of the hall. "I tried to reach you. Didn't you get my message?"

"No, what's up?"

"I came in early, met with Rudy." Tucking his hand under her elbow, Gage led her toward the boardroom doors as he spoke. "We're good to go. So I borrowed his boardroom to show you the setup."

Setup? He'd set things up for her?

Hailey all but clapped her hands together, she was so excited.

Together, they stepped into the boardroom. There, to one side by a set of open doors, were the samples she'd sent ahead for her presentation.

On the opposite end was a huge whiteboard. On it was a list of company names, some she recognized as huge. A marketing schematic covered one half of the board. She squinted. The schematic had her name at the top.

Trepidation started to overtake excitement in her stomach.

"What is this?"

"Rudy's going with Milano for the spring account, of course. He wanted to all along, but knew Cherry was leaning toward Merry Widow. But she's been so out of the loop, he's decided not to depend on her input any longer."

He said that as though he hadn't sold her out. As if just because Rudy would have chosen him in a head-on battle, that meant it was okay that he hadn't stepped down like he'd promised.

"You're kidding, right?"

"Nope. No joke. I got this all put together for you. You've got guaranteed orders, double the clientele as I'd suggested earlier and enough interest in your lingerie to translate into a fat load of new business." He pointed to the two-dozen names he'd listed on the board. Next to each was a dollar figure. Not shabby figures, either.

Hailey's head was buzzing.

"I put together a marketing plan for you. Now, granted, this is a first draft since we haven't talked it through and I don't have your actual figures or your business plan to integrate into it. But with it, and the prospectus I created, you have enough to take to the bank and get a big enough loan to stave off those greedy assholes."

His smile was huge, his eyes dancing. He looked as if he'd just handed her a pony covered in glitter with rainbow ribbons tied to its mane.

Instead of killing her dreams and stomping all over them.

"I can't believe you did this." Her head spinning, she shook it and hoped everything would shift. Change. Turn out to be a big fat hot-chocolate-induced mirage.

But it didn't.

Nope. Still there, on the board in bright colors, was proof that Gage had screwed her over.

And there he stood, grinning and looking as if he expected a thank-you note.

13

HAILEY WAS PACING the boardroom, from one end piled high with lingerie samples to the other with its whiteboard and presentation details.

As gorgeous as she was, with her skirt swishing to show a tempting length of thigh with each turn, he didn't think she was happy.

"What's up?" he asked, grabbing one of the leather chairs and pulling it out from the table so he could sit.

Then he caught the look on her face.

Pure fury, wrapped in a layer of hurt.

Nope. He was better standing.

"You stabbed me in the back." The accusation was made through clenched teeth.

"What the hell?" He reared back, shocked at both the accusation and the fact that his sweet Hailey could pull together this much anger.

"I thought you said you were going to let me have the contract."

"I said I was going to make sure you were taken care of," Gage countered. "I offered this before, and now it's an even better deal. I've got a dozen stores, venues and even a TV show all lined up, each one ready to make huge purchases. The revenue in a year will be as much, if not even more, than the Rudolph deal."

He waited, sure she'd simmer down now.

But she didn't. If anything, the fury in her eyes got even more fierce.

Gage frowned, starting to worry a little. He hadn't misplayed this. He was sure of it. There was no question that he was going to have everything he wanted. It looked as though it was just going to take a few pats and soothes before he got there.

"Hey, you haven't heard the bonus yet. By getting the Rudolph contract, I get my freedom. I can take on any client I want. So not only are you getting a boatload of new clientele, you get me." His smile was pure triumph, and he held out his arms, ready for her to throw herself at him in gratitude.

She hissed. If she'd been a cat, he was pretty sure she'd be wearing his skin under her nails right now.

He dropped his arms.

"I don't get it," he said. "You want success, or do you want the Rudolph deal? Aren't you being a little shortsighted with this obsession of yours?"

"We had an agreement."

Gage nodded.

"Right. We agreed that I'd make sure you were taken care of, that you didn't lose your business."

"That's not what I agreed to."

He sighed, shoved his hand through his hair, trying to figure out where this had all gone wrong.

"I can't help what you thought," he said. "I never said I'd step off the campaign. I made it really clear why not."

"And I made it really clear what this meant to me, and why I had to get the account."

He'd be able to handle this a lot better if she didn't sound as if she was about to cry. Gage hated feeling like a jerk. Hated even more the sense that his perfect solution was turning all to hell right before his eyes.

Dammit, he wanted Hailey.

And he wanted his freedom.

She just had to get over this silly attachment to the Rudolph account, and he could have both.

HAILEY SHOVED BOTH hands through her hair, hoping that if she tugged hard enough, a solution would pop out of her head.

When she'd woken up that morning, her world had been perfect. She'd been sure her business was safe, her holidays were heading toward the most awesome of her life, and she was falling in love with the greatest guy in the world.

Hailey had a brief, pining wish to return to that moment. Whether to rejoice in its brief existence, or to slap herself for being so naive, she wasn't sure.

But the moment, and the hope, was gone.

And this was her damned reality.

"Why would you do this?"

"You always take care of everyone else. You're the fix-it girl. The sweetheart who sweeps in and makes everyone feel better. Your employees, your family. Hell, even me. But who makes *you* feel better?" Gage's grin was part triumph, part little-boy-at-Christmas excitement. "I want you to have everything, too. So I fixed it so you could."

"No, you fixed it for you," she said quietly.

"Babe, this way we both win. You get to keep your business. I get my freedom. We both get to be together. That's better than a win-win. It's a win-win-you-and-me-win."

He looked so happy, so pleased with himself.

A part of her, the part that wanted everyone happy, wanted to step forward and give him a big hug. To give him the praise and gratitude he clearly expected. But as Hailey chewed her lower lip until it felt raw, she couldn't force out the applause he expected.

It wasn't as though she wasn't used to betrayal.

It wasn't as if this was the first time someone had made her a promise, then blithely danced away from it.

But this time, it was too much.

This time, she couldn't smile and pretend she was okay with it.

Pretend she didn't mind always coming in second. Because when it came to a commitment between two people, coming in second meant coming in last.

"C'mon, Hailey, let's just move past this," Gage said, his smile pure charm.

"We can't just move past it. I can't." She shook her head. "You're like everyone else. Happy enough to say you're there for me, as long as it's convenient."

"That's not true."

In other words, he didn't want it to be true.

Hailey looked at her shoes, ready to give in. She caught a glimpse of the lingerie samples out of the corner of her eye. She was losing it. Without that contract, there was no guarantee she could keep her business. And she was about to brush that off because it might make Gage feel bad?

So she took a deep breath and met his eyes. And even though each word was painful, she forced herself to speak.

"I've spent my entire life afraid that if I ever spoke up, ever put myself and my needs ahead of my parents' self-interest, that I'd be rejected. That they'd prove, beyond just the whispers in the back of my mind, that they couldn't— that they wouldn't—set aside their own self-absorbed priorities for me."

His frown was ferocious. Whether the anger was directed at her, or at himself, didn't matter. Hailey didn't care. For the first time in her entire life, she only cared about her feelings. It was both liberating and absolutely terrifying.

"You're putting other people's crap between us here,"

he accused. "You have a good reason to have those issues. But I shouldn't need to pay for them."

"But you're doing the same thing." How could he not see it?

Gage shook his head, as if denying her words could deny the truth.

"You're saying you won't take this deal?" he asked, as if he needed to hear her spell it out in tiny letters before he'd believe it.

"I'm saying I will not take your consolation-prize accounts. They're not enough to save my business. They're not enough to pay off the Phillips kids and put an end to this drama," Hailey repeated. Then, even though it was hard to get the air past the knot of tears in her throat, she added, "And if you can't understand why, we can't be together."

In that very second, she felt so miserably selfish.

It wasn't exactly an encouraging feeling to do this kind of put-herself-first crap again, she had to admit.

"You're not thinking straight. C'mon, seriously? You'd throw us, and a golden array of contracts, over? For what? Ego?"

Nope. Not encouraging at all.

But thankfully, anger stepped in and kept the apology on Hailey's lips from spilling out.

"Ego? How is my refusing to take second—no, last place and make the best of it ego driven?"

"You just said it yourself. You have to win, so you have to have first place."

"Me?" Hailey thumped herself in the chest so hard, she almost fell over. "Are you kidding? You're the one who won't walk away from this because you're afraid to go it alone."

"Don't be ridiculous," he dismissed. He looked derisive, but his hunched shoulders and scowl told her she'd scored a direct hit. "It's not as simple as leaving a lucrative job for a start-up. If I walk out, I'm giving up my heritage. I'm giving up any future claims on a company that's been in the family for a half century."

Maybe it was because she'd never had that kind of familial obligation—and definitely never had anyone in her family feel obligated to her—but Hailey couldn't wrap her mind around it.

"You're doing a job you don't like, at the beck and call of people you say don't respect you, because…what? You're afraid you won't get your share of the pie somewhere down the road?"

"Don't try to make it sound so stupid."

"I didn't have to try."

Gage ground his teeth, probably to hold back the cussing, but couldn't keep still. He paced. He grumbled. He did everything but look at Hailey.

"I just tried to hand you the best of everything, and you're tossing it aside. You have a bad habit of that, I've noticed."

Nice way to turn it around on her. But Hailey wasn't playing that game.

"Oh, please. I've never had anything handed to me," she snapped.

"No? What about Merry Widow?"

Before she could tell him how stupid and off base that was, he continued, stepping closer, butting right into her personal space to look down into her face.

"Your old mentor gave you the business. Yes, you had to work hard. You had to make payments. But if it wasn't for him, you wouldn't have had it."

"That's not the same. He and I had an agreement. One that if he were alive would mean I could walk out this door and not have to deal with you, this stupid contract or jumping through any of these ridiculous hoops." Hailey dropped back onto her heels, a little surprised—and a tiny bit ashamed—to realize that last had been offered at a full-on scream, from tiptoes so she could better get in his face.

Hmm. Maybe she had a few issues to resolve.

"Right. You had an understanding. You with obligations on your end. Him with obligations on his end. He didn't meet his, did he?"

"He met his obligations," she retorted, biting off the words. Eric would never have deliberately hurt her.

"Why didn't he draw up a contract for the purchase of the business, then? Why do you, all of a sudden, have to fork over the remaining balance if you had an agreement?"

"Because his kids—"

"If you had a contract, they couldn't do a damned thing."

Hailey pressed her lips together, trying not to burst into tears.

She'd trusted Eric. Just like she'd believed her father when he said she was always his little girl and had faith in her mother's vow to keep their family together.

But Eric, her mentor, her friend, her confidant, hadn't wanted to put it in writing because it'd upset his kids if they found it. And he didn't want to deal with their drama, as he put it.

Hailey should have insisted.

She should have pushed.

But she'd been so grateful to have the business, so grateful to be making her dream a reality, that she hadn't wanted to rock the boat. As always, she hadn't wanted to ruin a good thing by appearing greedy.

By trying to take care of herself.

When would she learn that nobody, ever, put her needs over their wants?

"Will you please leave?" she asked, near tears.

"No. We need to settle this."

"I don't want to discuss it. I don't want to talk to you." She clenched her jaw to keep her lips from trembling, but couldn't keep the tears from filling her eyes.

"Hailey—"

"Just go. I can say my goodbyes to Rudy without you. You've done enough. You can't give up this account— even though you admit my designs are better—because you won't get your perfect outcome wrapped in a perfect ribbon and your daddy won't love you anymore. Fine."

Before he could respond, before she rushed to apologize for the unfairness of her words, she waved him away.

"Please. Go."

"We haven't settled this." Gage's hand was warm on her shoulder as he tried to turn her to face him, but she shrugged it off. "There's more between us than just some silly business issue. Don't throw this away, Hailey."

She took a deep breath, then another to try to control her sobs. She'd never felt so good as she did with him. So wanted. But she couldn't be with him. Not now. It took all her strength, but she forced herself to turn and face Gage.

"We're through. Whatever we might have had, or could have been, it's over now." She gave a tiny, helpless sort of shrug. "Call it a quirk of mine. I don't want anything to do with the person responsible for pounding that final nail in my business's coffin."

Unable to resist, she indulged herself one last time by reaching out to cup her hand against his cheek. His eyes full of anger and pain, Gage leaned into her fingers, turning just a little to nuzzle a kiss against her palm.

It was too much. Hailey had to go.

Without looking at him again, she pulled her hand away, skirted around him and ran through the open door at the far end of the boardroom so fast, she was surprised she didn't fall and break her neck.

She'd leave. Oh, God, she wanted to leave. But she had

to be a good businesswoman. Smart women didn't burn bridges. She had to say her goodbyes, leave on a good impression.

But she couldn't until she got hold of herself.

Telling herself to get a grip, the sooner she stopped freaking out, the sooner she could get the hell out of here and go home, she hurried through the small anteroom she'd left her lingerie samples and supplies in. She shut the door behind her, blocking off Gage and the boardroom.

And almost screamed, her boots skidding across the carpet as she tried to stop her forward momentum.

"Cherry?" Hailey winced. She'd had no idea the other woman was even there. After how many attempts to get the torch singer to show up and listen to one of her brilliant pitches, and she finally did. And what did Hailey do? Have a total emotional breakdown, throw over her lover and kiss her career goodbye. All in one screaming match.

Lovely.

"You're smart to let him go," the other woman said, her voice huskier than usual.

Hailey was about to agree when she looked closer at Cherry. Dark grooves circled her eyes. Her skin had a pallid cast, made all the worse by the ugly overhead fluorescent lights. Despite the misery coursing through her, it was all Hailey could do not to go over, wrap her arms around the woman and pull her into a tight hug.

"It's none of my business, but are you okay?"

Hailey waited to be rebuffed. Just because Cherry had just been privy to her personal humiliation didn't make them bosom buddies.

"I feel bad. I didn't realize how much you had on the line with this deal," Cherry said, not looking at Hailey as she ran her hand over the heavy satin of a forties-inspired nightgown.

"My future was riding on it," Hailey said quietly. Not

to add any pressure to the woman, but for crying out loud, maybe it would be nice if people started considering someone else for a change in this little scenario. Rudy was all about self-indulgence. Cherry was totally self-absorbed. And Gage? Hailey ground her teeth together. Well, he was simply greedy and selfish.

So despite her dislike for emotional manipulation, she gave Cherry a direct look. "I have a dozen people who are depending on me, on my business, for their jobs. They have kids, families to support. We've put everything into this, and I really, really think Merry Widow is the best choice for this contract."

Cherry's nod was slow, her sigh deep.

"You're right. It is best." Then, with a loud swallow, she sighed again. "Actually, I've been on the fence, but today pushed me over. I'm not going to do the spokesmodel gig."

Oh, hell.

Hailey wanted to cry.

Or scream.

Screaming would be good.

But she only screamed inside her head. Never outside, where someone might hear her and be upset.

God forbid Hailey upset anyone with her petty personal issues.

But dammit, she'd tried so hard. She'd banked everything on this. She'd truly believed she'd get it, that all she needed was to get Cherry on her side.

And now?

Now it didn't matter. Rudy had already decided on Milano. Without Cherry's vote, he'd simply do what he wanted.

Still, Hailey dropped to a chair, her butt hitting the hard wood surface with a thump.

She was done.

It was over.

"I'm sorry," Cherry murmured, her voice seeming to come from much farther away than just across the room.

Hailey shrugged. She tried to pull out her brave face. Shouldn't be hard, right? She seemed to live in it. But she couldn't. Not this time.

She tried to find some happy words to brush off the whole thing, to make Cherry feel better.

But she couldn't. Not this time.

This time, she really wanted to scream.

On the outside.

"I needed this," she murmured instead. "I knew Rudy would take the sexy sell. That was pretty much a given once Milano got mixed up in the deal. But I needed this."

"You thought I was your answer." Cherry's statement wasn't a question. It was a simple acceptance. "You figured I'd see the merits of your line versus the leather."

"Didn't you?" Hailey lifted her head from her hands to stare through dull eyes.

Cherry nodded. "Yes. Of course I did. Given the scope of the launch and the variety your designs offered, I felt yours would be the much stronger line to feature."

Hailey tried to find some comfort in that.

All her life, she'd searched for the silver lining, holding tight to it when she was being deluged by the cloud. But this time, the lining meant nothing. It could have been pure gold, and it still wouldn't have helped her.

"Why'd you drag this out? Why'd you let Rudy, let me, think you were on board? Why couldn't you have just been honest from the beginning and said you didn't want me?"

Hailey winced as those last words escaped, knowing they weren't Cherry's to own. They were more a summary of every freaking time she'd been screwed over in her life. By her mom, who was always off chasing her dream, running after the next exciting thing and too busy to care about her daughter. By her father, who'd built his new life and liked to pretend that Hailey was a part of it, but who never—ever—tried to make her one of the family. By her mentor, who'd sworn he'd file the paperwork for the business.

And by Gage, who made her feel things she'd only read about. Who made her hope for more. Hope for everything. And then who made her think that maybe, just maybe, this time she'd get it.

"It wasn't fair," Hailey finally said, for the first time in her life, letting herself express how disappointed she was.

"I thought I could handle it," Cherry said, lifting both hands in the air. "I thought I could juggle it all."

"Juggle what? Your career obligations? Your love life? Holiday shopping? What did you need to juggle here? All you had to do was make a decision, wear some outfits for a weeklong photo shoot and do one simple fashion show." Yelling the last word, Hailey realized she was standing on tiptoe in her attempt to put as much force behind the words as possible.

Cringing, she immediately dropped back to her heels.

Lovely. She'd just yelled at a very nice, very influential woman. Good thing her business was ruined. Otherwise she'd be freaking out in paranoia over the probable outcome of finally letting loose.

"I've been diagnosed with cancer. Breast cancer. Right before Thanksgiving." Cherry's voice, husky with pain, was barely audible. The redhead looked down at her fingers, twining them together then pulling them apart, then starting over again. Her swallow was audible from across the room, echoed by the sound of the outer door closing.

Gage was gone.

But Hailey could only stare, her heart devastated.

But not for herself.

For the woman sitting in front of her.

"How bad…? I mean, what's the prognosis?"

"It's metastasized." Cherry gave a shaky smile, then gestured to her ample curves. "Looks like these babies are going bye-bye. That's the oncologist's recommendation. I've been fighting it, thinking somehow, if I just believed hard enough, I could change things."

She sniffed, then lifted her shoulder.

"All my life, I beat the odds because I believed I could. I did what everyone said was impossible. My career, my recording contract, moving into the movies and modeling." She looked down at her hands again, then gave Hailey a tremulous smile. "I thought I could believe this away. Silly, huh?"

Oh, God.

"No," Hailey whispered, her throat clogged with tears. "Not silly at all."

This time, Hailey couldn't stop herself. She rushed across the room and took the other woman into her arms. Together, they held tight, tears flowing in an aching river of misery.

Talk about perspective.

14

GAGE STRODE THROUGH his father's house, anger propelling his every step.

Damn Hailey for not jumping at his deal.

Damn Rudolph for making it so easy to steal the account away from her.

And damn his father for boxing him in, forcing him into this position. All because the old man had some twisted idea of heritage. A man who, Gage realized with a growl, hadn't ever once decorated a damned Christmas tree with his sons.

He stomped into the lounge, glaring at this year's tree in the corner, then sharing that look with his brother, who was cozied up with his newspaper and a glass of brandy.

"Where's the old man?" he asked, preferring to get it all over at once.

Devon's shrug made it clear Gage's preference wasn't going to matter. "No clue. I think he might have a date."

Both brothers slanted a look at the tree. Decorated in its customary red-and-green balls, it looked like it always did when it was just the three men. Gage was sure their thoughts were in sync. If the old man was on a date, what was the tree going to look like next year?

"Did we ever decorate the tree ourselves?" he heard himself ask. At Devon's puzzled expression, he elaborated,

"I don't remember decorating. I know we always had a tree. But did we have any kind of, you know, tradition or part in it? Or was it always like the wives, simply showing up one day as a big surprise, causing an uproar for its limited time here, then the old man tossing it away when it started to droop."

Devon's smirk faded into a squint as he thought about the question.

"I don't remember decorating. That's a girlie thing, though, so it can go right there with wearing makeup and going to dance class on the list of things we're glad we missed out on."

Girlie. Right. Along with traditions, emotions and anything that couldn't be tracked on a ledger sheet.

"Today was the meeting, right?" Devon asked, as if he were reading Gage's mind. "You nailed down the deets on the Rudolph deal?"

Still staring at the tree, Gage shrugged.

"I've got a new venture I just bought into. Another club, but more S and M focused, less pussycat fluff," Devon said after a minute or so. The silence was obviously bugging him. "You want in? You can take a look at the prospectus, write up a marketing plan, make us both rich."

When Gage's laugh came a second too late, Devon scowled.

"What's the problem?"

"Do you ever get tired of chasing new ventures? Of hopscotching from project to project?"

"I'm at Milano long-term, so everything else is about short-term. That's how you should be looking at your little marketing start-up, too. Get it going, have fun with it, then once it's solid, sell it off." Devon grinned. "Should make for a fun year. And who knows, maybe you'll finally beat my side earnings. Probably not, but you can try."

Rather than incur another scowl, Gage offered up the

expected smile. But he just wasn't into it anymore. The competition, the constant searching for something new, the next big thing. He wanted to settle in, manage his business and see how far he could take it. He wanted to build some traditions, and yes, maybe even learn from a few failures.

He thought of Hailey, of her determination and drive to do everything she could to succeed. He wanted that.

Hell, he wanted *her*.

"What's your problem tonight?" Devon snapped, clearly not happy with the mood Gage had brought into the room. "Did you get the account or didn't you?"

Gage opened his mouth to snap that of course he had. Then he frowned and shrugged instead.

"I want out."

"That's the deal. You get the account, you get out for a year." Devon folded his paper in neat, tidy creases and slapped it against his knee. "The terms were clear."

"I don't care about the terms, or that offer," Gage said, realization dawning. He shoved his hands into his pockets and stared at the tree. Unable to stop himself, even though he knew he was probably cutting his own throat, he repeated, "I want out."

His brother laughed and gave him a derisive look.

"You'd give it all up? Your future? The future of any rug rats you happen to have? Don't you think your kids would someday be a little pissed to find out you threw away their heritage?"

"I'm so freaking sick of hearing about the Milano legacy. We've heard it all our lives and what's it got us? We don't have a heritage. We don't have family memories. We have a despot at the head of the dinner table and the board table, calling the shots on the business and on our lives."

Gage glanced around. "Is this heritage? We've never decorated a tree together. We've never had fun family memories. We're stockholders, assets, prime Milano resources." Gage gestured to the tree, as if it epitomized his every point. "I'd like to think that if I someday have rug rats, as you put it, they'll want more than shares in the company. They'll want holidays and traditions and cookies for Santa. They'll want more than a cold, choking tie with a million conditions on it."

"Money, success, a family name," Devon countered. "Those all buy a hell of a lot of memories and make the holidays a lot more enjoyable. All thanks to those ties you're bitching about."

"Shouldn't ties be deeper than that?" Gage growled, throwing his arms in the air in frustration. "Shouldn't they be more than a fragile thread, easily snapped because I refuse to continue giving up my own goals, my own dreams, to toe the line?"

Shouldn't they be important enough to care that he didn't want to screw over a woman who meant a lot to him, just to snag the company yet another feather for its overstuffed freaking hat?

"Well, that's an interesting take on the traditions I've handed down to you."

Shit. Gage cringed. Even Devon winced as they both shifted their gazes to the doorway.

"Dad. I didn't know you were there."

"Obviously." Marcus crossed the room to pause in front of the tree, inspecting it much as his sons had earlier, then turning to take his favorite seat by the fire. "So you want to break tradition, do you?"

Devon's look was pitying, as though he felt as if he should leave the room so Gage could be shredded in private, but couldn't resist the show. Or, if Gage were in a generous mood, maybe his brother was sticking it out for moral support. The reality was probably propped somewhere in between.

Gage met his father's stare with an unwavering one of

his own. Well, one way or another, Hailey was right. It was time to step up and stand up.

THERE. HAILEY CLAPPED her hands together to indicate a job well done and stepped back from the tree to admire her handiwork. Beads and balls and dainty lace roses, a garland of ribbon and a few scatters of crystals here and there for accent.

The perfect, beautiful tree.

She sighed, letting her smile drop.

She'd rather have the paper snowflake, popcorn and condom-covered one. Of course, she'd rather have it because it came with a very sexy, usually naked man underneath.

And with a promise.

She dropped to the couch, the tree a blur.

"The tree is lovely."

"Thanks." She offered a warm smile to Cherry, who was curled up in the corner chair. The other woman still looked fragile. As if a loud noise would shatter her. But she had an air of peace about her now, too.

Hailey figured that probably had more to do with the ice-cream sundae and Christmas-cookie binge than anything Hailey had done. But if a few hours of listening, another few of hugs and tears and a couple of vats of hot fudge had helped, she was thrilled.

"You're upset about Gage?" Cherry observed after a few minutes of silence.

They'd talked about her cancer, about the holidays, about their favorite junk food and the hottest actors. They'd covered lingerie, a mutual shoe obsession. And now, apparently, they were on guys.

Lovely. But as they'd silently established at the beginning of this bonding session, nothing was off-limits. Hailey knew it wouldn't be fair to sidestep just because she didn't want to talk about Gage yet.

But *upset* was an understatement.

Heartbroken, devastated, miserable. Those came closer.

"Disappointed," Hailey finally said. "But Gage, the lingerie deal, they're minor. Especially compared to what you're facing."

"What I'm going through doesn't mean your pain is any less, you know," Cherry chided, pushing her hand through that luxurious mane of red hair as if appreciating every strand.

"Maybe not, but it definitely puts my heartbreak and business woes into perspective."

Cherry's phone buzzed, the tenth or so time that evening. She looked at it and sighed.

"I've got to go. I have a show at eleven and my car is on its way." Cherry gave her a warm smile, then offered, "This was wonderful, though. And now we have it down pat for our next visit. First I whine, then you whine? We just keep taking turns."

Hailey laughed. Then, remembering the reason she'd brought Cherry back to her place instead of going to the other woman's—besides the ample supply of cookies here—she jumped up and, with a murmured excuse, hurried into the other room. She was back in a quick minute with a gift-wrapped box.

"I intended to give this to you after we'd signed the deal, but, well, that's out the window," she said with a shrug as she handed Cherry the beribboned gift. "It's just a little something I thought would suit you. Go ahead, open it now."

Excitement, and the special joy that came from giving a gift that meant a lot, filled Hailey as Cherry tugged at ribbon, pulled at paper. When the woman opened the box and pulled out the hand-beaded, royal-blue forties-esque nightgown Hailey had designed just for her, it felt fabulous. Even better was the wide-eyed look of amazed appreciation on the redhead's face.

"Oh, this is gorgeous," she breathed. She pulled it close, holding it against her chest as if to assess the fit. Then, with a sniffle, she lifted tear-filled eyes to Hailey's.

"It's cut to drape from the shoulders," Hailey pointed out, having to push the words past the lump in her throat. "It'll flow to the hips, then swirl to the floor. No matter what your size, it'll look amazing."

"It's as if you knew…"

"No," Hailey quickly denied. "It's simply the design. Too often, women are objectified. We're made to feel beautiful only if we fit a specific mold, if we wear a specific size. But beauty, sexuality, that comes from within. Not from what fills our bra."

Hailey sniffed, wishing she had the right words to let Cherry know that she'd always be gorgeous, always be sexually appealing.

So, instead, she shrugged and offered a smile. "It'll be beautiful on you. Always."

"I wish there was something I could do," Cherry murmured, her fingers sliding over the heavy satin, then trailing along the delicate lace. "You're so sweet, and I feel like I just destroyed your world."

"No," Hailey objected quietly. "My designs suit you, suit a woman who wants to feel beautiful, feel feminine. That's not the direction Rudy is going. Even if I'd got the deal, the message would get lost in all the sloppy sex stuff he was going to throw in there. Leather panties, dinosaur shoes. The man has seriously horrible taste."

They shared a grimace.

"You're right. Your designs make women feel great. Sexy and strong." Cherry's words trailed off and she gave Hailey a considering look.

"What?"

"Well, I know you needed the contract. And I have no idea what position your company is in now that you didn't get it. But, and I'm not saying I'm sure of this, but I was just thinking that it might be interesting if we…" Her words trailed off, her gaze intent on the nightie in her hands. After a few seconds and a deep breath, she lifted her eyes to Hailey's. "What if we did a line together? You design. I model. Through all of these pitches, I've loved your message, your passion for how romance and emotion are sexier than lust."

"Launching a line together would mean you're putting yourself, your struggle and your body, on display," Hailey pointed out quietly. She knew Cherry knew that, but it was one of those things that needed to be said out loud. A few times.

"I know. I think this might be what I need, though." The redhead arched an elegant brow at Hailey. "And maybe it can be what you need."

Could it be? Hailey's mind spun in a million directions at once, all of them excited, none of them sure.

"Together?"

"Tentatively," Cherry said, swallowing hard. "I'll be damned if this disease is going to beat me, destroy my confidence or my career. I was going to agree to the Rudolph deal because I wanted exposure."

"Our launching a line together, based on your story, might mean a lot more exposure than you bargained for," Hailey said carefully.

She didn't want to get too hopeful. She definitely didn't want to profit from the other woman's struggles. But oh, the possibilities. The idea of sharing her vision, the concept of expanding people's views of femininity and sexual appeal, it made her want to cry with joy.

Somewhere between a grimace and relief, Cherry checked her buzzing phone.

"My ride is here. I've got to go. Let's both think about this. A couple of days, maybe through next weekend. I don't want to make promises I can't keep. And you need to be sure this is enough to save your company." The red-head rose, her nightie draped over one arm and both hands outstretched to take Hailey's.

"I think this could be incredible," she murmured.

Hailey's mind was spinning. It would be amazing.

But she'd have to step up herself. She'd have to find a way to keep her business, without the Rudolph account.

But if Cherry could face this and find a way, so could she.

"I think it could be, too," Hailey finally said.

With that and one last hug, Cherry smiled and floated out of the room. Hailey grinned. The woman was pure glam, even at her lowest.

As the echo of the shutting door faded, so did Hailey's smile.

She did miss Gage.

His smile and his tight ass. His laugh and his sexy shoulders. His belief in her, his acceptance of her and his outrage on her behalf. Right up until he'd done the exact thing he was so outraged over.

She sniffed.

Still, something good had come of it all.

Optimism paid off.

Sure, things weren't turning out the way she'd expected and held out for. But they were turning out. She should be happy. She should be excited.

She'd stood up for herself.

She'd made a new friend in Cherry.

She'd found a way to save her business, and to empower someone else in the process.

But all she could think of were Gage's words. How he'd forced her to see how much damage she'd caused herself, her life and her business. All because she was always too worried about upsetting someone else instead of standing up for herself.

He was right.

And telling him off when she'd stood up for herself had felt good. Losing him hadn't. But for the first time in her life, she understood that old saying.

If you love something, set it free. If it comes back it's yours. If it doesn't, it never was.

If she was always too afraid to stand up, to take a chance that someone might leave, then did it matter if she had them in her life?

It wasn't until she felt the chill on her chin that she realized she was crying. Hailey blinked fast, wiping her face. Then, knowing she owed it to herself to make the most of the lesson—because she'd be damned if she'd lose the most important guy in her life for nothing—she picked up the phone.

"Mom? Hi. We need to talk."

HAILEY STARED AT the thick expanse of wood, alternating between wanting to turn tail and run, and puzzling over the view.

Was that a wreath hanging there?

It was round.

It was green.

It had a red bow and—she leaned forward and sniffed—it smelled like pine.

Seriously?

Gage had a wreath hanging on his front door?

It was so out of character for a man who until last weekend had never even decorated a Christmas tree, she wasn't sure what to make of it.

Maybe it'd be better if she left, thought about it for a while, then when she figured out what it meant, came back and tried to talk to him then.

Her fingers tightened on the ornately wrapped box in her hands, and, since her heart was racing fast enough to run off by itself, she gave a nod.

Yep, come back later.

She turned to leave.

Her way was blocked by a large male body.

Hailey screamed. The package flew a half foot and her feet almost slipped out from under her. Thankfully this was one of those rare occasions that she was wearing flats instead of heels. Just in case she had to run.

"What the hell are you doing?" she asked, her words a gasp.

"Coming home?" Gage said, his eyes dancing and his grin huge. "What the hell are *you* doing?"

Hailey debated.

Running now, given that it would require doing a dash around him, was a little silly. Still, silly had a lot of appeal compared to putting her heart on the line.

Her eyes eating him up as if it'd been months instead of a few days since they'd seen each other, Hailey almost sighed.

Damn, he was gorgeous.

"I brought you this," she said, holding up the gift. "So here. Merry Christmas."

She shoved it in his hands and, figuring she'd side-stepped silly, started to leave. She'd tell him all the heart-baring stuff later. When he thanked her for the gift, maybe.

"C'mon in."

Hailey winced. But her feet froze and her body, always ready to do his bidding, turned to follow. Oh, man, this was harder than standing up to him had been.

"I didn't have time to wrap yours," he said after helping her off with her coat. The feel of his fingers, lightly brushing her shoulders, burned right through her sweater.

"You got me a present?"

Hailey gave up trying to look calm and casual, dropping to the couch and staring at him in shock.

"You really got me something? But I yelled at you."

Her mother still wasn't talking to her after hearing Hailey's feelings about being dumped at Christmas. *Again.* And her father? He'd apologized all over the place, then blamed it all on her mother. She still hadn't untwisted that.

But Gage acted as if he wasn't mad. More, he acted as though he'd known he'd see her again, and that they'd be in a gift-exchanging kind of place.

It was as though nothing had happened.

Hailey wanted to grab that, to simply let it all slide. Just pretend everything was peachy, that he hadn't hurt her or screwed her over in the Rudolph deal. Act as if she hadn't said mean things and yelled accusations at him.

It'd be so much easier.

All her life, she'd gone the easy emotional route. Smiles were better than frowns, happy times preferable to angry.

But…she wanted more.

She wanted a future with Gage. To give them a chance and see where things went.

And she couldn't do that the same old, easy way.

Then he asked, "Why wouldn't I get you a gift?"

"Because we had an ugly fight."

"So? People fight. Then they make up, right? At least, that's how I've always heard relationships went."

Relationships. They were in a relationship.

Joy, giddy and sweet, rushed through her. She wanted to stop talking now. To skip right over all this soul-searching chitchat and get down to the naked makeup fun.

But they deserved more than that.

Dammit.

Taking a deep breath, Hailey looked at her hands, then met his baffled gaze.

"I don't know. I've only had one ugly fight, and it resulted in a big family rift. After that, I was afraid to fight. I was too worried that I'd lose whatever crumbs I had if I stood up for wanting more. Or that the person would walk away."

His nod was slow and considering, and the look in his eyes intense. As if he were seeing all the way into those little cubbies and closets in her brain, the ones where she hid all her secrets.

"So where does that put us? That you didn't mind losing what we had? Or that you were sure I'd stick around?"

She peered closely at his face, wishing she could see a hint of which he'd prefer she say. Then, since they'd already established that she was all about telling him like it was, she gave a little lift of her hands.

"Because you let me be me. You seemed to appreciate my strengths, my opinions. Me. I never felt like I wasn't important with you. Or that there were conditions on our being together." She swallowed, hard, then took a deep breath. Big admission time. "I wouldn't say I blew up at you for no reason. I really was angry. And hurt. But maybe, sort of, I was pushing because a part of me wondered how fast you'd walk away once I got in your face."

He arched both brows and gave her an assessing look. "A test?"

Hailey opened her mouth to deny it, then had to close it. Why deny it.

"Maybe. Sorta." She looked at her hands again, wishing she had something to do with all this nervous energy. Like run her fingers over his body, or touch his hair. But both of those actions would probably change the subject. And as much as she wanted to, she'd rather get this out of the way before they got on the subject of being naked.

"You really did offer me a better deal than I was getting from Rudolph. I could have easily taken a ledger of sales like that to the bank and negotiated a loan. Add to it your marketing package, something with such great long-term possibilities? Turning away from it was the worst business decision I could make. I accused you of putting business, your own ambitions, over what we were making together. But I was the one doing that."

Hailey winced when Gage's face creased into a ferocious frown and he looked for a second as if he wanted to hit something. What? He couldn't take an apology?

"You're killing me," he finally said, pushing off the couch to pace the room. "I had these big plans. I spent the last few days putting everything into place, fine-tuning and perfecting things. And you sweep in here with your pretty smile and fancy gift and blow it all."

She shook her head, wondering if all that humility had ruined her hearing.

"What are you talking about?"

"I quit Milano. Not a break, not a sabbatical, not a sanctioned-but-still-contracted reprieve. I quit." He threw his hands in the air, as if tossing aside his heritage, his family and his commitments. But he didn't look upset. Instead, he seemed relieved. Or maybe that was just what she was hoping to see?

"Is that a good thing?" she asked hesitantly.

"It doesn't matter now. I've busted my ass building a pitch, crafting the perfect way to show you how much you mean and how important you are, and you sweep in here and outdo me. Again. Every damned time I think I've got the upper hand, you outmaneuver, outflank and outplay me."

Hailey had to pull her chin off her chest and force her mouth closed. He was ranting, but he didn't seem upset at all. Instead, he sounded proud. As if he was thrilled with her. As if he admired her. As if he really cared.

"Oh" was all she could say.

Then, as much as she didn't want to, Hailey burst into tears.

"HELL." GAGE CRINGED.

Not tears.

Anything but tears.

"Look, that isn't a bad thing. I'm not upset about being outflanked and outmaneuvered. It's like you being on top. I like that, too."

Well, that got a smile, but didn't stop the tears.

Dammit.

Gage pulled in a deep breath. He wanted to kiss the wet tracks off her face. He wanted to distract her with a naughty promise. But he was a man who knew the importance of timing. He had to do this now. Even though it was probably going to get him more tears, he manned up and took both her hands.

"That's one of the things I admire about you," he said, keeping his words low and quiet so she had to quit sobbing to hear him. "You're incredible at what you do. You're passionate about what you believe in. And you're smart. Smart enough to call me on being a jackass. Smart enough to see my fears and push me to get over myself and go for the dream."

She sniffed, her eyes wide and wet but, thank God, not pooled up any longer.

"You think I did all of that? You actually like that I called you on being a jackass?"

"Well, I'm not saying I want it to be my new nickname or anything. But I appreciate that you see me, that you understand me. And that you believe in me."

She smiled. It was a little shaky at the edges, but filled

with so much sweetness that Gage had to smile back. Figuring he deserved a reward for not running like a sissy boy at the first sign of tears, Gage lifted her hands to his lips, brushing a kiss over the knuckles of one, then the other. She was so sweet. So delicious. Then, his eyes locked on hers, he leaned in and brushed her mouth next.

So soft.

So incredible.

Her sigh was a gentle wash of emotion. Delight and relief, excitement and joy.

All good.

But he wanted her passion.

And he knew how to get it.

Gage shifted his lips, just a bit, and changed the angle. With a barely there moan, she opened to him, meeting passion with passion. Desire with desire. And, yes, baby, tongue with tongue.

He wanted to stay here. It felt good here. Safe. No emotional risk. A part of him figured he'd already risked plenty this week. His career. His standing with his family. His heritage.

There was nothing wrong with waiting a little while before putting everything else on the line.

Then Hailey gave a tiny moan. Her fingers, warm and gentle, grazed his cheek. Slowly, as if hearing his thoughts and giving him a chance to decide, she pulled back.

Her lashes fluttered, and then she gazed up at him. Those huge green eyes were filled with so many emotions. The lust made his already-steel-hard dick happy, and the delighted joy gave his heart a little buzz. But it was the trust there, the total faith in him, that made Gage want to groan.

With happiness. And in frustration.

Because there was no way he could back down when she was looking at him like that.

"So," he started, pretty sure this was the first time in his life he'd struggled with the right words to sell his point. "I talked to Rudy this morning."

The excitement shifted in her gaze, a frown leaving a tiny crease between her brows.

Nice job, Gage thought. Maybe next he could tell her Santa was fake and that Christmas cookies made women fat. She'd probably look just as happy.

"I wanted to tell him I was off the Milano account. I couldn't throw Milano under the bus, but did suggest he take a hard look at what sexy really was to women, and to men who didn't use *Playboy* to measure their relationships."

Her lips twitched, but the frown didn't fade.

"He's sick of the whole thing. Said he'd rather the models strut down the runway nude than have to worry any more about lingerie." Gage's lips twisted in a rueful smile. "But he said he was going to think about it. That he'd probably be giving you a call."

Gage waited, ready for her to, oh, maybe throw her arms around him. Squeal with excitement. Offer up her undying gratitude and maybe a little love.

Instead, she pulled away and bit her lip before giving him a grimacy sort of look.

"You're so sweet to do that. I really, really appreciate it." So much so that she looked as if she wanted to throw up, he noted. "But I don't think Rudy is going to want to work with me."

Gage knew for sure the guy didn't want to work with either one of them. But that was beside the point.

"Why not?"

"Because I stole his star," she said, watching her fingers twist together for a second before she met his eyes with a gleeful look. "For a lot of reasons, she didn't want to work with Rudy. So Cherry and I are launching a line together."

Gage burst into laughter. Poor Rudy. Looked as though his models were going to have to strut down the runway naked after all.

"What are you going to do about the payoff?" he asked. He'd already talked to his banker, arranged for a loan if she wanted it. He'd figured on wrapping up the payoff in a bright red box, but knew she wouldn't accept it, so the loan was his backup. Just in case she wanted help.

"Well, after chewing into you, I called my mother and told her off for just about everything," Hailey said, sounding proud. "Then, figuring I was on a roll, I called my father and did the same. And then, since I had nothing else to lose, I called Dawn Phillips and told her that revised contract or not, her father and I had an agreement and I'd met it faithfully for three years. That she'd either renegotiate the terms or my attorney would be in contact and we'd settle it in court."

Gage was pretty sure his grin was wide enough to pop his ears off.

"'Atta girl. You kicked ass. I take it everyone stepped up and took responsibility?" About damned time, too.

Hailey shook her head.

"Nope. My mother cried and blamed me for ruining her holiday. My father said he'd take my complaints under consideration and discuss them with my stepmother."

Damn them. Gage was afraid to ask, but figured he'd started this so he didn't have a choice.

"And the Phillips woman?"

"Dawn?" Hailey pursed her lips before giving him a smile that lit the room brighter than the tree they'd decorated. "She agreed to the terms Eric and I had set. After I'd told her how fabulous the business was doing, and how much more money she stood to make if she let the terms play out for another two years, and then I pay fair-market value on the balance due, she saw the wisdom in waiting."

And here he'd thought he'd have to rescue her.

Gage grinned.

Once again, she'd outdone him.

He loved that about her.

"You're amazing," he said with a wondrous smile.

"I couldn't have done it without you. Without you pushing me, showing me that there's more to a relationship than convenience." She swallowed hard enough for him to hear the click, then took a deep breath and met his gaze. Her own eyes were huge. "I think I'm in love with you."

He'd never heard those words.

Ever.

Gage's heart melted. And then, like the Grinch he'd dressed up as once, it seemed to grow huge. So huge he wasn't sure what to do with it.

All he could do was pull her close.

Before his lips met hers, he whispered, "I think I'm in love with you, too."

As they fell into the kiss, the lights of the condom-covered Christmas tree twinkled.

And Gage had to admit, the holidays pretty much rocked.

* * * * *

THE NURSE'S
CHRISTMAS GIFT

TINA BECKETT

To my kids, who are always willing to give me
space – and time – when I'm under deadline.
I love you!

CHAPTER ONE

MAX AINSLEY WAS happy to be back on familiar soil.

Opening the door to his new cottage in a brand-new city, he hefted his duffel bag and tossed it over his shoulder, enjoying the warmth he found inside. Six months was too long; the days and nights spent helping displaced children in war-ravaged North Africa had eaten into his soul—one painful bite at a time. Trying to meet each desperate need had drained his emotional bank account until there was nothing left. He'd needed to come back to recharge and decide what he wanted to do next.

What better season than winter? The icy weather and the festive lights of the approaching holiday should help him push aside the thoughts of what he hadn't been able to accomplish on this trip. At least he hoped so.

Three years of running from his past had changed nothing. Maybe it was time to start living in the present. To sign the papers he'd left behind and to finally let go of the past once and for all.

Shedding his parka and throwing his belongings onto a nearby leather sofa with a sigh, he surveyed the place. With its white-painted walls and comfortable furniture, it wasn't huge or fancy, but it was big enough for a landing place, at least until he could figure out where he wanted to park his butt for the long haul. Sienna McDonald had sent pictures of several possibilities that were just a short distance from the hospital, and he'd settled on this one, the cottage's quaint one-bedroom floor plan made more attractive by the small private garden off the back. This was the place.

He could finally sell his flat back in London.

And maybe it was time to call his solicitor and have him complete the process—to cut any remaining ties with a certain dark period in his life.

He spied a piece of paper on the table in the dining room and stiffened, before he realised it couldn't be from her. She had no idea where he was right now. And she hadn't tried to find him over the last couple of years. At least not that he knew of.

Wandering over to the note, he placed a finger on the pink stationery and cocked his head as he made out the cheerful words.

'Welcome to Cheltenham and to Teddy's! I've put some milk, cheese and cold meat in the fridge, and there is bread and sweets in the cupboard along with some other staples to help get you started. The boiler is lit, instructions are on the unit. I hope you're ready to work, because I am more than ready for a rest!'

She'd signed her name with a flourish at the end.

Sweets, eh? That made him smile. But he was glad for the boiler, as snow was expected to hit any day and the temperatures had been steadily dropping. His body was still trying to adjust to the chill after all those months dealing with the hot temperatures of Sudan.

He was due at Teddy's in the morning to start his contract, replacing Sienna McDonald when she went on maternity leave. She'd sent him a letter as he was packing for the flight telling him to get ready for a wild ride. There was a winter virus running through the halls of the hospital, affecting patients and staff alike. They were short-staffed and overworked.

He was ready. Anything to keep his mind off his previous life.

And the timing couldn't have been more perfect. Sienna would be there to show him the ropes, and Max would have time to adjust to being back in a modern hospital, where day-to-day life was not always a life and death struggle.

Well, that was not entirely true. In the world of paediatric cardiothoracic medicine, things were often about life and death, but they were caused by the battle raging within the person's body, not the cruel deeds done by one human against another. And with Doctors Without Borders, he had seen his share of war and the horrific results of it.

His mind headed to a darker place, and Max forced it back to the mundane tasks he had to accomplish before his first shift tomorrow morning: shave the scruff of several weeks off his face, unpack, hunt down a vehicle to use.

With that in mind, he headed to the refrigerator to find something to eat. And then he would face the day, and hopefully get ready to face his future…and his first step towards banishing the past, once and for all.

* * *

Annabelle Brookes couldn't believe how crowded the ward was. All the beds were full, and patients were seemingly crammed into every nook and cranny. The winter virus was not only sending people flooding into the hospital, but it was sending staff flooding out—multiple nurses and doctors had all become ill over the past several days. So far she had steered clear of its path, but who knew how long that would hold? She was frankly exhausted and, with six hours left to her shift, she was sure she would be dead on her feet by the time she headed home.

Despite it all, she was glad Ella O'Brien had pestered her until she'd agreed to come to Cheltenham a year ago. Maybe because her friend had recognised the signs of depression and the deadly spiral her life had taken after her husband had left for parts unknown. Whatever it had been, Annabelle felt she was finally getting her life back under control. She had Ella to thank for that. And for helping her land this plum position.

Head neonatal nurse was a dream come true for her. She might not be able to have children of her own, but she was happy to be able to rock, hold and treat other people's babies all day long. Working at the same hospital as her midwife friend also meant there was plenty of time for girlie outings and things to take her mind off her own problems.

She let her fingers run across a draping of tinsel against a doorway as she went by, the cool slide of glittery metal helping relax her frazzled nerves.

Tucking a strand of hair back into the plait that ran halfway down her back, she dodged people and patients alike as she made her way towards the nursery and her next patient: Baby Doe, aka Baby Hope.

The baby had been abandoned by her mother—who was little more than a baby herself—and Annabelle felt a special affinity with this tiny creature. After all, hadn't Annabelle been dumped by the person who should have loved her the most but left her languishing with a broken heart? No. Actually, Annabelle had done the dumping, but her heart had still splintered into pieces.

Baby Hope's heart was literally broken, whereas Annabelle's was merely...

She stiffened her jaw. No. Her heart was just fine, thank you very much.

Was that why that paperwork was still sitting on a shelf gathering dust? And it was too. Annabelle had cleaned around the beige envelope over the past couple of years, but hadn't been able to bring herself to touch it, much less open it and read the contents. Because she already knew what they said. She had been the one to do the filing.

But Max had never responded. Or sent his signed copy back to her solicitor.

And if he had? What then?

She had no idea.

As she rounded the nurses' station to check the schedule and see what other cases she'd been assigned for the day, the phone rang. A nurse sitting behind the desk picked up the phone, waving at her as she answered the call.

'Baby Doe? Oh, yes, Annabelle just arrived. I'll send her in.' She set the phone down.

Maybe the first order of business after her divorce

should be to officially get rid of her married name. It still hurt to have it attached to her, even though she no longer went by Annabelle Ainsley.

'Miss McDonald and her replacement are doing rounds and are ready to examine the baby. Do you mind filling them in on what's happened over the last few hours?'

'On my way.' Annabelle had already been headed towards the glass window that made up the viewing area of the special care baby unit, so it was perfect timing. Arriving on the floor, she spotted a heavily pregnant Sienna McDonald ducking into the room. The neonatal cardiothoracic surgeon had been overseeing Baby Doe's care as they waited for an available heart for the sick infant. Another man, wearing a lab coat and sporting dark washed jeans, went in behind Sienna. She could only catch a glimpse of a strong back and thick black hair, but something inside her took a funny little turn at the familiar way the man moved.

Shaking her head to clear it, she reached the door a few seconds later and slid inside.

She headed towards the baby's cot, finding Sienna and the other doctor—their backs to her—hovering over it.

About to step around to the other side, the stranger raised the top of the unit. 'Her colour doesn't look good.'

Annabelle stifled a gasp, stopping in her tracks for several horrified seconds. She lifted her eyes and stared at the man's back.

That voice.

Those gruff masculine tones were definitely not

the feminine Scottish lilt belonging to Sienna, that was for sure. This had to be Sienna's replacement. Had she actually seen the name of the new doctor written somewhere? She didn't think so, but she was beginning to think she should have paid more attention.

She swallowed down the ball of bile before the pressure built to dangerous levels.

The new doctor spoke again. 'What's her diagnosis?'

The ball in Annabelle's throat popped back into place with a vengeance.

It couldn't be.

Sienna glanced over at him. 'Hypoplastic left heart syndrome. She's waiting on a donor heart.'

The other doctor's dark head bent as he examined the baby. 'How far down is she on the list?'

'Far enough that we're all worried. Especially Annabelle Brookes—you'll meet her soon. She's the nurse who's been with our little patient from the time she was born.'

Annabelle, who had begun sliding back towards the door, stopped when the new doctor slowly lifted his head, turning it in her direction. Familiar brown eyes she would recognise anywhere met hers and narrowed, staring for what seemed like an eternity but had to have been less than a second. There wasn't the slightest flinch in his expression. She could have been a complete stranger.

But she wasn't.

He knew very well who she was. And she knew him.

No. It couldn't be.

For a soul-searing moment she wondered if she'd been mistaken, that he wasn't Sienna's replacement at all, but was here to say he'd finally signed the papers. Maybe he'd heard about Baby Hope's case and had just popped in to take a look while they hunted for Annabelle.

Or…maybe he'd met someone else.

Her whole system threatened to shut down as she stood there staring.

'Annabelle? Are you all right?' Sienna's voice startled her enough to force her to blink.

'Oh, yes, I…um…' What was she supposed to say?

Max evidently didn't have that problem. He came away from Hope's incubator, extending his hand. 'I didn't realise you'd moved from London.'

'Yes. I did.' She ignored his hand, tipping her chin just a fraction, instead. So he hadn't come here to find her.

Sienna glanced from one to the other. 'You two already know each other?'

One side of Max's mouth turned up in a semblance of a smile as he allowed his hand to drop back by his side. 'Quite well, actually.'

Yes, they knew each other. But 'quite well'? She'd thought so at one time. But in the end… Well, he hadn't stuck around.

Of course, she'd been the one to tell him to go. And he had. Without a single attempt to change her mind—or to fight for what they'd once had.

Sienna's brows went up, obviously waiting for some kind of explanation. But what could she say, really?

She opened her mouth to try to save the situation, but a shrill noise suddenly filled the room.

An alarm! And this one wasn't in her head.

All eyes swivelled back to Baby Hope, who lay still in her incubator.

It was the pulse oximeter. Hope wasn't breathing!

'Let's get some help in here!' Max was suddenly belting out orders in a tone that demanded immediate response.

Glancing again at the baby's form, she noted that the tiny girl's colour had gone from bad to worse, a dangerous mottling spreading over her nappy-clad form. Annabelle's heart plummeted, her fingers beginning a familiar tingle that happened every time she went into crisis mode.

Come on, little love. Don't do this. Not when we're just getting to know each other.

Social services had asked Annabelle to keep a special eye on the infant, since she had no next of kin who were willing to take on her care. Poor little thing.

Annabelle knew what it was like to feel alone.

In Max's defence, it had been her choice. But he had issued an ultimatum. One she hadn't been prepared to accept.

Right now, though, all she needed to think about was this little one's battle for life. Max shot Sienna a look. The other doctor nodded at him. Whatever the exchange was, Max took the lead.

'We need to tube her.'

Annabelle went to the wall and grabbed a pair of gloves from the dispenser, shoving her hands into them and forcing herself to take things one step at a time. To get ahead of yourself was to make a mistake.

She hurried to get the trach tube items, tearing into sterile packages with a vengeance. Two more nurses rushed into the room, hearing the cries for help. Each went to work, knowing instinctively what needed to be done. They'd all been through this scenario many times before.

But not with Baby Hope.

Annabelle moved in next to Max and handed him each item as he asked for it, her mind fixed on helping the tiny infant come back from the precipice.

Trying not to count the seconds, she watched Max in motion, marvelling at the steadiness of his large hands as he intubated the baby, his face a mask of concentration. A look that was achingly familiar. She swallowed hard. She needed to think of him as a doctor. Not as someone she'd once loved.

And lost.

He connected the tubing to the ventilator as one of the other nurses set the machine up and switched it on.

Almost immediately, Baby Hope's chest rose and fell in rhythmic strokes as the ventilator did the breathing for her. As if by magic, the pulse ox alarm switched off and the heart-rate monitor above the incubator began sounding a steadier *blip-blip-blip* as the heart reacted to the life-giving oxygen.

The organ was weak, but at least it was beating.

But for how much longer?

Thank God they hadn't needed to use the paddles to shock it back into rhythm. Baby Hope was already receiving prostaglandin to prevent the ductus in her heart from closing and cutting off blood flow. And they had her on a nitrogen/oxygen mix in an attempt to help the oxygen move to the far reaches of her body.

But even so, her hands and extremities were tinged blue, a sure sign of cyanosis. It would only get worse the longer she went without a transplant.

'She's back in rhythm.'

At least a semblance of rhythm, and she wasn't out of the woods, not by a long shot. Her damaged heart—caused by her mum's drug addiction—was failing quickly. Without a transplant, she would die. Whether that last crisis arrived in a week or two or three, the outcome would be the same.

Annabelle sent up a silent prayer that a donor heart would become available.

Even as she prayed it, though, she hated the fact that another family would have to lose their child so that Baby Hope might live.

They watched a few more minutes as things settled down. 'We'll leave her on the ventilator until we figure out exactly what happened. We can try adjusting the nitrogen rate or play with some of her other meds to see if we can buy her a little more time.'

Sienna nodded. 'I was thinking the exact thing.' She glanced at Annabelle. 'Are you okay?'

It was the second time she'd asked her that question. And the second time she had trouble coming up with a response.

'I will be.'

'I know this one's special to you.'

Of course. Sienna was talking about the baby. Not about Max and his sudden appearance back in her life.

'I just want her to have a chance.'

'As stubborn as you are, she has it.' Sienna gave her a smile.

'Annabelle is nothing, if not tenacious.' Max's

voice came through, only there wasn't a hint of amusement in the words. And she knew why. Because he wasn't referring to Hope. He was referring to how she'd clung to what she'd thought was *their* dream only to find out it wasn't.

'You said you know each other?'

When Annabelle came to work this morning, never in her wildest imaginings had she pictured this scene. Because she already knew how it was going to play out. She braced herself for impact.

'We do.'

There was a pause as the other doctor waited to be enlightened.

Annabelle tried to head it off, even though she knew it was hopeless. 'We've known each other for years.'

'Yes,' Max murmured. 'You could say that. Your Annabelle Brookes is actually Annabelle Ainsley. My wife.'

'Your…' Sienna suddenly looked as if she'd rather be anywhere else but here. 'It didn't even dawn on me. Your names…'

'Are not the same. I know.' Max's mouth turned down at the corners, a hard line that she recognised forming along the sides of his jaw. 'I see you've gone back to your maiden name.' He pinned her with a glance.

'We're separated. Getting a divorce.' She explained as quickly as she could without adding that going back to her maiden name had been a way to survive the devastation that his leaving had caused.

Even though you're the one who asked him to go.

They hadn't spoken since the day he'd found her temperature journal and realised that, although she'd stopped doing the in-vitro procedures as he'd demanded, she hadn't completely given up hope. Until that very minute.

When she'd seen the look on his face as he'd thumbed through the pages, she'd known it was over. She'd grabbed the book from his hands and told him to leave.

And just like that, he'd walked out of their front door and out of her life.

Just like Baby Hope's mother.

And like that lost soul, Max had never come back.

Until now.

She frowned. 'Did you know I was at Teddy's when you accepted that contract to take Sienna's position?'

Even as she asked it, she knew it made no sense for him to have come here. Not without a good reason.

Like those papers on her shelf?

'No.'

That one curt word told her everything she needed to know. If he'd known she was working at the Royal Cheltenham, this was the last place he'd have chosen to come.

Sienna touched a gloved hand to the baby's head. 'If you two can finish getting her stabilised, I need to get off my feet for a few minutes.' She eyed Max. 'Why don't you give me a call when you're done here and I'll finish showing you around the hospital?'

'Sounds good. Thanks.'

Annabelle was halfway surprised that he hadn't just said he was ready now. He had to be as eager to get away from her as she was to get away from him. But they had their patient to consider.

Their?

Oh, God. If he was Sienna's replacement, that meant they would share this particular case. And others like it.

As soon as Sienna had left the room along with the other nurses, Max took a few moments to finish going over the baby's chart, making notes in it while Annabelle squirmed. She couldn't believe he was here. After all this time.

And for the tiniest second, when those intelligent eyes of his had swept over her, she'd entertained the thought that maybe he really had come here looking for her. But it was obvious from his behaviour that he hadn't.

He hadn't seemed all that pleased that she'd dumped his name. How could he expect otherwise, though? She'd wanted no reminders of their time together, not that a simple name change could ever erase all the pain and sadness over the way their marriage had ended.

'Why don't you fill me in on the details of her care? Miss McDonald seemed to indicate you know the baby better than anyone else on staff.' The cool way he asked the question made heat rush to her face.

Here she was agonising over the past, while he was able, as always, to wall off his feelings and emotions. It had driven her crazy when they were together that he could behave as if their world weren't imploding as she'd had miscarriage after miscarriage.

'Social services needed someone who could report

back to them on what was happening with her care. And since I'm head nurse, it kind of fell to me to do it.'

'Somehow I didn't think you would remain a neonatal nurse. Not after everything that happened.'

She shrugged. 'I love my job. Just because I can't... have children doesn't mean I want to go into another line of nursing. I'm not one to throw in the towel.'

'I think that depended on the situation.' His words had a hard edge to them.

She decided to take a page from his book and at least try to feign indifference. 'What do you want me to tell you about her?'

'Do you know anything about her history? Her mother?'

Annabelle filled him in on everything she could, from the fact that Baby Hope's mother had been hooked on heroin to the fact that she'd fled the hospital soon after giving birth, staff only discovering her absence when they went in to take her vitals. They'd found her bed empty, her hospital gown wadded up under the covers. They'd called the authorities, but in the two weeks since the baby's birth no one had come forward with any information.

The drug use had caused the baby to go through withdrawals in addition to the in-utero damage her heart had sustained. It was getting weaker by the day. In fact, every ounce she gained put more strain on it. Normally in these children, Annabelle considered weight gain something to be celebrated. Not in Hope's case. It just meant she had that much less time to live.

'Does any of that help?' she asked.

'It does. I'm going to up her dose of furosemide and see if we can get a little of that fluid off her belly.

I think that's why she stopped breathing. If it's not any better in an hour or two, I'm going to try to draw some of it off manually.'

'We did that a few days ago. It seemed to help.'

'Good.'

They looked at each other for a long moment, then Max said, 'You've let your hair grow.'

The unexpectedness of the observation made her blink. 'It makes it easier to get out of the way.'

Annabelle used to tame her waves rather than pulling them back. Between blowing them out and using a straightening iron, she'd spent a lot of time on her appearance. Once Max had left, though, there'd seemed little reason to go through those contortions any more. It was only when she stopped that she realised she'd been simply going through the motions for the last half of their marriage. Having a baby had become such a priority that her every waking moment had been consumed with it. It was no wonder he'd jumped at the chance to get out. She hadn't liked who she'd become either.

She opened her mouth to say something more, before deciding the less personal they made their interactions, the better for both of them. They'd travelled down that road once before and it hadn't ended well. And she definitely didn't want to give him the impression that she'd been pining for him over the past three years. She hadn't been. She'd got well and truly over him.

'Since you're working here now, maybe we should set down some ground rules to avoid any sticky situations.' She paused. 'Unless you'd like to change your mind about staying.'

His eyes narrowed. 'I signed a contract. I intend to abide by the terms of it.'

Was that why he hadn't moved to complete the process of terminating their union? Because he viewed their marriage as a contract rather than an emotional commitment? She'd been the one to actually file, not him.

Her throat clogged at the thought, but she pushed ahead, needing to finish their conversation so she could leave. Before the crazy avalanche of emotions buried her any deeper.

'Most people at Teddy's don't know that I was married. They just assume I'm single. All except for Ella.'

Since she no longer wore her ring, it made it that much easier to assume she had no one in her life.

His brows went up. 'Ella O'Brien?'

'Yes.' He would know who Ella was. They'd been best friends for years. She was very surprised her friend hadn't got wind of Max's arrival. Then again, maybe Annabelle would have known had she paid more attention during staff meetings. She'd known Sienna was going on maternity leave soon but had had no idea that Max was the one who'd be taking her place. Maybe because Baby Hope had taken up most of her thoughts in the last couple of weeks.

'How is she?'

'Ella? She's fine.' She looked away from him, reaching down to touch Hope's tiny hand over the side of the still-open incubator. 'Anyway, Ella knows about us, but, as you could see from Sienna's reaction, that information hasn't made its way around the hospital. I would appreciate if you didn't go around blurting out that you're my husband. Because you're not. You haven't been for the last three years.'

One side of his mouth went up in that mouth-watering way that used to make her tremble. But right now, she was desperate to put this runaway train back on its tracks.

'I have a paper that says otherwise.'

'And I have one that says I'm ready to be done with that part of my life.'

'The divorce papers. I'm surprised you haven't followed up on them with your solicitor.'

She should have had that solicitor hound Max until he signed, but she hadn't, and she wasn't quite sure why. 'I've been busy.'

His eyes went to Hope. 'I can see that.'

'So you'll keep our little…situation between us?'

'How do you know Miss McDonald isn't going to say something to someone?'

'She won't.' Sienna was secretive enough about her own past that Annabelle was pretty sure privacy was a big deal to the other doctor.

'And Ella? You don't think she'll say anything?'

'Not if she knows what's good for her.' She said it with a wryness in her voice, because her friend was obstinate to the point of stubbornness about some things. But she was a good and faithful friend. She'd mothered Annabelle when she'd come to her crying her eyes out when Max had walked out of the door. No, Ella wouldn't tell anyone.

Annabelle pulled her hand from the incubator and took a deep breath. Then she turned back to face Max again.

'Please. Can't we try to just work together like

the professionals we are? At least for the time you're here.' She wanted to ask exactly how long that would be, but for now she had to assume it was until Sienna was finished with her maternity leave. If she thought of it as a finite period of time she could survive his presence. At least she hoped she could.

But she already knew she'd be seeing a lot more of him. Especially if he was going to be the doctor who either opened Hope's chest and placed a donor heart in it or who signed her death certificate.

She closed her eyes for a second as the remembered sound of that alarm sliced through her being. How long before that sound signalled the end of a life that had barely begun?

'I don't know, Anna.' His low voice caused her lids to wrench apart. 'Can we?'

Her name on his lips sent a shiver through her, as did his words. It was the first time she'd heard the shortened version of Annabelle in three years. In fact, during their very last confrontation he'd reverted to her full name. And then he was gone.

So it made her senses go wonky to hear the drawled endearment murmured in something other than anger.

She'd wanted a simple answer...a promise that Max would do his best to keep their time together peaceful. He hadn't given her that. Or maybe he was simply acknowledging something that she was afraid to admit: that it was impossible for them to work together as if they'd never crossed paths before. Because they had.

And if those old hurts and resentments somehow came out with swords drawn?

Then, as much as she wanted to keep their past relationship in the past, it would probably spill over into the present in a very real way.

CHAPTER TWO

'AND THIS IS where all of that wonderful hospital food is prepared.'

Sienna's easy smile wasn't able to quite penetrate the shock to his system caused by seeing Anna standing over that incubator. Why hadn't he kept track of where she was?

Because he hadn't wanted to know. Knowing meant he had to do something about those papers her solicitor had sent him. And he hadn't been ready to. Maybe fate was forcing his hand. Making him finally put an end to that part of his life in order to move forward to the next phase.

Wasn't that part of the reason he'd come home? To start living again?

Yes, but he hadn't meant to do it quite like this.

He decided the best way to take his mind off Anna was to put it on something...or someone else.

'The ubiquitous hospital food.' He allowed his mouth to quirk to the side. 'But it's probably better than what I've been eating for the past six months.'

She laughed. 'I'm sure Doctors Without Borders feeds you pretty decently.' She paused to look at him as they made their way down the corridor. 'What was it like over there?'

'Hard. Lots of pressing needs, and not knowing where to start. Not being able to meet all of those needs was a tough pill to swallow.' Memories of desperate faces played through his head like a slide show. Those he saved...and those he couldn't.

'I can imagine it was. And living in another country for months at a time? It couldn't have been easy being away from the comforts of home.'

'I heard you had a little experience with that as well. What was the kingdom of Montanari like?' Someone had mentioned that the other cardiothoracic surgeon had visited the tiny country on an extended stay, but that she had returned quite suddenly.

Sienna stared straight ahead. 'It was different.'

Different. In other words, move on to another subject. He was happy to oblige, since he knew of one particular subject he was just as eager to avoid. 'How about your cases here? Anything interesting?'

The other doctor's shoulders relaxed, and she threw him a smile that seemed almost grateful. 'Well, we actually have a mum who is expecting quadruplets. We're keeping an extra-close eye on her but so far she's doing well and the babies are all fine.'

'That's good.' He didn't ask any more questions. Someone carrying that many foetuses made him think of fertility treatments—another subject he wasn't eager to explore.

'Apparently they might bring in a world-renowned neonatal specialist if any complications develop.'

How many times would he have loved to fly in a specialist when he was in Africa? But, of course, there were only those, like him, who had volunteered their time and expertise. Doctors Without Borders sometimes took pot luck as far as who was willing to go. As a result there were often holes in treatment plans, or a patient who needed help from a specialist that wasn't on site. That was when the most heartbreaking scenarios occurred.

Yet despite that he was already missing those brief, and often frantic, interactions with the team in Sudan, which surprised him given how exhausted he'd been by the end. Or maybe it was the shock of having to work with Annabelle that had him wishing he could just fly back to Africa and a life where long-term connections with other people were neither expected nor desired. It was more in line with the way he'd grown up. And far removed from what he'd once had with Anna. He'd decided that keeping his distance from others was the safer route.

'Who is the specialist?'

'Hmm…someone told me, but I can't remember her name. I do remember it's a woman. I'd have to look.' She stopped in front of a set of double doors. 'And this is where we work our magic.'

The surgical unit. The epicentre of Max's—and Sienna's—world. Even with all the prep work that went on before the actual surgery, this was still where everything would be won or lost. Annabelle had once said she didn't know how he did it. He wasn't completely sure either. He just did it. The same way she did her job, standing beside the incubators of very sick babies and taking the best care she could of them.

Why was he even thinking about Annabelle right now? 'Can we go inside?'

'Of course.' She hit a button on the wall and the doors swung wide to allow them through. Glancing at the schedule on the whiteboard at the nurses' station, she said, 'Do you want to scrub up and observe a surgery? There's a gallbladder being taken out in surgical unit two.'

'No, I'm good. But I would like to observe your next cardiac surgery.'

Sienna gave a sigh and put a hand to her belly. 'Sure, but I'm really hoping to scale back by about seventy-five per cent over the next week so I can leave without worrying that you haven't carried an actual caseload.'

Maybe he should have been offended by that, but he wasn't. Sienna didn't know him from Adam. He was pretty sure that she could still carry her share of the patient load, but her comment had been more about wanting to see him in action. To reassure herself that she was leaving her little charges in the best possible hands. He was determined not to disappoint her.

'That sounds fair enough.' He paused. 'And the baby who was in crisis? Baby…Hope?'

'She doesn't have an official name. Hope is Annabelle's pet name for her. I think it's a fingers-crossed kind of thing. Whatever it is, it's stuck, and we all find ourselves calling her that now.'

That sounded just like Annabelle. Refusing to give up hope, even when it was obvious that the procedures were not going to work.

'Annabelle mentioned social services. And that the mum took off?'

'Yes. The mum came in while she was in labour.

She was an addict and abandoned the baby soon afterwards. We have no idea where she is.'

Max's chest tightened. His parents had never actually abandoned him physically, except for those long cruises and trips they'd taken, leaving him in the care of an aunt. But emotionally?

'Anyway,' Sienna went on, 'I'm assigning the case to you. Make sure you become familiar with it. Your best bet for doing that is to get with Annabelle and go over her patient file. She has followed that baby from the beginning. She knows more about her than anyone, maybe even me, and I'm Baby Hope's doctor.'

Max's heart twinged out a warning. The last thing he wanted to do was spend even more time with Annabelle, because it was...

Dangerous.

But what else could he do? Say no? Tell Sienna that he couldn't be a professional when it came to dealing with his almost-ex? Not hardly.

Maybe Sienna saw something in his face. 'Is that going to be a problem considering the circumstances? I'm sorry, I had no idea you two even knew each other.'

If there was one thing Max was good at, it was disengaging his brain from his heart.

'It won't be a problem.'

'Good.'

He'd work with Anna. Until it was over. Because one way or the other it would be. The baby would either have a new heart, or she wouldn't. The twinge he'd felt seconds earlier grew to an ache—just like the one he'd dealt with on an almost daily basis while working in the Sudan. He rubbed a palm over the spot for a second to ease the pressure.

'How often do hearts come available?'

'Do you mean here in Cheltenham? Some years there are more. Some years, less.'

'How many transplants have you done?'

'One. In my whole career. We deal with lots of holes in the heart and diverting blood flow, but hypoplastic cases are rare at Teddy's.'

So why was she handing the case over to him? This was a chance that she'd just admitted didn't come across her desk very often. 'Are you sure you don't want it?'

'Very.' Something flashed through her brown eyes. A trickle of fear? His gaze shifted lower. Was she worried about the health of her own baby?

He remembered well the worry over whether a foetus would make it to term. In fact he remembered several times when he'd prayed over Annabelle as she'd slept. Those prayers had gone unanswered.

'When are you due?'

'Too soon. But right now it feels like for ever.' Her glance caught his. 'Everything is fine with the baby, if that's what you're wondering. My handing that case over has nothing to do with superstition. I just don't think I have the endurance right now for what could be a long, complicated surgery.' She pressed a hand to the small of her back. 'And if for some reason I go earlier than I expect, I don't want to pass Baby Hope over to someone else at the last second. I want it to be now, when it's a deliberate decision on both of our parts.'

That he could understand. The need to be prepared

for what might happen. Unlike in his relationship with Annabelle when he'd impulsively issued an ultimatum, hoping to save her from the grief of repeating a tragic cycle—not to mention the dangerous physical symptoms she'd been experiencing.

It had worked. But not quite in the way he'd expected.

This was not where he wanted his thoughts to head. He'd do better to stick with what he could control and leave the rest of it to the side at the moment.

'Your patients will be in good hands. I'll make sure of it.'

'Thank you. That means a lot to me.' She sent him a smile that was genuine. 'Do you have any other questions before we officially end our tour and go on to discuss actual cases?'

'Just one.'

'All right.' The wariness he'd sensed during his mention of Montanari filtered back into her eyes. She had no need to be worried. He was done with discussing personal issues.

'Is the food as bad here as it was at my last gig?'

Sienna actually laughed. 'I'll let you be the judge of that. I don't mind it. But then again, I eat almost anything, as long as it isn't alive or shaped like a snake.'

'Well, on those two points we can agree. So I take it Teddy's doesn't serve exotic fare.'

'Nope. Just watery potatoes and tasteless jelly.'

He glanced at his watch and smiled back at her. 'Well, then, in the name of science, I think I should go and check out the competition. Can we save the case discussion until later?'

'Yes, I'm ready for a break as well. And you can

tell me what you think once you've sampled what the canteen has to offer. Just watch out for the nurses.'

'Sorry?'

'Some of them have heard you were coming. While you're checking out the food, don't be surprised if they're checking you out.'

Would they be? He'd made it a point not to get involved with women at all since his separation. And he wasn't planning on changing that.

And what of Annabelle? She was a nurse. Had she been checking him out as well?

Of course not. But on that note, he'd better go and get something into his stomach. Before he did something stupid and went back down to the first floor to check on a very ill baby, and the protective nurse who hovered over her.

Annabelle wasn't good for his equilibrium. And she very definitely wasn't good for his objectivity. And no matter what, he had to keep that. Because if he allowed his heart to become too entangled with her as he cared for his patients, he would have trouble doing his job.

What Baby Hope and the rest of his patients needed was a doctor who could keep his emotions out of the surgical ward. No matter how hard that might prove to be.

Annabelle grabbed a tray and headed for the line of choices. She wasn't hungry. Or so she told herself. Her stomach had knotted again and again until there was almost no room in it for anything other than the big bowl of worry she'd dished up for herself that morning. Baby Hope was getting weaker. The crisis she'd had this morning proved it. If Max hadn't been there, Hope might have…

No, don't think about that. And Max had not been the only one in that room who could have saved her. Sienna would have called for the exact same treatment protocol. She'd seen the other woman in action.

Once upon a time, Annabelle had expected Max to play the role of saviour. It hadn't been fair to him. Or to her. He'd finally cracked under the pressure of it all. And so had she. At least her body had.

A few days after she'd lost her last babies, her abdomen and legs had swelled up with fluid from all of the hormones she'd been on and she'd been in pain; Max had rushed her to A&E. They'd given her an ultrasound again, thinking maybe some foetal tissue had been left behind. But what they'd found was that her ovaries had swelled to many times their normal size from harvesting the eggs.

There'd been no magic-wand treatment to make it all go away. Her body had had to do the hard work. She'd worn support hose to keep the fluid from accumulating in her legs, and had had to sleep sitting up in a chair to make it easier to breathe as her hormone levels had gradually gone back to normal. And the look on Max's face when the doctors had told him the cause…

It had come right on the heels of him telling her that he was done trying to have babies. It had made everything that much worse. But she'd still desperately wanted children, so she'd started keeping secret recordings of her temperature. Only the more secretive she'd got over the coming weeks, the more distant he'd become. In the end, the death knell had sounded before he'd ever found that journal.

Back to food, Annabelle.

She set her tray on the metal supports running parallel to the food selections and gazed into the glass case. Baked chicken? No. Salad? No. Fruit? Yes. She picked up a clear plastic container of fruit salad and set it on her tray, pushing it a few feet further down the line. Sandwiches? Her stomach clenched in revulsion. Not at the food, but at the thought of trying to push that bread down her oesophagus.

Broccoli? Healthy, and she normally loved it, but no. She kept moving past the selection of veggies until she hit the dessert section.

Bad Annabelle. What would your mum say?

She peered back down the row, wondering if she should reverse her steps and make better choices. Except when she glanced the way she'd come, her gaze didn't fall on food. It fell on the very person she was trying to forget. Max.

And he was with Sienna. Both were holding food trays, which meant...

Oh, no! They were eating lunch too.

It's what people do. They eat. They sleep. Her throat tightened. *They move away to far-off places.*

Sienna waved to her. 'Hey, Annabelle. Hold on. Would you like to join us? We can talk about Baby Hope, and you can help catch Max up on the case.'

It was on the tip of her tongue to say she was going to eat back in her office, but she'd just been worrying about the baby. Any light they could shed on her prognosis should outweigh any awkwardness of eating with her ex. Right?

Right.

'Sure. I'll save you a spot.' She tossed a container of yoghurt onto her plate and then a large slice of chocolate cake for good measure. Handing her personnel card to the cashier and praying she scanned it before the pair caught up with her, she threw a smile at the woman and then headed out towards the crowd of people already parked at tables.

Setting her tray on one of the only available tables in the far corner, she hesitated. Should she really be doing this?

Yes. Anything for Baby Hope.

She shut her eyes. Was she becoming as obsessed with this infant as she had been with her quest to become pregnant all those years ago?

No. Looking back now, those attempts seemed so futile. Desperate attempts by a desperate woman. Max's childhood had been pretty awful, and she'd wanted to show him how it should be. How wonderful hers had been. And since he had no blood relatives left alive, she'd wanted to give him that physical connection—for the roots she'd had with her own extended family to take hold and spread. Only none of it had worked.

If her sister hadn't had a devastating experience when trying to adopt a baby, Annabelle might have gone that route after her first miscarriage. But if the grief she'd felt after losing a baby she'd never met was horrific, how much worse had it been for her sister, who'd held a baby in her arms for months only to have to hand him back over to the courts weeks before the adoption was finalised? The whole family had been shattered. And so Annabelle had continued on her quest to have a biological child, only to fail time and time again.

She popped open the lid to her fruit, realising it was the only truly healthy thing on her plate. She'd just wanted to get out of that canteen line at any cost.

Her mouth twisted sideways. It looked as if the final cost would be paid by her waistline and hips. She shoved a huge blueberry into her mouth and bit down hard just as Max and Sienna joined her. Juice spurted over her teeth and drummed at the backs of her lips, seeking the nearest available exit.

Perfect. She covered her mouth with her napkin as she continued to fight with the food, finally swallowing it down with a couple of coughs afterwards.

Max frowned as he sat. 'Okay?'

'Yes.' Another cough, louder this time, a few people at neighbouring tables glancing her way. Probably wondering who they were going to have to do the Heimlich on this time. She swallowed again, clearing her throat. 'Just went down the wrong pipe.'

Sienna, who arrived with only some kind of green bottled concoction that made Annabelle horrified at what her own plate contained, twisted the lid to her liquid lunch and sat down. She nodded at the selection. 'I'm finding smaller portions are easier to handle when I'm working. I'll eat a proper meal when I go off duty.'

Forcing herself to cut a chunk of melon into more manageable pieces, she wished she could be just as disciplined as the surgeon. Well, today was not a good day to stand in judgement of herself. Was it any wonder she was seeking out comfort food? Her husband had just landed back in her life.

She couldn't even pretend to have a boyfriend, because if there'd been anyone serious she obviously would have wanted to pressure Max into signing the divorce papers. But she hadn't.

Ugh! She chewed quickly and then swallowed, thankful that at least this time she wasn't choking.

A phone chirped and all three of them looked down at their devices, making her smile. Her screen was blank, so it wasn't Ella, who she hadn't heard from all day, which was unusual. Maybe she hadn't heard that Max was back.

Or maybe she had.

Sienna frowned, setting her drink down on the table so quickly the contents sloshed, almost coming over the rim of the bottle. She stared at her phone for several seconds, not touching the screen. Either it was very good news...or very...

The other doctor stood up, her tongue flicking out to moisten her lips. 'I'm sorry, I have to go.' She glanced at Max. 'Can you carry on without me?'

'Of course. Is everything all right?'

'It will be.' Her hand went to her midsection. And rather than responding to whoever had sent a message, she dropped her phone into the pocket of her scrubs and picked up her drink, screwing the cap back on. 'Page me if you have any questions or need help.'

'I think I'm good.' Max sent Annabelle a wry glance. 'I'm sure Anna can answer any questions about Hope or the hospital I might have.'

Or about why he hadn't severed those final ties that bound them together?

Somehow, though, she doubted he was any more eager to revisit their past than she was. But still, the last thing she wanted today was to play hospital adviser to a man who still made her knees quake. She had no idea why that was so. She was over him. Had been for the last couple of years. In fact, she hadn't thought of him in…

Well, the last fifteen seconds, but that didn't count, since he was sitting right across from her. Before today, she'd gone weeks at a time without him crossing her mind.

But since Sienna was glancing her way as if needing reassurance that it was indeed okay to leave them alone without a referee, Annabelle nodded. 'Go. It'll be fine.'

Looking a little doubtful, but evidently not enough to want to stick around, the cardiothoracic surgeon gave a quick wave and headed towards the entrance of the canteen. Annabelle noticed she slid her phone out of her pocket and stared at the screen again as she rounded the corner.

She wondered what that was all about. But it was really none of her business.

But Baby Hope was, and since that was why Sienna had wanted to sit with her…

'Is there some news about the baby?' Maybe that was what the message was about. Could it be that…? 'Could a heart have become available?'

Hope sparked in her chest, flaring to life with a jolt that had her leaning forward and sent her plastic fork dropping back onto her tray.

Max must have seen something in her face because he shook his head. 'No. Not yet. I think she would have told us if that message had anything to do with a donor heart.'

She sagged back into her chair. 'I was hoping…'

'I know. Why don't we work on things we can control until one is available? Tell me anything else you can think of about her. The events surrounding her birth, et cetera.'

'Are you looking for something in particular?' She'd told him pretty much everything she knew back in the special care baby unit.

Max pulled a small notebook out of one of the pockets of his jacket. 'I can look at her chart and get the mechanics. But tell me about *her*. Anything out of the ordinary that you've noticed that you think might help.'

She picked up her fork and pushed around a few more blueberries, not trying to really stab any of them but using the empty gesture as a way to sort through her thoughts about Hope.

'She's a fighter. She came into this world crying as hard as her tiny lungs would let her.' She sucked down a quick breath. 'Her mother didn't even touch her. Hope was very sick and might not have survived the night, but she never asked to hold her or tried to keep us from taking her away. Maybe she already knew she was going to leave her behind and was afraid to let herself get attached.'

'You were there when she was born.'

'Yes. When the mum came in—already in labour—the doctor examined her. He didn't like the way the baby's heartbeat sounded so they did an ultrasound. They immediately saw there was a problem, so they called Sienna down.' Annabelle gripped her fork tighter. 'She knew as soon as she looked at the monitor that it was serious. So when she delivered there was a roomful of staff, just in case Hope coded on the table. They did a Caesarean section, trying to save the baby any undue stress during delivery.'

'It worked. She's still alive.'

'Yes. But she's all alone. Her mum has never even called to check on her. Not once.'

'And say what?' Max's jaw tightened. 'Maybe she didn't want to have to deal with the fallout of what might happen if it all went wrong.'

'It was her child. How could she not want to be there for her?'

'She could have felt the baby was better off without her.'

Something about the tight way he said those words made her wonder if Max was still talking about Baby Hope and her mum, or something a little closer to home.

Had he felt she was better off without him?

Rubbish. It hadn't been his idea to leave. It had been hers. If he'd truly loved her, he would have fought for her.

But Max had always had a hard time forming attachments, thanks to parents who did their utmost to avoid any show of affection. And those long trips they'd taken without him—leaving Max to wonder if they were ever coming back. If they missed him at all. Annabelle had cried when he'd told her in halting words the way things had been in his home. Her own family's open affection and need to be with each other had seemed to fascinate him.

Maybe he really could understand how a mum could abandon her own child. In many ways, Max had felt abandoned. Maybe even by her, when she'd told him to leave.

She should have just given up when he'd given her that last ultimatum. But she hadn't—she'd wanted Max to have what his parents had denied him. And when he'd found her journal… God, he'd been so furious that night. To forestall any more arguments, she'd told him to get out. The memories created a sour taste in her mouth.

'I guess I'll never know what her true motivation was for leaving. If I had, maybe I could have changed her mind, or at least talked her into coming back to check on Hope.'

'She probably wouldn't have. Come back, that is. Maybe she felt that once she walked out, there was no going back.'

This time when his eyes came up to meet hers there was no denying that he was talking about something other than their patient.

Unable to come up with anything that wouldn't inflame the situation further, she settled for a shrug. 'Maybe not. I guess people just have to learn to live with the consequences of their choices.'

As Annabelle had had to do.

And with that statement, she made the choice to stab her fork into the slab of chocolate cake on her plate and did her best to steer the conversation back to neutral territory. Where there was no chance of loaded statements or examining past regrets too closely.

But even as they spoke of the hospital and its patients and advances in treatment, she was very aware that nothing could ever be completely neutral as far as Max went.

So she would try to do as she'd stated and make the very best choices she could while he was here. And then learn to live with the consequences.

CHAPTER THREE

'ELLA, LET'S NOT have this discussion right now.'

'What discussion is that?' Her best friend batted her eyes, while Annabelle's rolled around in their sockets. 'The prodigal returns to the scene of his crime?'

'That doesn't even make any sense.'

'It doesn't have to. So spill. I haven't seen you since I heard the big news. Not from you, I might add. What's up with that?'

She tried to delay the inevitable. 'What news are you talking about?'

Ella made a scoffing sound as she leaned against the exam table. 'That a certain ex has crashed back onto the scene.'

Crashed was a very good word for what he'd done. 'There's nothing to tell. He showed up yesterday at the hospital.'

'Out of the blue? With no advance notice?' Her friend lifted the bottle of water she held, taking a quick drink. She then grimaced.

'Are you okay?'

'Fine. Just a little tummy trouble. I hope I'm not coming down with whatever everyone else has. Wouldn't that be a wonderful Christmas present?'

She twisted her lips and then shrugged. 'Anyway, you had no idea he was coming?'

'Of course not. I would have told you, if I'd known.' And probably caught the next available flight out of town. Annabelle sighed, already tired of this line of questioning. When had life become so complicated? 'I'm sure someone knew he was coming. I just never thought to ask because I never dreamed...'

'That Max Ainsley would show up on your door-step and beg for your forgiveness?'

'Ella!' Annabelle hurried over to the door to the exam room and shut it before anyone overheard their conversation. She turned back to face her friend. 'First of all, he did not show up on my doorstep. He just happened to come to work at the hospital. I'm sure he had no idea I was working here any more than I knew that he was the one taking Sienna's place. And second, there's no need for him to apologise.'

'Like hell there's not. He practically abandoned you without a word.'

Oh, Lord, she'd had very little sleep last night and now this. As soon as she'd finished lunch with Max yesterday, she had got out of that canteen as fast as she possibly could. Even so, he'd come down to the special care baby unit a couple of hours later to get even more information on Baby Hope. Clinical information this time about blood types and the matching tests they'd done in the hope that a heart would become available.

She'd been forced to stand there as he shuffled through papers and tried to absorb any tiny piece of information that could help with the newborn's treatment. With his head bent over the computer screen, each little shift in his expression had triggered memories of happier times. Which was why she'd lain in bed and tossed and turned for hours last night. Because she couldn't help but dissect the whole day time and time again.

Sheer exhaustion had finally pulled her under just as the sun had begun to rise. And then she'd had to get up and come into work, knowing she was going to run into him again today. And tomorrow. And three months from now.

How was she going to survive until his contract ended?

'He didn't abandon me. It simply didn't work out between us. We both had a part in ending it, even though I asked him to leave.'

It was true. She couldn't see it back then, and Ella had had to listen to her long-distance calls as she'd cycled through the stages of grief, giving sympathy where it was needed and a proverbial kick in the backside when she was still wearing her heart on her sleeve six months after the separation.

'Enough!' she'd finally declared. 'You have to decide whether you want to start your life over again or if you're going to spend it crying over a man who isn't coming back.'

Those words had done what nothing else had been able to. They'd convinced her that she needed to climb out of the pity pit she'd dug for herself and start giving back to society. What better way to forget about your own heartache than to ease the suffering of someone else?

Ella had talked her into moving from London to

the Cotswolds soon afterwards. It had been one of the best decisions of her life.

Well. Until now. But that hadn't been Ella's fault. It had been no one's. Not even Max's.

Annabelle's pager suddenly beeped at the same time as Ella's, and they both jumped at the noise. Peering down to look at what had caused the alert, Annabelle read.

A multi-vehicle accident on the M5 has occurred. A hired bus for a nursery school outing was involved. Several of those patients are en route—eta five minutes. All available personnel please report to A&E.

'Oh, God,' she said, reaching for her friend's hand.

'I know. Let's head over.' Her friend stopped and gripped the edge of the table for a second.

'Ella?'

'I'm okay.' She ran a hand through her hair, her face pale. 'Let's go.'

'Maybe you should go home instead.' Almost a third of the hospital staff was out due to a virus that had spread through their ranks. Hopefully Ella wasn't the latest person to fall victim to the bug.

Her friend blew out a breath. 'I hope to God I'm not...' She stopped again. 'I'll be all right. If I start feeling worse, I'll go home, okay?'

'Are you sure?'

'Yes. Now, let's get our butts in gear and go and help whoever is coming.'

Max spotted her the second she came out of the lift. She and a familiar redhead hurried past a small

Christmas tree towards the assembled staff who were waiting for the first of the ambulances to arrive. The other woman sent him a chilling glare. Perfect. It was Ella. She'd always had it in for him.

It didn't matter.

His ex moved over to him. 'Any word yet?'

'I don't know any more than you do.'

Just then, he caught the sound of a siren in the distance. And then another. Once they hit, they would have to do triage—the kind he'd done during his stints with Doctors Without Borders. This hospital might be more modern than the ones he'd worked in over the last six months, but that didn't mean that the process of sorting patients from most critical to least would be any easier. Especially not when it came to those involving high-speed crashes. He had to be ready for anything, including cardiac involvement from chest trauma.

He'd never got used to the cries of suffering while he was in Africa. And it would be no easier here than it had been there.

A nursery school outing! Of all things.

Right now, they didn't even know exactly how many patients were coming in, much less the seriousness of the injuries.

Then the first emergency vehicle spun into the space in front of the hospital, another stopping right behind it. And, yes, the screams of a child as those back doors were opened cut through him like a knife.

He moved in to look as the stretcher rolled backwards and onto the ground. A child who couldn't be more than three came into view, blood covering the sheet of the stretcher. And her right arm… Her shirt sleeve had been cut and parted to reveal the raw flesh of an open fracture, the pearly edge of a bone peeking through.

One of the orthopaedists moved in. 'Take her to exam room one. Take vitals, check her for other injuries. I'll be there in a minute.' He knew that doctors hated assigning priorities to treatment, but it was the only way to save as many lives as possible. If they treated these patients according to the order they came in, they might condemn a more seriously injured patient to death. It couldn't work that way. Max knew that from experience.

A nurse directed the paramedic back towards the interior of the hospital where other staff were preparing to receive whoever came through those doors.

The assembled doctors met each stretcher as it arrived, specialists matched up with the appropriate accident victims. When Annabelle tried to follow one of the other doctors, Max stopped her. If a critical case came his way, he would need a nurse to assist. And who better than a nurse who dealt with crises on a daily basis? He'd seen her in action when Baby Hope's pulse ox levels had plummeted. She'd been calm and confident, exactly what he needed.

It wasn't an unreasonable request.

And it had nothing to do with their past, or the fact that working with someone he knew would be easier than a complete stranger. He already knew that he and Annabelle made a great team on a professional level. They'd worked together many times before, since they'd been employed by the same hospital in London during their marriage.

The next ambulance pulled into the bay. The driver

leaped out just as the doors at the back of the vehicle swung open.

'How many more are coming?' Max called. So far they'd had thirteen patients ranging in age from two to four years in addition to three nursery school workers who'd also sustained injuries. The rescue in the frigid November temperatures had taken its toll as well. Despite being wrapped in blankets, many of the patients were shivering from shock and exposure.

'This is the last one. She was trapped between seats. She sustained blunt force trauma to the chest. She threw PVCs the whole way over.'

When the wheels of the stretcher hit the ground and made the turn towards them, Max caught sight of a pale face and blue-tinged lips, despite the oxygen mask over her face. A little girl. Probably two years old. Disposable electrode pads had been adhered to a chest that heaved as she gasped for breath.

'How bad?'

The paramedic shook his head. 'Difficulty breathing, pulse ox low as is her BP. And her EKG readings are all over the chart. PVCs, a couple of quick ventricular arrhythmias, but nothing sustained.'

'Possible cardiac contusion. Let's get her inside.'

As soon as they ran through the doors, Max glanced at her. 'We're going straight to ICU. You'll have to tell me where to go.'

With Annabelle calling out instructions they arrived on the third-floor unit within minutes. The paramedic had stayed with them the whole time, assisting with moving the stretcher.

They burst through the entrance to the unit, and Max grabbed every staff member who wasn't already treating someone and motioned them to the nearest empty room. Together they worked to get the girl hooked up to a heart monitor and take her vitals. The child was conscious, her wide eyes were open, and, although there were tears trickling from the corners of her eyes, her struggle to breathe took precedence over crying.

Somehow that just made it worse.

'We need to intubate, and then I want to get some X-rays and a CAT scan.'

He was hearing some crepitus as she breathed, the popping and crackling sounds as her chest expanded indicative of a possible sternal fracture. It could also explain some of her cardiac symptoms. The faster he figured it out, the better the prognosis.

He leaned down to the child, wishing he at least knew her name. 'We're going to take good care of you.'

Within minutes they'd slid a trach tube into place to regulate her breathing. Her cardiac function was still showing some instability, but it hadn't worsened. At least not yet.

Max was a master of remaining objective during very difficult surgeries. But there was something about children who were victims of accidents that threatened to shred his composure. These weren't neat put-the-child-to-sleep-in-a-controlled-setting cases. These were painful, awful situations that wrung him out emotionally.

Needing to come home from the Sudan to maintain his certification couldn't have come at a better time. He'd desperately needed a rest; the abject poverty and suffering he'd seen had taken their toll on him.

And yet here he was, his second day on the job, feeling as if he'd been thrown right back onto the front lines.

Mentally and emotionally.

Annabelle helped him get the girl ready to move to the radiology section, glancing at him as she did. She touched the youngster every chance she got, probably as a way to reassure her. He'd noticed her doing the same thing with Baby Hope.

Those tiny gestures of compassion struck at something deep inside him.

Strands of hair stuck to a face moist with perspiration, and yet Annabelle was totally oblivious to everything except her patient.

Just then, as if she sensed him looking at her, her head came up. Their gazes tangled for several long seconds. Then they were right back at it. Annabelle was evidently willing to set any animosity aside for the benefit of their young patient.

The CT scan confirmed his suspicion. The force of the little girl striking the seat in front of her had fractured her sternum, putting pressure on her heart and lungs. A half-hour turned into an hour, which turned into five as they continued to work the case.

It had to be way past time for Annabelle's shift to end, but she didn't flinch as they struggled to stabilise the girl.

Sarah. He'd finally learned her name. And unlike Baby Hope's mum, or even his own parents—who'd been more angry than concerned when he'd been injured in a bike crash—Sarah's mum and dad were frantic, desperate for any shred of news.

Annabelle came in from her fifth trip to see them. 'I told them they could come see her in a few minutes.'

'Good.' Sarah was already more comfortable. They'd given her some pain medication, and although she was still on a ventilator they'd be able to wean her off in the next day or two, depending on how much more swelling she had. 'Why don't you take a break? Get off your feet for a few minutes.'

'Sarah needs me. I'll rest when she does.'

'Have you eaten today?'

This time she smiled, although the edges of her mouth were lined with exhaustion as she repeated the same thought. 'I'll eat when you do.'

If she thought he was calling her weak, she was wrong. She was anything but. Of course, he already knew that. He'd watched Annabelle go to hell and back in her effort to have a child. She was as stubborn as they came. It was one of the things he'd loved most about her, and yet it was ultimately that very thing that had driven them apart.

'Is that a dinner invitation?' He cocked a brow at her.

Her smile faded. 'Of course not. I just meant—'

'I know what you meant.' His jaw stiffened. 'I was joking.'

'Of course.' Annabelle began collecting some of the discarded treatment items, not looking at him. It was then he realised how harsh his voice had been. It reminded him of the time he'd finally had enough of the procedures and the heartache. He'd been harsh then too. Very harsh, if he looked back on it now.

Max moved in closer, lifting a hand to touch her arm, then deciding better of it.

'I'm sorry for snapping at you. I would say chalk it up to exhaustion, but that's no excuse.' He could envision this scene repeating itself ad nauseam unless he put a stop to it. 'Maybe we really should grab a bite when we're done here. We can figure out how we're going to work together for the next several months without constantly being at each other's throats.'

She glanced up at him. 'I think we can manage to bump into each other now and then without having a meltdown.'

This time the sharpness was on her side.

'I know we can.' He took a deep breath and dragged a hand through his hair. 'Look, I'm trying to figure out how to make this easier on both of us, since I assume neither one of us is going to resign.'

It wasn't just because of his contract. He'd known for a long time that this day was coming. When he'd have to face his past and decide how to move forward. Maybe that time was now. He could go on putting it off, as he had over the past three years, but this wasn't Africa where he could just immerse himself in work and not have to see her day after day. They were looking at months of working together. At least.

'I love my post.' The sharpness in her voice had given way to a slight tremor. Did she think he was going to cause trouble for her or ask her to leave?

'I know you do. And I don't want to make you miserable by being here.' This time, he touched her gloved hand. Just for a second. 'Will it really be so very hard, Anna?'

'No. It's just that I never expected to…'

'You never expected to see me again.'

'No. Honestly I didn't.'

'But we both knew we would eventually have to finalise things. We can't live in limbo for ever.' This wasn't the direction he'd wanted to go with this discussion. But now that he was here, he had to see it through.

'You're right.' She glanced down at the items in her hand and then went over to throw them in the rubbish bin. Then she moved over to the exam table and pushed the little girl's hair out of her face. The tenderness in her eyes made his stomach contract. She would have made such a wonderful mum. It was a shame that biology—and fate—kept her from being one. No power known to medical science had seemed able to work out what the problem was. Or how to fix it.

What he hadn't expected was for her to shove him out of her life the second she realised he was serious about not trying again. That bitter pill had taken ages to go down. But it finally had. And when it did, he realised his parents had taught him a valuable lesson. Keeping his heart to himself really was the better way.

When she looked up at him again, all hints of tenderness were gone, replaced by a resolute determination. 'You're right. We can't live in limbo. So this time the invitation is real. If you don't have plans, I think we should have dinner. And decide where to go from here.'

Suddenly that discussion didn't look quite as attractive as it had moments earlier. But since he'd been the one to suggest sitting down and talking things over, he couldn't very well refuse. 'Okay, once Sarah's parents have had their visit, we'll head out.'

A half-hour later, Max had scrawled the last of his instructions in Sarah's chart and set it in the holder

outside her door. The girl's parents were still sitting
by her bedside. He'd sent Annabelle on ahead to get
her things.

As he stretched his back a couple of vertebrae
popped, relieving the tension that had been building along his spine. He was dog tired. Maybe having dinner with Annabelle wasn't such a good idea.
The discussion should probably wait until they were
both rested.

Except there'd never seemed to *be* a right time to
approach their unfinished business. So they had to
make time.

He went to the men's changing room and washed
his hands and then bent down to splash his face. Blot-
ting it dry with a paper towel from the dispenser, he
caught a glance at his reflection.

Dark hair, still cut short from his time overseas,
was just starting to grey at the temples. Where had
the years gone?

One minute he'd been a happily married man, and
the next he'd been on the brink of divorce and living
like a nomad, going from place to place but never really settling down. Maybe he should have joined the
military. Except he hadn't wanted to give up the possibility of coming back to work in his field, and he
would have either had to retrain for his speciality or
settled for a position as a general surgeon. He loved
paediatric cardiology in a way he couldn't explain to
anyone but himself. So he'd gone with Doctors Without Borders.

Only his travels had simply delayed the inevitable.
He still had to face the ghosts of his past.

He didn't want to hurt Annabelle. And he wasn't

quite sure why he'd never signed the papers the second he'd realised what the packet of documents contained. Maybe he'd used them as a cautionary tale of what could happen when you opened your heart up to someone. Or maybe marriage had been an easy excuse for not getting involved with anyone else—not that he ever planned on it. Some day, though, Annabelle would meet Mr. Right and would want to be free to be with him. Their old life would stand in the way of that.

So, were they going to discuss their past tonight? Or discuss how to work together in the future?

He wasn't sure. They were both tired. And probably overly emotional.

Maybe he should just let Annabelle take the lead as far as topics went. And if she decided she wanted those divorce papers signed post haste, he might just have to tackle a tough conversation after all.

CHAPTER FOUR

THE PUB WAS PACKED. And with the clanging of plates and raucous laughter, it was hard to think, much less carry on a civilised conversation. Not the kind of place to go after dealing with a twelve-hour day of work.

But the place was also dark, with just some dim wall sconces lighting the way towards the tables. A few coloured bulbs along the bar were the only concession to the upcoming Christmas season.

O'Malley's wasn't a normal hospital hangout, but that was okay. She wanted privacy. Which was one of the reasons Annabelle had suggested it. If they were going to have The Talk, opening up the subject of their past, she didn't want anyone to overhear the conversation.

And the low lighting would keep Max from seeing her expression. In the past, he'd always been able to read her like a book. It had been no different in that treatment room an hour earlier, when he'd known instantly that he'd hurt her with his words and apologised. She hated that he could still decipher her expressions. And when he'd touched her...

No doubt he'd seen the heat that washed into her

face. Well, this time she was going to make it a little harder on him, if she could.

They followed the waitress to a small table for two in the very back of the place. Max waited for her to sit down before pulling his own chair out.

The server plonked a menu down in front of each of them, having to speak loudly to be heard above the din. 'What would you like to drink?'

Annabelle tried to decide if she wanted to risk imbibing or if she should play it safe. Oh, what the hell? Maybe she should dull her senses just a little. 'I'll have white wine.'

Writing her request down in a little book, the woman then turned her attention to Max. And 'turned her attention' was evidently synonymous with turning on her charm. Because suddenly the waitress was all smiles, fiddling with her hair. 'And you, sir?'

'I'll have a whisky sour, thank you.' He sent her a quick smile, but to his credit there was nothing behind it that hinted of any interest in whatever the waitress was offering. And she was offering. As a woman, Annabelle recognised the signs, even though she had never gone the flirting route.

At least not until she met Max.

Evidently realising she was out of luck, the woman shifted her gaze to Max's left hand, then she snapped her little book shut and flounced off.

Max didn't wear his ring any more. But then again, neither did she.

'Thank you for that.'

Max tilted his head. 'For what?'

'Not responding to her in front of me.'

Up went one brow. 'Not my type.'

That made her laugh, and her muscles all loosened. 'Really? Because she seemed to think you were hers.'

'I hadn't noticed.'

'Oh, come on.' She sat back in her chair and studied him. Max had always been handsome. But in the three years since she'd seen him, he'd grown even more attractive, although there was a deep groove between his brows that she didn't remember seeing when they were together.

'Seriously. She was probably just being friendly.'

'Seriously, huh? I don't know. Maybe we should make a little bet on it.'

'I don't bet on things like that.' The furrow above his nose deepened. 'Not any more.'

He didn't bet on what? Relationships? Because of her?

That wasn't what she wanted for Max. His childhood had been rough as it was, devoid of affection… love. He deserved to be happy, and she wanted that for him. Even now.

'We never really talked about it. What happened all those years ago.' Suddenly she wished she'd chosen a place a little less loud as she fingered the plastic placemat in front of her.

'I seem to remember a *lot* of talking. Most of it angry.'

Yes, there had been the arguments. Especially at the end, when he'd found her journal, the smoking gun that she was still hoping against hope that she would become pregnant.

Even before that, though, Max had become someone she didn't recognise. Impatient. Short. And somehow sad. That was the worst of all the emotions she'd seen in him. She'd tried so hard to have a child, thinking it would make everything better between them. That it would bind Max to her in a physical way—give him a sense of roots. Instead, it had only made things worse. The pregnancy attempts had ended up becoming a vicious cycle of failure and then increased desperation. Instead of binding them together, her attempts had torn them apart.

The waitress came and set their drinks in front of them. 'Are you ready to order?' Her voice wasn't nearly as friendly this time.

'Fish and chips for me and a glass of water, please.' Annabelle was craving good, old-fashioned fare.

'I'll have the same. And a dark ale to go with it, please.'

Annabelle didn't remember Max being a big drinker. Not that two drinks constituted an alcoholic. He just seemed…harder, somehow. Less approachable. Like his parents?

Once the waitress was gone, Annabelle picked up her wine, sipping with care.

Max, however, lifted his own glass and took a deep drink. 'I haven't had one of these in a long time. This place was a good choice.'

'Ella and I like to come here every once in a while. It's out of the way and loud enough that you don't have to think.'

He seemed to digest that for a moment. 'Not as loud as some of the places I've been.'

Interesting.

'Where *have* you been? If you don't mind my asking.' She didn't feel like talking about the arguments or failures of the past.

'I don't. I joined up with Doctors Without Borders. In between contracts in England, I've gone wherever they've needed me. Kenya, a time or two, but mostly the Sudan. I spent the last six months there.'

Annabelle listened, fascinated, as he shared what he'd done in the years since he'd left their flat. Some of the stories were horrifying. 'Isn't it hard to see that?'

'Yes.'

'And yet you keep going back. After this contract is up and Sienna is back from maternity leave, will you return there?'

The waitress arrived with their food and drinks, quickly asking if they needed anything else.

'I think we're good, thank you.'

When they were alone again, he drank the last of his whisky. 'I don't know what I'm going to do once this contract is up. I've been thinking about settling someplace on a more permanent basis.'

From what he'd told her, he'd hopped from city to city, country to country as the whim took him.

She was on her first bite of fish when he asked, 'How long have you lived in Cheltenham?'

It took her a second to chew and swallow. 'A year. I went to live with my mum for a while after...well, after you left.'

'Suzanne told me you didn't stay in the flat for long.'

Annabelle had missed their cleaning lady. 'Did you think I would?'

'I didn't really know what you would do. I went back after my first trip, almost a year later, and you were gone.'

'I just couldn't…stay.'

'Neither could I.' He paused. 'Even if you hadn't asked me to go, I would have. Things were never going to change.'

This was the most she'd ever been able to drag out of him. And she wasn't even having to drag. Back then they would fight, and then Max would clam up for days on end, his tight jaw attesting to the fact that he was holding his emotions at bay with difficulty.

He'd once told her that his parents had been the same way with him—their anger had translated into silence. He'd struggled with breaking those old patterns their entire marriage. But in the last six months of it, those habits had come back with a vengeance. If she'd tried to probe or make things right between them—with the offer of physical intimacy—he'd always seemed to have some meeting or suddenly had a shift at the hospital. She'd finally got the message: he didn't want to be with her, except when absolutely necessary for the in-vitro procedures. And then, after her last miscarriage, he was done trying for a baby.

Actually, Max had been done. Full stop. He'd left their relationship long before he'd actually walked out of the door.

She took another sip of her water to moisten her mouth as she got ready to tackle the most difficult subject of all.

'You haven't signed the papers.'

There was a pause.

'No. I've been overseas on and off.' He shrugged. 'After a while, I forgot about them.'

That stung, but she tried not to let it. 'Doesn't it make going out on dates awkward?'

'I've been busy. No time—or inclination—to jump back into those waters.'

His answer made Annabelle cringe. 'I'm sorry if I'm the reason for that.'

'I just haven't seen many happy marriages.'

'My parents are happy.'

He smiled at that. 'They are the exception to the rule. How are they?'

'They're fine. So are my sisters. Jessica had another boy while you were gone—his name is Nate.' She didn't want to delve into the fact that her parents' and siblings' relationships had all seemed to work out just swimmingly. Except for hers.

'That's wonderful. I'm happy for them.'

Popping a chip into her mouth, she tried not to think about how different their childhoods had been. Max's parents had seemed unhappy to be tied down with a child. They'd evidently loved to travel, and he had cramped their style.

Annabelle's home, on the other hand, had been filled with love and laughter, and when her parents had travelled—on long road trips, mostly—their kids had gone with them. She had wonderful memories of those adventures.

She'd hoped she and Max could have the same type of relationship. Instead, she'd become so focused on a single aspect of what constituted a family that she'd ignored the other parts.

Had she been so needy back then that she'd damaged Max somehow?

Well, hadn't their breakup damaged her?

Yes, but not in the way she'd expected. Annabelle had grown thicker skin over the past three years. Before, it seemed as if her whole life had been about Max and their quest to have a family. When that had begun breaking down and she'd sensed a lack of support on Max's side to continue, she'd become more and more withdrawn. She could see now how she'd withheld love whenever Max hadn't done exactly what she'd wanted. Just as his parents had.

She regretted that more than anything.

'So what do you want to do about it?'

He set his glass down. 'About what?'

Did she need to spell it out? 'About the paperwork. Maybe this is the reason we've been thrown back together. To tie up loose ends.'

A smile tilted up one side of his mouth. 'So I'm a loose end, now, am I?'

Nothing about Max was loose. He'd always been lean and fit, but now there was a firmness to him that spoke of muscle. Like the biceps that just peeked out from beneath the polo shirt he'd changed into before leaving the hospital.

They'd checked on Baby Hope before taking off. She was still holding her own, against all odds. But if a donor heart was not found soon…

She shrugged off the thought. 'You're not a loose end. But maybe I'm one of yours. You could be happy, Max. Find the right woman, and—'

'You're not a loose end, either.' His hand covered hers, an index finger coaxing hers to curl around it. The sensation was unbearably intimate and so like times past that she was helpless not to respond to the request. Their fingers twined. Tightened. The same heat from the exam room sloshed up her neck and into her face.

'Are you done with your meal?'

Her eyes widened. 'Yes. Why?'

'Would you mind coming with me for a minute?' He threw some notes onto the table, and, without even waiting for the bill, got to his feet.

She swallowed hard, wondering if he'd had enough of this conversation. Maybe he even had his signed divorce papers back in his office. If so, she hoped she wouldn't burst into tears when he presented her with them.

But he'd just told her she wasn't a loose end. And he'd held her hand in a way that had been so familiar it had sent a sting of fear through her heart.

So she picked up her coat and followed him through the pub, weaving through tables and people alike. When their waitress made to stop them, Max murmured something to her. She nodded and disappeared back among the tables of customers.

At the door, Max helped her into her coat and they went out into the dark night. It was chilly, but it wasn't actually as cold as she expected. When Max kept on walking, rather than stopping to let her know why they'd left the restaurant, she remained by his side. She had no idea where they were going, but right now she didn't care.

A taxi stopped at the kerb. 'You looking for a fare?'

'I think we're okay.' Max glanced at her as if to confirm his words. She gave a quick nod, and the cab driver pulled away in search of another customer. The bar was probably a perfect spot to do that, actually, since anyone who'd had a few too many drinks would need a way to get safely back to their flat. Putting her hands in her pockets, she waited for him to tell her why he'd brought her out here. Maybe something was wrong with him physically. Could that be why he'd come home from the Sudan?

A few minutes later, she couldn't take not knowing. 'Is everything okay?'

'It's still there, isn't it, despite everything?'

She frowned, moving under one of the street lamps along the edge of a park. 'What is?'

'That old spark.'

She'd felt that spark the second she'd laid eyes on him all those years ago. But he wasn't talking about way back then. He was talking about right now.

'Yes,' she whispered.

She wished to hell it weren't. But she wasn't going to pay truth back with a lie.

'Anna…' He took her hand and eased them off the path and into the dark shadows of a nearby bench.

She sat down, before she fell down. His voice… She would recognise that tone anywhere. He sat beside her, still holding her hand.

'You've changed,' he said.

'So have you. You seem…' She shook her head, unable to put words to her earlier thoughts. Or maybe it was that she wasn't sure she should.

'That bad, huh?'

'No. Not at all.'

He grinned, the flash of his teeth sending a shiver over her. 'That good, then, huh?'

Annabelle laughed and nudged him with her shoulder. 'You wish.'

'I actually do.'

When his fingers shifted from her hand to just beneath her chin, the shiver turned to a whoosh as all the breath left her body, her nerve endings suddenly attuned to Max's every move. And when his head came down, all she felt was anticipation.

Max wasn't sure what had come over him or made him want to leave the safety of the bar, but the second his lips touched hers all bets were off. The fragrance of her shampoo mixed with the normal sterile hospital scents, and it was like coming home after a long hard day.

His fingers slid up her jawline, edged behind the feminine curve of her ear and tunnelled into her hair. Annabelle's body shifted as well, turning into him, her arms winding around his neck in a way he hadn't felt in far too long. Or with any other woman.

The truth was that simple. And that complicated. No woman would ever be able to take Anna's place— so he'd never even tried to find one.

He deepened the kiss, tongue touching her lips, exulting in the fact that she opened to him immediately. No hesitation.

They'd always been good in bed, each instinctively knowing what the other wanted and each had been more than willing to oblige. Soft and sweet or daring and adventurous, Anna had always been open to trying new things. Until it had become all about...

No. No thinking about that right now.

Not when she was clutching the lapels of his jacket as if she could tug him into her very soul.

He angled his head, thrusting a little deeper into the heat of her mouth. Maybe they should just forget about the cold park and head back to the warmth of his cottage and the heat they'd find in his bed. There were taxis on practically every corner.

That was what he wanted: to have her. In bed. Skin to skin. With nothing between them but fire and raw need.

Just as he was getting ready to edge back enough to ask her to go with him, the sound of voices broke through the haze of passion.

Not Anna's voice, but someone else's. Close enough that he could tell they were man and woman.

Annabelle beat him to the punch, pulling back so suddenly that it left him reeling for a few seconds. She glanced at him and he looked back at her. They both smiled. Young medical students caught necking. It had happened before, when they'd been dating. Only that had been a police officer, who'd not been quite as amused by their antics.

'Caught again,' he murmured.

'So it would seem.'

He looked over to see who was walking past and his smile died, icy fingers walking up his spine. It was indeed a man and a woman, but they were pushing a pram. Bundles and bundles of blankets were piled on top of what had to be a young infant. And their faces.

God. They were happy. Incredibly happy.

His gaze went back to Anna's to find that all colour had drained from her skin, leaving her pasty white. The young man threw them a smile and a quick hello.

Somehow Max managed to croak something back, but the mood was spoiled. He could tell by Anna's re-action that she'd been thrown back to the tragedy that had been their shared past. At least that was what he took her stricken gaze to mean—the way her hungry eyes followed that pram as it went past and disappeared into the darkness.

His teeth gritted together several times before he had the strength to stand up and say what needed to be said. 'I think we've both had a little too much to drink. Maybe it's time to call it a night.'

Anna's one glass of wine and his two weightier beverages did not constitute drunkenness by any stretch of the imagination. Unless you considered being drunk on memories of the past as over-imbibing. It had to be all the reminiscing they'd done in the restaurant and the way her face had softened as she'd looked across the table at him. He'd always had trouble resisting her, and tonight was no exception. After one smile, he'd been putty in her hands. But he'd better somehow figure out how to put a stop to whatever was happening between them before one of them got hurt.

He'd opened his heart to her once before only to have it diced into tiny pieces and handed back to him. Never again. He would do whatever it took to keep that stony organ locked in the vault of his chest.

Far out of reach of her or anyone else.

CHAPTER FIVE

'I JUST HEARD. There's a heart. Get to the hospital.'

It took several seconds before a still-groggy Annabelle realised who was on the phone and what he was talking about. Once she did, she leaped to her feet, glancing at the clock on her nightstand to see what time it was. Three a.m.

Once a donor organ was located time was of the essence. It had to be transplanted within hours. 'I'm on my way.'

Scurrying around as fast as she could, she found clothes and shoved her limbs into them, not worrying about how she looked other than a quick brush of her teeth and putting her hair up into a high ponytail. Then she was out of the door and on her way to Teddy's. It was pitch black as she pulled her car out onto the roadway, and there were almost no other vehicles out this late. Blinking the remaining sleep from her eyes, she thought about the tasks she needed to do once she arrived.

Max evidently wasn't at the hospital yet, since he'd said he'd just heard. Which meant they'd tracked him down at home. Wherever that was.

Last night after that disastrous kiss, he'd seen her

home in a taxi, before giving her a tight wave as the driver pulled away. What had she been thinking letting him kiss her?

Letting him? More like her yanking him to her as tightly as she could. Once his lips had made contact with hers, he'd have been hard pressed to get away from her. She'd been that desperate to have him keep kissing her on into eternity.

Only that hadn't happened.

She tightened her grip on the steering wheel. No, that couple with the baby had walked by ruining everything. It hadn't been their fault, nor could they have known that Max's face had hardened instantly, reverting back to the mask she remembered from the end of their marriage. Was he remembering how badly he'd wanted what she couldn't deliver? No, he'd told her he no longer wanted children—maybe he didn't want to see reminders of what could have been.

And the way he'd looked at her after the young couple had walked away...

As if he couldn't wait to get away from her. He'd pulled her up from that bench so fast her head had spun. And no mention of when they would see each other again.

They wouldn't, obviously. Not outside the hospital. Or outside surgical suites. Last night had been a mistake. A remnant of embers long since extinguished. Except for one tiny spark...

Wasn't that what he'd called it? A spark?

Why had he even called her about the heart? He could have operated on Hope in the middle of the night, and she would have known nothing about it until the next morning. Had he been worried about how upset she would be that he hadn't told her?

Or was it simply the courtesy of a doctor to another member of a patient's medical team?

That was probably it.

Well, it didn't do any good to think about it now. This call was what Annabelle had been waiting for during the past two weeks. News that this particular baby might have a chance to live and grow.

She could put aside any discomfort working beside Max might bring. He and Sienna were both top in their field. She halfway wondered if the other doctor would be performing the transplant surgery. But Sienna had turned the case over to Max. Which meant he would be doing it.

Would he let her in the operating room? She wasn't a surgical nurse, but she had done a rotation in the surgical suite. And she wanted to be there for Hope, even though the baby would have no idea she was there. And wouldn't care.

She reached the hospital and made her way to the staff car park area. From the looks of the empty spaces, people still hadn't recovered from the virus. Hopefully Max would be able to find enough healthy bodies to be able to perform the surgery in the middle of the night. Well, by the time things were all prepped, it would probably be closer to six o'clock in the morning. Still early, but not so far out that it would be hard to talk people into coming in to assist.

Hurrying to the main entrance, she was surprised to find Max waiting for her. 'I thought you'd be in prepping for surgery.'

'We're still waiting on the medevac to get here with the heart.'

She walked with him, his long steps eating the distance. 'Do you know anything about it?'

'It typed right for Hope. The donor was an infant… the victim of a drunk driver. The family signed off just a few hours ago.'

Signed off. Such an impersonal term for what was a very personal decision. That baby had been someone's pride and joy. Their life. She'd mourned the foetuses she'd miscarried. But how much more would she ache if she'd held those children in her arms only to have them taken away by a cruel set of circumstances?

Kind of like the devastation her sister had experienced when she'd tried to adopt. But at least that child was still alive somewhere in the world.

A telltale prickle behind her eyelids warned her to move her thoughts to something else. Like the way Max had sounded saying Baby Hope's name.

Max had always been good at making sure parents knew that he thought of his tiny patients as people, painstakingly remembering even the names of extended family members. It was one of the things she'd truly loved about him. How special he made people feel.

It was what had drawn her to him when they'd first met. He'd acted as if she were the most beautiful girl in the room. Well, Max had certainly been the best-looking guy she'd ever laid eyes on, and when he'd said her name it had made her—

'Anna? You okay?'

She scrubbed her eyes with her palms. 'Still fighting the last bits of sleep, but I'll be fine.'

It was a lie. Annabelle was wide awake, but she was not going to tell him that she'd been standing there remembering the way they'd once been together.

'Well, you'd better finish waking up. We have a lot of work to do before that heart arrives.'

'Were you able to assemble a transplant team?'

He nodded, looking sideways at her as they continued down the brightly painted corridor. Annabelle had always loved the way Teddy's was so cheerful, almost as if it were a wonderful place for kids to laugh and play rather than a hospital that treated some of the most desperately ill children in the area.

'You're part of that team.'

Annabelle stopped in her tracks. She'd hoped he would include her in some way, but to put her on the actual team... That strange prickling sensation grew stronger. 'Are you serious?'

'I wouldn't have said it if I weren't.'

'Thank you. You don't know what this means to me.'

'I think I do.' He smiled, no hint of awkwardness in his manner, unlike Annabelle, who could barely look at him without remembering what had happened last night. 'But I didn't put you on it out of some sense of pity. I need you. You know Hope better than probably anyone else here at the hospital. I want you monitoring her, letting me know of anything out of the ordinary you see as we get her ready. And I want a sense of how she is when the surgery is finished, and she's coming out of the anaesthetic.'

More beautiful words had never been spoken. Max acted as if it were a given that the baby would survive the surgery and actually wake up on the other side.

As if there were no question about it. Done for her sake? Or because he really believed it? 'You've probably studied her case as much as I have.'

'I've studied it, but you've lived it, Anna.'

She *had* lived it. Some of it joyful, like when Hope opened those sweet blue eyes of hers and stared into Annabelle's. Some of them terrifying…like the day before yesterday when she had gone into respiratory failure. Annabelle had thought for sure those were the last moments of the baby's life. And now this. The sweet sound of hope…for a precious baby who was fighting so hard to live.

And now she just might get that chance.

'Thank you. For letting me be a part of it.'

Max started moving again, his steps quicker, more confident. 'I wouldn't have it any other way.'

'Ready for bypass.'

Max glanced back at the perfusionist seated at the table across from him, its myriad tubing and dials enough to make anyone nervous. But Gary Whitley—an expert in his field, Max had been told—was at the helm, his white goatee hidden beneath the surgical mask. 'Tell me when.'

Once they put Baby Hope on the bypass machine, the race with time would begin once again. The sooner the donor heart was in place and beating, the better chance the baby had for a good outcome. The risk for post-perfusion syndrome—the dreaded 'pump head'—grew the longer a patient was on bypass. Most of the time, the symptoms seemed to resolve after a period of weeks or months, but there were some new studies that suggested the attention and memory problems could be long-reaching for some individuals. Hopefully the baby's young age would preclude that from happening.

'Let's start her up.'

Gary adjusted the instrumentation and looked up just as the centrifugal pumps began whirling, sending the blood through the tubes and over into the oxygenator. 'On bypass.'

Max then nodded at Anna, who noted the time. She would keep an eye on the maximum time allowable and notify the team as they arrived at certain critical markers: one-quarter, the halfway mark and the three quarters mark, although he hoped they didn't cut it that close.

Using a series of clamps and scalpels, they finished unhooking Hope's defective heart, and, after checking and double checking the great vessels, they removed the organ from the opening in her chest wall.

'Ready for donor heart.' The new organ carefully changed hands until it reached Max. He checked it for damage, despite the fact that it had already gone through rigorous testing. He preferred to inspect everything himself…to know exactly what he was dealing with.

Was that one of the reasons he'd asked Annabelle to be involved in the surgery? Because he knew what to expect when they worked together?

Yes. But it was also because he knew this patient meant so much to her. Leaving her out after all the time, effort, and—knowing Annabelle—love she'd put into Baby Hope seemed a terrible act. Almost as if he were discarding her once she'd served her purpose.

That thought made him wince, but he quickly recovered.

Everything looked good. He measured the new heart for fit on the patient's left atrium and trimmed a tiny bit of tissue to ensure everything went together as it should. Then he set about the painstaking process of suturing it all back together.

'One half.' Annabelle's voice was calm and measured, giving no hint of what must be going through her mind. Things like, *Are we on track?* Or, *How long until I see those beautiful eyes of hers open?*

Max knew those fears all too well. He experienced them on each and every surgery. But for him to do his job, he had to put those thoughts aside and move systematically through the process. The worst thing he could do was waste precious time worrying about each and every possible outcome.

But Max couldn't help giving her a tiny piece of reassurance. 'We're a little ahead of schedule. As soon as I finish these final sutures we can begin warming her up.'

In his peripheral vision, he saw Annabelle's eyelids close as if she was relieved by the words. Then she squared up her shoulders and continued to watch both him and the clock.

When the last stitch was in place, Max looked at every vessel and each part of the heart, making sure he'd forgotten nothing. Only when he was completely satisfied did he give Gary the okay to start the warming process and begin weaning Hope off the bypass machine. Sometimes the weaning process itself would coax the new heart into beating, the return of blood flow triggering the electrical impulses, which would then start firing. The surgical suite was silent until Annabelle's voice again counted down the time. 'Three quarters.'

This time there was the tiniest quaver to her tone. *Don't worry, sweetheart. Just give her a few minutes.*

Sweetheart?

He hadn't used that endearment when thinking about her in ages. And he shouldn't be thinking it now.

His gaze zeroed in on his patient's open chest to avoid glancing up at Annabelle, knowing something in his expression might reveal emotions he wasn't even aware of having.

Two more minutes went by. If the heart didn't start soon, they would have to shock it with the paddles. Even if it came to that, they could still have a good outcome, but something made him loath to use more aggressive measures.

Just one more minute. Come on. You can do it.

This time he couldn't resist glancing at Annabelle. Her face was tight and drawn, no colour to be seen, even in her lips. It was as if she were sending her own lifeblood over to the baby so that she could live.

His assessment of his wife's thoughts was interrupted by a quick blipping sound from a nearby machine. Everyone's attention rocketed to the heart monitor. *Blip-blip.*

Looking directly at the new heart, he saw a beautiful sight. The organ contracted so strongly it seemed to want to leap out of its spot.

Within a few more seconds, it had settled into a normal sinus rhythm. Strong. Unfaltering. Unhesitating. The most beautiful sight he'd ever seen.

'It's working.'

There were cheers of relief throughout the operating theatre, but one voice was missing. When he looked up to see why, Annabelle's hand was covering her mouth and tears were streaming down her face. His instinct was to go to her, wrap her in his arms and say everything was going to be okay. But he couldn't promise her that. Not ever again. It was why they were no longer together, because he couldn't bring himself to say those words. He'd been at the end of himself by that point and had to let her go in order to save her.

At least that was Max's reasoning at the time.

Had it been valid?

It didn't matter now. What was done was done. There was no going back. Not that he wanted to.

So he turned his attention to the patient in front of him, assessing her needs and checking the sutured vessels for any sign of leakage. Everything looked tight and steady. And that beautiful heart was still beating.

Five minutes later, the decision was made to close her up. Max could have passed that work over to someone else. In fact it was customary after a long surgery to let an intern do the final unglamorous job. But Max wanted to do it himself. Needed to follow the path all the way to the end before he would feel right about passing her over to the team of nurses who would watch over her all night long.

'Let's finish it.'

Soon the room was alive with different staff members doing their appointed tasks, the atmosphere much different now than it had been twenty minutes ago when that heart had sat in Baby Hope's chest as lifeless as her old heart was now. They would start the immunosuppressant medication soon, to prevent her body from turning on her new organ and killing it, mistaking it for an invader. She'd be on medication for the rest of her life, which Max hoped would be a long and healthy one.

He set up the drainage tube system and then closed the sternum, using a plating technique that was made up of tiny screws and metal joiners. He carefully tightened each and every screw. Once that was done, muscle was pulled back into place and finally the skin, leaving space for the tubes that would drain off excess fluid. And the ventilator would remain in place for the next day or so, until they were sure everything was still working the way it should.

An hour later, an exhausted but jubilant Max cleared the baby to head to Recovery and then to the critical care ward to be closely observed over the next couple of days. Six hours of surgery had seemed like an eternity, at least emotionally. He was worn out.

When the baby was wheeled away, he congratulated his team, aware of the fact that Annabelle was standing in the corner. She looked as tired as he felt. A cord tightened in his gut as he continued thanking everyone individually.

The last person he went to shake hands with was the perfusionist, who had done his job perfectly, with stellar results. Only when he reached the man, his head was swivelled to the side, looking with interest at...

Annabelle.

He frowned.

Max peeled off his gloves and tossed them in the stack of operating rubbish that sat in a heap a few feet away, watching Annabelle. She was gathering instruments, seemingly unaware of the other man's gaze.

Gary's attention finally swung back to him and he smiled, stretching his hand out. 'Were you waiting for me? Sorry. It was great working with you.' He nodded in Annabelle's direction. 'I was just wondering who the nurse was. She looks vaguely familiar, but I don't think I've seen her in surgery before.'

One of his biceps relaxed, and he accepted the man's quick handshake.

She wasn't using her married name any more, but he decided to use a tactful approach and see if the perfusionist understood his meaning. 'That's Annabelle Brookes-Ainsley. She works down in the neonatal unit, but was interested in this particular case.'

'Because...' The drawn-out word said Gary hadn't connected the last names yet.

'Because she's been working with this patient. And it's my first surgery here at the hospital. It was a chance to see me in action.' He connected the two phrases, even though one had nothing to do with the other. He certainly didn't want to spell out that Annabelle was his wife. He was pretty sure she wouldn't appreciate that, but the guy had put him in a tough spot.

'To see you in...' Gary's eyes widened and a hint of red crept up his neck. 'Of course. I should have realised.'

'Not a problem. I'll let you get back to what you were doing, but I wanted to come over and say how much I appreciate the smooth handling of this surgery.'

'I—well, I appreciate it.'

With a ghost of a smile, Max swung away from the man and spoke briefly with the intern who'd been observing, answering a couple of questions he had. He kept that easy smile, but his insides were churning to get to Annabelle before she disappeared. And she would, if he knew her. She would want to go see how Baby Hope was doing.

The heart transplant marked the third patient 'crisis' that she'd assisted him with, and in each instance she'd done her job with precision and without hesitation. Max found it amazing that two people who'd been through what they had could still pull together and work for the good of someone else.

No rancour. No snide remarks, just an uncanny ability to know what the other was thinking, probably ingrained from years of living together. Whatever it was, they'd worked well together.

Except it evidently didn't carry over to their 'off times' because Max had no idea what she was thinking now. He answered one final question and then glanced at where Annabelle had been a second ago. Except, just as he'd suspected, she wasn't there. She'd already left the room. Without a single word.

CHAPTER SIX

ANNABELLE WASN'T SURE where she was going, but she had to get away from that room. It wasn't just the pile of bloody gauze and surgical tools that bothered her. Or the sight of Hope's still form being wheeled out of the surgical suite. It was Max's easy handling of both the case and the surgical staff.

And the aftermath of an adrenaline high that would probably send her crashing back to earth over the next hour or so. She didn't want Max to see her like that. He'd seen it enough over the course of their marriage.

She got ten steps down the hallway when she heard her name being called. Annabelle stopped in her tracks.

Max. Of course it was.

He had always been too good at ferreting out her emotional state, picking up on the nuances of what she was feeling. Maybe if he hadn't been quite so adept at it, she would have been able to hide her anguish over her repeated miscarriages. Only she hadn't. So she'd resorted to pulling away emotionally in an attempt to hide it from him. And in doing so had driven a wedge between them that had been impossible to remove.

Steeling herself, she turned to face him.

He came even with her, looking down into her face. Searching for something. She had no idea what.

'Good job in there.'

That made her lips twitch. 'I didn't have a very difficult task.'

'No, but I know you had a vested interest in that baby. It couldn't have been easy watching the clock ticking without any idea of what to expect.'

'I've watched transplants being done before.'

He frowned. 'You have? Because Gary, our perfusionist, doesn't seem to remember seeing you before.'

'I haven't actually watched one done at this hospital. Well... I mean, I've watched videos of them.' Lots of them actually. She'd wanted to see exactly what Hope would experience from start to finish.

'And did I measure up to what you saw in those videos?'

She sensed a slight hint of amusement in his voice. But yes, Max had measured up, damn him. Except she'd desperately wanted him to be as good as or better than anything that had passed across her computer screen. And he had been. His fingers had been nimble and yet gentle as he'd handled Hope, both before surgery and during it. There'd been a steely determination about him as those brown eyes had inspected the new heart. She'd seen it again as he'd waited for that same heart to begin beating. And then the smile he probably hadn't even realised he'd flashed when that tiny organ had started pumping oxygen-rich blood through Hope's tired body.

Watching him work had caused something warm to flood through her own insides. Just as the warmth had washed through Hope's veins as the surgery had neared completion. And that scared her.

'You already know the answer to that. Hope is alive because of you.'

That same devastating smile slid across his lips. 'It's been a while since I've done surgery in a hospital setting. Actually it's been a while since I've done anything in a modern hospital.'

Annabelle matched his smile. 'I'm sure it takes some getting used to after what you've seen.'

'It does.' He paused for a long moment and his eyes dipped to her mouth.

Annabelle's breath caught in her lungs. 'I can't imagine what it must have been like.'

Slowly his glance came back up to hers. 'You'd have to be there to really understand.' He paused for a moment. 'I actually have a Christmas fundraising gala to attend with Doctors Without Borders the day after tomorrow in London. If you're interested in learning more you could always come with me. Or are you slated to work two nights from now?'

'No, but...' Was he asking her to travel to London with him? Because it sure sounded like—

'I know we haven't made any hard and fast decisions about the future, but maybe we should. We could talk on the drive over.'

She stood there paralyzed, afraid to say no, but even more afraid to say yes.

'I would like you to come, Anna. Please.'

Oh, Lord. When he asked her like that, with his head tipped low to peer into her face, it was impossible to find the words to refuse him. So she didn't try. 'What about Hope?'

'We should be able to tell by tomorrow how things are going, and Sienna has already agreed to cover for me that night—along with her team, which she assures me is the best in the area. We'll just be gone overnight. Hope will never even know we're gone.'

Overnight? That word sent a shiver through her, even though it shouldn't. Memories of other nights in London swirled to life in her head despite her best efforts. Of them in their flat, making love as if there were no tomorrow.

Of course, in the end, there hadn't been.

She shook herself back to reality. This was no big deal. And they did have a lot to discuss. Most fundraisers were held at night. By the time the festivities wound down and they got back on the road it would be late. Probably much later than Max would want to drive. And if there was alcohol involved...

They could stay at a hotel. Annabelle had done that on several occasions when she'd gone into London for a seminar or lecture in her field. It was no big deal. She'd travelled with colleagues before. They'd simply taken care of their own sleeping arrangements.

Would he bring the divorce papers with him and sign them on the dotted line in front of her? If so, she should just let him. They both needed some closure, and maybe this would give it to them.

Even if the thought of taking that final step made her throat clog with emotion.

Why? It was time. Past time, actually.

'Okay, I'll go.' And she would just suck it up and muddle through the best she could. 'What kind of dress is it?'

'Black tie, actually.'

'Really? Isn't it too late to tell them you're bringing along a guest?'

'No.' He shrugged, the act making his shoulder slide against hers, a reminder of just how close he was standing. 'The invitation is for me and a guest. Most people bring a significant other.' That devastating smile cracked the left side of his mouth again. 'You're as close as I have to one of those.'

As in close, but no cigar? As in an almost-ex significant other?

'Ditto.' Her brows went up. 'I think.'

His hand came up, the backs of his knuckles trailing down the side of her face, leaving fire in their wake. 'We did good in that surgical suite. We gave her a chance that she wouldn't have otherwise had.'

'*You* did good. You made this happen.'

'Sienna could have done just as well.'

Annabelle was sure the other surgeon could have. But there had been something about the way Max had looked at that baby that had turned her inside out. Something more than simply a surgeon treating a patient. Hope had touched him as much as she'd touched Annabelle.

A wrench of pain went through her. Max would have made such a great father.

She'd wanted to do that for him more than anything. To give him what he hadn't been given by his own parents: the chance to watch a normal, happy childhood unfold. To love. And be loved. Only it hadn't worked out that way.

'Sienna didn't do it, though. You did.'

The fingers that had been slowly caressing her face curved around to the back of her neck.

Oh, Lord. He was going to kiss her. Right here in the hospital corridor. Was that the act of a man who was about to finalise a divorce?

Maybe. Weren't there exes who had sex as they travelled down the path to divorce?

Not her.

And yet, every nerve ending was quivering with awareness. With acceptance. Her lips parted.

'Sorry. Is your last name Ainsley?'

'Yes.' Their necks cranked around at the same time, foreheads colliding as they did so. Ouch. Damn it!

Only then did she remember that she didn't go by Ainsley any more.

She slid away from Max as a male nurse came towards them, horrified that she'd been caught red-handed flirting with her ex-husband.

He's not your ex. Not yet. And she wasn't flirting. She'd been… Oh, hell, she had no idea what either of them had been doing.

The nurse's eyes went from one of them to the other. Of course. He wasn't sure exactly who he was looking for. '*Max* Ainsley?'

'That would be you,' Annabelle said, glancing sideways at Max.

The nurse frowned. 'There's been a complication with the transplant patient.'

'Oh, God.' Annabelle's stomach clenched. She should have been in that room monitoring Baby Hope, not hanging around in the corridor mooning after her ex.

She hadn't been mooning. And she'd been heading for the recovery area when Max had stopped her to talk. Had asked her to go with him to some gala.

Neither of them had expected the moment to morph into something more.

Didn't it always, though, where Max was concerned?

They hurried down the hallway following the retreating nurse. 'What do you think it is?'

'I have no idea.' He took his smartphone out of his pocket. 'No one tried to page me that I see.'

They arrived in Recovery, and Max slid through the door with Annabelle close behind. 'What's the problem?'

Two nurses were at the baby's head watching the heart monitor on the side. Annabelle saw it at once.

'A-fib.'

Her eyes swung to Max, waiting for his assessment. And the concern on his normally passive face sent a wave of panic through her.

Damn it!

Max went into immediate action. While postoperative atrial fibrillation was a fairly common complication of cardiac surgeries, POAF wasn't the norm for heart transplants, and, when it did show up, it typically showed up a couple of days down the line. That made it a very big deal. Especially in an infant that had already been in crisis in recent days.

The possibilities skated through his head and were legion. Problem with the pulmonary vein? Probably not. The isolation of that vessel usually helped prevent POAF. Acute rejection? Not likely this soon after transplantation. Pericardial inflammation or effusion? Yes. It could be that. Fluid could be building around the heart—the body's reaction to inflammation. And it could cause a-fib, especially if it came on this quickly.

'Let's see if she's got some effusion going on and work from there.'

The baby, awash in tubes and bandages, looked tiny as she lay in the special care incubator, a tuft of soft blonde hair turning her from a patient into a person. He glanced to the side to see that Annabelle's face was taut with fear, her hands clenched in front of her body.

Was she worried about losing this one, the way she'd lost baby after baby due to miscarriage?

He'd been helpless to prevent those, but he damned well wasn't right now. He could do something to turn this around. And if he had anything to do with it, this baby was going to live.

He belted out orders and over the next three hours they ran several tests, which confirmed his diagnosis. They pumped in anti-inflammatories, and he and Annabelle settled in to wait for a reaction. Four hours after the initial alarm was raised, Baby Hope's heart had resumed a normal sinus rhythm.

Annabelle sank into a rocking chair, her elbows propped on her knees, her back curving as she sat there with her eyes closed. 'Thank God.'

Unable to resist, Max went over and used his palm to move in slow circles between her shoulder blades. 'We'll keep a close eye on her over the next twenty-four hours, but I'm pretty sure we've got this licked. As long as the fluid doesn't start building again, the rhythm should hold.'

'And if it starts building?'

'We'll cross that bridge when we come to it, Anna.'

The other nurses had moved on to other patients, now that the crisis was over, leaving Max and Annabelle alone with the baby.

Annabelle reached into the incubator and smoothed down that tuft of hair he'd noticed earlier. The gesture caught him right in the gut, making it tighten until it was hard to breathe. 'I think you're too close to this case. Maybe you need to take a step back.'

'Social services handed me her care.' She glanced up at him. 'Please don't make me stay away.'

He could do just that. Let someone know that her emotions were getting in the way of her objectivity. And he probably should. But Max couldn't bring himself to even mention that possibility. He hadn't been able to comfort her during those awful times in their marriage, but he could give her this. As long as it didn't take too big a toll on her.

She was a grown woman. She could make her own decisions. Unless it adversely affected their patient.

'I won't. But I'm going to count on you to recognise when your emotions are getting the better of you and to pull back.'

He didn't say the words 'or else', but they hung between them. Anna acknowledged them with a nod of her head. 'Fine. But I don't think I should go to the Christmas party with you.'

'Miss McDonald will take good care of her. If she starts taking another turn tomorrow, we'll both stay here. But it's only for one night. We'll be back the next day.'

She looked up, her hand still on the baby's head. 'Are you sure?'

Why he was so insistent on her going with him he

had no idea. But these first few days at the hospital had been crazy. With the staff shortages, Annabelle had probably worked herself almost into the ground. A little Christmas cheer was in order. For both of them. They could count it as a celebration of Hope's successful surgery.

He told her as much, and then added, 'I'll tell you what. As long as she's holding her own, we'll go to London. If we hear the slightest peep out of Sienna, we'll come back immediately. It's not that long a drive.'

Her thumb brushed back and forth over the baby's tiny forehead. 'Okay.'

She probably had no idea how protective she looked right now. As if her very presence were enough to keep anything bad from happening to that baby. If it worked like that, Annabelle might have three or four children by now.

His children.

Max's throat tightened, a band threatening to cut off his airway. There would be no children. Not for Annabelle. And not for him.

That had nothing to do with this case. Or with either of them. Max needed to remember that, or the past would come back and undo all the progress he'd made over the last three years.

Progress. Was that what it was called? His stints in Africa seemed more like running away.

No. He'd helped a lot of children during those trips. Kids that might have had no chance had he not been there.

Like Baby Hope?

It wasn't the same at all. Hope could have had any

number of doctors perform her transplant. He'd just happened to be here at the time.

And he was glad he was.

His fingers gave Annabelle's shoulder a squeeze. 'She needs her rest.'

A ridiculous statement, since Hope was in a drug-induced sleep. He had a feeling his words were more to help Annabelle rest than the baby.

'She's just so...helpless.'

'She might be. But we're not. She's got a great team of experts who are pretty damned stubborn.'

'Like you.'

That made Max smile, the band around his throat easing. 'Do I fall on the expert side or the stubborn side?'

'Both.' She tilted her head back and smiled up at him. 'Hope is extremely lucky to have you on her team.'

'Thank you.'

When she stayed like that, he gave in to temptation and bent down to give her a friendly kiss, hoping to hell no one was looking through the observation window at them right now.

He straightened, his fingers moving beneath her hair to the warm skin of her neck, damp despite the chilly temperatures in the room. From the stress of working to keep Hope's a-fib from turning into something worse. She had to be absolutely exhausted. 'You need to get some rest too, Anna. Before you collapse.'

'I will.' Her attention moved back to the baby. 'I just want to sit here a little longer, okay?'

He had a feeling nothing he said was going to move her out of that chair, so he did something he shouldn't have done. Something that would only test his equilibrium more than it already had been.

He pulled up a second rocking chair and settled in beside her.

'How are the quads?'

Ella and Annabelle walked towards the front doors of the local café just like they did every Friday morning. Only today big flakes of snow were beginning to fall around them, sifting over the Christmas decorations that had been strung to the lamp posts. It should have felt festive, like something out of a postcard. But it didn't.

She had too much on her mind for that.

She tightened the scarf around her neck, needing her friend's advice today. The midwife hadn't steered her wrong when she'd convinced her to move to the Cotswolds a year ago. The change in scenery had done her a world of good. At least until Max had come barrelling back into her life. But no one could have predicted that he would be the one taking Sienna's place. Well, Sienna had known, but, from her reaction when she realised they knew each other, the cardiothoracic surgeon had had no idea who he was when the hospital had contracted him.

Annabelle just had to think about how to broach the subject. So she'd started with something work related until she could figure out how to bring up Max's name.

'They're fine so far. Mum and babies all doing well. It's very exciting.'

Ella had seemed distracted over the last couple of weeks. But every time Annabelle tried to gently probe to see what was bothering her, her friend clammed up. 'I hope everything goes well for them.'

'Me too.' Ella pushed open the door to the café and got into line along with probably ten other people who were all ordering speciality coffees and breakfast sandwiches. 'So what's going on with Max?'

Whoa. So much for casually introducing the subject after an appropriate amount of small talk. But she should have known that wasn't going to happen. Ella tended to jump right to the heart of the matter. Except when it came to talking about her own issues, evidently. But at least she seemed to be feeling better than she had a couple of days ago. Maybe she wasn't catching the virus after all.

'What do you mean?'

'Are we really going to play this game, Annabelle?'

Her? Her friend had been pretty evasive herself recently.

'I guess we're not.' She gripped the wrought-iron rail that kept customers headed in the right direction. 'It's no big deal. He asked me to go to a Christmas fundraiser with him. It's in London.'

'He did? When did this happen?' Ella's face was alight with curiosity. And concern.

Annabelle couldn't blame her. Max had only been at the hospital a few days, but he'd already managed to turn her neat and orderly world on its head. Just as he always did. She'd sworn she was immune to him, that she could stay objective.

But just like with Baby Hope, it seemed that Max had the uncanny knack of being able to separate the fibres of her emotions and stretch them until Annabelle was positive they would snap.

He'd warned her about getting too emotionally attached to Hope. But who was going to warn her about him?

Max was a master at keeping his feelings under wraps. She knew the way she—and the rest of her family—wore her heart on her sleeve made him uncomfortable. His background had made him much more cautious about big emotional displays when they'd started dating. But with a lot of work and time spent with her parents that personality trait had turned around to the point that Max didn't think twice about slinging his arm around her shoulders. That was when Annabelle knew she could love him.

His parents had died when he was in his early twenties, before he and Annabelle met. Even his grieving had been a private affair. And when she'd lost her babies...

He'd gone back to being clinical. Probably because she'd been so overwrought the first time or two. Then she'd begun pulling away as well and it had snowballed from there. She'd called him heartless that last time.

No more, Anna.

Wasn't that what he'd said?

But had he really been as heartless as she'd thought? Maybe his grief—like with his parents' deaths—had been worn on the inside.

'Anna?'

Her friend's voice called her back. She tried to remember the question. When had Max asked her to the charity event? 'He asked me yesterday, after Hope's surgery.'

When he'd almost kissed her in the hospital corridor.

If the male nurse hadn't interrupted them when he had...

God! She was setting herself up for disaster.

The redhead moved forward several feet in line. 'How did he ask you?'

'Um...with his voice?'

Ella jabbed her with her elbow. 'That's not what I mean and you know it. Was he asking you to a fundraiser? Or was he asking you to something else?'

Something else?

'I'm not sure what you mean.'

Ella turned her attention to the barista, ordering her usual beans and eggs breakfast with coffee.

Unlike her friend, Annabelle's stomach was churning too much to go for a hearty breakfast so she ordered a cup of tea and a couple of crumpets with butter and marmalade.

'What in the world are you having?' Her friend curled her nose, her Irish accent coming through full force, as it did when she was amused.

'I'm trying to eat lighter these days.'

Ella tossed her hair over her shoulder, taking the coffee the woman at the counter handed her. 'I'll go find us a table.'

It would do no good to try to hide anything from the midwife. She had always been far too good at seeing through her. Then again, there was that heart-on-the-sleeve syndrome that Annabelle just couldn't shake. The barista handed her a teapot and cup, promising that she would be along with their breakfast orders soon. There was nothing left but to join Ella and try to sort through all of her feelings about spending time alone with her husband tomorrow evening. After all the years they'd been apart, he shouldn't still leave her weak at the knees, but he did. And there was no denying it.

The second she sank into her chair, the midwife wrapped her hands around her chunky white mug and leaned forward. 'So tell me what's going on.'

'I'm not sure.'

Ella didn't respond, just sat there with brows raised.

Okay, so this was worse than just spilling her guts. 'Like I said, it's Max.'

This time her friend laughed. 'I thought we'd already established that. If the rumours about the newest—and sublimely hot—member of Teddy's tight-knit family are true, then he was spotted with his lips puckered, ready to swoop in on the always untouchable Annabelle. Some accounts of that story included a ringing slap to the face.'

Annabelle's eyes widened, shock moving through her system. 'People think I slapped him?'

'Not everyone. Some think you disappeared into the nearest supply cupboard with him.'

'Oh, heavens!' She poured tea into her cup and took a quick sip, letting the hot liquid splash into her empty stomach, hoping it would give her some kind of strength. 'Do they know who he is?'

She hoped Ella would understand the question. Did everyone at the hospital know that Max was her husband? Not that he actually was, except for on a piece of paper. The second she'd told him to get out, the marriage had been over.

'If they don't yet, they're going to work it out soon enough.' A waitress stopped by and dropped off their plates of food. 'The only thing stopping them is that you're using your maiden name. But of course, that makes it even more delicious as it heads down the gossip chain. Who wants to hear about an old married couple doing naughty things?'

'Great. So what do I do about it?'

'You might want to think about putting your own version of events out there so that you—and Max, for that matter—don't wind up with a real mess on your hands.'

'And what version of events is that? That I'm married to Max, but that we're on our way to dissolving the marriage? Talk about winding up with a mess on my hands.'

She already had. And she wasn't exactly sure what she could do to fix it. Especially since some people had evidently seen their display after the transplant surgery, when she was as sure as the next person that Max had been about to kiss her. If not for the nurse...

She presumed that he had been one of the ones to start the rumour. Then there was the situation of the actual kiss that had passed between them. But that had been outside the pub, and she was pretty sure no one from the hospital had been there. It was why she'd chosen the place.

Quickly telling Ella about that incident as well as all of the confusing feelings and emotions she'd been dealing with up to this point, she shrugged. 'Maybe I should have told him I wouldn't go to London with him.'

'Are you kissing... I mean kidding?' Ella grinned

to show that the slip had been anything but an accident. 'You two have got to figure this thing out. There's obviously something there. That's what people are picking up on. Tell me you're not still in love with him.'

Annabelle didn't miss a beat, although her fingers tightened on the handle of her teacup. 'Of course not. But that doesn't mean I don't care what happens to him. I want him to be happy.'

'And you don't think he will be with you?' Ella took a deep breath. 'You've been locked in the past, Anna, whether you realise it or not. I think you have a decision to make. If you really believe you shouldn't be together, and you want him to be happy, then maybe it's time to do something about it. Remove yourself as an obstacle, as hard as that might be.'

When she'd asked Max to leave, she'd made no effort to go after him. And he'd made no effort to come back and work things out. Besides, she'd been so devastated by the fact that he wasn't willing to sit and wallow in misery with her that she hadn't been thinking straight.

But he evidently hadn't needed to wallow. He could have fought for their marriage—offered to go with her to counselling. But he hadn't. He'd simply seemed relieved it was all over with.

Her heart clutched in her chest. She'd been relieved too. And now?

Now she didn't know how she felt.

Their food was long since gone, although Annabelle couldn't remember actually eating her crumpets. But she must have since the spoon from the little pot of marmalade was sitting on her bread plate, remnants of orange rind still clinging to its silver bowl.

'Maybe you're right. Maybe it is time to do something.' She could contact her solicitor and ask him to prod Max to sign, since she couldn't seem to get the nerve up to ask him herself.

'Unless you decide you still love him. Then I say you fight.' Ella reached across and squeezed her hand. 'I know that doesn't help, but maybe you need to take a closer look at your heart. See what it's telling you to do.'

'I don't think I can.' That kiss went through her mind. He was certainly still attracted to her, he'd said as much, but Annabelle had always assumed that he'd stopped loving her when he'd left their home. So even if she cared about him, would it matter?

'Maybe that gala will give you the strength to do just that. If it does, then you have a decision to make. And this time you'd better act on it, one way or the other. Unless you're content to remain in stasis for the rest of your life.'

No. Of that Annabelle was sure. She had been locked in a kind of suspended animation for three years now. It was time to move forward.

Even if that meant leaving Max behind. For ever.

CHAPTER SEVEN

MAX SAT ON the stairs, listening to his parents argue.

Again.

For the first time in his fifteen years he was scared about what might happen to him. Would they leave him here by himself?

'I am going on that cruise, whether you come with me or not.'

His dad's angry voice carried easily, just as it always did. Even if Max had been upstairs in his room, he would have heard those words.

'And what about Maxwell?'

'What about him? If you're worried, ask your aunt Vanessa to come and stay with him. I'm sure she'll be happy to lounge around the pool and do nothing.'

'Doug, that's not fair.'

'What's not fair about it? I consider it an equitable trade. I worked hard for this bonus, and I'm not going to give it up.'

There was a pause, and he held his breath as he waited for his mother's answer. 'Okay, I'll ask her. But we can't keep doing this. Vanessa has accused me more than once of not wanting him.'

'Just ask her.'

No reassurance that his parents actually did want him. They never took him on any of their so-called trips.

His hands tightened into fists as they rested on his knees. Then he slowly got up from his spot and crept back up the stairs. To pretend he didn't care.

Except when he got to his room and opened the door there was someone already in there. A woman... crouched on the floor beside his bed, crying. She looked up. Blue eyes met his.

Annabelle!

Suddenly he was grown up and his childhood bedroom morphed into the bathroom of their London flat. Anna held a small plastic stick in one hand, her eyes red and swollen. When he went to kneel down beside her to comfort her, she floated away. Through the door. Down the stairs, where everything was now eerily quiet. No matter how hard he tried to reach her, she kept sliding further and further away, until she was a tiny blip on the horizon. Then poof! *She was gone. Leaving him all alone. Just as his parents had.*

Max's eyes popped open and encountered darkness. He blinked a couple of times, a hand going to his chest, which was slick with sweat.

God. A dream.

He sat up and shoved the covers down, swinging his legs over the side of the bed.

Well, hell!

He didn't need a dream to tell him what he already knew.

But maybe his subconscious had needed to send

him a clear and pointed message about going to that Christmas party with Anna: that he needed to tread very, very carefully.

Baby Hope was still holding her own. And he'd finally shaken off the remnants of that dream he'd had that morning.

He'd also received some positive news about the accident victims they'd treated a couple of days ago. Several of the patients had already been released to go home, and the rest of them were expected to recover. Sarah, who'd been one of the most badly injured, might have to have surgery to stabilise the sternal fracture. But everyone was hopeful that she'd heal up without any lasting damage.

That was some very good news.

He hadn't seen Annabelle yet this morning. Which was another good thing.

Right, Max. Just because you've passed the entrance to the hospital multiple times since your arrival this morning, means nothing.

A thought hit him. Maybe she'd come down with the same virus that had plagued other hospital staff.

It didn't seem likely. A few of those had trickled back to work today, and no one else had called in sick. At least, that was what one of the nurses had told him. So it seemed that the outbreak might be dying down. A good thing too. The closer they got to Christmas, the more patients they'd probably be seeing. Everywhere he looked, there were doctors and nurses whose faces appeared haggard and tired.

Frayed nerves were evident everywhere, including the operating room this morning, where he'd had to repair a hole in a young patient's heart. The anaesthetist had snapped at a nurse who'd only been trying to do her job. He'd apologised immediately afterward, but the woman had thrown him an irritated glance, muttering under her breath. It was probably a good thing that he'd understood none of the words.

All of a sudden, Annabelle came hurrying down the hall, a red coat still belted tightly around her waist. When she caught sight of him and then glanced guiltily at the clock to his right, one side of his mouth cranked up in spite of himself. She was late.

The Annabelle he knew was never late. Ever.

He moved a few steps towards her. 'Get held up, did you?'

'I'm only six minutes late.'

For Anna, that was an eternity. He held up his hands to ward off any other angry words. 'Hey, I was only asking a friendly question.'

'Sorry, Max. It's just been quite a day already.'

'Yes, it has.' His had started off with that damned nightmare, followed by a surgery at five o'clock this morning. Fortunately, the procedure had been pretty straightforward, and he'd been out of the surgical suite an hour later.

Her glance strayed to his face. 'What time did you get here?'

'A few hours ago.'

'I thought shift changes were at eight.' Her fingers went to her belt, quickly undoing the knot.

He nodded. 'They are. I had an emergency to see to, so I came in early.'

Her breath caught with an audible sound, her hands stopping all movement. 'Hope?'

'No, another surgery. It was urgent, but it came out fine.'

'I'm so glad.' She finished shifting out of her jacket and stepped into her office, where she hung the garment on the back of the door. Her lanyard was already hanging on a cord around her neck. 'Have you been to see Hope yet?'

'Once. She's still stable. I was just getting ready to check on her again. Care to join me?'

'Yes. I was halfway afraid something would go terribly wrong during the night.'

A cold hand gripped his heart. It had indeed. He shook off the thought.

'I would have called you, if something involving Hope had come up.'

She nodded. 'Thank you.'

'So your day has already been tough?'

'Kind of. I've been on the second floor.'

'Oncology?' Some kind of eerie premonition whispered through his veins.

'Yes.' Her voice quavered slightly. 'We found out this morning that one of my nephews has been diagnosed with a brain tumour. I went to ask Dr Terrill a few questions about the type and prognosis. Just so I could hear first-hand what he might be facing.'

He hadn't yet met any of the doctors or nurses on the second floor, as each area was kind of insulated from each other. 'I'm sorry, Anna. Who is it?'

'It's Nate. Jessica's son…the one I mentioned.'

A band tightened around his chest. 'How old is he?'

'Just two.'

Jessica, the youngest of Annabelle's sisters, had already had a couple of children by the time he'd left. In fact, the huge size of Anna's family was one of the things that had created such pressure on her to have children of her own. She would never admit it, but with each new niece or nephew the shadows in his wife's eyes had grown. She'd wanted so desperately what her sisters had…what her parents had had. If the family hadn't been so close, it might not have mattered quite so much. But they were—and it did.

He wanted to ask what Dr Terrill had said, but, at two years of age, the tumour had to be something that didn't take years to emerge.

'Jessica noticed he wasn't keeping up with his peers on the growth charts like he should. And recently he'd been complaining that his head hurt. So they ran a series of tests.'

Headaches could be benign or they could signal something deadly. 'Do they have the results?'

Annabelle could say it was none of his business. And it wasn't. Not any more. He'd lost the right to know anything about her family when he'd walked out of their home and flown to Africa.

'A craniopharyngioma tumour. They're in discussing treatment options with their doctor today.'

He went through the catalogue in his head, searching for the name.

Found it.

Craniopharyngiomas were normally benign. But even though they didn't typically spread outside the original area, they could still be difficult to reach and treat.

'Why don't you get someone to cover you for a few hours, so you can be on hand if they need you? Or maybe you should go to London early.'

That might solve his dilemma about the Christmas party.

'I need to work. And Mum and Dad are there with Jessica and her husband. At this point there are too many people. Too many opinions.'

Kind of like with Annabelle's in-vitro procedures. There had always been someone in her family stepping up with an opinion on this or that. It hadn't bothered him at first, but as things had continued to go downhill Max had come to wish they would just mind their own business. A ridiculous mind-set, considering Max himself had hoped to have a family as large and connected as Annabelle's had been—and evidently still was.

'If you'd rather not go to the party—'

'I want to go. It'll give me a chance to run by and check in on Nate while I'm in London.'

'Of course.'

Well, if fate didn't want to help him, he was stuck. Besides, he didn't blame her for wanting to go, if it meant making a side trip to see them. It was doubtful her family would want him there, though. Not with everything that had happened. But he could think about that later.

He decided to change the subject. 'Are you ready to go see Hope?'

'Yes, just let me check in and make sure there are no other urgent cases I need to attend to.'

Five minutes later, they were in Hope's room, gowned and gloved to minimise exposure to pathogens that could put the tiny girl in danger. She was still sedated, still intubated. But her colour was good, no more cyanosis. Something inside Max relaxed.

Her atrial fibrillation hadn't returned after the scare yesterday, and her new heart was beating with gusto.

The empty chair next to the baby's incubator made a few muscles tense all over again. This child would never have a concerned loved one sitting beside her to give her extra love and care. At least not her mum.

As if Annabelle knew what he was thinking, she lowered herself into that seat, her gaze on the baby inside. She murmured something that he couldn't hear and then slid her hand through one of the openings of the special care cot. She stroked the baby's hair, cooing to her in a quiet voice. More muscles went on high alert.

Had she done this for each of her nieces and nephews? The fact that she would never hold a child she'd given birth to made him sad. And angry. Sometimes the world was just cruel, when you thought about it. Here was a woman who could give unlimited amounts of love to a child, and she couldn't have one.

But life wasn't fair. There were wars and starving children and terrible destructive forces of nature that laid waste to whole communities.

Annabelle glanced up at him. 'The difference between how she looked thirty-six hours ago and right now are like day and night.'

He remembered. He also remembered how they'd almost lost her an hour after her surgery.

But this tiny tyke was a fighter, just as Anna had said she was. She wanted to live. Her body had fought hard, almost as if she'd known that if she held on long enough, relief would come.

And it had.

Maybe life was sometimes fair after all.

He laid a hand on top of the incubator. 'And so far she's handling all of this like a champ.'

'Where will she go after this?'

The question wasn't aimed at him. But he felt a need to answer it anyway. 'I'm sure there are a lot of people who would take Hope in a second. She'll get a lot of love.'

'I hope so.'

'There's no chance that her mum will come back and want her later?'

'It's been over two weeks. She knew that Hope was born with a heart defect. There's always a chance, but if she'd wanted to find her, surely she would have come back to the hospital by now?'

He nodded. 'What do social services say?'

'That if her mum doesn't return, she'll be placed in a foster home and then put up for adoption.'

That brought up another point. He took his hand off the cot. 'You've never thought again about adopting?'

That had been another sticky subject towards the end of their marriage. She'd refused to even entertain the idea.

'My sister's experience made me afraid of going that route. But after spending so much time with Hope, I'm more open to it than I was in the past. Not every case ends in heartache, like Mallory's did. I don't know if I'd be able to adopt Hope, but surely they would let me consider another child with special needs. I love my nieces and nephews, but...' She stopped as if remembering that she had a very ill nephew.

She withdrew her hand, staring into the special care cot.

'But it's not the same. I get it.' He wanted to make sure she knew that there was nothing wrong with wanting someone of your own to love. He'd once felt that way about Anna. That she made his life complete in a way nothing else could, not even his work in Africa, as worthy as that might be. But in the end, his dream had been right about one thing: she hadn't wanted him to stay.

'You've probably seen plenty of needy children in Africa.'

'Yes. There are some incredible needs on that continent. I've sometimes wished...' He'd sometimes wished he could give a couple of kids a stable home without poverty or fear, but with the way his parents had been... Well, it wasn't something he saw himself tackling on his own.

Then there was the unfinished business with Annabelle. It didn't lend itself to making a new start. Especially when the previous chapter was still buzzing in the background. It was another thing his dream had got right. Annabelle was out of reach. She had been for a long time. He needed to sign those papers. Only then could he move forward.

He'd been thinking more and more along those lines over the last several days. She was here. His excuse of old was that he wasn't quite sure where to find her. But that no longer held water.

He couldn't have hired a solicitor to track her down back then? Or have gone through her parents?

Probably. But he'd believed if she wanted that divorce badly enough, she would find him.

'You've sometimes wished what?'

'That I could make life better for a child or two.'

She swivelled in her chair, her face turning up to study his. 'You once told me you no longer wanted children.'

Yes, he had. After her last miscarriage, he'd told her that to protect her health and to save what was evidently unsalvageable: their marriage. So he'd told a lie. Except when he'd said the words, they hadn't been a lie. He'd just wanted it all to stop.

And it had.

'I was tired of all the hoops we had to leap through. Of all of the disappointment.'

'I'm so sorry, Max.' Her face went from looking up at him as if trying to understand to bending down to stare at the floor.

What the hell?

Realising she might have misunderstood his words, he knelt down beside her in a hurry, taking her chin and forcing her to look at him. 'I wasn't disappointed *in* you, Anna. I was disappointed *for* you. For both of us. I wanted to be able to snap my fingers and make everything right, and when I couldn't... It just wore me down, made me feel helpless in a way I'd never felt before.'

'Like Jessica must feel right now with Nate.' Her eyes swam with moisture, although none of it spilled over the lower rim of her eyelids.

'She has a great support network in you and the rest of the family.' Something Max hadn't felt as if he'd given to Annabelle. He'd withdrawn more and more of his emotional support, afraid to get attached to a foetus that would never see the light of day. And towards the end, that was what he'd started thinking of them as. Foetuses and not babies. And he'd damned himself each time he'd used that term.

'She does. Her husband has been her rock as well.'

Unlike him? His jaw tightened, teeth clenching together in an effort to keep from apologising for something that he couldn't change.

Her eyes focused on him. And then her hand went to his cheek. 'Don't. I wasn't accusing you of not being there, Max. I was the one who pulled away. You did what you could.'

'It wasn't enough.'

Her lashes fluttered as her lids closed and her hand fell back to her side. 'Nothing would have been enough. I was a mess back then. I'm stronger now.'

She was. He saw it in the way she cared for Baby Hope and the rest of her patients. She'd called Jessica's husband a rock. She could have been describing herself.

'You were always strong. They were just difficult days.'

Baby Hope stirred in her cot, one of her arms jerking to the side until her fingers were pressed against the clear acrylic of the incubator. Annabelle touched her index finger to the barrier separating her from the baby. 'This is the strong one. I'm envisioning a bright future for her.'

'She has a great chance.'

Annabelle sucked down a deep breath and let it out in a rush. 'Thank you for all you did to help her.'

'She did most of the work. She stuck around until we could find a donor heart.'

'Yes, she did.'

Max stood up and held out his hand, the ominous

warning of his dream fading slightly. 'Let's let her get some rest.'

'Good idea. I need to get to work and then check in with my sister.' She took his hand, their gloves preventing them from feeling each other's skin, but it was still intimate, her grip returning his. He found himself continuing to hold her hand for several seconds longer than necessary. 'You'll let me know if there's any change in her condition, won't you?'

'You know I will.' He paused, not sure how she would feel about what he was about to say. 'You'll let me know about Nate, won't you? I know I've never met him, but I care about your family.'

He had loved her parents and siblings, had liked seeing what it was like to be part of a large and caring family. It had had its downsides as well, the births of her nieces and nephews seeming to increase Annabelle's anguish over her own lack of having babies, but that hadn't been anyone's fault. As upset as he'd been at times over what he'd seen as meddling, he was grateful her family had been there to give her the support he'd never had as a child and couldn't seem to manage as an adult.

'I will. And thank you.'

With that, Annabelle peeled off her gloves, threw them in the rubbish bin, and went out of the door.

'You go to the party, honey.'

Annabelle clenched her phone just a little tighter. 'Are you sure, Mum? I can spend the night there with you instead.'

'Don't do that. Nate is fine. He's resting comfortably right now.'

'And Jessie and Walter?' Her sister had to be frantic with worry. With a husband who travelled five days a week, it couldn't be easy to deal with a child's health crisis while his father worked to make a decent living.

'Walter is staying home this week. They're setting up timetables with their team of doctors. It looks like Nate's prognosis is better than it could have been. The tumour is not malignant, and they're hopeful they can get all of it with surgery.'

Even though it wasn't malignant, meaning it wouldn't spread wildly through Nate's body, it could still regrow, if they didn't get absolutely every piece of it when they operated. But resecting a tumour and differentiating between tumour cells and healthy tissue was one of the hardest jobs a surgeon had. At least with Baby Hope's surgery, once the transplant was done, there was no growth of foreign tissue to contend with. There were other problems that could arise, yes, like her a-fib, but cells of the old heart wouldn't hang around and cause trouble later. Once it was out of the body, it was gone for good.

She hadn't told her mum yet that Max was working at her hospital or that he was the one she was going to the party with. Somehow she needed to break the news to her. But she wasn't sure if she should do it now, with the worry of Nate hanging over her head. The last thing her mother needed was to lose sleep over another of her children. Her family had been shocked—and horrified—when they'd heard that she and Max had separated. So she had no idea how her mum would react. She'd probably be thrilled...and hopeful. Something else Annabelle didn't want her family being. She and Max were not getting back together.

'Who are you going with? Ella?'

Oh, great. Here it came.

'No. Not Ella.' She'd better just get it over with. 'I'm actually going with Max.'

There was a pause. A long one. Annabelle could practically hear the air between their two phones vibrating.

'Mum? Are you there?'

'I'm here.' Another hesitation. 'I didn't know he was back in England.'

'He came back a week ago.' She bit her lip. This was turning out to be harder than she'd expected.

'Okay, then. I didn't know you'd been in contact with him.'

Oh, yes. Much harder.

'By coincidence, he's come to work at the same hospital as I am, here in Cheltenham.' Before her mother could jump to conclusions, she hurried to finish. 'He wound up here quite by accident. He's taking another surgeon's place while she goes on maternity leave.'

'You're positive he didn't know you were there?'

And there was that note of hopefulness she'd been hoping to avoid.

'Yes, I'm absolutely positive.'

'I wonder…' Her mother let whatever she was going to say trail off into nothing. Then she came back. 'Why don't you and Max come to London a little earlier? We're just getting ready to put up the tree and decorate it. You didn't help us put on the ornaments last year, and you know everyone would love to have you there. And Max, of course. Nate… Well, he would love it.'

Oh, Lord, how was she going to get out of this? She'd had no idea her mother would suggest she come over and help decorate the tree. Especially not with her ex in tow.

'I'm not sure Max will want to—'

'It certainly can't hurt to ask. And if he doesn't want to join us, he can just pick you up at the house later and off you'll go to the party.' Another pause, quicker this time. 'What kind of party did you say it was?'

'A Doctors Without Borders fundraiser.'

'Isn't that who Max left—I mean worked with?'

Her mum was right. Annabelle might have been the one to ask him to leave, but Doctors Without Borders had been Max's escape route. They had used to talk about going and working together. But in the end, Max had gone alone.

'Yes.'

'Is he going back with them once he's finished his contract at the hospital?'

Something in Annabelle's stomach twisted until it hurt. No, that had been her, clenching her abs until they shook. She'd asked him that same question at the pub. 'I don't know what his plans are after that, Mum.'

'So this might be our last chance to see him for a while?' Her mum called something to her father, but she couldn't hear what it was. Great. She could only hope that she wasn't telling him that Max was back and that it would be good to have the family together again.

Her mum knew that Max had left, but she'd never

told her that she'd served him with divorce papers soon afterwards. It had been a painful time in her life and she'd kept most of it to herself. And then as time had gone on and Max hadn't sent his portion of the paperwork back, it was as if Annabelle had put it to the back of her mind like a bad dream that had happened once and was then forgotten.

This probably wasn't a good time to bring up the fact that a reconciliation was highly unlikely. Max had given no indication that he wanted to get back together with her. In fact, even when he'd towed her from the restaurant and kissed her in the park, he'd referred to what was going on between them as 'the spark'. Physical attraction. People could be attracted to each other without it going any deeper than that.

'I'll ask him. But don't be disappointed if he'd rather not come, Mum.'

'I won't. But you'll come, even if he chooses not to, won't you?'

There was no way she was going to be able to get out of it. And actually she didn't want to. This was a family tradition that she'd participated in every year except for the last one, when she'd just been getting situated at Teddy's and had been too busy with all the changes to be able to take a train home to London. With Nate's diagnosis, though, she had to go. 'I'll be there, Mum, but I probably won't be able to stay for dinner.'

'Of course not. Tell Max I'm looking forward to seeing him.'

Okay. Hadn't she just explained that he might not want to come?

She would invite him. And then let him decide

what he wanted to do. And if he agreed to go? Well, she'd have to decide how to tell him that her family wasn't privy to one small detail of their relationship: that not only had she asked him to leave, but she'd also asked him for a divorce. And the only thing lacking to make that happen…was Max's signature on a piece of paper.

'You what?'

Sitting in front of Annabelle's mum and dad's house, Max wasn't sure what on earth had possessed him to say yes to this crazy side trip. Because he was suddenly having second thoughts.

Especially now.

'You didn't tell them we're divorcing?' The words tasted bitter as he said them, but how could she have neglected to tell her parents that their marriage was over, and that it had been her choice?

Surely they'd realised, when he'd never come home…

'There just never seemed to be a good time to mention it. Someone was always being born. And then my aunt Meredith passed away a year and a half ago. My dad retired six months after that. It's just been—'

'Life as usual in the Brookes' household.' He remembered well how frenetic and chaotic things got, with lots of laughter and some tears. It had taken him a while to get used to the noise—and there was a lot of it—but the love they had for each other had won him over. Especially when they had drawn him into the fold as if he'd always been a part of their close-knit group. It was what he'd always wanted, but never had. He'd been in heaven. While it lasted.

'Please don't be angry. I'll tell them eventually. Probably not tonight, since it's Christmas time, and with Nate's illness…'

'It's okay. Maybe it's easier this way. They did know we weren't living together any more.'

'They knew we'd separated, yes, of course. I left our flat and came home before moving to the Cotswolds.'

'Yes, the flat…' He almost laughed. Well, he guessed they were even, then, because there was something he hadn't told her either. That he hadn't sold the flat once she'd moved out of it, even though his monthly cleaning lady had called him to let him know Annabelle was moving home and that she'd said he could do what he wished to with the flat. Those words had hit him right in the gut. Somehow he'd never been able to picture her moving out of the place they'd turned into a home. He'd assumed he would sign the place over to her once the paperwork was finalised. But then she'd moved out. And the paperwork had never been signed.

Why was that?

'What about it?' Annabelle turned to him, her discomfiture turning to curiosity.

'We still have it, actually.'

Her head cocked. 'Still have it?'

'I never got around to selling it.'

Her indrawn breath was sharp inside the space of his small sports car. 'But why?'

That was a question he wasn't going to examine too closely right now. 'I was overseas on and off and it got pushed to a back burner. As time went on, well, it just never happened.'

'Who's living there?'

'No one. I never sublet it. Suzanne cleans it once a month, just like always. When repairs are needed, her husband comes over and does them.' He shrugged. 'I halfway thought maybe I'd return to London at some point.'

Except every time he'd got close to thinking about his home city, he somehow hadn't been able to bring himself to come back and visit. Instead, he'd landed in several different cities in between his stints with Doctors Without Borders.

Annabelle smiled and it lit up the inside of the car. 'I'm glad. I loved that place.'

'So did I.' Well, they were going to look awfully out of place at a tree-decorating party with their fancy clothes on. But she'd seemed so uncomfortable when she'd relayed her mother's request that he hadn't wanted to make her feel even worse—or have to go back to her mum and tell her that he'd refused to take part. That would have been churlish of him. At least now he knew why the invitation had been extended. If they'd been divorced, Max was pretty sure he'd have been persona non grata in this particular family, even if he hadn't been the one to initiate it.

Climbing out of the car, he went around to Annabelle's side and opened it for her. Out she stepped, a vision in red. Until she tried to move to the side so he could close the door and tripped over the hem of her gown, careening sideways. He grabbed her around the waist, his fingers sliding across the bare skin of her back as he did so.

Her momentum kept her moving and her arms

went around his neck in an effort to regain her footing. 'Oh! Max, I'm so sorry...'

Just then the front door to the house opened, and people poured out of the opening, catching them tangled together.

Not good.

Because it didn't look as if he'd just been saving her from a fall. It looked as if they were having a private moment.

Not hardly.

Annabelle saw them at the same time as he did and quickly pulled back. So fast that she almost flung herself off balance all over again. He kept hold of her for a second or two longer to make sure she had her footing. Then they were surrounded by her family, and Annabelle was hugging various adults and squatting down to squeeze little ones of all sizes. He couldn't prevent a smile. This was the Annabelle he remembered, uncaring of whether or not her dress got dusty. The people she loved always came first.

Just as he once had.

He'd forgotten that in all of the unhappy moments that had passed between them. These had been good times. Happy times. And...he missed them.

George Brookes came around and extended his hand. 'Good to see you, Maxwell.' His booming voice and formal use of his name was just like old times as well. There wasn't a hint of recrimination on the man's face. Or in his attitude. Just a father welcoming his son-in-law for a typical visit.

Max squeezed his hand, reaching over to give him a man's quick embrace, then gave himself over to greeting the family he'd once been a part of.

Bittersweet. He shouldn't have come. And yet he was very glad he had.

Jessica came up to hug him. He held her shoulders and looked into her face. 'How are you and Walter holding up?'

Her chin wobbled precariously, but she didn't start crying. 'We're doing better now that you and Annie are home.'

Home.

Yes, he'd once considered this the home his childhood abode never was. And the Brookeses had been the family he no longer had. Despite his own parents' faults, he suddenly missed them. Regretted never once visiting their graves.

Once he'd lost the right to be a part of Annabelle's family, the children of Africa had become his family. And they had loved more freely and with more joy than anything he'd ever seen. They'd taught him a lot about unconditional love.

Something he'd never really given to anyone. Even Anna. He'd always held something back, afraid of being hurt. And in the end, he'd demanded she give up something she dearly wanted.

He'd been wrong in that. Even though he'd told himself time and time again that it had been to save Annabelle the pain of future miscarriages, maybe he'd been more interested in saving himself.

He didn't have time to think about it for long, though, because he was soon whisked back into the bosom of a family he'd dearly missed, sitting on the arm of the sofa while Annabelle and her sisters held up ornament after ornament, reminiscing about where each had come from. Some were home-made. Some were fancy and expensive. But each held some kind of special meaning to this family.

Anna was gorgeous in her flowing red gown. Off the shoulder, but with some loose straps that draped over her upper arms, it fitted her perfectly, the snug top giving way to a full loose skirt that swished with every twitch of her hips. And they twitched a lot. Every once in a while she threw him a smile that was more carefree than any he'd seen from her in a long, long time. He knew that smile. She'd once worn it almost constantly. When he'd come home from work. When they'd gazed at each other across the dinner table. When they'd made love deep into the night...

His throat tightened, and he dipped a finger beneath his bow tie in an effort to give himself a little more room to breathe, even though he knew that wasn't the problem. In his hands, Max held the long white gloves Anna planned on wearing to the party, but had taken off so she wouldn't drop and break any ornaments. In the back of all their minds was Nate and his diagnosis, but when Max looked at the little blond boy, he was smiling and laughing on the floor as he played with his siblings and cousins. Suddenly Max wished he could commit this scene to memory so that he would never forget this moment.

When Nate got up from his place on the floor and came to stand in front of him, looking at him with curious eyes, the tightness in his throat increased.

'Where's my ball?'

He blinked. Max wasn't sure why the boy was asking him, but he was not about to refuse him. 'I don't know.'

'You help find?'

'Sure.' Getting to his feet, he tucked Anna's gloves into his pocket and held out a hand to the little boy. As he did, his doctor's mind took in the subtle signs of illness. Nate's small stature, the frailness of his fingers beneath Max's. Jessica sent him a look with raised brows.

'He's looking for his ball?' Max had to raise his voice to be heard.

'It's in the basket by the far wall in the dining room.' Jessica glanced at her son, the raw emotion in her eyes unmistakable. 'Thanks, Max.'

'Not a problem.'

Together he and the boy made their way into the dining room. It looked the same as it always had, polished cherry table laid with glistening china and silver for the meal they would be having later. Gloria had never been worried about breakage, even with such a large and active family. His own mum had rarely set out the good china.

'There's the basket, Nate. Let's see if Mum was right.'

A white wicker chest was pushed against a wall, a large contingent of photographs flowing up and around it until they filled the space with black and white images.

Above the pictures ornate black letters gave a message to all who dined there.

In Stormy Seas,
Family Is A Sheltered Cove.

And it was. This family represented safety. Too many faces to count, but there must have been thirty frames, each telling a story. The birth of a child. The winning of trophies. The weddings of each of the girls. Jessica and Walter, Paula and Mark, Mallory and Stewart…

No. His heart caught on a stuttered beat, and he couldn't stop himself from moving closer. Annabelle and Max.

That day was pinned in his memory, superseding even his most recent ones. Anna, fresh from his kiss, was staring up at him with eyes filled with love. And he was… He had his arm wrapped around her waist as if he was afraid she might wander away from him if he didn't keep her close.

And she had. They'd both wandered.

Annabelle said she hadn't told her parents about the divorce. He wasn't sure if Gloria just hadn't had a picture to replace this one with, or if she'd left it up in hopes that one day he and her daughter might mend their fences and get back together.

Little did she know that those fences had been irrevocably broken. His gaze moved over the rest of the pictures. There were no others of them. Maybe because they hadn't had all that much to celebrate during their marriage.

Part of that was his fault. They'd been fixated on having a baby for so long, they'd never made time to look at the other things they'd shared.

A small hand tugged on his. 'My ball? In basket.'

That was right. He'd forgotten about Nate and his ball. Forcing the lump in his throat to shift to the side, he gave the child a smile. 'Let's see if it's where Mum said it was.'

He opened the basket to find children's toys of

every shape and size. Gloria must keep them for all of the grandkids to play with while they visited. And all of Annabelle's sisters now had children. Except for her.

He glanced through the doorway to see her still helping to decorate the tree, laughing at something someone had said. She was truly beautiful. Inside and out.

She seemed to have made her peace with not having kids. At least from what he could tell. So maybe it was time for him to accept that as well and start finding the joy in life. Turning back to his task, he found Nate trying to lean over the basket to get a green spongy ball the size of a football. 'Is that it, buddy?'

Grabbing the object from the chest, he handed it to Nate, who let go of his hand and gripped the item to his chest. 'Ball!'

'I guess we got the right one. Watch your fingers.' He carefully lowered the lid and latched it to keep small hands from getting pinched. They made their way back to the room and Nate went straight to Jessica, showing her his prize.

'Wonderful. You've found it!' She glanced up at Max with a mouthed, 'Thank you.'

He gave her a nod in return. Annabelle handed an ornament to her dad, who still stood ramrod straight and tall, probably from his days in the military. He gave her a quick hug and took the item, stretching up to put it on the very top of the tree. The man then turned towards the rest of the people assembled. 'Shall we light it before Annie and Max have to leave?'

A roared 'Yes!' went up from all the kids, making the adults smile. He glanced at his watch. Seven-thirty. The gala started in half an hour, so they did need to leave soon, since the party was on the other side of the city.

Annabelle came over to stand beside him.

With the flick of a switch all the lights in the living room went off, leaving them in darkness. An affected *'oooooh'* went up from the people gathered there.

Max stood there, the urge to put his arm around Anna's waist almost irresistible. The way he'd done in years past. He fought it for a moment or two, then gave up. His contract wasn't for ever. Once Sienna came back from maternity leave, he would be on his way again. So why not do this while he still could?

He slid his hand across the small of her back, the warm bare skin just above the edge of the fabric brushing against his thumb. Curving his fingers around the side of her waist, he was surprised when she reciprocated, her arm gliding around his back, leaning into him slightly as she smiled at something else her father was saying.

Then, just as suddenly as the overhead lights had been turned off, another set of lights flicked on. Swathed in layers of tiny glowing bulbs, the Christmas tree lit up the whole room like magic.

Not 'like' magic. It *was* magic. The tree. The night. The family. It was as if he'd never left three years ago. He didn't know whether to be glad or horrified. Had he not moved forward even a little?

No, he'd done nothing to forge a life without Anna. But he needed to either do just that, or...

Or try to do something to make things right between them.

Only, Max wasn't sure that was a good idea. They'd

wounded each other without even trying. Wouldn't they just take up where they'd left off and do it all over again, if given half a chance? Wouldn't she ask him to leave once again?

He didn't know. All he knew was that he wanted to live here in this moment. Surrounded by Annabelle's family and the life and love they shared between them.

Except they needed to leave, if they were going to make it to the gala in time.

As if reading his thoughts, Annabelle looked up at him, her eyes shining with a strange glow that was probably due to the lights on the tree. 'We should go.'

'Are you sure you don't want to stay here and eat with your family?'

She lifted a handful of the fabric of her dress. 'We got all dressed up, so let's just enjoy the night. Okay? No expectations. No preconceived ideas.'

That shocked him. Annabelle was by nature a rigid planner. The attempts to get pregnant had been accomplished with clinical precision—the spontaneity wiped out more and more with each new wave of treatment.

If she hadn't just said those last words, he would have assumed she was following through with what they'd planned to do. But something about the way she said it…

Well, if that was what she wanted, who was Max to disagree? And maybe it was the twinkle lights messing with some rational part of his brain, or the fact that her dress clung in all the right places, but he suddenly wanted to have Annabelle all to himself.

CHAPTER EIGHT

THE GALA HAD some twinkle lights of its own. Everywhere she looked there were signs of Christmas. From the garland-draped refreshment tables to the large ornate tree in the corner, filled with presents. Those boxes, mostly filled with toys and hygiene supplies, would make their way to needy kids all over the globe. Max had brought a small gift too, placing it gently under the tree.

'What is it?'

'A couple of toy cars.' He smiled at her. 'Not very practical.'

She smiled back at him, touched by his thoughtfulness. 'Some little boy is going to love it. Especially since it's *not* practical.'

When Max had suggested staying at her parents' house, she'd heard what she thought was a note of yearning in his voice. She'd been so tempted to just fall back into old patterns, but her parents might have started asking some harder questions if they'd stayed for the meal. Questions she didn't have the answers to. Or maybe she simply hadn't wanted to face those answers.

So here she was, with her ex-husband, at a party. And she had no idea what she was going to do about him.

No expectations. Wasn't that what she'd said?

Yes. So she was simply going to enjoy this night. Max was right. She'd worked herself into the ground over the last couple of weeks. Didn't she deserve to just let her hair down and have a little fun? He'd suggested using this time to celebrate Hope's successful surgery, so she would. And maybe she'd even send a wish up to the universe that the baby have a long and happy life.

That was what she'd do. She'd worry about what happened tomorrow when it came.

But for now, they had the whole evening in front of them, and she intended to enjoy it.

'Do you want something to drink?' Max's voice brought her back from wherever she'd gone.

'I'd love a glass of red wine, if they have it.'

'Wait right here. I'll go and see.'

He went off in the direction of the bar where there was quite a large crowd waiting to get something. He'd be up there for a while. She took the opportunity to study her surroundings.

Were all of these people doctors who volunteered with the organisation? Surely not. Some of them must just be donors who were here to pledge their support. Or people like her who simply wanted to know more about what happened in the places those volunteers served.

A leader board hovered over the raised platform to the left. Annabelle assumed they would unveil an amount at the end of the evening. There were also wooden boxes at all of the doors where you could drop in either a pledge card or a one-time donation. She'd gone to do just that when they'd arrived at the building, but Max had stopped her. 'I didn't bring you here for that.'

'I know you didn't.'

She'd wanted to give. Annabelle had often thought of going on one of the medical missions with the organisation, but, once she and Max had separated, the idea had been put on a back burner. Maybe she should rethink that. She glanced at the bar again. He was still waiting so maybe she could find some more information in the meantime.

She took the opportunity to move over to one of the doors where the boxes were, along with some colourful brochures about the organisation. Taking her purse out of her clutch bag, she pulled out several notes and dropped them into the slot of the box in front of her, then she went to peruse the pamphlets.

'What can I help you with?' A voice to her right made her look up.

A man in a tuxedo stood there, hand outstretched. 'I'm Dale Gerrard.' He flashed a set of very white teeth. 'I should warn you that I'm a recruiting agent for Doctors Without Borders. And I'm very good at my job. Are you in the medical profession?'

'I'm a nurse.' She accepted his handshake, although it felt weird doing so with her long white gloves in place.

The man epitomised the meaning of 'tall, dark and handsome.' With raven-black hair and tanned skin, he probably had more than his share of female admirers. He smiled again, giving her hand a slight squeeze before releasing it. 'Have you been on a mission with us before?'

'No. But I've thought about it in the past.'

'Really?' His level of interest went up a couple of notches. 'What stopped you?'

And that was something she wasn't about to tell him. It was too personal. And too painful. She glanced back at the line. Max was still over there. But just as she caught sight of him he suddenly turned, his eyes sweeping the crowd. Probably wondering where she'd gone.

And then he saw her. Just as the man next to her touched her arm to get her attention. Even from this distance she saw Max's brows pull together.

She looked away in a hurry, trying to focus on what the person beside her was saying. He was trying to hand her a clipboard and a pen.

Taking it with fingers that suddenly shook, she tried to corral her emotions. So what if Max had seen her? Surely he didn't think she'd stood around pining for him year after year.

What had started off as an enjoyable evening morphed into something different as a wave of irritation slithered through her innards. They weren't together any more, so Max had no say in her life. None.

Lifting her chin, she focused again on the man next to her. 'Yes, I would love to fill one out.'

'Great. Why don't you come behind the table with me and you can have a seat while you do?'

So Annabelle did just that, following Dale around the edge of the table where there was a line of seats, although no other representatives were there at the moment.

She sat down, suddenly glad to let her shaking legs have a break. Then she ducked her head and did her best to concentrate on the questions on the form, filling them in and hoping that Max didn't storm over here and embarrass her.

He wouldn't.

Her ex had never been a particularly jealous type. And there was no reason for him to start now. Especially since they were no longer a couple.

She was scribbling something in the box of the sixth question when a glass of red wine appeared in front of her. Swallowing hard, she glanced up. How had he got back that fast?

Sure enough, Max was standing in front of the table, taking a sip of whatever amber liquid was in his glass. 'Are you thinking of going on a medical mission?'

'I… Well, I…'

Dale, probably realising something was amiss, smoothly filled in the blanks. 'Annabelle was filling out a form to get more information on what we do.' He glided to his feet and offered his hand. 'I don't know if you remember me. I'm Dale—'

'I remember you. You were in Sudan with me two years back.'

'That's right. I haven't been back in a while. I'm doing recruiting work now.'

Max was gracious enough to smile at the man. 'And you're doing a great job of it, from what I can see.'

Looking from one to the other of them, Dale thanked him, and then said, 'I take it you two know each other.'

'You could say that.' His smile grew. 'Annabelle and I are married.'

'You're…' All the colour leached out of the man's face, leaving it a sickly grey colour. 'I didn't realise…' He glanced down at the form she was filling out. She had indeed put Annabelle Ainsley. She'd thought about using her maiden name, like at the hospital, but Ainsley had just seemed to flow out of the pen of its own accord. She had no idea why, but right now she could clobber Max for making this poor man feel like an idiot. Except a tiny part of her wondered why he'd spoken up and claimed she was his wife. He could have just played it off with a laugh and said that, yes, they knew each other from long ago. It would have been the truth, and it might have saved everyone some embarrassment. And yet he hadn't. He'd spoken the truth, without actually speaking it. Because they had not been husband and wife for almost three years.

Dale recovered, though. 'Well, maybe you can go on the next mission together, then. And since you already know the ropes, I'll let you help Annabelle finish filling out the form. I'm sure you can answer any questions as well as I can.'

With that, the man headed over to another person who was glancing at the literature, engaging him in conversation.

'Why did you do that?' She peered up at him.

'He's a flirt. I was trying to save you from being hit on.'

'Maybe I wanted to be hit on.' That was unfair. She didn't want to be. But she also didn't want Max taking it upon himself to be her rescuer when he hadn't been in her life for almost three years.

His gaze hardened. 'Did you?'

And it now came down to telling the truth. Or lying just to get back at him. 'No. But I could have handled it on my own.'

'I'm sorry, then.'

Annabelle let her emotions cool down. No harm done. And maybe he really had been trying to keep her from landing in an awkward situation. 'It's okay. And thank you for the wine.' She picked up the glass and took a sip.

'Did you really want to fill out a form?'

'I did. I've thought about volunteering in the past, but it never worked out.'

Max came around the table and dropped into the chair that Dale had vacated. 'I remembered us talking about it years ago. I thought you only said that because it was something I wanted to do.'

'It's been in the back of my mind for a while. I just never got around to doing anything about it.'

The sleeve of his tuxedo brushed against her upper arm as he leaned over to see what she'd filled out so far, his warm masculine scent clinging to her senses in a way that no one else's ever had. If Max had been worried about Dale, he needn't have. She had no interest in the other man. While she could recognise that the recruiter was good-looking and charming, she'd felt no spark of attraction.

In fact, those sparks—as Max had called them—had been few and far between. And they'd never been strong enough to make her want to be with someone else. Not while there was still a piece of paper that had gone unsigned for far too long.

Maybe it was time to confront the issue. 'Do you want to sign the divorce papers? Is that why I'm here?'

His gaze darkened, lips thinning slightly. 'I brought you here so you could see what I've been doing with myself for the past three years. If I remember right, you were the one who expressed an interest.'

The soft anger in his voice made her fingers clench on the pen. Okay, so maybe it had been rude to come out and ask, but the subject was like the elephant in the room that no one wanted to talk about.

And evidently, Max still didn't want to talk about it. Something in her heart became lighter, though, at the words. So he wasn't any more anxious than she was to finally close the chapter on their failed relationship.

But why?

Did she really want to sit here and dissect all the possible reasons? Or was she simply going to take another sip of wine and go back to filling out the papers? She lifted the glass to her lips.

A few seconds went by, and then a warm hand touched her arm. 'Hey. I'm sorry. I didn't want to come here alone, and you were the person I chose to bring. Can't that be enough?'

Yes. It could.

She drew in a deep breath and let it out in a whisper of sound. 'I'm sorry. And I wanted to come too. So yes, let's just leave it at that for now, shall we?'

His fingers moved slowly down her arm, along her glove, until his hand covered hers on the table. 'Then as soon as you're finished with that form, will you dance with me?'

Letting her fingers circle his for a brief second, she lifted them with a nod. 'Yes. I'd love to.'

Max's hand slid around her waist and swung her around the room for a second time, the music pulling him into a world where nothing else existed but her touch and the synchronised movements of their bodies as they danced together. It had been ages since he'd held her like this.

It felt good and right, and he wasn't exactly sure why. What he did know was that he didn't want this night to end any time soon.

Maybe it didn't have to.

Annabelle had said she didn't want any expectations or any preconceived ideas.

Had she meant that she didn't want the past to stand in the way of them being together tonight? He had no idea. But if she was willing to just take tonight as it came, then maybe he should be okay with doing the same.

And with her cheek pressed against his left shoulder, he wasn't in a hurry to do anything to change the situation.

He'd been an idiot about Dale being there with her at the table. But the man—a general physician—had somehow charmed his way into more than one bed when they'd served on the medical mission in Sudan that year. The women hadn't complained, but back then Max had been too raw from his own heartache to take kindly to someone jumping from one person to the next.

He'd fielded some veiled invitations of his own from female volunteers, but he hadn't taken any of them up on their offers. In reality, he hadn't wanted anyone. The sting of rejection when Anna had asked him to leave had penetrated deep, leaving no room for anything else but work. In reality, he'd been happy to be alone. It was a condition he was well acquainted with.

And something he didn't want to think about right now.

'Are you okay?' He murmured the words into her hair, breathing deeply and wondering what the hell he was playing at.

'Mmm.'

It wasn't really an answer, but the sound made something come alive in his gut. How long had they been here, anyway?

Not that he wanted to look at his watch. In fact, he didn't want to leave at all. But they couldn't stay here all night, and once they left...

It was over.

'Anna?'

'Yes?'

He paused, trying to figure out what he wanted. 'Are you still okay with spending the night in London?'

Her feet stopped moving for a second. 'Yes. I can stay with my folks if you don't want me at the flat, although I didn't ask Mum if she had room.'

'We can share the flat. I just wasn't sure if you'd decided you wanted to get back to Cheltenham—'

'No. As long as we can check on Hope at some point, I have no plans until my shift starts midday tomorrow.' She eased back to look into his face. 'Unless *you've* changed your mind.'

Not hardly.

But he should have told her he had. Because holding her brought back memories of dancing with her other times, when life was simpler and all that mattered was their love for each other. Seeing that picture on the wall at Anna's parents' house had made all those feelings come back in a rush. He'd been having trouble tamping them down again, but he'd better work out how.

Because, as of now, he and Anna were going to be sharing their flat one last night.

And the memories and feelings that haunted that place were a thousand times more powerful than anything he might have felt as he'd looked at that wall of pictures. His heart thudded heavy in his chest as the music changed, the singer they'd hired shifting to a lower octave, his voice throaty with desire. The mood in the place changed along with it, dancers beginning to hold each other a little closer.

Right on cue, the arms around his neck tightened just a hair, bringing his face closer to hers. And suddenly all he wanted to do was kiss her.

'Anna…'

Her eyes slowly came up and focused on his. He saw the exact same longing in them that he felt in his gut. Tired to hell of fighting what he'd been wanting to do for days, Max lowered his head and pressed his lips to hers.

Nothing was fast enough.

Annabelle's body couldn't keep up with the ricochet of emotions as Max spun her back into his arms the second they were inside the lift at their old flat, heading towards the fourth floor. Thank heavens no one else was in the compartment, because it felt as if she were on fire, and the only one who could quench the blaze was having none of it. He was keeping the flames fanned to inferno-like proportions.

Her gloved fingers gripped the expensive fabric of his tuxedo jacket as she tried desperately to return kiss for kiss…to respond to his murmured words. In the end, all she could do was hang on and pray they reached the flat before the dam totally broke and the camera caught them doing something that could get them arrested.

Ping! Ping!

Finally. The soft sound signalled they had arrived at their destination. The only thing left was to… The doors opened.

'Max.' His name came out as half chuckle, half moan as she tried to tug him to the side. 'We need to get off.'

His fingers tunnelled into her hair, his lips nibbling on the line of her jaw and making her shiver with need. 'And if I don't want to move out of the lift?'

'Then…*ooh!*…then we're going to be stuck riding it for the rest of the night.'

'Bloody hell.' His pained smile put paid to his words, but he stuck a hand between the doors just as they were getting ready to close. 'The image of you "riding it for the rest of the night…"'

They slid into the foyer, a ring of doors lining the fourth floor. She tried to call to mind the number of their flat, but, with her head this fuzzy with need, she was having trouble. 'I don't—'

'Four-oh-three.'

Gripping her hand as if afraid she might try to flee before they made it inside, he came up with a set of keys from one of the pockets of his trousers.

No way. She wasn't about to run.

Somehow Max got the key fitted into the lock and turned it. They practically fell inside the door.

Home!

No, not home. But close enough.

Dumping the keys onto the marble table in the foyer, he navigated through a hallway, switching lights on as he went, towing her behind him. She glanced around as they went through the flat.

It was immaculate. He'd said that Suzanne came once a month to clean. Annabelle didn't even want to think about how much money that added up to over the course of the last couple of years.

The place looked just as she'd left it. Her mum had told her to take the furniture with her to her new flat, but Annabelle hadn't wanted anything to do with the sad remains of their marriage. So she'd just left it all for Max to dispose of. It looked as if he hadn't wanted to be left in charge of that task any more than she had.

Down the hallway, past a bathroom and two guest bedrooms, until they arrived at their old room. Three years later, the brown silk spread still adorned the bed, looking brand-new. It could have been a mausoleum preserving a slice of her life that had been both happy and filled with anguish.

'I can't believe it's all still here.'

That seemed to stop Max for a moment. He looked around as if seeing it all for the first time. 'I haven't been here in ages. I always meant to change things, but...'

He hadn't been able to any more than she had.

'Let's not think about that right now.' She wrapped her arms around his waist, unwilling to ruin what had been building between them ever since they'd come face to face in the corridors of Teddy's. It seemed as if every tick of the clock had been leading to this.

Whatever 'this' was.

He cupped her face in his hands. 'Let's not,' he agreed before moving in to kiss her once more.

Again and again, his lips touched hers until the fire was back and this time there was nothing to hold them back.

Annabelle pushed his tuxedo jacket from his shoulders, moving to catch it when it started to drop to the floor.

'Leave it.' His knuckles dragged up the length of her neck, smoothing along the line of her jaw until he reached her ear. He toyed with one of her chandelier earrings, making it swing on her lobe in a way that made her shudder. He'd always known exactly how to make her melt like a pot of jelly that had been exposed to a heat source.

And he was the ultimate heat source, his body generating temperatures that threatened to scorch her until nothing was left but smouldering embers.

And she was fine with that.

He reached around and found the zipper on her dress—began edging it downward.

'Wait!'

She wasn't sure quite why she said that word, other than the fact that she wasn't wearing a bra under the gown, and if he got her dress off—well, she would be standing there in only her underwear while Max was almost fully clothed.

He evidently misunderstood because he went very still. Too still.

'Max?'

'Do you want me to stop?' He leaned back to look at her face.

'Yes. I mean no.' She shook her head, trying to form her words in a way that wouldn't sound completely off the wall. 'I'm not wearing...um...anything under this. I was hoping to even up the odds a little bit first.'

'You're not wearing *anything*?' He took a step back and dragged a hand through his hair. 'I am very glad I didn't know that while we were out on the dance floor. Or driving over here. Or in the lift.'

'I'm not totally naked. There was just no way to wear a bra with the back of the dress the way it is.'

He moved in again, his fingers trailing up the length of her spine and then walking back down it. 'Very glad I didn't know that, either. But now that I do...' His fingers again reached for the zipper and tugged it down, while Annabelle scrambled to hold up the front of her dress.

'What happened to evening up the odds?'

'I kind of like the odds the way they are.'

'You mean when they're in your favour?'

Max grinned at her but took a step back and began undoing the knot of his bow tie. 'You want even? You've got it.'

Not fair!

'But I wanted to do that.'

'It's much safer this way.' He pulled the tie through

the starched white collar of his shirt and let it drop on top of his jacket.

'Safer for whom?'

'For me. And for you.' His fingers went to the first button of the shirt.

This time she groaned. Then a thought came to her. He'd done this on purpose. If she was holding up the front of her dress, she wouldn't be able to touch him, which meant...

That the thought of her doing so was making him as crazy as he was making her.

Well, two can play at that game, Max Ainsley!

'Oh, Max...' She let his name play over her tongue.

His hands stopped where they were, his brows coming together.

With what she hoped was a saucy smile, she let go of her dress, glad when it whispered down her body and pooled at her feet, instead of just staying put and forcing her to awkwardly push it to the ground.

His reaction was more than worth it. A blast of profanity-laced air hissed from his mouth as he stood there and stared. And when she started to move a step forward, he lurched backwards.

Annabelle was glad she'd decided to wear her laciest underwear ever, the red matching her dress to a tee. They rode high up on her hips and, while not quite a thong, they'd been advertised as Brazilian cut, which meant there was only a narrow band of fabric that covered her behind.

She peeled one of her gloves off in a long smooth move, and then the other, letting each of them land on top of her dress. 'Now the odds are even, don't you think?' She moved forward again, and this time

Max stayed put. Maybe he was just incapable of thought right now, which had been her exact intent. She pressed her palms against his chest, gratified to feel the pounding of his heart beneath her touch. 'Let me help you with those buttons, since you seem to be having trouble.'

He still didn't say anything as she somehow managed to flip open one white button after another, until she reached the one at the top of his cummerbund. Pressing herself against his chest and gratified to hear yet another gust of air above her head, she reached around him to find the fastening at the back that held the wide satin band in place. It too hit the floor.

Evidently, Max had had all he could take, because his hands wrapped around her upper arms and eased her away from him. 'You're a witch, you know that?'

'Mmm-hmm. Be careful, or I might cast an evil spell on you.'

'A spell? Yes. I think you already have.' He swooped her up into his arms and dumped her in the middle of the bed, the brown silk rippling out from her landing spot. 'Although whether it's evil or not is yet to be seen.'

Max backed up several paces and made short work of the rest of his buttons, undoing the fastening on the front of his black trousers. And this time it was Annabelle who got to enjoy the show, as his strong chest appeared along with those taut abs. Off came his shoes and black socks.

The man made her mouth water. Even his feet were sexy.

Then he hesitated, and her attention shot back to his face.

'What are you doing?'

His smile this time was a bit forced, the lopsided gesture she loved so much tipped a little lower than normal. 'I'm trying to hold it together.'

Annabelle's relieved sigh was full of pure joy. He wasn't having second thoughts. He wanted this just as much as she did. 'Then why don't you come over here and let me hold it for a while?'

'Did I call you a witch yet?' His laughter came out sounding choked, but at least his voice had lost that weird edge he'd had moments earlier.

'Yes.' She leaned up on one elbow and crooked a finger at him. 'Time to stop stalling and let me help you finish.'

'That's exactly what I'm afraid of, Anna: that you'll help me finish before I'm ready.'

'Hmm...we can take care of that on the next round.'

'Next?' He came forward until he was close enough for her to go into action. She sat up and scooted her butt to the edge of the bed until he stood between her thighs.

'Yes, next.' She said the word with conviction, reaching again for his waistband. This time the zipper went down, and he made no effort to stop her. Pushing his trousers down his legs, she let him kick them out of the way. 'And now, Maxwell Ainsley, we're finally even.'

They both still had their underwear on.

'You first, then.' Max leaned over her, planting his hands on the bed on either side of her thighs, but he made no effort to strip her bare. Instead, his lips found hers, his touch soft and sweet and somehow just as erotic as the more demanding kisses had been. She tipped her head up, absorbing each tiny taste, each brush of friction as they came together over and over. Soon, though, the V between her parted legs began to send up a protest, a needy throbbing making itself known. She pushed herself even closer to the edge of the bed, her thighs spreading further. It didn't help.

Well, his 'you first' might mean she was supposed to strip him first, right? So that was exactly what she would do. Hooking her thumbs in the elastic band on his hips, she gave a quick tug before he could say or do anything, pushing them down to his knees.

'Cheater,' he murmured, not moving from his spot, every syllable causing his lips to brush against hers.

'We never set any ground rules, if I remember right. And if you'll just stand up, I'll finish the job.'

'I don't trust you.'

'No?' She gave him a smile full of meaning. 'Well, there's more than one way to skin a cat…or undress a man.'

With that she lay back on the bed, kicked off her high-heeled pumps and slid her bare feet up the backs of his calves. When she reached the spot where his boxers were still clinging to his legs, she pushed them as far down as she could. Max still hadn't moved a muscle…except for the one currently ticking away on the side of his jaw.

What she didn't expect was for his hands to whisk up her sides and cover her breasts, the warm heat and promise of his touch making the nipples harden instantly. He didn't stay there, however; his fingers were soon travelling down the line of her belly until he reached her own underwear and dragged them down her thighs, moving backwards as he inched them over her legs, across her ankles and finally pulled them free of her body. He stepped out of his boxers while he was at it. Or at least she assumed he did, since she couldn't actually see him do it.

This time when he parted her legs, there was no mistaking his intent.

'You want to play with fire, Anna? Well, you've got it.'

With that, he put his hands beneath her bottom and tugged. Hard. Hard enough that she slid forward to meet his ready flesh. 'Is this what you want?'

The part of her that had been throbbing in antici-pation clenched, thinking he was going to give it to her right away. Instead, he slid up past it, eliciting a whispered complaint from her. It ended in a moan when he found that nerve-rich area just a little higher.

He repeated the act. Words failed her, a jumble of sensations eclipsing her ability to think, much less talk.

Her eyes fluttered closed, the release she'd sought just seconds ago now rushing at her much too quickly.

His voice came from above her. 'I think it is.'

His fingertips found her nipples once again and squeezed, the dual assault wracking her body with a pleasure so sharp it made her arch up seeking him. 'Max.'

He gave her what she wanted then, thrusting for-ward and finding her immediately. The movement was so sudden it made her gasp, her fingers clutch-ing his shoulders as he set up a quick rhythm that didn't give her any room to catch her breath. Instead it tossed her high into the air and held her there for several seconds, and then she was over the edge, her body spasming around his. Max groaned, his mouth finding hers as he plunged again and again before finally slowing, the sound of his heavy breathing wonderfully loud in her ears.

She wrapped her arms around his neck, holding him tight as the emotions she'd been holding back finally bubbled over, tears slipping silently down her cheeks. Annabelle came to a stunning realisation.

She loved her husband.

She didn't just *love* him. She was *in* love with him. She'd never stopped being in love with him. She'd submerged the truth—buried it far out of sight—and tried to lose herself in caring for sick children instead. Only it hadn't worked. Not entirely.

Because here it was. In plain sight.

Annabelle loved him. Deeply. Entirely. And she had no idea what she was going to do about it.

CHAPTER NINE

IT HADN'T FELT like goodbye sex.

The deep sleep that had finally pulled Max under in the early hours of the morning released him just as quickly.

He blinked a couple of times, trying to bring to mind exactly what had happened last night, but it all blurred together to form a scene of decadence and exhausting satisfaction.

Annabelle.

He turned his head to look at her side of the bed only to find it empty—the nightstand bare of anything except a clock. No note. He frowned before remembering that they'd come to London together, so it wasn't likely that she'd slipped out and caught a train back to Cheltenham. So she was still here. Somewhere.

She was here.

He relaxed and rolled onto his back, settling into the pillows with his hands behind his head. It was just seven in the morning. They might even have time for another session before they had to be on their way.

And do what afterwards?

He wasn't sure. But maybe they could start again.

In the crush of timetables and thermometers and ovulation charts, Max had forgotten just how good sex—real sex, not something with a goal in mind—had been between them. Last night had brought it all rushing back. Their first year had been out of this world. They'd been so in tune with each other's needs that it had seemed nothing would be able to come between them.

Until it had.

Maybe they could get back to the 'before' part of the equation.

Was he actually thinking of getting back together with her? Could they erase what had torn them apart and start over? If so, they could just put off signing any papers for a while and wander down this lane for a few miles and see what happened.

Unless Annabelle didn't want to do that.

Didn't someone say that couples who were getting divorced would sometimes fall into each other's arms one last time as a way of saying goodbye or having closure? What they'd done hadn't seemed like that. At least not to him.

Vaguely he was aware of the sound of running water. Ah, that answered the question as to where she was. She was taking a shower.

Naked.

She probably had soap streaming down her body. *Naked.*

When the word popped up a second time, he smiled. Hadn't he just thought about how it was still early?

Well, they could kill two birds with one stone. He could soap her back, while doing a few other things.

Throwing the blankets off, he realised the flat was chilly. The heat must be turned down, since Suzanne hadn't expected anyone to be living here.

He'd have to call her this morning and let her know he'd spent the night so she didn't come into the flat, realise someone had been in there and assume there'd been an intruder. And he'd promised he would call the hospital first thing to see how Baby Hope was doing. This was a good time to do that.

Bringing up the number on his smartphone, he rang the main desk of the hospital.

'This is Mr Ainsley. Is Miss McDonald in yet?'

'Let me check.'

The voice clicked off and became elevator music as he was put on hold. The shower was still running. Even if she came out before he was done with his call, he would just coax her back under the spray.

The music stopped and Sienna's voice came over the line. 'Hi, Max. Everything okay?'

It was more than okay, but that wasn't something he was going to tell anyone. Not yet.

'Fine. I'm just checking on our patient.'

He could practically hear a smile form on the other doctor's lips. 'We have several patients. Which one are you referring to?'

This time the smile was on his end. 'A certain young transplant patient.'

'She's fine. No more episodes of a-fib.' There was a pause. 'I do seem to remember telling you I would call you if there was any change.'

'You did. But I wanted to be able to tell…' This time it was Max who stopped short. He wasn't really ready for anyone to know that he and Annabelle had spent the night together. 'I just wanted to see if I needed to rush back this morning or not.'

'No need to rush at all. She's doing brilliantly.'

'Good. Thank you for taking over her case during my absence.'

'Not a problem at all. Are you coming back today?'

'Yes.' Which brought back to mind what he'd set out to do when he got out of bed. 'I'll be in around four o'clock this afternoon. Call me if you need me.'

'I will. Have a safe trip.'

'Thank you.'

Max rang off, scrubbing a hand through his hair. And now back to his previous thoughts of Annabelle and that shower.

Before he headed for the bathroom, though, he made a quick detour down the hallway and turned the heating up to a tolerable level—the amazing thing was they hadn't noticed the cold last night when they'd been making love. Then he padded back to the bathroom, stopping just outside the door.

The shower was definitely running.

He hadn't put on any clothes before falling asleep so that saved him a step. His mouth watered. He could certainly use a shower. Now more than ever.

Trying the doorknob and finding it unlocked, he eased into the room. Steam enveloped the space. She'd been in here a while. But then again, he remembered Annabelle had loved long, luxurious baths and showers. Her skin would be soft and moist...

Gulping, he removed his watch and placed it on the counter and then turned towards the shower enclosure. He could just barely make out Annabelle's form through the frosted glass. His body hardened all over again. How did she do that to him?

It was almost as if they'd been given a clean slate. Something he'd needed—they'd both needed.

With that thought in his head, he wrapped a hand around the handle of the door just as the water switched off.

Damn!

Yanking the door open, he found a pink-faced Annabelle, her hair streaming down her back, eyes wide with surprise.

'Max! I thought you were still asleep.'

'I was. But then I heard the shower and thought I might take one too.'

Her slow smile lit up the enclosure. 'I think I might have left you a little hot water. If you can be quick.'

'Did you forget? We had an on-demand unit put in. I can be as slow as I want to be.'

'Can you?' Her smile widened. 'I may have missed a spot or two, then. Do you mind if I join you?'

'I was counting on it.'

With that, Max closed the door and turned on the shower. Then, with the sting of hot water pelting his back, he put everything else out of his mind as he moved to turn on Anna.

Annabelle stretched up to kiss Max's shoulder one last time, her body warm and limp as she stood on the warm tiles of the shower enclosure. 'Were you able to call the hospital yet?'

'How did I know you were going to ask that?' He gathered her hair in his hand and squeezed the excess water out. 'I've missed doing this.'

'Showering?'

'Showering…with you.'

'I've missed it too. Along with…' Her hands swept down his chest, heading to regions below, only to have him catch her before she reached her destination.

'Witch. Is that all you've missed?'

Was there a hint of insecurity in that voice? Impossible. Max was never insecure. He always knew exactly what he wanted. Or didn't want.

A chill went over her.

No. He'd said he'd missed her. Or had he? Hadn't his exact words been that he'd missed showering with her? Having sex with her?

Not exactly. He'd stopped her from stroking him. Had asked if that was all she'd missed. Maybe he was seeking reassurance.

'No, it's not all I've missed. I've missed…us.' She tried to let the sincerity in her voice ring through.

Threading his fingers through hers, he nodded. 'So have I. And yes, I called the hospital. Hope is doing fine.'

'Thank God. Maybe this will be a happy Christmas after all.' She wasn't above seeking a little reassurance herself.

'I'm hoping it will.' Letting her go, he stepped out of the shower, leaving her alone. Just when the worry centres began firing in her head, he came back, a thick white towel in his hands. Another one was wrapped around his waist.

'I guess this means fun time is over?'

'Didn't you say you had a shift this afternoon?'

'Oh! That's right.' How could she have forgotten that? Maybe because when Max was around, she tended to forget everything.

When she went to grab the towel from him, he held it just out of reach. 'Not so fast. There's something else I've missed.'

With that, he opened the fluffy terry and proceeded to pat her dry, starting with her face and gently moving down her body, until he was kneeling before her, sweeping the towel down her thighs and calves. A familiar tingling began stirring in her midsection. 'You'd better be careful, or I'm never going to let you out of this room.'

'I can think of worse things than being kept as your prisoner.'

The towel moved between her legs, teasing more intimate territory.

A low moan came from her throat before she could stop it. 'That's so not fair. You didn't let me touch you.'

His eyes came up to meet hers. 'You have more control than I do.'

'Wanna bet?' She tangled her fingers in his hair, letting the warm moist strands filter between them. 'I've never been able to resist you. I really do need to get to work, though.'

He stood. 'See? More control. Bend over.'

'Wh…what?' The word sputtered out on a half-laugh.

'Naughty girl. Not for that.' He grinned, the act taking years off his face. 'Now bend over.'

She did as he asked, and Max flipped her hair over until the strands hung straight down. Then he wrapped the towel around her head and twisted it, enveloping her wet locks in it. A glimmer of disappointment went through her. Max had it all wrong. She had no control when it came to him. She wanted him. All the time.

And now that things seemed to be easing between them, maybe she'd be able to have him whenever she wanted him. At least that was what she hoped. Surely he felt the same way as she did.

She tightened the towel and then stood upright again, letting the end of it slide down the back of her head. Luckily there was still a hairdryer in the flat. She'd found it when searching through the drawers.

Max opened the shower door for her and let her step out. A wave of steam followed her as he wrapped her in a second towel. 'Good thing we don't have an alarm that is triggered by heat.'

'Yes, that's a very good thing.' He encircled her waist and pulled her back against him. 'I can think of several times during the night when we might have set it off, if so.'

'I can think of several times that you went off too.'

He dropped a kiss on her hair, and she felt something stir against her backside. He gave a strangled laugh. 'Maybe we'd better not talk about that right now.'

Maybe they shouldn't. Because the tingling that had started when he'd towel-dried her was getting stronger. 'Okay, let me get dressed and dry my hair, and I'll be ready.'

He tipped up her head and gave her a soft kiss. 'Okay, but it's under duress.' Letting her go, he dragged his hands through his own wet hair, which settled right into place.

'That is so not fair. You don't have to do anything to look great.'

'Neither do you.' He tapped her nose with his finger. 'You are perfect just as you are.'

'I don't know about that, but I do feel perfectly satisfied.' She went over and opened a drawer, finding the hairdryer she'd discovered earlier. She picked it up, laughing as a thought hit her. 'After all those contortions we did years ago, wouldn't it be funny if last night or this morning did what all the hormone treatments couldn't? So...do you want a boy or a girl?'

It was only when she picked up her hairbrush that she realised Max wasn't laughing. He had gone very still.

He slipped his watch around his wrist, before looking up. His eyes were completely blank, although a muscle ticked in his jaw. 'A boy or a girl?'

A sliver of alarm went through her at the slow words. Where was the man who had just made love to her as if he couldn't get enough?

She forced a smile to her face. One she didn't feel. 'It's just that it would be ironic, if I got pregnant when we weren't even trying.'

Actually, it wouldn't be funny. Or ironic. Or anything else. Why had she even said that?

Max turned and went into the bedroom. With a panicked sense of déjà vu, Annabelle followed him, finding the bed was perfectly made. So perfectly that if she hadn't remembered writhing like a maniac beneath those sheets, she might have thought it was all a dream.

Only that exquisite bit of soreness in all the right places said it had been very real.

Except there was that weird vibe she'd picked up after joking about getting pregnant. He hadn't looked or sounded like someone who would be thrilled about that happening. Maybe she should put his mind at ease. She moved closer.

'Hey, are you afraid I might get pregnant because of what we did?'

His pupils darkened, expanding until they seemed to take up his entire iris. 'I think the more appropriate question would be: are you afraid you *won't* get pregnant?'

She blinked. 'No, of course not. I was joking.'

'Were you? Because right now, I don't feel like laughing.'

Neither did she. She had no idea why the pregnancy thing had crossed her mind. Maybe because it had been so long since they'd had sex that was totally spontaneous.

Nothing like bringing up a whole slew of bad memories, though.

He turned away and picked up his overnight bag, setting it on the bed.

Annabelle caught at his arm, forcing him to face her again. 'Look, I'm sorry. Obviously it's still a touchy subject.'

'Touchy would be an understatement.' The thin line of his mouth was a warning she remembered from days past. 'Is this why you were so eager to get back to the flat last night—were you trying to hit a certain magic window? If so, you've got the wrong man.'

'I wasn't doing anything of the sort! You're being ridiculous.'

It was as if everything they'd done last night had

been swept away, dropping them back into the same angry arguments from their past.

'I'm being ridiculous?' His tone was dangerously soft. 'Funny you should say that, because I seem to remember a whole lot of ridiculousness that went on during our marriage. That journal you kept being one of them.'

The words slapped at Annabelle, leaving her speechless for several seconds. He considered their attempts to have a baby 'ridiculousness'?

The pain in her gut and the throbbing in her chest were duelling with each other, seeking the nearest available exit: her eyes. But she couldn't let the gathering tears stop her from trying one last time.

'Max, I wasn't serious about what I said in the bathroom.'

It was as if he hadn't heard her at all. 'We should have used some kind of protection. I meant what I said three years ago. I don't want children.'

His words stopped her all over again.

'Ever?'

'Ever. I thought I made that perfectly clear.'

He had. But that had been three years ago. A lot had changed since then. Maybe more than she'd thought. He'd never once mentioned still loving her. Not last night. Not this morning. The closest he'd come was the word 'spark'.

Oh, God, how could she have been so stupid? And just to prove that she was, the words kept pouring out.

'I don't understand what you're saying.'

'No? I'm saying this was a mistake, Annabelle.' He glanced one last time at the open bag on the bed. 'When we get back to Cheltenham, I'm going to find those divorce papers and sign them.' There was a long pause, and she suddenly knew the hammer was going to fall and crush her beneath its blow. 'And if you haven't already, I'm going to ask that you sign them too.'

'Please don't say that, Max. Let's talk about it.'

'There is nothing to talk about. You wanted a divorce? Well, guess what, honey, so do I.'

CHAPTER TEN

THE TRIP BACK to Cheltenham had been made in total silence. She could have tried to plead her case, but she doubted that Max would have heard anything she had to say.

Just as in their marriage, he had shut down emotionally. His face and the tight way he'd gripped the wheel had seemed to confirm that, so Annabelle had stared out of the window at the passing countryside, doing her best not to burst into tears.

He wasn't any more willing to fight for her—for *them*—than he had been three years ago. And she was done trying.

She loved him, but she was not going to kneel at his feet and beg him not to leave.

After working her afternoon shift—during which she hadn't seen Max a single time, not even to check on Hope—she'd spent a long sleepless night, first in her bed, and when that hadn't worked she'd lain on the sofa.

This morning, she was exhausted, but resigned. If he wanted to sign the papers, she was going to let him. She unpacked her bag, staring at herself in the mirror for a long time.

Was he right? Had some subconscious part hoped she might become pregnant because of what they'd done? Maybe. And if she was honest with herself, there was probably some long-lost side of her that would always harbour a tiny sliver of hope. How could she just extinguish it?

She couldn't. And evidently Max would not be able to love the side of her that wanted children.

Okay. She would just deal with it, as she had the last time.

She went to the shelf and picked up the manila envelope, blowing three years' worth of dust off it. Sitting at her desk, she withdrew the papers inside, her hand shaking as she laid them out flat, realising she'd never really looked at what her solicitor had sent over. Max wasn't the only one who had put off walking this through to the end.

Petition for dissolution of the marriage between
Maxwell Wilson Ainsley
and
Annabelle Brookes Ainsley

She was listed as the petitioner and he was the respondent. In other words, she was asking for the divorce and it was up to Max to respond.

Which he had, yesterday.

The night before last she'd felt such hope. And now here she was, back where she'd started three years ago.

Only worse. Because back then, when he'd issued his ultimatum about discontinuing the IVF attempts, she hadn't completely believed him. Until she'd caught him looking at that ovulation journal. She'd seen his face and had known it was over.

But that was all in the past. At least she'd thought so until yesterday. She'd had no idea he harboured such terrible resentment of their time together.

After they'd made love, Annabelle could have sworn that those old hurts had been healed. Obviously she'd been wrong.

Annabelle stared at the document.

She was the petitioner.

The word swirled through her mind again and again. Just because someone asked for something didn't mean the other person had to give it to them, did it? No, but Max seemed more than willing to let her have what she wanted. Only she wasn't sure she wanted it any more.

Why? Because he'd hurt her pride? No. That hurt went far deeper than that.

What if she, the petitioner, *withdrew* her request? Was that even possible? She could try to stop the process and, if Max insisted, let it turn into a long drawn-out battle in the courts. She could try to hurt him the way he'd hurt her. But that wasn't what Annabelle wanted. She didn't want to hurt him. Or to fight with him.

She didn't want to fight at all.

But that didn't mean that wasn't what should happen.

Hadn't her parents always taught her to fight for what she believed in? And wasn't that what she'd expected of Max all those years ago?

Yes.

Even now, despite his angry words, she believed

they had a chance if they let go of the past. But did Max believe the same thing? After yesterday, she wasn't sure.

Why had he got so angry after she'd joked about her getting pregnant?

Because he thought she still wanted children and he didn't?

That was what he'd implied when he'd mentioned hitting the 'magic' window: *If so, you've got the wrong man.*

She didn't know for sure, because Max had *refused to talk to her*!

So, she had a choice. Let him sign and be done with it. Or go and have it out with him. Whether he wanted to or not.

Where? She had no idea if he'd even gone in to work yesterday afternoon.

She could always go to his house. If she knew where that was. She realised she didn't have a clue where he lived.

But she knew someone who did.

Max circled his living room for what seemed like the hundredth time, trying to find some kind of peace with his decision. If he could leave the country, as he had three years ago, he would. But he had a contract to fulfil, and he was dead tired of running.

He loved Annabelle. More than life itself.

But the thought of standing by a second time while she destroyed her health and more over a dream that was never going to come true was a knife to the heart. That time she'd retained fluid and had been so sick, he'd been afraid he was going to lose her. It had all turned into one huge ball of misery. The empty promises from fertility doctors. The tears. The torment. There had been no holy grail. No miracle.

And when she'd finally realised he was serious that last time? She'd told him to leave. Had sent him packing, cutting him off from the only real and good thing he'd ever known. And he'd been willing to walk away to make it all stop.

His statement about there being no miracle wasn't entirely true. There had been. But it hadn't been in what he or any of the doctors could give to Anna. It was what Anna had given to him: a love like none he'd ever known.

And what had he done? He'd thrown it away a second time. Because he'd been afraid.

Could he undo the things he'd said? Maybe, but how did he convince her to be happy with what she had? With him?

A cold hand clutched his chest. Was that what it had been? Had he been jealous of her attempts to have a child?

No. He could answer that honestly. That wasn't his reason for walking out on her yesterday. And yes, even though he hadn't physically left the vicinity, he had walked away from the burgeoning hope of a new beginning.

And for what?

For a few careless words uttered in a bathroom? Had he really stopped to listen to what she was saying, or had he simply assumed she was headed down the same old path?

The problem was, he hadn't actually heard her out,

he'd simply blurted out that he didn't want children and that he wanted to finalise the divorce.

Was she waiting for him to sign the papers? Was she even now informing her solicitor to finish what she'd started?

His throat tightened until it was difficult to breathe. She should. She should leave him far behind and forget all about him.

But he didn't want her to.

So what should he do?

Probably what he should have done three years ago. Stand in front of her and listen to her heart, rather than issue ultimatums. Hear what it was she wanted out of life. If it came out that they wanted completely different things, then he could walk away with no regrets. It was just that Max wasn't so sure they did. They had worked together—had loved together—in a way that had made him hope that this time might be the charm.

Weren't those almost the exact same words that Annabelle had said in that bathroom?

Yes.

So why was he standing here wondering if he'd done the right thing? He needed to find her and pray that he wasn't too late.

Opening his wardrobe, he grabbed a leather jacket and headed towards the front door. He could always camp in front of Baby Hope's hospital room and wait for Annabelle to show up. Because if he knew one thing about the woman it was that she loved that baby. She had fought for the infant's survival time after time. Maybe it was time that someone—him—decided to fight for Annabelle.

Just as he reached for the doorknob his bell rang, startling the hell out of him.

He frowned. *Come on. I really need a break here.*

Wrenching the door open to tell whoever it was that he didn't have time for chit-chat, he was shocked to find the person he'd just been thinking about standing on his front mat.

No. That couldn't be right.

He forced his gaze to pull the image into sharp focus. Still the same.

'Anna?' Her eyes looked red, and she carried a packet under her arm. 'Are you okay?'

'No. No, I'm not, actually.' She took a deep breath and then held up an envelope. 'But I brought my copy of the divorce papers. If you have yours, you can sign them, and I'll take them both to my solicitor.'

His throat clogged with emotion. He was too late. He'd brought the axe down on something that could have made him happy for the rest of his life. He should tell her he wasn't going to sign them, that it wasn't what he wanted at all, but somehow the words wouldn't form.

Because she was going to leave him all over again.

It's not like you didn't tell her to.

'Are you going to ask me in?'

Realising she was standing in the cold, he took a step back, motioning her inside his cottage.

'Let me take your coat and hat.'

Annabelle shed both items, handing the gear to him, but retaining her hold of the envelope. 'Thank you.'

He led her into the living room and made her a cup of tea, while she perched on the couch, the packet resting across the knees of her jeans. He wanted to take it from her and toss it into the gas fireplace he'd switched on, but hadn't he decided to listen to her heart? To hear her out without jumping to any conclusions?

But she said he could sign his copy of the papers right there in front of her.

If he wanted to.

He waited until she'd had her second sip of tea before wading into the waters. 'You didn't have to bring your copy. I have one of my own.'

He couldn't imagine saying anything more stupid than that.

'I know. But I wanted to come by and get a few things off my chest. In person.'

Taking a gulp of his coffee and feeling the scald as it went down his throat, he paused to let her talk.

Reaching deep into her handbag, she pulled out a notebook. Max recognised the green floral cover and immediately stiffened. Why did she even still have that?

'When I was packing my things to come to Cheltenham, I found this, and realised the enormity of the mistake I'd made all those years ago. Keeping this a secret was wrong on so many levels.' Her chest rose as she took a deep breath. 'What I said in the bathroom had nothing to do with this. I meant the words as a joke, but they backfired horribly and ended up shooting me in the heart. I wasn't scheming to get pregnant after the fundraising party, I swear.'

'I'm just beginning to realise that.' One side of his mouth tilted slightly. 'I think you used the word "ridiculous" to describe my reaction. You were right.'

Her eyes searched his. 'I never should have said that. And just so you understand, I know I'm not going to get pregnant from having sex with you. Not two days ago. Not three months from now. Not ten years from now. I'm sorry if you thought that was what I was after. I'm not. Not any more.'

A pinpoint of hope appeared on the horizon. 'So you're not interested in having a baby?'

'If it happened, I would be ecstatic. But I'm not going to chase after it ever again. Especially knowing you don't want kids.'

'I never said that.' Even as the words came out, he realised he had. He'd said that very thing. Maybe he wasn't the only one who'd misunderstood. 'Okay, I did. But I meant I didn't want to go through the procedures any more. It hurt too much to see how they ripped you apart emotionally. Physically. Especially after that last attempt.'

He swallowed hard, forcing the words out. 'I thought you were going to die, Anna. And in the end, that's why I agreed to leave.'

'What?' The shock on her face was unmistakable.

He nodded. 'I've never done anything harder than walk through that door. The only thing that kept my feet moving was the thought that I might be saving your life. With me gone, you'd have no reason to go through any more treatments.'

'I—I never knew.'

If he'd been hoping she'd leap into his arms after that revelation, he was mistaken. Instead, she looked down at the journal in her hands, smoothing her fingers over the embossed cover. 'You hurt me, Max, when you came into that bathroom all those years ago and issued an edict that it was over. That I wasn't to try to get pregnant any more. I felt I had no control over anything, not even my own decisions.'

He knew he'd hurt her. 'You're right. We should have discussed it together.' He stood and walked towards a bank of windows that overlooked a park, stuffing his hands into his front pockets. 'It's just that seeing you in such torment… Well, it ripped my heart out.'

'And it killed me that I couldn't give you what you wanted.'

'What *I* wanted?' He turned back towards her.

'A family. You used to talk about how you wanted a big family, just like mine. So you could give our children what your parents hadn't given to you. And I wanted so desperately for you to have that. Then, when it came down to it—' her voice cracked '—I couldn't give it to you.'

He sat down next to her on the couch, horrified by her words. Had she really thought that? 'Anna, *you* were my family. Yes, I was disappointed that you couldn't get pregnant. But only because it seemed to be something you wanted so desperately.'

'I wanted it because of you.'

Could it be? Had he misread the signs all those years ago? Had he been so focused on the fights that had swirled around her efforts at conceiving that he'd missed the real reason she'd been so anguished after each failed attempt?

'I had no idea.' He took one of her hands.

'I asked you to leave because I was hurt and trying to protect myself the only way I knew how. I took the coward's way out.'

'You're not a coward.' He took the journal from her, his thumb rubbing the edges of the little book. 'I am. Because I love you too much to watch you go through this again.'

'You love me?'

He stared at her. 'You didn't know?'

'I thought I did. At one time. But now?' She swallowed. 'I'm not sure.'

He set the journal on the coffee table and caught her face in his hands. 'I'm so sorry, Anna. Hell, I...' He bowed his head, trying to control the stinging in his eyes. Then he looked back up at her. 'I screwed everything up back then. And I screwed it up again at the flat yesterday morning.'

'So you don't want a divorce?'

He had to tread carefully. He wanted there to be no more misunderstandings. 'I don't. But I have to be sure of what you want out of life.'

'You aren't the only one who screwed up, Max. I wanted so badly to give you the things you didn't get as a child: roots and a huge amount of love.'

'You gave me those when you married me. That, along with your amazing, crazy family.'

'They all love you, you know. It's one of the reasons I couldn't bring myself to tell them about the divorce.' His eyes weren't the only ones stinging, evidently, judging from the moisture that appeared in hers. 'So where do we go from here?'

He thought for a minute.

'Maybe we should look at counselling. Find out how to handle everything we've been through. And after that?' He picked up her left hand and kissed the empty ring finger. 'I'd love to put something back on this.'

'I still have my rings.' She smiled. 'I don't think I've ever quite given up on us. It's why I never asked my solicitor to find you and demand those signed papers back. I think I was hoping that one day you would find your way home. And you did.'

He smiled back, linking his fingers with hers. 'It would seem we have fate—and Sienna McDonald—to thank for that. Although I would like to think I would have come to my senses if your solicitor ever *had* hunted me down.'

She leaned her head on his shoulder. 'I guess I should have sicced him on you sooner, then.'

'Maybe you should have.' He dropped a kiss on her temple. 'I have to tell you that picture of us in your parents' dining room brought back memories of how happy we were. Of how things could have been had not things got so...'

'Insane.' She finished the sentence for him.

'I don't mean that in a bad way.'

'I know. But it was.' She lifted her head and motioned to the packet. 'That brings me back to my original question. Do you want me to hold onto these just in case it doesn't work out?'

'No.' Max got up from his seat and went over to a cabinet under his television. Opening the door, he retrieved an envelope that looked identical to hers. He sat back down, but didn't take the papers out. Instead, he folded the packet in half, trapping the journal in between. 'May I?'

He held out a hand for her envelope. When she gave it to him, he opened the flap and dropped the other items inside. Then he got up from the sofa. 'What I really want to do is toss these into the fireplace and watch them burn to ashes, but, since it's a gas fireplace, I'm afraid I'd set the cottage on fire.'

'That wouldn't be good.'

'No, it wouldn't. Especially since I'm hoping to move out of it very soon. I might not get my security deposit back.'

'Y-you're moving?' The fear on her face was enough to make him pull her from the sofa and enfold her in his arms.

'I'm sorry. I didn't mean I was moving away. I'm just hoping to change locations.'

'I don't understand.'

'Well, it might seem a little odd to your family and everyone at the hospital if you put your rings on and we continue living in separate homes, don't you think?'

Wrapping her arms around his neck, she pressed herself against him. 'Yes. It would. If you're thinking of coming to live at my place, I have to warn you that it's not as fancy as our flat in London, and—'

'It will be perfect, Anna. Just like you.'

With that he led her into the kitchen and stopped in front of the rubbish bin. Pushing the foot pedal, he waited until the top lifted all the way up. 'It's not as impressive as sending them up in a puff of smoke, but it'll be just as permanent. Once this lid falls, I don't want to mention these papers ever again.'

'Deal. But let's both do it.' She held one side of the envelope, while Max kept hold of the other end. Then they dropped it, along with all the hurts from the past, right where they belonged. Where they could never again poison their relationship.

Max released the pedal and let the lid drop back into place. 'Maybe in a couple of years we could move back to London. Or talk about adoption.'

'Adoption? You'd be okay with that?'

'As long as you are. I know with your sister—'

'I'm definitely open to that option.' She squeezed his hand. 'You might even be able to talk me into going on a medical mission, just like we used to dream about.'

'Are you serious?'

'Yes. I want to see what you've seen. Walk where you've walked. And I know that, this time, we'll be right in step with each other.'

He turned her until she faced him. 'I would be honoured to work alongside you, Mrs Ainsley.'

'And I, you.'

'How long before you have to be at Teddy's?'

She glanced at her watch. 'I have about two hours. I wasn't sure how long this was going to take or what state I would be in by the end of it.'

'Hmm… I think I might be able to answer both of those questions.' He gripped her hand and started leading her through the living room. 'This will take just about two hours…or however long you have left. And as for the state you'll be in by the end of it—I'm hoping you'll be in a state of undress and that you'll be very, very satisfied.'

'That sounds wonderful.' She caught up with him and put her arm around his waist. 'As for the satisfied part, I can't think of how I could be any more satisfied than I am at this very moment.'

They went through the bedroom door and he pushed it shut behind them. 'In that case, I plan to keep you that way for the rest of your life.'

EPILOGUE

ON EITHER SIDE of her, a small hand clutched hers as she walked slowly towards the waiting plane. After a ton of paperwork and countless trips to their solicitor's office, Annabelle and Max finally had their answer. Two boys with special needs were on their way to a brand-new life on a brand-new continent. Ready to join their sister, who was being cared for by Annabelle's mum.

Six months after Hope's surgery, the baby had come home to live with Annabelle and Max. The same solicitor who had handled this adoption had done a bit of digging and found a similar case where a preemie baby had been adopted by her nurse. It was enough to convince the courts that Hope belonged with them. Now two years old, she was growing and thriving and had brought such joy into their lives.

She glanced to the side where Max was making the final arrangements for the flight back to England. He stood tall and proud, no sign of the angry, frustrated man who'd walked out of her door all those years ago. And Annabelle had finally made her peace with never having a biological child. If it happened, it happened.

They'd compromised on that front. Max had agreed

to not using birth control—with a sexy smile as they'd lain in bed after making love one night—and she'd agreed not to seek extraordinary means to have a child.

The life they now had was enough. More than enough.

Max meant the world to her. As did Hope, who had given them the best Christmas gift of all: a chance to rekindle their romance and to fix what was broken between them.

And now these two small gifts had come into their lives, both with heart defects that had needed surgery. Max and Annabelle had met Omar and Ahmed on a brief Doctors Without Borders trip they'd made four months earlier. A colleague of Max's had performed the surgeries and Annabelle had fallen in love. With those two boys, and with Max all over again. His self-less need to help ease the suffering of others had been more than evident. Then and now.

They'd both vowed to communicate. And they'd learned how with the help of a counsellor right after they'd moved into Annabelle's home. At the end of the process, Max had promised to stick with her no matter what. As had she.

'Baba anakuja!' said Omar, and he gripped her hand even tighter.

Annabelle glanced up, her eyes watering to see that 'Papa' was indeed coming towards them. It was the first time one of the boys had referred to Max that way, and she envisioned many more years of it as they all grew to know one another even more.

He came and stood in front of her, his gaze searching her face. 'You're sure this is okay?'

'Do you even need to ask? Hope will be so happy to finally meet them. So will the rest of the family.'

Glancing down at the two kids flanking her, he then leaned in and kissed her, his lips warm with promise. A small giggle burst from Ahmed at the PDA.

'It means we'll have even less privacy.' He tucked a strand of hair behind her ear, the gesture making her smile.

'No, it just means we'll have to be more inventive.'

'More? I don't see how that's possible.' Luckily the kids didn't have a strong grasp of English yet, but they would learn. Just as they would learn about their own heritage, possibly even returning to Africa one day to give back to their culture.

'You'll just have to wait and see. I have some ideas.'

Max leaned in and kissed her again. 'I think we'd better leave this topic of conversation for another time, or I'm going to be pretty uncomfortable on the trip home.'

Home.

Max had explained how seeing their wedding photo on her parents' wall had made something inside him shift, had made him realise he still loved her.

That picture now hung over their bed as a reminder of what they stood to lose. It was something that Annabelle kept in mind each and every day.

There were no more jokes about getting pregnant. She knew just how painful a subject it was, and she was more than willing to leave it behind. For Max's sake.

Besides, they were complete just as they were.

Adding Omar and Ahmed to their household was just icing on an already beautiful cake.

And Nate... Her nephew's surgery had been a complete success, and there was no reason to think the brain tumour would ever return. Jessica was ecstatic, as was everyone else. It seemed they'd all got their happy endings.

It's enough.

Those two words were now the motto of her life. No matter what her problems or difficulties, she would weigh everything against that phrase. Because it was true. Life with Max, no matter what it brought, was enough.

She wanted to reach up and touch him, but the fingers squeezing hers prevented it. But there were other ways to touch. 'I love you.'

'I love you too, Anna.' He kissed her again before moving to the side and gripping Ahmed's hand, forming an unbreakable, unified line.

Then they walked towards the open door of the plane, knowing it would soon carry them to a brand-new phase of their lives.

Where they would wake up to face each and every day.

Together.

* * * * *

THE SHEIKH'S CHRISTMAS CONQUEST

SHARON KENDRICK

To the amazing Anni MacDonald-Hall – who taught
me SO MUCH about horses.

Sheikh Saladin Al Mektala is very grateful for
her expertise!

CHAPTER ONE

LIVVY WAS HANGING mistletoe when the doorbell rang. Expensive, mocking mistletoe tied with ribbon the colour of blood. The sudden sound startled her because the heavy snow had made the world silent and she wasn't expecting anyone until Christmas Eve.

Go away, whoever you are, she thought as several white berries bounced onto the floor like miniature ping-pong balls. But the doorbell rang again—for much longer this time—because whoever was outside had decided to jam their thumb against the buzzer.

Livvy wished the unwanted caller would vanish, because there was still so much to do before the guests arrived, and the snowfall meant that Stella, her part-time help, hadn't turned up. But you couldn't run a successful business and behave like a prima donna—even if it was only four days before Christmas and you didn't have any room vacancies. She climbed down the ladder with a feeling of irritation that died the instant she opened the door.

She was unprepared for the man who stood on her doorstep. A stranger, yet not quite a stranger—although it took a moment for her to place him. He was famous in the horse-racing world she'd once inhabited. Some might say infamous. He was certainly unforgettable with eyes like gleaming jet and rich olive skin that showcased his hawklike features. His hard body spoke of exercise and discipline, and he was the kind of man who would make you take a second glance and then maybe a third.

But it wasn't just his appearance or his undeniable charisma that made Livvy blink her eyes in disbelief— it was his lofty status. Because it wasn't just any man who stood there surveying her so unsmilingly—it was Saladin Al Mektala, the king of Jazratan. A real-life desert sheikh standing on *her* doorstep.

She wondered if there was some sort of protocol for greeting one of the world's wealthiest men, especially when they also happened to be royal. Once upon a time she might have been intimidated by his reputation and his presence—but not anymore. She'd had to do a lot of growing up these past few years and her experiences had made her strong. These days she lived an independent life she was proud of—even if currently it felt as if she was clinging on to that independence by her fingernails.

'Didn't anyone ever tell you,' she said, tipping her head to one side, 'that it's polite to wait for someone to answer the first ring, rather than deafening them with a repeated summons?'

Saladin raised his eyebrows, unable to hide his surprise at her feisty response. It was an untraditional greeting to receive, even here in England where the demands of protocol were less rigid than in his homeland. But even so. His royal presence was usually enough to guarantee total deference, and although he sometimes complained to his advisors that people were never *normal* around him, he missed deference when it wasn't there.

He narrowed his eyes and studied her. 'Do you know who I am?'

She laughed. She actually laughed—her shiny ponytail swaying from side to side, like the tail of a chestnut horse.

'I thought that was the kind of question B-list celebrities asked when they were trying to get into the latest seedy nightclub,' she said.

Saladin felt a flicker of annoyance and something else. Something that was a little harder to define. He had been warned that she was difficult. That she could be prickly and stubborn—but these were qualities that were usually melted away by the sheer force of his personality and his position in society. And, not to put too fine a point on it, by his impact on the opposite sex, who usually melted like ice in the desert whenever he was around. His instinct was to bite back a withering response to put her in her place, but Livvy Miller had something he badly wanted so that he was forced to adopt a reasonable tone, something that didn't come easily to him. 'It was a genuine question,' he said. 'I am Saladin Al Mektala.'

'I know who you are.'

'And my office have been trying to contact you.' He paused. 'Repeatedly.'

She smiled, but Saladin noted that the smile did not reach her eyes.

'I know that, too,' she said. 'In fact, they've been bombarding me with emails and phone calls for the past week. I've barely been able to switch on my computer without a new message from palace@jazratan.com pinging into my inbox.'

'Yet you chose to ignore them?'

'That is my prerogative, surely?' She leaned on the doorjamb, her unusual eyes shaded by their forest of lashes. 'I gave them the same answer every time. I told them I wasn't interested. If they were unable to accept that, then surely the fault lies with them. My position hasn't changed.'

Saladin could barely disguise his growing irritation. 'But you don't know what it is they were asking of you.'

'Something to do with a horse. And that was enough for me.'

She drew herself up to her full height but he still towered over her. He found himself thinking that he could probably lift her up with one hand. When he'd heard about her ability to soothe huge and very temperamental horses, he'd never imagined she could be so...petite.

'Because I don't have anything to do with horses anymore,' she finished gravely.

Dragging his gaze from her slender frame to eyes that were the colour of honey, he fixed her with a questioning look. 'Why not?'

She gave a little clicking sound of irritation, but not before he had seen something dark in her eyes. A flash of something uncomfortable that he stored away for future reference.

'That's really none of your business,' she said, tilting her chin in a gesture of defiance. 'I don't have to offer any kind of explanation for my decisions, particularly to people who turn up unannounced on my doorstep at one of the busiest times of the year.'

Saladin felt the first flicker of heat. And of challenge. He was not used to resistance, or defiance. In his world, whatever he wanted was his. A click of his fingers or a cool glance was usually enough to guarantee him whatever he desired. Certainly, this kind of opposition was largely unknown to him, and certainly when it came from a woman, because women enjoyed submitting to his will—not opposing it. His response was one of renewed determination, which was quickly followed by the first sweet shimmer of sexual arousal and that surprised him. Because although Olivia Miller was reputed to have a magical touch when it came to horses, she certainly hadn't applied the same fairy dust to her appearance.

Saladin's lips curled. She was one of those women who the English called tomboys—and he didn't approve, for weren't women supposed to look like women? Her hair was pale brown, touched by red—a colour named after the great Italian painter Titian and a colour rare enough to be admired—but it was tied back in a functional ponytail, and her freckled face was completely bare of artifice. Why, even her jeans failed to do the only commendable thing that jeans were capable of—they were loose around her bottom instead of clinging to it like syrup. Which made the undeniable stir of lust he was feeling difficult to understand. Because why on earth should he be attracted to someone who sublimated her femininity as much as possible?

He narrowed his eyes. 'Are you aware that your attitude could be termed as insolence?' he questioned softly. 'And that it is unwise to answer the king of Jazratan in such a way?'

Again, that defiant tilt of the chin. He wondered if

she was aware that such a positioning of her face made her look as if she were inviting him to kiss her.

'I wasn't intending to be insolent,' she said, although the message in her eyes told him otherwise. 'I was simply stating a fact. What I chose to do with my life has nothing to do with you. I owe you no explanation. I am not one of your royal subjects.'

'No, you are not, but you might at least grant me the courtesy of hearing what I have to say,' he bit out. 'Or does the word *hospitality* mean nothing to you? Are you aware that I have travelled many miles in the most inclement weather in order to meet you?'

Livvy eyed the remaining bunches of mistletoe still waiting to be hung and thought about all the other things that needed to be done before her guests arrived. She wanted to make more cake to fill the house with sweet smells, and there were fires to make up in all the bedrooms. Her to-do list was as long as her arm and this handsome and vaguely intimidating stranger was hindering her. 'You could have chosen a more convenient time than just before Christmas,' she said.

'And when would have been a more *convenient* time?' he retorted. 'When you have consistently refused to be pinned down?'

'Most people would have taken the hint and cut their losses.'

'I am a king. I don't do *hints*' came his stony response.

Livvy hesitated. His behaviour confirmed everything she'd ever heard about him. He had been known for his arrogance on the racing circuit—seemingly with good reason—and she was so tempted to tell him to go. But she *was* running a business—even if it was currently a struggling business—and if she angered Saladin Al Mektala any more than he was already clearly angered, he might just spread a malicious word or two around the place. She could imagine it would be easy for someone like him to drip a little more poison onto her already damaged reputation. And adverse publicity could be death if you worked in the hospitality industry.

Behind him, she could see the falling snow, which had been coming down in bucketloads since before breakfast. Fat flakes were tumbling past like a never-ending slide show. Lawns that earlier had been merely spattered with the stuff now sported a thick white mantle—as if someone had been layering on cotton wool while she hadn't been looking. If it carried on like this, the lanes would soon be impassable and she'd never get rid of him. And she wanted to get rid of him. She didn't like him dominating her doorway and exuding all that *testosterone* and making her think about stuff she hadn't thought about in a long time. *She didn't like the way he made her feel.*

Farther up the drive stood a black four-wheel drive and she wondered if anyone was sitting shivering inside.

'What about your bodyguards—are they in the car?' Her gaze swept around the wintry garden. 'Hiding in the bushes, perhaps—or waiting to jump from a tree?'

'I don't have any bodyguards with me.'

So they were all alone.

Livvy's anxiety increased. Something about his powerful body and brooding features was making her skin prickle with a weird kind of foreboding—and an even more alarming sense of anticipation. For the first time she found herself wishing that she had a dog who would bark at him, rather than a soppy feline mop called Peppa, who was currently stretched out in front of the fire in the drawing room, purring happily.

But she wasn't going to allow this man to intimidate her. And if she wasn't intimidated, then it followed that she shouldn't keep avoiding a meeting with him. Maybe this was the only way he would understand that she meant what she said. If she kept repeating that she wasn't interested in whatever he was offering, then surely he would have no choice other than to believe her. And to leave her alone.

'You'd better come in,' she said as an icy gust brought a flurry of snow into the hall. 'I can give you thirty minutes but no longer. I'm expecting guests for Christmas and I have a lot to do before they arrive.'

She saw his faintly triumphant smile as he stepped inside and noticed how the elegant proportions of the airy entrance hall seemed to shrink once she had closed the front door on the snowy afternoon. There was something so intensely *masculine* about him, she thought reluctantly. Something that was both exciting and dangerous—and she forced herself to take a deep breath in an attempt to slow the sudden galloping of her heart. *Act as if he's a guest*, she told herself. *Put on your best, bright smile and switch on your professional hospitality mode.*

'Why don't you come into the drawing room?' she suggested politely. 'There's a fire there.'

He nodded and she saw his narrowed gaze take in the high ceilings and the elaborate wooden staircase as he followed her across the hallway. 'This is a beautiful old house,' he observed, a note of approval deepening his voice.

'Thank you,' she said, automatically slipping into

her role as guide. 'Parts of it date back to the twelfth century. They certainly don't build them like this anymore—perhaps that's a good thing, considering the amount of maintenance that's needed.' The building's history was one of the reasons why people travelled to this out-of-the-way spot to hire a room. Because the past defined the present and people hungered after the idea of an elegant past. Or at least, they had—until the rise of several nearby boutique hotels had started offering the kind of competition that was seriously affecting her turnover.

But Livvy couldn't deny her thrill of pleasure as the sheikh walked into the drawing room, because she was proud of her old family home, despite the fact that it had started to look a little frayed around the edges.

The big fire was banked with apple logs, which scented the air, and although the huge Christmas tree was still bare there weren't many rooms that could accommodate a tree of that size. At some point later she would have to drag herself up to the dusty attic and haul down the decorations, which had been in the family since the year dot, and go through the ritual of bringing the tree to life. Soon it would be covered in spangles and fairy lights and topped with the ancient little angel she'd once made with her mother. And for a while, Christmas would work its brief and sometimes unbearable magic of merging past and present.

She looked up to find Saladin Al Mektala studying her intently and, once again, a shiver of something inexplicable made her nostalgic sentiments dissolve as she began to study him right back.

He wasn't dressed like a sheikh. There were no flowing robes or billowing headdress to indicate his desert king status. The dark cashmere overcoat that he was removing—without having been invited to— was worn over dark trousers and a charcoal sweater that hugged his honed torso. He looked disturbingly *modern*, she thought—even if the flinty glint of his dark eyes made him seem disturbingly primitive. She watched as he hung the cashmere coat over the back of a chair and saw the gleam of melted snow on his black hair as he stepped a little closer to the fire.

'So,' she said. 'You must want something very badly if you're prepared to travel to the wilds of Derbyshire in order to get it.'

'Oh, but I do,' he said silkily. 'I want you.'

Something in his sultry tone kick-started feelings Livvy had repressed for longer than she cared to re-member and for a split second, she found herself imag-ining what it would feel like to be the object of desire to a man like Saladin Al Mektala. Would those flinty eyes soften before he kissed you? Would a woman feel *helpless* if she was being held in arms as powerful as his?

She swallowed, surprised by the unexpected path her thoughts had taken her down because she didn't fall in lust with total strangers. Actually, she didn't fall in lust at all. She quickly justified her wayward fan-tasy by reminding herself that he was being deliber-ately provocative and had made that statement in such a way—as if he was *seeking* to shock her. 'You'll have to be a little more specific than that,' she said crisply. 'What do you want me to do?'

His face changed as the provocation left it and she saw a shadow pass over the hawklike features. 'I have a sick horse,' he said, his voice tightening. 'A badly injured stallion. My favourite.'

His distress affected her—how could it fail to do so? But Livvy hardened her heart to his problems, because didn't she have enough of her own? 'I'm sorry to hear that,' she said. 'But as a king of considerable wealth, no doubt you have the best veterinary surgeons at your disposal. I'm sure they'll be able to work out some plan of action for your injured horse.'

'They say not.'

'Really?' Linking her fingers together, she looked up at him. 'What exactly is the problem?'

'A suspensory ligament,' he said, 'which has torn away from the bone.'

Livvy winced. 'That's bad.'

'I know it's bad,' he gritted out. 'Why the hell do you think I'm here?'

She decided to ignore his rudeness. 'There are revolutionary new treatments out there today,' she said placatingly. 'You can inject stem cells, or you could try shockwave treatment. I've heard that's very good.'

'You think I haven't already tried everything? That I haven't flown out every equine expert to examine him?' he demanded. 'And yet everything has failed. The finest specialists in the world have pronounced themselves at a loss.' There was a pause as he swallowed and his voice became dark and distorted as he spoke. 'They have told me there is no hope.'

For a moment, Livvy felt a deep sense of pity because she knew how powerful the bond between a man and his horse could be—especially a man whose exalted position meant that he could probably put more trust in animals than in humans. But she also knew that sometimes you had to accept things as they were and not as you wanted them to be. That you couldn't defeat nature, no matter how much you tried. And that all the money in the world would make no difference to the outcome.

She saw the steely glint in his dark eyes as he looked at her and recognised it as the look of someone who wasn't intending to give up. Was this what being a king did to a man—made you believe you could shape the world to your own wishes? She sighed. 'Like I said, I'm very sorry to hear that. But if you've been told there's no hope, then I don't know how you expect me to help.'

'Yes, you do, Livvy,' he said forcefully. 'You know you do.'

His fervent words challenged her nearly as much as his sudden use of his name.

'No. I don't.' She shook her head. 'I don't have anything to do with horses anymore. I haven't done for years. That part of my life is over, and if anyone has told you anything different, then they're wrong. I'm sorry.'

There was a pause. 'May I sit down?'

His words startled her as he indicated one of the faded brocade chairs that sat beside the blazing fire—and his sudden change of tactic took her by surprise. And not just surprise. Because if she was being honest, wasn't there something awfully flattering about a sheikh asking if he could prolong his stay and sit down? Briefly, she wondered if he would let her use his endorsement on her website. 'The Sheikh of Jazratan loves to relax in front of the old-fashioned fire.' She met the cold glitter of his eyes. Probably not.

'If you want,' she said as she turned on one of the

lamps so that the fading afternoon was lit with something other than firelight.

But her heart began to race as he sat down—because it seemed disturbingly intimate to see his muscular body unfold into a chair that suddenly looked insubstantial, and for those endlessly long legs to stretch out in front of him. He looked like a panther who had taken an uncharacteristic moment of relaxation, who had wandered in from the wild into a domestic domain, but all the time you were aware that beneath the sheathed paws lay deadly claws. Was that why her cat suddenly opened its eyes and hissed at him, before jumping up and stalking from the room with her tail held high? Too late she realised she should have said no. She should have made him realise she meant what she said before ejecting him into the snowy afternoon before the light faded.

'So,' she said, with a quick glance at her watch. 'Like I said, I have things I need to do, so maybe you could just cut to the chase?'

'An ironic choice of words in the circumstances,' he commented drily. 'Or perhaps deliberate? Either way, it is unlikely that my stallion will race again, even though he has won nearly every major prize in the racing calendar. In fact, he is in so much pain that the vets have told me that it is cruel to let him continue like this and...' His voice tailed off.

'And?'

He leaned his head back against the chair and his eyes narrowed—dark shards that glinted in the firelight. 'And you have a gift with horses, Livvy,' he said softly. 'A rare gift. You can heal them.'

'Who told you that?

'My trainer. He described to me a woman who was the best horsewoman he'd ever seen. He said that she was as light as a feather but strong as an ox—but that her real skill lay in her interaction with the animal. He said that the angriest horse in the stables would grow calm whenever she grew close. He said he'd seen her do stuff with horses that defied logic, and astounded all the horse vets.' His voice deepened as his dark eyes grew watchful. 'And that they used to call you the horse whisperer.'

It was a long time since Livvy had heard the phrase that had once followed her around like mud on a rainy day at the stables. A phrase that carried its own kind of mystique and made people believe she was some kind of witch. And she wasn't. She was just an ordinary person who wanted to be left to get on with her life.

She bent to pick up a log so that her face was hidden, and by the time she straightened up she had composed herself enough to face his inquisitive stare and to answer him in a steady voice.

'That's all hocus-pocus,' she said. 'Nothing but an old wives' tale and people believing what they want to believe. I just got lucky, that's all. The law of probability says that the horses I helped "heal" would have got better on their own anyway.'

'But I know that sometimes nature can contradict the laws of probability,' he contradicted softly. 'Didn't one of your most famous poets say something on those lines?'

'I don't read poetry,' she said flatly.

'Maybe you should.'

Her smile was tight. 'Just like I don't take advice from strangers.'

His eyes glittered. 'Then, come and work for me and we'll be strangers no longer.'

With a jerky movement she threw another log onto the grate and it sparked into life with a whoosh of flames. Had he deliberately decided to use charm—knowing how effective it could be on someone who was awkward around men? She knew about his reputation but, even if she hadn't, you needed only to look at him to realise that he could have a woman eating out of his hand as easily as you could get a stroppy horse to munch on a sugar cube.

'Look,' she said, trying to sound less abrasive, because he was probably one of those men who responded best to a woman when she was cooing at him. 'I'm sorry I can't help you, but I haven't got a magic wand I can wave to make your horse better. And although I'm obviously flattered that you should have thought of me, I'm just not interested in your offer.'

Saladin felt a flicker of frustration. She didn't sound flattered at all. What was the matter with her? Didn't she realise that accepting this job would carry a huge financial reward—not to mention the kudos of being employed by the royal house of Al Mektala?

He had done his research. He knew that this ancient house she'd inherited was written up in all the guidebooks as somewhere worth visiting and that she ran it as some kind of bed and breakfast business. But the place was going to rack and ruin—anyone could see that. Old houses like this drank money as greedily as the desert sands soaked up water, and it was clear to him that she didn't have a lot of cash to splash about. The brocade chair on which he sat had a spring that was sticking into his buttocks, and the walls beside the fireplace could have done with a coat of paint. His eyes narrowed. Couldn't she see he was offering her the opportunity to earn the kind of sum that would enable her to give the place a complete facelift?

And what about her, with her tomboy clothes and freckled face? She had turned her back on the riding world that had once been her life. She had hidden herself away in the middle of nowhere, serving up cooked breakfasts to the random punters who came to stay. What kind of a life was that for a woman who was nearly thirty? In his own country, a woman was married with at least two children by the age of twenty-five, because it was the custom to marry young. He thought of Alya and a spear of pain lanced through his heart. He remembered dreams crushed and the heavy sense of blame, and he cursed the nature of his thoughts and pushed them away as he looked into Olivia Miller's stubborn face.

'You might not have a magic wand, but I would like you to try. What is it that you say? Nothing ventured, nothing gained. And I think you will discover that the financial rewards I'm offering will be beyond your wildest dreams.' He tilted the corners of his mouth in a brief smile. 'And surely you don't want to look a gift horse in the mouth?'

She didn't respond to his attempt at humour, she just continued to stare at him, only now there was a distinct flicker of annoyance in her amber eyes. Saladin felt another rush of sexual attraction, because women didn't often glare at him like that and he was finding her truculence a surprising turn-on. Because no woman had ever refused him anything.

'How many ways do I have to say no before you'll believe I mean it?' she said.

'And how long will it take you to realise that I am a very persistent man who is used to getting what I want?'

'Persist away—you won't change my mind.'

And suddenly Saladin did what he'd told himself he was only going to do as a last resort, which he seemed now to have reached. He leaned back, his eyes not leaving her face. 'So is this how you are intending to spend the rest of your life, Livvy?' he questioned softly. 'Hiding yourself away in the middle of nowhere and neglecting a talent that few possess—and all because some man once left you standing at the altar?'

CHAPTER TWO

AT FIRST LIVVY didn't react to Saladin's cruel taunt because not reacting was something she was good at. One
of the things she'd taught herself to do when the man
she'd been due to marry had decided not to bother turning up. She'd learned not to show what she was feeling. Not to give the watching world any idea what was
going on inside her head, or her heart. But the sheikh's
words hurt. Even now, they hurt. Even though it was
a long time since anybody had been crass enough to
remind her that she had once been *jilted*. That she had
stood at the altar wearing a stupid white dress and an
eager smile, which had faded as the minutes had ticked
by and the silence had grown into hushed and increasingly urgent whispers as it had dawned on the waiting congregation that the groom wasn't going to show.

She looked at the man sitting there with firelight illuminating his hawklike face and in that moment she
actually *hated* him. How dare he bring up something
so painful just so he could get what *he* wanted? Didn't
he care about hurting people's feelings and trampling
all over them—or was he simply a master of manipulation? Didn't he realise that such a public humiliation had dealt her self-confidence a blow from which

it had taken a long time to recover? And maybe it had never completely recovered. It had still been powerful enough to make her want to leave her old life behind and start a new one. To leave the horses she'd once adored and to view all subsequent advances from men with suspicion.

She would like to take a run at him and *shake* him. To batter her fists against that hard, broad chest and tell him that he was an uncaring beast. But she suspected her rage would be wasted on such a powerful man, and mightn't he regard such a strong response as some petty kind of victory?

'My abandoned marriage has nothing to do with my reasons for not wanting to work for you,' she said, with a coolness she'd cultivated to cope with all the questions she'd had to deal with afterwards. And she'd needed it. She remembered the badly disguised glee in the voices of the women—those wafer-thin blondes who couldn't understand why Rupert de Vries had proposed to someone as unremarkable as her in the first place. *He didn't say why? You mean you honestly had no idea?* No. She'd honestly had no idea. What woman would ever subject herself to that kind of public ridicule if she'd had any inkling the groom was going to do a runner?

She glared into Saladin's glittering dark eyes. 'Though the fact that you even asked the question is another mark against you.'

His dark brows knitted together. 'What are you talking about?'

'I'm talking about the fact that you've obviously been delving into my private life, which isn't making me feel very favourable towards you. No person likes to feel they're being spied on, and you're not doing a very good job of selling yourself as a prospective employer.'

'I don't usually have to sell myself,' he replied, with a coolness that matched hers. 'And surely you can understand why I always investigate people I'm planning to employ.'

'When are you going to accept that you won't be employing me?'

He opened his mouth and then shut it, turning to look around the room, his gaze coming to rest on the faded velvet curtains, as if he'd only just noticed that the sun had bleached them and that moths had been attacking some of the lining.

Had he noticed?

'So is your bed and breakfast business thriving?' he questioned casually.

It was quite clear what he was getting at and suddenly Livvy wanted to prove him wrong. So just *show him*, she thought—though it didn't occur to her until afterwards that she wasn't obliged to show him anything. She wondered if it was pride that made her want to elevate her image from jilted bride to that of budding entrepreneur, even though it wasn't exactly true.

'Indeed it is. It's been a very popular destination,' she said. 'Historic houses like this have a wide appeal to the general public and people can't get enough of them. Speaking of which…' Pointedly, she looked at her watch. 'Your half hour is almost up.'

'But it must be hard work?' he persisted.

She met the mocking question in his black eyes. 'Of course it is. Cooking up to eight different breakfasts to order and making up beds with clean linen most days is not for the faint-hearted. But I've never been afraid of hard work. You don't get anything for nothing in this life.' She paused, her smile growing tight. 'Although I suppose someone like you might be the exception to the rule.'

Not showing any sign of moving, he surveyed her steadily. 'And why might that be?'

'Well, you're a sheikh, aren't you?' she said. 'You're one of the richest men in the world. You own a string of prizewinning racehorses and a palace—for all I know, you might own hundreds of palaces. You have your own plane, I imagine.'

'And?'

'And you've probably never had to lift a finger to acquire the kind of wealth you take for granted. You've probably had everything handed to you on a plate.'

There was silence as Saladin felt a flicker of exasperation. It was an accusation levelled at most people born to royal status, but never usually voiced in his presence because usually people didn't dare. Yes, he was unimaginably rich—but did she think that he had grown up in a bubble? That he'd never had to fight for his country and his people? That he'd never known heartbreak, or stared into the dark abyss of real loss? Once again, Alya's beautiful and perfect face swam into his memory, but he pushed it aside as he met the Englishwoman's quizzical gaze.

'Materially I do not deny that I have plenty,' he said. 'But what about you? You're not exactly on the breadline, are you, Livvy? This place is hardly your average house. You, too, have known privilege.'

Livvy wished he would move away from her, because his presence was making her feel distinctly uncomfortable. As if her plaid shirt had suddenly become too small and her breasts were straining against the tightening buttons. As if those watchful eyes could somehow see through her clothes to the plain and functional underwear that lay beneath.

'It's a rare Georgian house,' she agreed, her fingers playing with the top button of her shirt. 'And I'm lucky to live here. It's been in my family for many years.'

'But the maintenance costs must be high,' he mused.

'Astronomical,' she agreed. 'Which is why I open the house to paying guests.'

He was glancing up at the ceiling now. Had he noticed the ugly damp stain then, or did the firelight successfully hide it? His gaze was lowered and redirected to her face, where once again it seemed to burn its way over her skin.

'So how's business, Livvy—generally?'

Her smile was bland. 'Business is good.'

'Your guests don't mind the fact that the paint is peeling, or that the plaster is crumbling on that far wall?'

'I doubt it. People come looking for history, not pristine paintwork—you can find that almost anywhere in some of the cheaper hotel chains.'

'You know, I could offer you a lot of money,' he observed, after a moment or two. 'Enough to pay for the kind of work this place is crying out for. I could throw in a little extra if you like—so that you could afford the holiday you look as if you need.'

Livvy stiffened. Was he implying that she looked washed out? Almost without her thinking, her fingers crept up to her hairline to brush away a stray strand that must have escaped from her ponytail. It was true she hadn't had a holiday in ages. And it was also true that her debts continued to grow, no matter how many new bookings she took. Sometimes she felt like Canute trying to turn back the tide, and now she couldn't remember how Canute had actually coped. Had he just admitted defeat and given up?

She wished Saladin would stop looking at her like that—his black eyes capturing her in their dark and hypnotic spotlight. She wasn't a vain woman by any definition of the word, but she would have taken a bit more trouble with her appearance if she'd known that a desert sheikh was going to come calling. Suddenly her scalp felt itchy and her face hot, and her shirt still felt as if it had shrunk in the wash.

'Is that your answer to everything?' she questioned. 'To write a cheque and to hell with anything else?'

He shrugged. 'Why wouldn't it be—when I have the capability to do exactly that, and money talks louder than anything else?'

'You cynic,' she breathed.

'I'm not denying that.' He gave a soft laugh. 'Or maybe you're just naive. Money talks, Livvy—it talks louder than anything else. It's about the only thing in life you can rely on—which is why you should do yourself a favour and come with me to Jazratan. My stable complex is the finest in the world and it would be interesting for you to see it.'

He smiled at her, but Livvy sensed it was a calculating smile. As if he had only produced it because it would add a touch of lightness to conversation that wasn't going the way he intended.

'Come and work with my horse and I'll give you whatever you want, within reason,' he continued. 'And if you cure Burkaan—if you ensure that a gun will not be held to his head while I am forced to stare into his trusting and bewildered eyes as the life bleeds out of him, you will walk away knowing that you need never worry about money again.'

The heartfelt bit about the horse got to her much more than the financial incentive he was offering. In fact, she hated the mercenary progression of his words. As if everything had a price—even people. As if you could wear them down just by increasing the amount of money on the table. Maybe in his world, that was what happened.

But despite her determination not to be tempted, she *was* tempted. For a minute she allowed herself to think what she could do with the money. Where would she even start? By tackling the ancient wiring in some of the bedrooms, or sorting out the antiquated boiler that badly needed replacing? She thought about the icy corridors upstairs and the lack of insulation in the roof. Most of the heat was pumped into the guest bedrooms, leaving her own windows coated with a thin layer of ice each morning. She shivered. It had been a bitter winter and they were still only a third of the way through it, and she was getting fed up with having to wear thick socks to bed at night.

'I can't,' she said. 'I have guests who are due to spend the holidays here who are arriving in a couple of days. I can't just cancel their Christmas and New Year when they've spent months looking forward to it. You'll just have to find someone else.'

Saladin's mouth tightened, but still he wasn't done. Didn't she realise that he would get what he wanted in the end, no matter how he had to go about it? That if it came to a battle of wills, he would win. Spurred on by the almost imperceptible note of hesitation he'd heard in her voice, he got up from his chair and walked over to the window. It was almost dark, but the heavy clouds had already leached the sky of all colour and all you could see was snow. It had highlighted all the leafless trees with ghostly white fingers. It had blanketed his parked car so that all that was visible was a snowy mound.

His eyes narrowed as fat flakes swirled down, transformed into tumbling gold feathers by the light streaming from the window. He ran through the possibilities of what he should do next, knowing his choices were limited. He could go and get his car started before the snow came down any harder. He could drive off and come back again tomorrow. Give her time to think about his offer and realise that she would be a fool to reject it. Or he could have his people deal with it, using rather more ruthless back-room tactics.

He turned back to see her unsmiling face and he was irritated by his inability to get through to her. Logic told him to leave, yet for some reason he was reluctant to do so, even though she had started walking towards the door, making it clear that she expected him to trail after her. A woman who wanted him gone? Unbelievable! When had any woman ever turned him away?

He followed her out into the wood-lined corridor, which was lit by lamps on either side, realising that she was close enough to touch. And bizarrely, he thought about kissing her. About claiming those stubborn and unpainted lips with his own and waiting to see how long it would take before she was breathlessly agreeing to anything he asked of her.

But his choices were suddenly taken away from him by a dramatic intervention as the lights went out and the corridor was plunged into darkness. From just ahead of him, he heard Livvy gasp and then he felt the softness of her body as she stumbled back against him.

CHAPTER THREE

As THE CORRIDOR was plunged into darkness, Saladin's hands automatically reached out to steady the stumbling Livvy. At least, that was what he told himself. He thought afterwards that if she'd been a man he wouldn't have let his hands linger on her for quite so long, nor his fingers to grip her slender body quite so tightly. But Livvy Miller was a woman—and it had been a long time since he had touched a woman. It had recently been the anniversary of Alya's death and he always shied away from intimacy on either side of that grim date, when pain and loss and regret overwhelmed him. Because to do so felt like a betrayal of his wife's memory—a mechanical act that seemed like a pale version of the real thing. With other women it was just sex— something a man needed in order to function properly. A basic appetite to be fed—and nothing more. But with Alya it had been different. Something that had captured his heart as well as his body.

But maybe for now a body would do…

He felt himself tense with that first, sweet contact— that first touch that set your hormones firing, whether you wanted them to or not. He could feel Livvy's heart beating hard as his hands curved around her ribcage.

The soapy scent that perfumed her skin was both innocent and beguiling, and the tension inside him increased. He found himself wishing he could magic away their clothing and seek relief from the sudden unbearable aching deep inside him. An anonymous coupling in this darkened corridor would be perfect for his needs. It might even have the added benefit of making the stubborn Englishwoman reconsider his offer, because a sexually satisfied woman automatically became a compliant woman.

For a moment he felt her relax against him and he sensed her welcoming softness—as if a split second more would be all the time he needed for her to open up to him. But then she pulled away. Actually, she *snatched* herself away. In the darkness he could hear her struggling to control her breathing and, although he couldn't see the expression on her face, he could hear the panic in her voice.

'What's happened?' she gasped.

It interested him that she'd chosen to ignore that brief but undeniable embrace. He wondered what she would say if he answered truthfully. *I am big enough to explode and I want to put myself inside you and spill my seed.* In his fantasy he knew exactly what he would like her response to be. She would nod and then tear at his clothing with impatient fingers while he dealt swiftly with hers. No need even to undress. Access was all that was required. He would press her up against that wood panelling, and then slide his fingers between her legs while he freed himself. He would kiss her until she was begging him for more, and then he would guide himself to where she was wet and ready, and push deep inside her. It would be quick and it would be meaningless, but he doubted there would be any objections from her.

She was flicking a light switch on and off, but nothing was happening. 'What's happened?' she repeated, only now her voice sounded accusatory.

With a monumental effort he severed his erotic fantasy and let it drift away, concentrating instead on the dense darkness that surrounded them, but his mouth was so dry and his groin so hard that it was several seconds before he was able to answer her question.

'There's been a power cut,' he said.

'I know that,' she howled illogically. 'But how did it happen?'

'I have no idea,' he answered steadily. 'And the how isn't important. We have to deal with it. Do you have your own emergency generator?'

'Are you insane?' Her panicked question came shooting at him through the darkness. 'Of course I don't!'

'Well, then,' he said impatiently. 'Where do you keep your candles?'

Livvy couldn't think straight. He might as well have asked her where the planet Jupiter was in the night sky. Because the sudden loss of light and heating were eclipsed by the realisation that she had been on the brink of losing control. She'd nearly gone to pieces in his arms, because his touch had felt dangerous. And inviting. It had only been the briefest of embraces, but it had been mind-blowing. She hadn't imagined feeling the unmistakable power of his arousal pressing firmly against her. And the amazing thing was that it hadn't shocked her. On the contrary—she'd wanted him to carry on holding her like that. Hadn't she been tempted to turn around and stretch up on tiptoe, to see whether he would kiss her as she sensed he had wanted to? And then to carry on kissing her.

'Candles?' he prompted impatiently.

She swallowed. 'They're…in the kitchen,' she said. 'I'll get them.'

'I'll come with you.'

'You don't think I'm capable of finding my way around my own house?'

'It's dark,' he ground out. 'And we're sticking together.'

Saladin caught hold of her wrist and closed his fingers over it, thinking that if only he had been accompanied by his usual bodyguards and envoys, then someone would now be attempting to fix whatever the problem was.

But he had undertaken this journey alone—instinct telling him that he would have a better chance of success with the Englishwoman without all the dazzle of royal life that inevitably accompanied him. Because some people were intimidated by all the trappings that surrounded a royal sheikh—and, in truth, he liked to shrug off those trappings whenever possible.

When travelling in Europe or the United States, he sometimes got his envoy Zane to act as a decoy sheikh. The two men were remarkably similar in appearance and they had long ago discovered that one powerful robed figure wearing a headdress in the back of a speeding car was interchangeable with another, to all but the most perceptive eye.

In Jazratan he sometimes took solo trips deep into the heart of the desert. At other times he had been known to dress as a merchant and to blend into the thronging crowds of the marketplace in the capital city of Janubwardi. It gave him a certain kick to listen to what his people were saying about him when they thought they were free to do so. His advisors didn't like it, but that was tough. He refused to be treated with kid gloves, especially here in England—a country he knew well. And he knew that the dangers in life were the ones where obvious risk was involved, but the ones that hit you totally out of the blue…

He could feel her pulse slamming wildly beneath his fingers.

'Let me go,' she whispered.

'No. You're not going anywhere,' he snapped. 'Stick close to me—I'm going first. And be careful.'

'I don't need you to tell me to be careful. Don't you have a phone? We could use it as a torch instead of stumbling around in the dark.'

'It's in my car,' he said as they edged along a corridor that seemed less dense now that his eyes had started to accustom themselves to the lack of light. 'Where's yours?'

'In my bedroom.'

'Handy,' he said sarcastically.

'I wasn't expecting to be marooned in the darkness with a total stranger.'

'Spare me the melodrama, Livvy. And let's just concentrate on getting there without falling over.'

Cautiously, they moved along the ancient passage. The flagged floors echoed as she led him down a narrow flight of stairs, into a large windowless kitchen that was as dark as pitch. She wriggled her hand free and felt her way towards a cupboard, where he could hear her scrabbling around—before uttering a little cry of triumph as she located the candles. He found himself admiring her efficiency, but noticed that her fingers were trembling as she struck a match and her pale face was illuminated as the flame grew steady.

Wordlessly, he took the matches from her and lit several more candles while she melted wax and positioned them carefully in tarnished silver holders. The room grew lighter and the flames cast out strange shadows that flickered over the walls. He could see the results of what must have been a pretty intensive baking session, because on the table were plates of biscuits and a platter of those sweet things the English always ate at Christmastime. He frowned as he tried to remember what they were called. Mince pies, that was it.

'What do you think has happened?' she questioned.

He shrugged. 'A power line down? It can sometimes happen if there's a significant weight of snow.'

'But it can't!' She looked around, a touch of desperation in her voice. 'I've still got so much to do before my guests arrive.'

He sent her a wry look. 'Looks as though it's going to have to wait.'

A sudden silence fell and he noticed that her hand was trembling even more now.

'Hadn't you better go, before the snow gets much worse?' she said, in a casual tone that didn't quite come off. 'There must be someone waiting for you. Someone who's wondering where you are.'

Incredulously, he stared at her. 'And leave you here, on your own? Without electricity?' He walked over to one of the old-fashioned radiators and laid the flat of his hand on it. 'Or heating.'

'I'm perfectly capable of managing on my own,' she said stubbornly.

'I don't care,' he said. 'I'm not going anywhere. What kind of man would walk out and leave a woman to fend for herself in conditions like these?'

'So you're staying in order to ease your own conscience?'

There was a pause, and when he spoke his voice had a bitter note to it. 'Something like that.'

Livvy's heart thundered as she tried to work out what to do next. 'Don't panic' should have been top of her list, while the second should be to stop allowing Saladin to take control. Maybe where he came from, men dealt with emergencies while the women just hung around looking decorative. Well, perhaps it might do him good to realise that she didn't need a man to fix things for her. She didn't need a man for anything. She'd learned to change a fuse and fix a leaking tap. She'd managed alone for long enough and that was the way she liked it.

She walked over to the phone, which hung on a neat cradle on the wall, but was greeted with nothing but an empty silence as she placed it against her ear.

'Dead?' he questioned.

'Completely.' She replaced it and looked at him but, despite her best intentions, she *was* starting to panic. Had she, in the rush to buy the tree and hang the mistletoe and bake the mince pies, remembered to charge her cell phone? 'I'll go upstairs and get my phone.'

'I'll come with you.'

'Were you born to be bossy?'

'I think I was. Why, does it bother you?'

'Yes.'

'Tough,' he said as he picked up a candle.

But as they left the kitchen Saladin realised that for the first time in a long time he was feeling *exhilarated*. Nobody had a clue where he was. He was marooned in the middle of the snowy English countryside with a feisty redhead he suspected would be his before the night was over. And suddenly his conscience and his troubled memories were forgotten as he followed her up the large staircase leading from the arched reception hall, where the high ceilings flickered with long shadows cast from their candles. They reached her bedroom and Saladin drew in a deep breath as she pushed open the door and turned to him, a studiedly casual note in her voice.

'You can wait here, if you like.'

'Like a pupil standing outside the headmaster's study?' he drawled. 'No. I don't like. Don't worry, Livvy—I won't be judging you if your room's a mess and I think I'm sophisticated enough to resist the temptation to throw you down on the bed, if that's what you're worried about.'

'Oh, come in, if you insist,' she said crossly.

But it was with a feeling of pride that she opened the door and walked through, with Saladin not far behind her. The curtains were not yet drawn and the reflected light from the snow outside meant that the room looked almost radiant with a pure and ghostly light. On a table beside the bed stood a bowl of hyacinths, which scented the cold air. Antique pieces of furniture glowed softly in the candlelight. It was a place of peace and calm—her haven—and one of many reasons why she clung to this house and all the memories it contained.

She walked over to the window seat and found her phone, dejectedly staring down at its black screen.

'It's dead,' she said. 'I was sending photo messages to a school friend when the snow started and then they delivered the Christmas tree...' Her words tailed off. 'You'll have to go out to the car and get yours.'

'I will decide if and when I'm going out to the car,' he snapped. 'You do *not* issue instructions to a sheikh.'

'I didn't invite you here,' she said, her voice low. 'We're here together under duress and in extremely bizarre circumstances—and I think it's going to make an unbearable situation even worse if you then start pulling rank on me.'

He looked as if he was about to come back at her with a sharp response, but seemed to think better of it—because he nodded. 'Very well. I will go to the car and get my phone.'

He left the room abruptly, and as she heard him going downstairs she felt slightly spooked—a feeling that was only increased when the front door slammed. Everything seemed unnaturally quiet without him— all she could hear was the loud tick of the grandfather clock as it echoed through the house. She stared out of the window to see the sheikh's shadowy figure making its way towards a car that was now completely covered in white. The snow was still falling, and she found herself thinking that at least he'd had the sense to retrieve his cashmere coat and put it on before going outside.

She could see him brushing a thick layer of snow away from the door, which he was obviously having difficulty opening. She wondered what would happen next. Would crack teams of Jazratan guards descend in a helicopter from the snowy sky, the way they did in films? Doubtfully, she looked up at the fat flakes that were swirling down as thickly as ever. She didn't know much about planes, but she doubted it would be safe to fly in conditions like this.

Grabbing a sweater from the wardrobe and pulling it on, she went back downstairs to the kitchen and had just put a kettle on the hob when she heard the front door slam, followed by the sound of echoing footsteps. She looked up to see Saladin standing framed in the kitchen doorway and hated the instant rush of relief— and something else—that flooded through her. What was the something else? she wondered. The reassurance of having someone so unashamedly alpha strutting around the place, despite all her protestations that she was fine on her own? Or was the root cause more fundamental—a case of her body responding to him in away she wasn't used to? A way that *scared* her.

Despite the warm sweater she'd pulled on, she could feel the puckering of her breasts as she looked at him.

'Any luck?' she said.

'Some. I've spoken with my people—and the roads are impassable. We won't get any help sent out to us tonight.'

Livvy's hand trembled as she tipped boiling water into the teapot. They were stuck here for the night— just the two of them. So why wasn't she paralysed with a feeling of dread and fear? Why had her heart started pounding with excitement? She swallowed.

'Would you like some tea?'

'Please.' His voice grew curious. 'How have you managed to boil water?'

'Gas hob,' she said, thinking how *domesticated* this

all sounded. And how the words people spoke rarely reflected what was going on inside their heads. She looked into the gleam of his eyes. 'Are you hungry? I'll put some mince pies on a plate,' she said, in the kind of babbling voice people used when they were trying to fill an awkward silence. 'And we can go in and sit by the fire.'

'Here. Let me.' He took the tray from her, aware that this was something he rarely did. People always carried things for *him*. They ran his bath for him and laid out his cool silk robes every morning. For diplomatic meetings, all his paperwork was stacked in symmetrical piles awaiting his attention, even down to the gold pen that was always positioned neatly to the left. He didn't have to deal with the everyday mechanics of normal life, because his life was not normal. Never had been, nor ever could be. Even his response to tragedy could never be like other men's—for he'd been taught that the sheikh must never show emotion, no matter what he was feeling inside. So that when he had wanted to weep bitter tears over Alya's coffin, he had known that the face he'd needed to show to his people must be an implacable face.

His mouth hardened as he carried the tea tray to the room where the bare Christmas tree stood silhouetted against the window and watched as she sank down onto the silky rug. And suddenly the sweet wholesomeness of her made all his dark thoughts melt away.

The bulky sweater she was wearing emphasised her tiny frame and the slender legs that were tucked up neatly beneath her. The firelight had turned her titian ponytail into a stream of flaming red, and all he could think about was how much he wanted to see her naked…

So make it happen, he thought—as the pulse at his groin began to throb with anticipation. *Just make it happen.*

CHAPTER FOUR

'WE HAVE A long evening ahead of us, Livvy. Any idea of how you'd like to fill it?'

Livvy eyed Saladin warily as he drawled out his question, thinking that he was suddenly being almost *too* well behaved, and wondering why. She almost preferred him when he was being bossy and demanding, because that had infuriated her enough to create a natural barrier between them. A barrier behind which she felt safe.

But now?

Now he was being suspiciously compliant. He had drunk the tea she'd given him and eaten an accompanying mince pie—declaring it to be delicious and telling her he intended to take the recipe back for the palace chefs, so that his courtiers and guests could enjoy the English delicacy. He had even dragged a whole pile of logs back from the woodshed and heaped them into the big basket beside the fire.

Despite the thickness of her sweater, a shiver ran down her spine as she watched him. His body was hard and muscular and he moved with the grace of a natural athlete. He handled the logs as if they were no heavier than twigs and somehow made the task look effortless. Livvy was proud of her independence and her insistence on doing the kind of jobs that some of her married school friends turned up their noses at. She never baulked at taking out the rubbish or sweeping the gravel drive. She happily carried logs and weeded the garden whenever she had time, but she couldn't deny that it felt like an unexpected luxury to be waited on like this. To lean back against the cushioned footstool sipping her tea, watching Saladin Al Mektala sort out the fire for her. He made her feel...*pampered*, and he made her feel feminine.

She considered his question.

'We could always play a game,' she suggested.

'Good idea.' His dark eyes assumed the natural glint of the predator. 'I love playing games.'

Nobody had ever accused Livvy of sophistication, but neither was she stupid. She'd worked for a long time in the testosterone-filled industry of horse racing and had been engaged to a very tricky man. She'd learned the hard way how womanising men flirted and used innuendo. And the only way to keep it in check was to ignore it. So she ignored the flare of light that had made the sheikh's eyes gleam like glowing coal and subjected him to a look of cool question. 'Scrabble?' she asked. 'Or cards?'

'Whichever you choose,' he said. 'Although I must warn you now that I shall beat you.'

'Is that supposed to be a challenge I can't resist?'

'Let's see, shall we?'

To Livvy's fury, his arrogant prediction proved correct. He won every game they played and even beat her at Scrabble—something at which she normally excelled.

Trying not to be a bad sport, she dropped the pen onto the score sheet. 'So how come you've managed to beat me at a word game that isn't even in your native tongue?' she said.

'Because when I was a little boy I had an English tutor who taught me that a rich vocabulary was something within the grasp of all men. And I was taught to win. It's what Al Mektala men do. We never like to fail. At anything.'

'So you're always triumphant?'

He turned his head to look at her and Livvy's heart missed a beat as she saw something flickering within the dark blaze of his eyes that didn't look like arrogance. Was she imagining the trace of sorrow she saw there—or the lines around his mouth, which suddenly seemed to have deepened?

'No,' he said harshly. 'A long time ago I failed at something quite spectacularly.'

'At what?'

'Something better left in the past, where it belongs.' His voice grew cold and distant as he threw another log onto the fire, and when he turned back Livvy saw that his features had become shuttered. 'Tell me something about you instead,' he said.

She shrugged. 'There's not very much to tell. I'm twenty-nine and I run a bed and breakfast business from the house in which I was born. My love life you already seem well acquainted with. Anything else you want to know?'

'Yes.' His hawklike features were gilded by the flicker of the firelight as he leaned forward. 'Why did he jilt you?'

She met the searching blaze of his black eyes. 'You really think I'd tell *you*?'

He raised his dark brows. 'Why not? I'm curious. And after the snow clears, you'll never see me again—that is, if you really are determined to turn down my offer of a job. Isn't that what people do in circumstances such as these? They tell each other secrets.'

As she considered his words, Livvy wondered how he saw her. As some sad spinster who'd tucked herself away in the middle of nowhere, far away from the fast-paced world she'd once inhabited? And if that was the case, then wasn't this an ideal opportunity to show him that she *liked* the life she'd chosen—to show him she was completely over Rupert?

But if you're over him—then how come you still shut out men? How come you must be the only twenty-nine-year-old virgin on the planet?

The uncomfortable trajectory of her thoughts made her bold. *So let it go,* she told herself. *Let the past go by setting it free.* 'Do you know Rupert de Vries?' she asked slowly.

'I met him a couple of times—back in the day, as they say.' His mouth twisted. 'I didn't like him.'

'You don't have to say that just to make me feel better.'

'I can assure you that I never say things I don't mean, Livvy.' There was a pause. 'What happened?'

She stared down at the rug, trying to concentrate on the symmetrical shapes that were woven into the silk. She pictured Rupert's face—something she hadn't done for a long time—fine boned and fair and the antithesis of the tawny sheikh in front of her. She remembered how she couldn't believe that the powerful racing figure had taken an interest in *her*, the lowliest of grooms at the time. 'I expect you know that he ran a very successful yard for a time.'

'Until he got greedy,' Saladin said, stretching his legs out in front of him. 'He overextended himself and that was a big mistake. You should always keep something back when you're dealing with horses, no matter how brilliant they are. Because ultimately they are flesh and blood—and flesh and blood is always vulnerable.'

She heard the sudden rawness in his voice and wondered if he was thinking about Burkaan. 'Yes,' she said.

'So how come it got as far as you standing at the altar before he got cold feet?' Black eyes bored into her. 'That's what happened, isn't it? Didn't he talk to you about it beforehand—let you know he was having doubts?'

Livvy shook her head as her mind raced back to that chaotic period. At the time she'd done that thing of trying to salvage her pride by telling everyone with a brisk cheerfulness that it was much better to find out *before* the wedding, rather than after it. That it would have been unbearable if Rupert had decided he wanted out a few years and a few children down the line. But those had been things she'd felt *obliged* to say, so that she wouldn't come over as bitter. The truth was that the rejection had left her feeling hollow…and stupid. Not only had she been completely blind to her fiancé's transgressions, but there had been all the practical considerations, too. Like paying the catering staff who were standing around in their aprons in the deserted marquee almost bursting with excitement at the *drama* of it all. And informing the driver of the limousine firm that they wouldn't be needing a lift to the airport after all. And cancelling the honeymoon, which she'd paid for and for which Rupert had been supposed to settle up with her afterwards. He never had, of course, and the wedding that never was had ended up costing her a lot more than injured pride.

And once the initial humiliation was over and everyone had been paid off, she had made a vow never to talk about it. She'd told herself that if she fed the story it would grow. So she'd cut off people's questions and deliberately changed the subject and dared them to continue to pursue it, and eventually people had got the message.

But now she looked into the gleam of Saladin's eyes and realised that there had been a price to pay for her silence. She suddenly recognised how deeply she had buried the truth and saw that if she continued to keep it hidden away, she risked making herself an eternal victim. The truth was that she was over Rupert and glad she hadn't married him. So why act like someone with a dirty secret—why not get it out into the open and watch it wither and die as it was exposed to the air?

'Because I allowed myself to do what women are so good at doing,' she said slowly. 'I allowed myself to be wooed by a very persuasive man, without stopping to consider why someone like him should be interested in someone like me.'

His eyes narrowed. 'What's that supposed to mean?'

'Oh, come on, Saladin—you haven't held back from being blunt, so why start now? He was known for dating glamorous women and I'm not. The only thing I had to commend me was the fact that my father owned a beautiful house. This house. My mother was dead and my stepmother long gone—and since I don't have any brothers or sisters, I stood to inherit everything. From where Rupert was sitting, it must have looked a very attractive proposition and I think he made the assumption that there was lots of money sitting in a bank account somewhere—the kind of money that could have bailed out his failing business.'

'But there wasn't?'

'At some point there was. Before my stepmother got her hands on it and decided to blow a lot of it on diamonds and plastic surgery and then demand a massive divorce settlement. By the time my father died there was nothing left—not after I'd paid for the nurses who helped care for him in his final years.'

'You didn't think to tell de Vries that?'

Livvy gave a snarl of a laugh as she picked up the poker and gave the fire a vicious stab. 'Most brides labour under the illusion that they're being married for love, not money. It would look a bit pathetic, don't you think, if one were to have a conversation on the lines of, "Look, I've just discovered that I'm broke—but you do still love me, don't you?" And the truth of it was that I didn't realise how little money there was—at least, not until just before the wedding.'

'And then you told him?'

'I told him,' she agreed. She would never forget the look on her prospective groom's face. That leaching of colour that had left him with a curiously waxy complexion and the fleeting look of horror in his eyes. In that illuminating moment Livvy hadn't been able to decide who she was angrier with—Rupert, for his unbelievable shallowness, or herself for having been too blind to see it before. Maybe she just hadn't wanted to see.

'I told him and he didn't like it. I wish he'd told me right then that he'd changed his mind, so that I wouldn't have to go through the whole pantomime of dressing up in a big white frock with my bridesmaids flapping around me in nervous excitement. But obviously that was something he couldn't face doing. So there.' She looked at him defiantly. 'Have you got the whole picture now?'

There was silence for a moment—the firelight flickering over his ebony hair as he studied her. 'Not quite,' he said.

Defensively, she stiffened. 'You want a blow-by-blow account of my subsequent meltdown?'

He shook his head. 'I meant that not everything you said is true.'

His words were softer than before, as if they'd suddenly been brushed with velvet. Or silk. Yet despite their softness, all the time Livvy was aware of the underlying steel underpinning them, and that made him sound even more attractive. Dangerously so.

'Which bit in particular?'

He smiled. 'That you have nothing to commend you other than a house.'

'Oh, really?'

Saladin heard the disbelief in her voice and felt a surge of rage that someone as worthless as de Vries had smashed her confidence and made her hide herself away like this.

'Yes, really.' His gaze drifted over her. 'Would you like me to list your more obvious attributes?'

Splaying her hands over her hips, she struck a pose. 'My old jeans and sweater?'

'Your complexion, for a start, which makes me think

of honey and cream.' His voice dipped. 'And, of course, your freckles.'

Her fingers strayed to her nose. 'I hate my freckles.'

'Of course you do, but in my country they are highly prized. We call them kisses from the sun.'

'Well, that's certainly not what we call them here.' She gave a nervous laugh and then shivered, as if she had only just registered the sudden plummet in temperature. 'It's cold,' she said, rubbing her hands up and down her arms. 'I should go and make us something to eat.'

'I'm not hungry.'

'You must be. I am. Starving, in fact.'

He could hear the lie in her voice as she jumped to her feet and picked up one of the candles, as if she couldn't wait to escape from the sudden intimacy that had sprung up between them.

'I'll come and help you,' he said.

'No.' The word was sharp, before she pulled it back with a smile. 'I'd prefer to do it on my own. Really. You stay here. You look very comfortable.'

He knew why she was trying to put distance between them and that it was a futile exercise. Didn't she realise that her darkened eyes gave her away and her body was betraying all the signs of sexual excitement? He felt the hard beat of anticipation cradling his groin and suddenly the bright beat of sexual excitement burned out everything except the anticipation of pleasure. 'Don't be long,' he said softly.

Livvy felt almost *helpless* as she made her way towards the kitchen through the now distinctly chilly corridors. She couldn't believe she'd just blurted out all that stuff—to Saladin, of all people—and wondered how he'd managed to cut through her defences so effectively. But he had. She had been surprised at his understanding—and then suspicious of it, because it made her feel vulnerable. And she didn't want to feel vulnerable. She didn't want to feel any of the stuff that was raging through her body like wildfire. As if she would die if he didn't touch her. As if her life wouldn't be complete unless she knew what it was like to have Saladin Al Mektala take her in his arms and kiss her.

Because she had made that mistake once before. She'd fallen for a powerful man who was way out of her league—and it was not something she intended repeating.

She set about preparing food she suspected neither of them wanted, putting a plate of newly baked bread onto a tray along with some cheese from the local shop, and adding some rosy apples that she absently polished with a cloth. She wondered if he drank wine but decided against it, making coffee instead. Wine was the last thing either of them needed.

When she returned to the drawing room, he hadn't moved from where he'd been sitting. In fact, his eyes were closed and he was so still that she thought he might have fallen asleep. For a moment she just stood there looking at him, trying to take in the unbelievable scene that lay before her. A real-life king was stretched out in front of *her* fire, his ebony head resting against the faded crimson silk of the brocade chair. He looked powerful and exotic—dominating his surroundings with a brooding sensuality, which shimmered from his powerful frame. His long legs were sprawled out in front of him and the material of his trousers was flattened down over the hard bulge of his thighs. And all her best intentions melted away because just looking at him made her want him—and it was *wrong* to want him.

Suddenly he opened his eyes and the crockery on the tray she was holding began to jangle as her hands began to tremble. Livvy hoped he hadn't noticed the rush of blood that was making her cheeks burn, but she was aware of the glint of amusement in his eyes as she walked across the room towards the fire. She waited for him to make some smart comment, but he said nothing—just watched in silence as she put the tray down. Her heart was pounding as she sat down on the rug beside him and tried to behave casually.

'Help yourself,' she said.

'Help yourself?' There was a pause. 'But I am used to someone serving me, Livvy.'

She heard the mockery in his voice and she turned her head to catch the provocative gleam in his eyes. *He's flirting with me*, she thought. And no way was she going to flirt back. 'I'm sure you are,' she said crisply. 'But something tells me you are a man who is perfectly capable of looking after himself.'

Saladin smiled, wondering if she was aware that her attitude was slowly sealing her fate. If she had been submissive and eager to please—as women always were—then his desire might now have faded. But she wasn't being in the least bit submissive. She was sitting munching her way through an apple, though she didn't look as if she was particularly enjoying it—and her body had stiffened with a defiance that he couldn't resist.

He could feel the sudden beat of anticipation. Apart from the protected virgins in his homeland who were expected to remain pure until marriage, he couldn't think of a single woman in this situation who wouldn't be coming on to him by now. She was a challenge—in a world where few challenges remained. Shifting his position slightly, he tried to alleviate some of the pressure on his rapidly hardening groin.

She had thrown the apple core into the fire and was holding out her hands in front of the flames again, spreading her fingers wide. They were *working* hands, he thought, and something made him lean over and pour coffee for them both—though she took hers with a look of surprise she couldn't quite disguise.

He watched as she ate a little bread and cheese, but he took no food himself and eventually she pushed her plate away.

'You're not eating,' she said.

'I told you I wasn't hungry.'

She hugged her arms around her knees and looked at him. 'So now what do we do? More Scrabble? Or do you want to try calling up your people to see if the roads are clear?'

'Forget about my people,' he said impatiently, his gaze straying to the pinpoint tips of her nipples. 'You're cold.'

Livvy saw the direction of his glance—bold, appraising and unashamed—and felt the instant quickening of her body in response. Her heart was fluttering as if it was trying to escape from the confinement of her ribcage, and she knew exactly what she should do. She should say goodnight and go upstairs to her icy bedroom and stay there until the morning brought snow ploughs, or his private helicopter or *something* to rescue them from their incarceration.

But she didn't. She stayed exactly where she was, seated on the rug, gazing back at him—as if she had no idea what was going to happen next. Yet despite her lack of experience and the sheer impossibility of the situation, she knew exactly what was about to happen because it was happening right now. Saladin Al Mektala was putting his hand on her shoulder and pulling her close before bending his head to kiss her.

Livvy reeled at that first sweet taste as he began to explore her mouth with the flickering tip of his tongue, and a great wave of desire and emotion swept through her in a stupefying rush. As his arms tightened around her she felt safe. She could taste coffee on his tongue and feel the warmth of his breath as he anchored her head to deepen the kiss and she opened her mouth beneath his seeking lips. His fingertips moved to whisper their way over her neck, but the first touch of his hand to her breast made her freeze as she wondered just what he would expect from her.

She knew exactly what he would expect from her—and it was a million miles away from the reality of what he would actually get. And wouldn't he be horrified if he knew the truth?

'Saladin—' The word came out as a barely intelligible sound as she broke the kiss.

'You're now going to list all the reasons why we shouldn't do this?' he said unsteadily.

'Yes.'

'Starting with what? Lack of desire?' He grazed the pad of his thumb over her bottom lip and it trembled wildly in response. 'I don't think so.'

With an effort she jerked away from him, her words tumbling out of her mouth as she struggled to do the right thing. 'Starting with the fact that you're a sheikh and I'm a commoner and we don't really know each other.'

'Something that can be solved in an instant,' he said unevenly.

'In fact, we don't even seem to *like* one another,' she continued. 'We've done nothing but argue since you arrived.'

'But conflict can make sex so piquant, don't you think?' he murmured. 'Such a blessed relief when all that tension is finally broken.'

Livvy didn't answer. She didn't dare. Would he laugh if he realised the truth? And now he was reaching behind her head to tug the elastic band from her ponytail—and she was letting him. Sitting there perfectly still as her hair spilled down over her shoulders and his eyes narrowed with appreciation.

'You could probably come up with a whole stack of reasons why we shouldn't,' he said. 'But there's one thing that cancels out every one of your objections.'

She knew she shouldn't, but Livvy asked it all the same. 'Which is?'

'Because we want to. Very, very badly. At least, I do. How about you?'

Livvy shut her eyes, afraid that she would be swayed by the desire that burned so blackly from his eyes. *Because we want to.* How simple that sounded to someone who hadn't followed her own desires for so long that she'd forgotten how. But maybe that was because she hadn't ever been tempted before—at least, not like this. After she had behaved so circumspectly with Rupert, his betrayal had come as a complete shock and had made her question her own judgement. She'd been cautious of men—and wary. After she'd packed up her wedding dress and sent it off to raise money for charity, she had felt empty inside—as if there were a space there that could never be filled. She had begun to think there was something wrong with her. That she wasn't like other women.

But now...

Now there was a hot storm of need within her and she felt anything was possible. That the powerful sheikh had all the knowledge required to give her pleasure. And was it such a terrible thing to want pleasure when it had been denied to her for so long?

She tipped her head back to expose her neck to him and instantly he covered it with a path of tiny kisses. Beneath the sweater, she could feel the increasing weight of her breasts and the denim of her jeans scraping against her newly sensitive thighs as sexual hunger began to pulse through her.

'Saladin,' she said again, her voice a throaty invitation as she felt his hand move slowly down her ribcage towards her waist.

'You are very overdressed, *habibi*,' he observed, peeling the sweater over her head with effortless dexterity.

Livvy held her breath with trepidation as he began to unbutton the shirt underneath and she wondered if he would be turned off by her boring white bra, because a man like this would surely be used to fine underwear. But he didn't appear to notice any obvious deficiencies in the lingerie department as he peeled away her shirt—he seemed too intent on bending his dark head to her exposed skin and she shivered again as she felt his tongue slide over her breastbone, leaving a moist trail behind.

'Your body is so tiny,' he said as he edged his fingers beneath the waistband of her jeans. 'I don't think I've ever been with a woman who is so small.'

And that was when reality hit her like an invisible punch to the solar plexus. She was making out with a man she barely knew. A ruthless sheikh who exuded a dark and dangerous sensuality—and she was seconds away from succumbing to him. Heart pounding, she wrenched herself away, grabbing at her scattered clothes and scrambling to her feet as he stared up at her with dazed disbelief.

'What's going on?' he demanded.

She began to button up her shirt with shaking fingers. 'Isn't it obvious? I'm stopping this before it goes any further.'

He raked his fingers through his hair, his expression one of impatience and frustration. 'I thought we'd already had this conversation,' he growled.

'It's an ongoing conversation,' she said, sucking in an unsteady breath. 'On every level, this would be a mistake and it's not going to happen. We're two people from completely different worlds, who won't ever see one another again once the snow melts. It seems you're stuck here until help arrives, but there's nothing we can do about it. We'll just have to make the best of a bad situation. Just so you know—there are seven bedrooms in this house and you're welcome to sleep in any of them.' She glared at him. 'Just stay out of mine.'

CHAPTER FIVE

SALADIN WAS CUPPING her breast again, only this time it was completely bare. His palm was massaging the peaking nipple and Livvy made a mewing little sound of pleasure.

'Please,' she moaned softly. 'Oh, Saladin. Please.'

He didn't answer, but now his hand was circling her belly—slowly and rhythmically—before drifting down towards the soft tangle of curls at her thighs and coming to a tantalising halt. Her throat dried as the molten heat continued to build and she felt her thighs part in silent invitation. *Just do it*, she prayed silently. *Forget all those stupid objections I put in your way. I was stupid and uptight and life is too short. I don't care whether it's right or wrong, I just want you.*

She opened her mouth to call his name again when she heard the loud bang of a door somewhere in the distance and she woke with a start, blinking in horror as she looked around, her heart banging against her ribcage like a frenzied drum. Disorientated and bewildered, she tried to work out what had happened, before the truth hit her. She was in her bedroom at Wightwick Manor with her hand between her legs, about to call out Saladin's name—and she'd never felt so sexually excited in her life.

Whipping the duvet away, she was relieved to see that the other side of the bed was smooth and unslept in—although her pyjama bottoms were uncharacteristically bunched up into a small bundle at the bottom of the bed. Heart still racing, she grabbed them and slithered them on, still trying to make sense of the warm lethargy and pervading sense of arousal that was threatening to overwhelm her. *So don't let it*, she told herself fiercely. *Just calm down and try to work out what's going on.*

Jumping out of bed, she scooted over to the windows and pulled back the heavy curtains—her heart performing a complicated kind of somersault as she looked outside. Because there, on the snow-laden lawns, was her sweetest dream and worst nightmare all rolled into one. Saladin Al Mektala knee-deep in snow. The man she'd dreamed about so vividly that she'd woken up believing he was in bed with her was outside, shovelling snow like a labourer.

He'd managed to find a spade from somewhere and had cleared the path leading to the front door, although the rest of the landscape was still banked with white. More snow must have fallen overnight and the beautiful gardens were unrecognisable—blotted out by a mantle that was so bright it hurt the eyes. Livvy blinked against the cold whiteness of the light. And once again, that sense of unreality washed over her, because it was beyond *weird* to see the desert-dwelling king standing in the middle of the snowy English countryside.

He must have found himself a pair of the wellingtons she always kept for the guests in case they wanted to go walking—because, in her experience, nobody ever brought the correct footwear with them. She wondered why he hadn't put on one of the waterproof jackets, because surely it was insane to be shovelling snow in a cashmere coat that must have cost as much as her monthly heating bill.

She was about to duck away from the window when he looked up, as if her presence had alerted him to the fact he was being watched. He was too far away for her to be able to read his expression correctly—and Livvy told herself she was imagining the glint of mischief in his eyes. Was she? With a small howl of rage, she turned away and headed for the freezing bathroom just along the corridor—only to discover that the lights still weren't working.

After a brief and icy shower, her worried thoughts ran round and round, like a hamster on a wheel. It *had* just been a dream, hadn't it? The aching breasts and heavy pelvis and the hazy memories of him in bed with her were all just the legacy of an overworked imagination, weren't they? Probably her subconscious reacting to the way he'd kissed her by the fire.

Pulling on a black sweater over her jeans, she piled up her hair into a topknot, wondering why he'd made a pass at her in the first place. Maybe she looked like someone who was crying out for a little affection. Or maybe he'd just felt sorry for her when she'd told him about Rupert.

He was arrogant and infuriating and dangerous and yet, when she closed her eyes, all she could remember was the sweet seduction of his kiss as he'd pulled her against his hard body.

She ran downstairs and checked the phone but the lines were still down. Which meant...

Meant...

The front door slammed and Saladin walked in, looking as if the wintry wilds of the snowy English countryside were his natural habitat. His golden skin was glowing after the physical exertion of shovelling snow, and Livvy flushed a deep pink as embarrassment coursed through her. Because suddenly all she could think about was her dream and how vivid it had felt. And it *was* a dream, wasn't it?

'Where did you sleep?' she questioned—and wasn't part of her terrified he'd answer 'in your bed'? That he would sardonically inform her that the reason the dreams had been so vivid was because they were real...

'Aren't you supposed to enquire *how* I slept, rather than where?' he questioned coolly, removing a pair of leather gloves and dropping them on a table. 'Isn't that the usual role of the hostess?'

She forced a smile. 'Okay. Let's start again. How did you sleep?'

'For a time I slept the sleep of the just,' he drawled, raking his fingers back through black hair that was damp with melting snow. 'But that was before you woke me up.'

Livvy's throat dried as she stared at him in growing horror. 'I *woke you up*?'

'Indeed you did.' He flicked her a glance from between the dark forest of his lashes. 'You were shouting something in your sleep.'

Her rosy flush was now a distant memory. She could feel all the colour leaching from her face and knew from past experience that her freckles would be standing out as if someone had spattered mud all over her skin. 'What,' she croaked, 'was I shouting?'

There was a split-second pause. 'At first I thought it was my name until I decided I was probably mistaken—given the abrupt way you drew the evening to a conclusion,' he said, his eyes sending out some sort of coded message she couldn't decipher. 'But I thought I'd better get up and investigate anyway.'

Livvy's heart pounded. 'Right,' she said breathlessly.

'So I walked along the corridor to your room, and you shouted it again but this time there could be no mistake, because it was very definitely my name and you were saying it as if you were in some kind of pain. Or something.' His eyes glittered. 'So I turned the door handle and...'

'And?' she squeaked, hating the way he had deliberately paused for dramatic effect.

He glimmered her a smile. 'And I discovered that you'd locked yourself in.'

'So I had,' she remembered, breathing out a shaky sigh of relief.

'Of course—' his eyes narrowed but she couldn't mistake the dangerous glint sparking from their ebony depths '—if there had been any real danger, no door would have kept me out—locked or otherwise. In the circumstances, I can't quite decide whether you were being prudent or paranoid. What did you think was going to happen, Livvy—that I was going to force my way into your room in the middle of the night, all on the strength of one little kiss?'

'Of course not,' she said stiffly, wondering if her words sounded as unconvincing to him as they did to her. What if she *had* left her door unlocked and he'd come running when she'd called out his name? It wasn't beyond the realms of possibility that she would have reached out for him, was it? Grabbed at him and kissed him as hungrily as before. It wouldn't take much of a leap of the imagination to work out what would have happened next...

She wanted to bury her face in her hands, or close her eyes and find that when she opened them he would be gone—taking with him all these confusing thoughts and this gnawing sense of frustration. But that wasn't going to happen, and it was vital she acted as if it was no big deal. As if it had been just *one little kiss*—as he had said so dismissively.

'I certainly didn't mean to disrupt your night,' she said.

'I can live with it,' he said softly. 'Would you like some coffee? There's a pot brewing in the kitchen.'

'You've made coffee?' she questioned.

'Last night you told me to make myself at home. You also made it very clear that you weren't going to wait on me, so it seems I shall have to fend for myself.'

He turned on his heel and began walking towards the kitchen, and Livvy felt obliged to follow him, wondering indignantly how he had managed to assume such a powerful sense of ownership in *her* home.

By daylight and without the mysterious glow of candles, the kitchen seemed a far less threatening environment than it had done last night. Livvy sat down at the table and watched as he poured coffee with the same dexterity as he'd demonstrated when removing her sweater. Oh, God—he'd taken off her sweater. And her shirt. Briefly, she shut her eyes. He would have taken off even more if she hadn't stopped him.

So stop letting him take control. Tell him he's got to stop shovelling snow and making coffee and to concentrate on getting himself out of here as soon as possible. She needed to remember that the response he evoked in her was purely visceral, and it would soon pass. He'd kissed her and made her feel good, and so her body wanted him to do it all over again. It was as simple as that—and it was to be avoided at all costs.

'So did you get through to your people?' she questioned.

Saladin slid the cup towards her. 'I did. On a very bad line and with a low battery, but yes. Sugar?'

'Just milk, thanks.' She took the coffee. 'And they're coming to get you, I presume?'

'Unfortunately, it's not quite that easy,' he said smoothly. 'Several trees are down and some of the lanes are blocked, and all the gritting lorries are needed for the arterial roads.'

Livvy only just avoided choking on her second mouthful of coffee. 'What does that mean?'

Saladin shrugged. He wondered if she realised he could have commandeered a whole fleet of gritting lorries with a click of his fingers—plus a helicopter prepared to swoop down and fly him away to anywhere he chose to go.

But he wasn't planning on leaving. At least, not yet. Not until she'd agreed to accompany him to Jazratan. And he realised there was something else that was making him stay put—and that was a desire for her so intense that he couldn't look at her without his groin aching. 'It means I'm staying here, Livvy,' he said.

Her eyes widened with alarm and with something else—something that was easily recognisable as de-

sire. He could see it in the self-conscious way her body
stiffened whenever he approached. He had tasted it
in that amazing firelight kiss last night even if—
incredibly—she had turned him down afterwards. And
it pleased him that her hunger matched his, even if
her reluctance to have sex with him astonished him.
Did she realise that resisting him was only fuelling
his determination to join with her? Why, he could
have exploded with frustration and excitement when
she'd banished him to his bedroom and barricaded herself into her own room last night. For passion-fuelled
seconds he'd actually considered behaving as one of
his ancestors would have done and broken down the
door—before sanity had prevailed and he had slunk
away with a sense of disbelief and a throbbing groin.

'You're staying here?' she echoed as a series of con-
flicting emotions crossed over her freckled face.

'It would seem so.'

'For how long?'

'Until it's safe to leave.'

'Surely someone like you could call for a helicopter,' she objected. 'I can't believe that the sheikh of
Jazratan, with all his power and influence, is stuck in
the snow in the English countryside.'

He smiled, because this was something else he
wasn't used to. People usually did everything to en-
tice him to stay because they loved the cachet of having a royal in their presence. They didn't stare at him
with a mulish expression on their face, not bothering to
hide their wish to see him gone. 'Anything is *possible*,'
he mused. 'But you wouldn't want me to put one of my
pilots at risk, would you, Livvy—just because having
me around makes you feel uncomfortable?'

She licked her lips, as if his soft tone had temporarily disarmed her—which was precisely what he intended it to do.

'You don't make me feel uncomfortable.'

Their eyes met.

'Well, then,' he said softly. 'There isn't a problem, is there?'

She glared at him and Saladin felt a heady sense of triumph. Surely she must realise by now that that resistance was futile?

'Just so you know,' she said, glancing up at the wall clock, 'I have things to do and I can't stand around entertaining you all day.'

'If this is what you term as entertainment, I'm happy to pass.'

She slanted him a furious look. 'I have to work on the assumption that the weather is going to clear and that my guests will be arriving on schedule.'

'So let me help you.'

Livvy put down her cup with a clatter. *'How?'*

'Are there logs that need chopping?'

'You chop logs?'

'Yes, I chop logs, Livvy. Or do you think I lie around on silken cushions all day doing nothing?'

'I have no idea. I hadn't given your daily routine a moment's thought.'

Exaggeratedly, he ran his hand slowly down over his biceps. 'You don't get a body like this by just lying around all day.'

'That's the most outrageous boast I've ever heard!'

He smiled. 'So? Logs?'

'A man from the village chops them.' She got up from the table. 'But you can bring some through to the drawing room from the big pile in the storehouse if you like. That would be very helpful. And if you'd like to light the fire, that would also be helpful.'

'And then?'

'Then I'm decorating the Christmas tree.'

She flung the words out like a challenge.

'Ah,' he said. 'Something at which I am a complete novice, which means you can order me round to your heart's content. I'm sure that will give you immense pleasure, won't it, Livvy? You seem to enjoy taking control.'

He watched as she appeared to bite back what she was about to say. She looked as if she wanted to tell him to go to hell.

'I suppose you can hold the ladder for me,' she said, and he almost laughed as she bit out the ungracious response.

Half an hour later he found himself gripping the sides of a ladder while she hauled dusty boxes from the loft and handed them to him. Saladin stared down at different labelled boxes bearing the words *Baubles* and *Tinsel* with the sense of a man entering uncharted territory. He had never decorated a Christmas tree in his life—it wasn't a holiday they celebrated in Jazratan—and unexpectedly he found he was enjoying himself.

From his position at the foot of the stepladder, he was able to study the slender curves of Livvy's body, and from this angle her jeans certainly looked a lot more flattering. Every step up the ladder hugged the denim against the curve of her buttocks and outlined each slender thigh. His gaze travelled up to the back of her neck, which was pale and dusted with a few freckles. He wondered if she had deliberately put her hair into that topknot, knowing he would want to remove the single clip that held it in place. So that it would tumble around her shoulders like a fall of flame, the way it had done last night...

Last night.

He swallowed as she leaned out to attach a sparkly silver ball to the end of a branch, his hands again gripping the sides of the ladder—not quite sure which of them he was keeping steady. He'd lied to her about sleeping well because the truth was that he'd barely slept at all—especially when he'd realised she'd meant what she said, and that she wouldn't be sharing a bed with him. In the silence of his icy room, he'd kept reliving their fireside kiss—thinking how unexpectedly *erotic* it had been. His fierce hunger for her had taken him by surprise—because nobody could deny that she was a very unassuming creature—but just as surprising was her determination to resist him.

At first he'd thought she was joking. Or that she was playing the old, familiar game because women often believed that a man was more likely to commit if they played hard to get. He gave a cynical smile. But if that was her plan then she was wasting her time, because there would be no commitment from him other than the guarantee of pleasure. His mouth hardened and his heart clenched with pain. He had walked that path before and he would not be setting foot on it again.

'Could you hand me that angel, please?'

Angel? Livvy's voice broke into his uncomfortable thoughts and Saladin picked up the figure she was pointing to—a plastic doll wearing a crudely sewn dress. A tiny ring of tinsel wreathed the flaxen hair, and she was holding a foil-covered matchstick, which he assumed was meant to be a wand.

'Homemade?' he ventured wryly, as he held it out towards her.

She hesitated before giving a brief, sad smile. 'I made it with my mum.'

That smile touched something deep inside him and he found himself wanting to kiss her again, but her rapid ascent up the ladder was clearly intended to terminate the conversation, and maybe that was best. *Yes, definitely for the best*, he told himself. Instead, he forced himself to concentrate on the way she brought the bare tree to life by heaping on the glittering baubles and tinsel while the fire crackled and spat. It was one of the most innocent ways he'd ever spent a morning, and Saladin was overcome by an unexpected wave of emotion, because wasn't it captivating to find a woman whose main focus wasn't sex? How long since he'd been in the company of a female who was behaving with restraint and with decorum? Not since Alya, he thought—and a wave of guilt washed over him as he made the comparison.

'Be careful,' he growled as she began to back her way down the ladder.

'I am being careful.'

But suddenly, he was not. He was giving in to what he could no longer resist. He caught hold of her as she made that last step and his hand closed over hers, and to his surprise she didn't pull away from him. She just stared at him as he turned her hand over and raised it slowly to his lips, his tongue snaking out over her palm to slowly lick at the salty flesh.

'Saladin,' she whispered, but he could see that her eyes had darkened.

'Don't talk anymore, because I'm going to kiss you,' he said, his voice deepening with sudden urgency. 'But you already know that, don't you, Livvy? You know that's what I have been longing to do since I got up this morning.'

As a stalling device it was pathetic, but Livvy said it all the same, lifting her gaze to the bare ceiling. 'There's supposed to be mistletoe,' she whispered.

'Damn the mistletoe,' he ground out as his head came down towards hers.

CHAPTER SIX

ONE KISS, LIVVY told herself as Saladin's mouth claimed hers. One kiss and no more. Just like last night—it didn't have to lead anywhere. She could call a halt to it any time she liked.

But deep down she knew she was fooling herself—because this felt *different*. Last night had been all about candlelight and firelight and a sense of other-worldliness that had descended on them as they'd sat around the sparking logs. Restaurants didn't dim the lights for no reason and call it *mood lighting*, did they?

But today...

In the cold clear light of today, in the harsh and blinding reflection of newly fallen snow—there was nothing but rawness and reality. And hunger. Oh, yes. A fierce hunger that had been building all night—even while she slept—and that was being fed by the sweet seduction of Saladin's kiss as he began to explore her mouth. He kissed her softly at first, and then he kissed hard and long and deep—with a warm urgency that was contagious. And she wanted him. She wanted him more than she'd ever wanted anything, because this was like nothing she'd ever experienced before.

Wrapping her fingers around his neck, she kissed

him back and, although he held her very tightly, it was almost as if she were floating free. She felt soft. Bone-less. As if every point of her body was a pleasure point. As if every inch of her skin was an erogenous zone. Wherever Saladin touched her she felt on fire. With each kiss he dragged her deeper into the silken web he was weaving. At some point she thought she must have groaned because suddenly he pulled back, sucking in a ragged breath, his eyes as bright as a man with a fever.

'Here?' he questioned succinctly. 'Or upstairs?'

It was a brutal question that killed off some of the romance she'd been feeling, but at least it was *real* and at least there could be no misinterpretation about his intentions. He wasn't dressing it up to be something it wasn't. This was sex, pure and simple. He wasn't *lying* to her, was he?

'Can't decide?' he murmured, and, when she didn't answer, he began to nuzzle her neck.

She tipped her head back while she skated through the possibilities. The bed would be better. She could hide beneath the concealing weight of the duvet, couldn't she? But this wasn't supposed to be about *hiding*. This was about taking control of her own des-tiny. About taking something she really wanted for once, instead of being influenced by other people's expectations.

She realised he was waiting for an answer, and her heart missed a beat as she stared into the blackness of his eyes. He was the wrong man on so many levels, but did that matter? Doing the *right* thing had never worked out for her, had it? Maybe it was time to run full tilt at glorious fantasy and forget all about reality for once, because this gorgeous man wanted to make love to *her*.

And when some bone-deep instinct warned her that he was capable of inflicting pain—real emotional pain, far worse, she suspected, than any she'd suffered with Rupert—she reminded herself that she was a different person now. She was no longer that innocent bride who looked at the world through rose-tinted glasses. She was independent and she could handle this. So what the hell was she waiting for?

'Here,' she managed from between swollen lips. 'I want to do it here.'

He brought his head down as if to seal her intention with another kiss, but she sensed his growing impatience as he led her over to the fire and pulled her close—close enough for her to feel every sinew of his powerful body. Pulling the pin from her hair, he watched as it tumbled around her shoulders.

'Your hair is like fire,' he murmured, letting silky strands slide through his fingers. 'You should wear it down all the time.'

She opened her mouth to tell him it wouldn't be practical but her words were forgotten as he removed her sweater, his eyebrows shooting upwards as a lacy bra of midnight-blue silk was revealed.

Tiptoeing his fingertip along the delicate edging of lace, he pushed her down onto the silken rug. 'What's this?' he murmured.

'It's…a bra. What does it look like?'

'Nothing like the one you had on last night, that's for sure.' Slowly, he expelled the air from his lungs as he flattened his palm over one peaking mound. 'Did you wear it specially for me?'

Had she? She'd never worn it before. A friend had given her birthday vouchers to an upmarket lingerie shop that didn't know the meaning of words like *sensible* or *refund*. The navy set had been the most practical thing on offer, but up until today it had seemed too delicate for everyday use. There had never been a reason to wear it before, yet something had made her put it on this morning…

'Maybe subconsciously,' she admitted.

He gave a glimmer of a smile. 'A woman only wears underwear like this if she wants a man to take it off. Is that what you want me to do, Livvy? Is that what you've been longing for me to do ever since you got up this morning? To run my fingers over your beautiful pale skin and get you naked?'

She closed her eyes as his hand strayed to the bra's front clasp. She wanted to tell him that his assumption was arrogant, but how could she protest when his fingers had loosened the clip and her breasts were spilling free? The cool air hit her skin and suddenly he was bending his lips to a nipple and he was sucking on it. Nipping at it and grazing his teeth all over the sensitised nub. She gave a little squeal of pleasure and he lifted his head.

'You are very vocal in your approval, *habibi*,' he observed softly. 'Does that feel good?'

Her tongue snaked out to moisten her parched lips. 'So good,' she breathed.

'And this? Does this feel good?'

Against the rug, Livvy writhed with pleasure as his hand moved between her legs, because her body suddenly felt as if was out of her control and words seemed to be beyond her. Did he really need her to tell him that she liked the way he was sucking her nipple? The way his finger was rubbing up and down the stiff seam of her jeans at the very point where she was acutely sensitive. The finger stilled.

'Does it?' he questioned silkily.

Did he want praise? Maybe she was expected to touch *him*. To reach out to where his crotch was straining so formidably against his trousers and to trickle her fingers over his hardness. Livvy's heart began to pound. Her experience of foreplay was limited, because Rupert had known she was a virgin and had wanted to wait until they were married and had said he didn't trust himself to touch her. It wasn't until afterwards that she had discovered the reason why...

Her sex life was something she regarded as an arid area of failure, but instinct told her that Saladin Al Mektala could be the person to change all that. She suspected that what the sheikh didn't know about pleasure wouldn't be worth knowing. Yet surely it would be deceitful to let him make love to her without telling him her secret.

'Does it?' he repeated silkily, and Livvy circled her hips with frustration and guilt.

What if she told him and he rejected her—if he left her shivering and aching with frustration in front of the fire?

She had to tell him.

She stared straight into his black eyes. 'It feels incredible,' she said. 'But maybe you ought to know that I'm—'

'Driving me crazy with desire, that's for sure,' he said, moving over her to silence her words with another breathtaking kiss.

And Livvy let him. That was the shame of it. She just let him. Wrapping her arms around his neck, she kissed him back with a slow, exploratory hunger as he began to slide down the zipper of her jeans.

'Mmm...' was his only comment as he tugged the denim away to reveal the lacy blue knickers that matched her bra, before concentrating his attention on kissing her body. He whispered his lips over her breasts—his breath warm against her skin—before travelling down to her belly. She held her breath as his head travelled downwards until his dark head was positioned between her thighs. For a moment she tensed, but when he licked almost lazily at the moist panel of her panties a spasm of pleasure so intense shot through her that for a moment Livvy was scared she might faint.

Was it the half-broken cry she made in response to that intimacy that made him suddenly stop? Her nails dug hard into his shoulders in protest but he didn't appear to care.

'Don't—' she gasped.

Had he read her mind?

'Don't stop?' He looked up from his decadent position between her thighs, and smiled. 'I have no intention of stopping, but I am hungry to feel my skin next to yours, *habibi*. And while you are almost naked—I am not.'

She didn't want him to move—terrified that any movement would shatter this precarious magic—but she had little choice except to lie there and watch as he stood up and began to strip off. His shirt was silk and so were his boxers and they floated to the ground like fine gossamer. Livvy's mouth dried as his body was revealed. His dark skin glowed like richest gold and the deep shadows cast by the flickering firelight emphasised his physical perfection. A hard and rippling torso, with powerful arms and muscular legs that seemed to go on forever. Narrow hips and rock-hard buttocks. Even the powerful evidence of his arousal wasn't as daunting as it should have been because by now Livvy was alive with a need that had been buried inside her for so long that she felt she would die if he didn't make love to her.

Her heart was pounding as she stared at his erection, but when he reached down into the pocket of his trousers and drew out a condom, she felt a flutter of misgiving. Did he always carry protection with him? Did he take it for granted that there would always be a willing woman lying waiting for him like this? She thought about the women who sometimes used to accompany him to the stables—those models and actresses with their suede boots and miniskirts and real fur. For a moment she wondered how she could possibly compare to those glamorous creatures, until she forced the dark clouds of insecurity from her mind. Maybe there *was* always an accommodating female wherever he went—like a sailor having a woman in every port—but this wasn't about *convention*, was it? She'd done all that stuff and look where it had got her.

She thought about the heartache of the past and the struggle her life had been for so long. She stared over Saladin's shoulder as he slithered her panties off and moved over her. Outside the world was white and still and silent, apart from the distant ticking of a clock. Time was passing, but they were completely alone and this moment would never come again. And she had to seize it—to grab it—and to hell with the consequences.

Yet once before she had blinded herself to the truth. She'd buried her head in the sand and allowed herself to be treated like a fool by the man she'd been engaged to. Was she going to repeat that pattern of behaviour all her life—to run away from what she was afraid to face?

'Saladin,' she whispered as he rubbed his thumb over her clitoris. 'There's something you should know.'

'The only thing I need to know is whether you like… this…'

She closed her eyes. *Like* it? She imagined that even a marble statue would have squirmed beneath his questing finger, but that wasn't the point. The words came out in a bald rush—but what other way was there to say them? 'I'm a virgin.'

His fingers—which had been working rhythmically against her heated flesh—now stilled. He raised his head to look at her, his eyes full of disbelief—but there was something else in their depths, too. Something she didn't recognise. Something dark and tortured. Something that scared her.

'Is this some sort of joke?' he demanded in a strangled kind of voice.

Wondering what had made him look so *bleak*, Livvy shook her head. 'It's no joke,' she said. 'Why would I joke about something like that? It's the truth. I might not be very proud of it—but it's the truth.'

He rolled away from her and she noticed that his erection had diminished. 'How can this be?' he bit out. 'You are nearly thirty years old. You were engaged to be married. I know what Western women are like. They lose their innocence early and they take many lovers!'

His crass generalisations dispelled some of her insecurity and made Livvy start to claw back some dignity—something that wasn't particularly easy when she wasn't wearing any clothes. Did she dare walk over to the sofa where the soft woollen throw she kept for cold winter nights was folded? Too right she did—because staying here completely naked was making her feel even more vulnerable than she already did. On shaky legs she rose to stand, aware of his heated gaze following her as she walked over to get the blanket and brought it back to the fireside. But as she wrapped it around herself and sat at the other end of the rug, she became aware that his erection was back. And how. Hastily averting her eyes, she turned to throw a log into the neglected fire.

'I hate to ruin your prejudices, but not all women conform to the stereotypes you've just described,' she said. 'The law of averages suggests that there will be some older virgins as well as young ones.'

Saladin's mouth thinned with displeasure, thinking that there couldn't have been a more inappropriate moment for her to try to dazzle him with statistics, and he was amazed she should even dare try. He felt the heavy throb of his heart. He had wanted sex. Simple, uncomplicated sex with a willing woman. He didn't want someone with *issues* or *baggage*. He didn't want someone who, with her purity, had stirred up memories he had locked away a long time ago. For he had only ever slept with one virgin before, and that virgin had been his beautiful wife. Pain and guilt clenched at his heart as he stared at her.

'I don't understand,' he said coldly.

'You don't have to. I'm…' And suddenly he saw the uncertainty that flickered across her pale and freckled face. 'I'm sorry if I led you on.'

An unwanted but persistent point of principle made him shake his head. 'We led each other on,' he said heavily. 'But it is true that you have left it a little *late* to drop this particular bombshell.'

Awkwardly, she shrugged. 'Do you want to get dressed?'

Saladin shook his head. What he wanted was to be back where he'd been less than five minutes ago, not stuck in the middle of some damned conversation! 'I don't believe it,' he breathed. 'I thought it was the custom in the West to have sex before marriage—and you were on the very brink of marriage. So what happened?'

'It's difficult to put into words.'

'You don't seem to have had much problem with words so far.'

She shifted uncomfortably beneath his gaze. 'I think I was born in the wrong age,' she said slowly. 'I was a tomboy who loved messing around in the countryside. I climbed trees and used to make dens with the boys from the village. I never had posters of pop stars on my walls like all the other girls in my class. I was more interested in horses—horses were my life. In fact, everything was just like one of those old-fashioned children's stories, until my mum died.'

'That must have been hard,' he said.

She shrugged again and suddenly he thought she looked much younger than nearly thirty.

'Lots of children lose their mothers,' she said. 'But not so many have a father who was left feeling very vulnerable. A rich widower who became perfect marriage fodder for the kind of woman commonly known as a gold-digger.'

'I have some experience of that breed myself,' he observed wryly. 'So what happened?'

She shrugged. 'He fell for a busty blonde with a penchant for diamonds and couture and then he married her. My father was a country gentleman and this house had been in his family for generations, but his new wife preferred luxury travel and sailing in sunny waters on a lavish yacht. She was the kind of woman who would buy an entire new wardrobe before every trip—and we weren't the sort of family who had a lot of ready cash. Most of it was tied up in the house. Would you...?' Again, she licked her lips. 'Would you like a blanket, or something?'

He would like *something*, but he suspected he wasn't going to get it right then. 'Why, is my nakedness bothering you?'

'A little.'

'Just a little?' He let his gaze slide down to his groin before raising his eyes to her flaming cheeks. 'I must be slipping. Very well, bring me a blanket if it makes you feel better.'

He wondered if she was aware that he was being treated to a tantalising glimpse of her bare bottom as she walked over to a second sofa and grabbed another blanket, though he noticed that she averted her gaze again as she thrust it at him before resuming her position at the other end of the rug.

'So what happened?' he questioned, watching as she huddled herself in a cocoon of soft wool. 'Or can I guess? Did she grow bored with marriage to an older man? Did she demand more and more money, until she'd bled him dry?'

Her eyes widened. 'How did you know?'

'Because I know what women are like,' he said. 'And your stepmother was conforming to a pattern that isn't exactly ground-breaking.' His eyes narrowed. 'And ironically, you met your own male version of the gold-digger in de Vries.'

She nodded before staring down at the pattern on the rug as if completely absorbed by it, but when she lifted her face he noted that her expression was calm—as if she had practised very hard to look that way.

'That's right. I can't believe that I didn't see it for myself, my only defence being that I was very young,' she said. 'His stables were in trouble—everyone knew that—but nobody realised quite how bad the problem was. He knew I was an only child and he saw this house and made the assumption we were rolling in money. Which, of course, we weren't. My father was quite an old man by then and he was ill. We had a lot of carers who were coming in and helping me look after him, and they cost an absolute fortune.'

'And I suppose that was also occupying a lot of your time and energy?' he said grimly.

She nodded again. 'He was very frail by then, and Rupert seemed so understanding about it all. He didn't seem to mind when I had to cancel dinner because one of the carers hadn't shown up. And because he was my first real boyfriend, I had nothing to compare him with. I just thought he was being kind. When he said…' She sucked in a deep breath. 'When he said that he wanted to wait until we were married before we had sex, I found that somehow reassuring.'

Saladin nodded. Yes, he could see that. A horse-mad, motherless tomboy whose only role models had been an old man who should have known better and an avaricious stepmother who was out for all she could get. No wonder Livvy hadn't known the rules about relationships, or men, or sex. Nobody had bothered to explain them to her, had they?

'Don't you realise that it reflects badly on him, not you?' he questioned savagely. 'That a man who dumps a woman on her wedding day because she has less money than he thought is not a *real* man. We have a name for that kind of man in Jazratan, but I will not sully your ears with it.'

'But it wasn't just the money. There was something else.' She twisted some of the blanket's tassels between her fingers. 'It turned out that he was sleeping with one of the female grooms and had been for some time, which was why he hadn't tried harder to get into bed with me. Not just any groom, either—but my best friend. And there was me thinking that he was displaying old-fashioned values of chivalry designed to win a woman's heart, not realising that I was being betrayed by the two people I considered closest to me.' She gave a short and bitter laugh. 'What a fool I was.'

'You shouldn't beat yourself up for wanting to believe the best in people,' he said, his voice growing hard. 'Though I hope you've learned your lesson now. It's always better to think the worst. That way you don't get disappointed.'

She stared at him. 'You've been very...' Her voice tailed off.

'Very what?'

'It doesn't matter.'

'I think it does.'

'*Understanding.*' She gave an embarrassed kind of shrug.

'What did you think I was going to do?' he questioned roughly. 'Carry on as if nothing had happened—

kiss away your protests and ignore your obvious reservations? Or maybe you *wanted* me to fulfil the fantasy of the exotic stranger who ravishes the willing but innocent woman. Who takes away the responsibility so you didn't have to make the decision for yourself. Is that what you would have liked? It's a common enough fantasy, especially where desert sheikhs are concerned. Would that have made it easier for you, Livvy?'

She licked her lips. 'I wasn't even going to tell you.'

'No, I gathered that,' he said drily. 'So what changed your mind?'

She shrugged again and the blanket slipped down over her shoulders, before she hauled it back up again. 'I thought it was dishonest not to. I thought you might be one of those men for whom virginity is a big deal.'

Saladin was silent as he considered her words. Was it? Her eyes were wide as she looked at him and he could read the faint anxiety in their depths. He supposed it was. For a man in his position, virginity was an essential requirement of any future queen. But he was not looking for a queen. He had been there, done that. What was it they said in the West? Bought the T-shirt.

His mouth hardened as she held his gaze with those startling amber eyes. Was she seeking reassurance? Holding out for an impossible dream? He felt the hard throb of desire at his groin and shifted his weight. This was a unique situation, but despite his undeniable lust—lust was interchangeable, because there was always another female eager enough to open her legs for him. If it were anyone else, he would get dressed, make a quick phone call and get the hell out of there—no matter how many damned snow ploughs it took.

And that was what he *should* do—he knew that. Because purity was something he always associated with just one woman—and wouldn't it dishonour Alya's memory if he were to take the innocence of another? Every instinct he possessed—except for the sexual instinct—told him to leave now and get away while he still could.

But Livvy Miller still had something he wanted. Something that only she could provide. And maybe he had something *she* wanted, because surely she didn't want to carry on like this. Was now the time for a little adult negotiation? If he fulfilled a need in her— then wouldn't she feel morally obliged to do the same for him?

On her face he could read trepidation warring with desire, and a genuine sense of injustice washed over him. How crazy was it that she had never known the joy of sex? That a woman who was known for her physicality and skill on a horse should have neglected her own body for so long?

He didn't move—he didn't dare—because it was vital he didn't influence her decision, even though he knew that another kiss and she would be melting beneath him. But it had to be *her* decision, not his. His gaze was unwavering as he looked at her.

'So,' he questioned silkily. 'Do you want me to take your virginity, Livvy?'

CHAPTER SEVEN

LIVVY DIDN'T ANSWER straight away. It seemed like something out of a dream—the powerful sheikh asking if she wanted him to take her virginity, with all the impartiality of someone enquiring whether she'd like a spoonful of sugar in her coffee.

As she stared into the provocative gleam of Saladin's black eyes, she thought about everything that had brought her to this moment. The public shame of being jilted that had hit her so hard, even though she'd done her best to hold her head up high afterwards. She'd walked away from the world of horses without a backward glance and had started a new life.

Out of a sense of loyalty to her father's memory and a determination that Rupert's rejection wouldn't destroy her completely, she'd done her best to keep Wightwick Manor going. On a shoestring budget she'd worked hard to make her bed and breakfast business a success. But now she could see that she had neglected her own needs in the process. She'd put her emotional life on a back burner, letting her twenties trickle away beneath the hard work of maintaining an old house like this. She hadn't done dates or parties or make-up— she'd spent any spare money on roof tiles, or getting the windows painted. She hadn't gone off for minibreaks or enjoyed sunny vacations with girlfriends, drinking lurid-coloured cocktails while they were chatted up by waiters. She hadn't even tried to find herself a new boyfriend. She'd told herself she didn't need the potential pain of another relationship.

Yet here she was—naked underneath a blanket while a similarly naked Saladin surveyed her from the other end of the rug. She stared into the dark smoulder of his eyes and wondered how best to respond to his question. She supposed she could say no. Act prim and outraged—and tell him that she wasn't interested in giving her virginity to him, like some kind of medieval sacrifice. He was certainly sophisticated enough to take it on the chin. She doubted he would feel more than a moment of regret, and she would probably be knocked down by the rush of women eager to take her place.

But it wasn't quite that straightforward, because she still wanted him. He'd kissed her passionately and made her feel she was part of something magical. He'd made her feel things she didn't think she was capable of feeling—a powerful passion that had overwhelmed her and a need that had flooded hotly through her veins. He'd set her body on *fire*. She thought about the way he'd touched her—whispering his mouth over each breast in turn, grazing them with his teeth and making her urge him on with writhing hips. She remembered the way his head had slid down between her thighs and something molten and sweet had begun to tug at the very core of her—something that was making refusal seem like a crazy idea. And she knew something else—that she would never get another chance like this.

Desert sheikhs promising untold pleasure didn't come along more than once in a lifetime.

She stared at him.

'Yes,' she said, in a low voice. 'Yes, I want you to take my virginity.'

His face showed no immediate reaction. The hawk-like features displayed no hint of triumph although his lips curved in the briefest of smiles.

'Come here,' he instructed softly.

She wondered briefly why he couldn't come to *her*, but his words were compelling and masterful and Livvy stood up and began to walk towards him, clutching the blanket against her skin like a makeshift dress. She could feel his eyes burning into her—as if that piercing black gaze was capable of scorching through the wool to the body beneath. Her footsteps faltered as she reached him, uncertain about what to do next, but he reached out and slid his thumb over her ankle, massaging briefly against the jut of bone there, before beginning to stroke his way up her calf. Livvy swallowed as pleasure began to ripple over her skin. It seemed such a light, innocuous movement to such an innocent part of the body and yet…yet…

'Saladin,' she whispered.

'Shh.'

The back of her knee was next—a tiny circular movement that must have made her loosen her grip on the blanket because he gave it a single tug and it slid to the ground, leaving her standing naked in front of him. Automatically, her hands flew up to conceal her breasts, before he shook his head.

'Do not cover yourself, Livvy,' he instructed softly. 'Your body is very beautiful. It is small and neat, yet strong and supple. It pleases me very much and I wish to look at it.'

She kept her hands exactly where they were, even though his words were making her nipples peak against her fingers. 'You're making me feel like an object.'

'Not an object,' he demurred, reaching up and pulling her down into his arms, so that her flesh met the comforting warmth of his. He pushed the mussed hair away from her face and used the edge of his thumb to trace the outline of her lips. 'Not even a subject, since I do not rule over you. So stop looking at me with those anxious eyes and relax, because I am going to give you pleasure such as you have never dreamed of.'

'But I don't have a clue what to do,' she whispered.

'And that,' he said unevenly, 'is part of your attraction.'

Only part of it, she wondered dazedly as his mouth came down towards her. What was the other part?

But his kiss was powerful enough to send any last doubts skittering from her mind, and the slow caress of his lips made further deliberations impossible. All she could think about was what he was doing. He was holding her close—so close—making her feel as if every cell in her body were sensitive to each seeking caress.

At first his touch wasn't overtly sexual. The hands that were cupping her face seemed more interested in exploring the thickness of her hair and the outline of her face. And when that innocent exploration made her relax, he started stroking his hands down the sides of her body—until she was moving restlessly against him.

He must have known that her impatience was growing, but he paid no attention to her squirming movements. He just took his time—drawing out the exquisite torture as his fingers slowly acquainted themselves with her skin. Inch by tantalising inch, he touched her. First her breasts and then her ribcage and the undulation of her waist. She held her breath as he turned his attention to her belly and teased her by brushing his fingers farther down to delve inside the soft fuzz of hair. Yet his hawklike features remained impassive even though she could feel the tension building in his powerful body. She could sense his restraint—as if he was battling his own desire in order to feed hers.

'Saladin,' she breathed, looking into his eyes to find herself ensnared by a smoky black gaze.

'Want me?' His thumb brushed against the moist and engorged bud hidden by the soft curls, and she let out a little murmur of assent as she nodded.

'I…I think so.'

'I think so, too,' he said, his voice suddenly growing harsh.

He moved over her, his hardness nudging against her wet heat as she opened her legs for him with an instinct that seemed to come from somewhere deep inside her. She became aware of so many things—his weight and his strength and the subtle scent of sandalwood and salt that clung to his skin.

'Look at me,' he urged softly.

Until he spoke, she hadn't even realised her eyes had closed again. She let the lids flutter open to meet his heated gaze as he made that first thrust deep inside her—a long, slow thrust that made her gasp and instantly he stilled, his eyes narrowing.

'It hurts?'

Breathlessly, she shook her head. 'Not really. It just feels…'

'What?'

'Big.'

Saladin smiled—he couldn't help himself. But her unintentional boost to his masculine ego only increased his hunger—if that was possible—and it was a moment before he could trust himself to move again. Already he felt close to a tipping point that had been reached the moment he had entered her. He could feel her flesh enclosing him as sweetly as an oyster clamped its shell around the glistening pearl. She was so tight. So wet. So...*unexpected*. But he reined back his sudden urgent desire to ride her as fiercely as he would ride one of his horses. Because this was her first time, he reminded himself. This was the touchstone by which she would measure all the men who would follow. And he must make it a good experience—the very best experience—for all kinds of reasons.

So he concentrated on kissing and fondling her. On doing all the things that women liked best and on holding back his own desire. And even though his sexual hunger was at a high that was almost unendurable, it felt exquisite. Maybe because it was the first time in a long time that he had put a woman's needs before his own. Usually he didn't have to, because he prided himself on being able to make a woman orgasm within moments of touching her, but this was different. Virgins were different...

The pain of memory shot through him like a dark streak of lightning and for a moment he screwed his eyes tightly shut, cursing the thoughts that crowded into his mind—and slamming down the barriers before they could take root there.

He drew in a deep breath and began to objectify

what was happening, in order to distract himself. He concentrated on Livvy's reaction rather than his own—watching as her eyes grew dark and her cheeks flushed. He felt the tension in her fingers as they kneaded against his sweat-sheened back. He could feel the urgency in her thighs, which were digging hard against his hips, and the way she instinctively angled her pelvis to encourage him to go deeper. He tipped his head back as she covered his shoulder with a flurry of frantic little kisses that seemed to grow in crescendo as he drove her towards her climax.

He knew when she was about to come. He could sense the change in her body—the unmistakable quiver of expectation and excitement edged with the sense of disbelief that heralded any orgasm. And that was when he kissed her again. Gripped her hips hard as he drove into her. Imprisoned her against his exquisitely aroused length as her back began to arch and he waited for the split second of stillness before she started spasming against his flesh. He thought she called out his name as he gave into his own release, which he could hold back no longer—his own pleasure increased by the sensation of her still quivering helplessly in his arms.

It took him a long time to come down and, unusually, he stayed where he was for a long time—withdrawing only when he felt the returning stir of an erection. He rolled away from her, pulling the discarded blanket over her, unable to resist a glance at her flushed face and the bright, honey-coloured eyes, before her eyelids fluttered sleepily down. But for once he did not want sleep—something his body habitually demanded after sex, which helped emphasise the distance he craved and lessened the chances of being asked pointless questions about the possibility of a long-term relationship.

For once he was wide awake and more alive than he could remember feeling in a long, long time. He wanted to hear what the feisty little redhead had to say about her first experience of sex, although he told himself that his interest was simply academic. He was not looking for praise because he knew how good he was—but he needed her to be satisfied with what had just happened. *He needed to keep her sweet.*

Stroking a slow finger over one flushed breast, he smiled. 'No need to ask whether you enjoyed that.'

His murmured words dissolved the clouds of contentment that had settled on her and, with an effort, Livvy blinked herself awake. Her eyes felt so heavy, it was as if someone had crept in and placed two tiny pebbles on them while she hadn't been looking. She met Saladin's dark gaze. His skin was flushed and his eyes were smoky, yet he sounded more concerned with his own performance rating than with anything else. She told herself that his arrogance didn't matter because nothing had felt this good in a long time—maybe ever—and she'd be a fool not to hold on to it while she could. She felt…warm. Complete. As if she were floating on a pink cloud that she never wanted to get off.

She studied his hawklike features and sensual lips and she wanted him all over again. All she had to do was to lean forward to kiss him, and she had to fight the longing to do just that because something warned her to tread carefully. She needed to remember that the sheikh was unlike other men—and her own track record was hopeless. She didn't want to make a fool of herself and, more important, she didn't want to give him the opportunity to reject her. Because hadn't she vowed that she would never get rejected for a second time?

She must not make the mistake of falling in love with him.

What would such a seasoned lover as Saladin normally require in such circumstances? she wondered, and something told her to play it straight. Just because her system was flooded with hormones that were making her want to do inappropriate things like stroke his face and be all *tender*—didn't mean she was going to listen to them.

'I don't think you'd need me to be wired up to a machine to register my heart-rate to realise that it was a very satisfying experience,' she said.

He looked surprised, there was no denying that—and neither could she deny the little rush of pleasure that gave her.

'So you don't regret it?'

Livvy chewed on her lip. Did she? She thought about the vow she had made to herself a long time ago.

'I don't do regrets,' she said quietly. 'Not anymore.'

Saladin's eyes narrowed. It was not the glowing endorsement he had expected, nor the compliancy of a woman who was eager for more. If he had been on territory he could call his own—a hotel suite, perhaps—then he might have taken himself off for a long shower and left her lying there to think about the wisdom of her words. But he wasn't. He was in *her* house on *her* rug—and she was still in possession of something he wanted. He gave a slow smile as he drew a thoughtful finger down over her breast and felt her shiver. Did she really think she would be able to deny him now that she had tasted the pleasure he could give her?

'I'm going to make love to you again,' he said.

But instead of being captured by his gaze, she was looking across the room at a radiating blue-white light.

'Your phone's vibrating,' she said.

And her damned *cat* chose that precise moment to stalk into the room and hiss at him.

CHAPTER EIGHT

LIVVY WATCHED AS Saladin walked across the room to answer his phone, not seeming to care that away from the fierce blaze of the fire the unheated room was icy cold on his naked body. Or maybe his careless, almost sauntering journey was deliberate. Perhaps he thought that the sight of him without any clothes would set her heart racing and cast some kind of erotic spell on her. And if that was the case, he was right.

Beside her Peppa gave a plaintive meow, but for once Livvy's stroking of the cat's abundant fur was distracted, because how could she concentrate on anything other than the sight of the magnificent sheikh?

She found herself watching him hungrily in the way that Peppa sometimes watched a beautiful bird as it hopped around the garden. The powerful shafts of his thighs rose to greet the paler globes of buttocks, leading to the narrow taper of his hips and waist. Livvy swallowed. The proud way he held his head and broad line of his shoulders reminded her of a statue she'd once seen in a museum. It seemed impossible that moments before he'd been deep inside her, making her cry out with pleasure.

A man she barely knew—yet one who ironically

knew her more intimately than anyone. She'd told him about still being a virgin and then, very slowly—he had made love to her.

She wrapped the blanket round her as he picked up the vibrating phone and, after clicking the connection, began speaking rapidly in an unknown language she assumed was his native tongue. She noticed that he listened for some—not much—of the time, but mostly he seemed to be barking out commands. She gave a wry smile as she lay back on the rug. She guessed that was what sheikhs did.

Resting her head against her folded arms, she waited—her newfound sense of torpor making her aware of her glowing skin and her sense of satisfaction. And Saladin was responsible for that. For all his arrogance and sense of entitlement, he had proved the most considerate and exciting first lover a woman could wish for.

Lazily, she turned her head and looked out of the window. The snow had stopped falling but there were no signs of a thaw. The landscape looked as pretty as a Christmas card—unreal and somehow impenetrable, as if they were in their own private little bubble and nobody else could get in. Inside, the lack of electricity was beginning to bite and it was starting to get cold. The decorated tree looked strange without the rainbow glow of fairy lights, and despite the blaze of the fire the room had taken a distinct drop in temperature. She dreaded to think how icy it must be upstairs. Some of her euphoria began to leave her as Livvy started to consider the more practical concerns of the power cut. Eight guests were due to arrive the day after tomorrow and she had no electricity!

Her torpor forgotten, she jumped up and grabbed the silky knickers that were lying in a heap on the floor, and had just slithered them on when she felt a light but proprietorial hand on her bottom.

'What do you think you're doing?'

She turned round and steeled herself against the glint of displeasure in Saladin's dark eyes.

'I'm getting dressed.'

'Why?' With possessive intimacy, he trailed his finger down over the silk-covered crack between her buttocks. 'When I want to make love to you again.'

'Because…' Furious at the way her concerns about the electricity should have morphed into concerns about the very different kind of electricity that was sparking from her skin where he touched her, Livvy tried to pull away. 'Because there's no power and my freezer will be defrosting, and the roads might be cleared at any time. And there are eight guests who will be arriving for Christmas who won't have any croissants for breakfast if the freezer defrosts!' She drew in a deep breath. 'And while these might not be the kind of problems that would normally enter your radar, this is the *real world*, Saladin—and it's a world in which I have to live!'

'And how does getting dressed solve anything when your guests aren't due today?'

She met the mocking expression in his eyes. *It stops me from getting too close to you again. It stops me from feeling any more vulnerable than I'm currently feeling.*

Livvy never knew how she would have answered his question because suddenly the electricity came on in a flurry of light and sound. The tree lights blazed into life and three small lamps began to glow. Somewhere in another part of the house a distant radio began playing and Peppa jumped to her feet and gave a growling little purr.

'The power's back on,' he said.

'Yes,' she answered, in a strange flat voice.

And then the landline started to ring—its piercing sound shattering the silence of their haven. Livvy stared at Saladin, aware of a sinking sensation that felt awfully like disappointment. The outside world was about to intrude and, right then, she didn't want it to.

'Better answer it,' he said.

Clad in just her knickers, Livvy scooted across the room to pick up the phone and nodded her head as she listened to the voice on the other end.

'No, no. That's quite all right, Alison,' she said, aware that Saladin was putting a guard in front of the fire. 'Honestly, it really doesn't matter. I quite understand. I would have done exactly the same in your position. Yes. Yes, I hope so. Okay. I will. Yes. Of course. And a merry Christmas to you, too. Goodbye.'

Slowly, she replaced the receiver as Saladin straightened up and suddenly a part of his anatomy was looking like no museum statue *she'd* ever seen, and it was all still so new to her that she didn't know whether it was rude to stare—even though she was finding it very difficult *not* to stare.

'Who was it?' he questioned and Livvy wondered whether she'd imagined that faint note of amusement in his voice, as if he was perfectly aware of her dilemma.

She shrugged. 'My guests. Someone called Alison Clark who was due to arrive with a load of her polo friends. They rang to say that the weather forecast is too dodgy and they're not coming after all. They've decided to spend Christmas at some fancy hotel in London instead.'

'And are you disappointed?' he questioned smoothly.

'I don't know if *disappointed* is the word I'd use,' she said, aware that a long and empty Christmas now loomed ahead of her. And wasn't that one of the reasons why she always stayed open during the holiday? Because being busy meant she didn't have to look at all the things that were missing in her own life. 'It means I won't get paid, of course.'

There was a pause as he glittered her a smile. 'But that is where you are wrong, Livvy,' he said softly. 'Don't you see that fate has played right into our hands? You are now free to take up my offer and return to Jazratan with me. You can forget about niggling domestic duties over the holidays and use your neglected healing powers on my horse, for which I will reward you handsomely.'

The sum he mentioned was so large that for a moment Livvy thought he was joking, and for a moment she was seriously tempted. Yet some stubborn sense of pride made her shake her head. 'That's far too much.'

He raised his eyebrows. 'First time I've ever heard anyone complain about being paid too much.'

'It should be a fair price,' she persisted stubbornly. 'Not one that sounds like winning the national lottery.'

'What is fair is what I am prepared to pay for your services,' he argued. 'If your gift was more widely distributed, then obviously the price would be a lot lower. But it isn't, and what you have is rare, Livvy— we both know that.'

She knew what he was doing. He was manipulating

her and he was doing it very effectively. He was making her an offer too good to refuse and she was scared. Scared to try. Scared of failing. Scared of his reaction if she *did* fail. And scared of so much else besides.

'But what if this so-called *gift* no longer exists?' she said. 'There's no guarantee that my intervention will work. Burkaan may not respond to my treatment, we both know that.'

'Yes, I know that,' he said. 'But at least I will have tried. I will have done all that is in my power to help my horse.'

She wasn't imagining the sudden hollowness in his voice, or the accompanying bleakness in his eyes, and it was that that made up Livvy's mind for her. Yes, Saladin Al Mektala had the kind of unimaginable riches and influence that other people could only dream of, but when it boiled down to it he was just a man who was desperate to save his beloved horse.

'Very well.' She bent down and picked up her bra. 'I'll come to Jazratan with you.'

'Now what are you doing?'

She straightened up. 'I'm getting dressed, of course. There's a lot I have to sort out. I need to organise someone to feed the cat, for a start.'

'I'm sure you do, but there is something of much greater urgency.' His voice had grown silky. 'And don't look at me with those big honey-coloured eyes and pretend you don't know what I'm talking about.'

Taking the bra from her unprotesting fingers, he dropped it to the floor and wrapped his arms around her waist, securing her to the spot, so that he could kiss her. And once he had started kissing her, she was hungry for more. She rose up on tiptoe to curl her hands possessively around his neck and he gave a low laugh of triumph.

But this time he didn't push her to the rug and slowly thrust himself inside her. Instead, he bent and slid his arm underneath her knees, lifting her up so that she was cradled effortlessly in front of his chest.

'Where are you taking me?' she whispered as he headed for the door.

'To bed.'

She looked up at him. 'Why?'

'Are you serious? You know exactly why. Because I want sex with you again, and once on a hard floor is quite enough when there is the promise of a soft mattress.'

'Actually, my mattress happens to be very firm.'

'That's good.' He slid his hand over her bottom and gave it a squeeze. 'I like firm.'

Her cheeks hot with embarrassment and excitement, Livvy turned her face into his chest. He was taking control and she was letting him. *I want sex with you again*, he'd said—in a way that could almost be described as abrupt. There were no euphemisms tripping off his tongue, were there? No tender words of affection to feed her romantic fantasies. *He's being truthful*, she reminded herself. *He's telling it as it is.*

Yet it was difficult to keep fantasy totally at bay when a naked sheikh was in the process of kicking open her bedroom door and depositing her on her bed.

'Now,' he said as he straddled her, his fingers hooking into the soft silk of her knickers.

She thought he was about to slide them down as he'd done before, but the sudden sound of delicate fabric being ripped made her eyes widen in astonishment and, yes, in excitement, too.

'I can't…' Her heart began to hammer against her ribcage. 'I can't believe you just did that.'

'Well, I did—and here's the proof,' he drawled, dangling the tattered fragments from his index finger like a trophy.

'Those are my best knickers,' she protested.

'Were,' he corrected. 'But they were an obstruction to my desire, and I don't do obstruction. Ever. You shouldn't have put them back on, Livvy.'

'That is…outrageous,' she spluttered.

'Perhaps it is,' he agreed unsteadily. 'But you like me being outrageous, don't you, *habibi*? You like the sense that I am now free to do this…' With a light and teasing movement, he began to brush his finger over her searing heat. Back and forth it went in a relentless rhythm so delicious that she almost leaped off the bed.

'Oh,' she breathed.

'And, of course, I shall make sure you have new panties,' he said unsteadily.

She felt his warm breath heating her face as he lowered his lips towards her. 'What, just so that you can rip them off again?' she managed indistinctly.

'Of course. Because I think we're both discovering what we like. You like me being masterful, don't you, my beauty?' His finger was continuing with its insistent, stroking movement. 'Which is very convenient, since being masterful comes very easily to me.'

Livvy was so aroused by this stage that she barely noticed he must have been in possession of another condom all the while he'd been carrying her upstairs, because he was now stroking it on with practised fingers and easing himself inside her, and she gasped—her cry catching in her throat like a crumb. But this time there was nothing but glorious anticipation coursing around her veins like thick, sweet honey as he entered her. Because this time she knew what was coming.

'Oh, Saladin,' she said, the tender words tumbling out of her mouth—driven by her sheer delight in the moment and wanting him to know how special this felt. 'You are…'

But her breathless words died on her lips as she felt him tense inside her, as if she'd wronged him in some way. She looked up to see that his face had become a mask—stony and forbidding.

'Don't say soft words to me, because I don't want to hear them,' he instructed harshly. 'I don't do tenderness, Livvy. Do you understand?'

'S-sure,' she said uncertainly, and closed her eyes so he wouldn't see her hurt and confusion.

But something had changed—although maybe it was just her own perception of what was happening. He seemed like a man on a mission. As if he was intent on demonstrating his sexual superiority—or demonstrating *something*. Why else did he seem to set about showcasing how many times he could have her orgasm? Of having her plead with him not to stop? Over and over again he made love to her in different ways, as if he intended to make up for all the sex she'd missed out on in her twenty-nine years. Or was it all about power? About showing her who was really the boss?

CHAPTER NINE

SALADIN HEARD THE whir of helicopter blades long before the craft entered the immediate airspace of the house. Moving his wrist carefully so as not to wake Livvy, he glanced at his watch and gave a small nod of satisfaction. Exactly on time and exactly as he had instructed.

He glanced over at the head that was lying next to him—Livvy's bright hair spread out over the pillow. Her lips were parted as she breathed and there was a rosy flush on her freckled cheeks. He felt another stir of desire and contemplated moving his fingertip down over one silken thigh as he thought back to the previous night and most of the subsequent day that he'd spent in her bed. They had taken short breaks for food and for a shared and very erotic shower, and at one point they'd even scrambled into their clothes and gone out tramping through the snowy countryside. But for the most part they had been shut in her bedroom, making love so often that he should have been exhausted, when all he felt was a delicious kind of high.

Because Olivia Miller had proved an exciting lover—more exciting than she should have been, given her lack of experience. Her light, strong body had bent beneath his with the suppleness of a young sapling as he'd driven into her over and over again. She had embraced sex with a passion and athleticism that had taken his sometimes jaded breath away. And if at one point she had made the mistake of going all tender on him, it was a mistake she would not be repeating, for he had warned her off starting to care for him—and royal protocol would ensure that the message was slammed home to her. For this was the last time they would lie together like this...

He felt a stir of something else and acknowledged the uncomfortable stab of his conscience, knowing he had manipulated her in a particularly ruthless fashion. He had taken her virginity because it seemed wrong that a relatively young woman should be living such a celibate existence. And because he had wanted her very badly. But there had been another reason why he had made love to her...knowing that a woman rarely refused a man something if he gave her enough pleasure. And it had worked, hadn't it? She would now be accompanying him to his homeland, as he had intended she would all along.

He felt another stab of conscience. His own doubts hadn't stayed around for long, had they? His guilt about taking her virginity and the symbolic betrayal of his wife hadn't lasted beyond that first, sweet thrust.

He felt the returning throb of an erection and wondered if there was time for another swift coupling prior to their flight before deciding against it. She was going to need to wash and brush up before the trip to his homeland, and he was going to have to deal with his advisors and bodyguards who would doubtless be angry about this solo trip, though they would never dare show it. And although they would invariably guess that he had been doing more than taking tea with the fiery-headed horse expert, there was no need to flaunt his affairs openly in front of such a notoriously conservative group of men. And besides, this would be the end of it. His conscience would trouble him no longer, for there would be no sexual relationship once they were in Jazratan. His mouth hardened. He never brought his lovers to his homeland for reasons that were practical and reasons that were painful.

The clatter of the helicopter blades interrupted his introspection and, gently, he shook Livvy awake. Her lashes fluttered open and he could see the momentary confusion that clouded her amber eyes as she looked around and realised she was naked in bed with him.

Much less shy than after their first encounter, she sat up, the duvet tumbling to her waist and highlighting the pert thrust of her breasts, and Saladin cursed the powerful wave of desire that shot through him.

'What's that noise?'

'My helicopter.'

She blinked at him. 'It's *here*?'

'It's about to land.'

'It's dark outside,' she said sleepily.

'That's because we've been in bed most of the day and it's late. You'll need to get showered, changed and packed,' he added. 'Because we have to leave—and as quickly as possible.'

Livvy felt disorientated as she brushed her untidy hair away from her face and wondered why Saladin was suddenly being so cool towards her. Because she'd obeyed his curt instructions to the letter, hadn't she?

She certainly hadn't been in any way tender towards him after he'd warned her off. She'd responded to his lovemaking with nothing more controversial than a newfound passion and enjoyment. She waited for him to touch her again—or to kiss her, or *something*—but he was already picking up his cell phone and tapping out a number, and she told herself not to make a big deal out of it. Because hadn't she been firm in her resolve last night that she wasn't going to do anything stupid like falling in love with him?

Sliding out of bed, she went along the corridor to the shower, grateful that the boiler was working again and there was plenty of hot water. She remembered the shower they'd shared some time after lunch, and her cheeks burned as she tipped shampoo into the palm of her hand and relived the memory of what had happened.

Because despite his emotional detachment, it had been amazing. Every single second of it. Better than she'd ever imagined, even in her wildest dreams. Suddenly she was *glad* that Rupert had never consummated their relationship. Glad that it had been Saladin who had been her first lover, because instinct told her that no other man could make her feel the way the desert sheikh had done.

She tried to envisage someone other than Saladin touching her, but the thought of another man's hands on her body made her stomach clench with distaste. She turned her face towards the hot jets of water, knowing she mustn't read anything into what had just happened, because that would be setting herself up to be a victim. And hadn't she sworn she would never be a victim again? It was sex, that was all. Nothing but sex—

beautiful and empowering, but ultimately meaningless. So why not just enjoy it while she could?

Back in her bedroom, she stuffed her ripped panties into the bin, dressed in jeans and a sweater and then found her old jodhpurs at the back of the wardrobe and began packing a suitcase. Layering in casual clothes and T-shirts plus a couple of smarter dresses, she went over to the bookcase and picked out a couple of long-neglected books. By the time she got downstairs, the helicopter had landed on the back field and Saladin was standing beside the Christmas tree, still talking into his cell phone.

He cut the connection immediately, but his eyes didn't seem particularly warm as he turned to look at her, and he made no attempt to touch her as she walked over to him. There was no lingering kiss acknowledging their shared intimacy. No arm placed casually around her shoulder. Anyone observing them would have assumed that they were simply boss and employee, not two people who, a short time ago, had been writhing around in ecstasy together upstairs.

Boss and employee.

Which was exactly what they were.

'Your hair is still wet,' he observed. 'You'll get cold.'

Trying to ignore his critical stare, Livvy forced a smile. 'I have a woolly hat I can wear.'

'As you wish.' He glanced around. 'Do you need to lock up the house?'

'No, I thought I'd leave the doors open to see if any seasonal burglar fancies taking their chances,' she replied sarcastically. 'Of course I need to lock the house up!'

She wanted him to stop talking to her as if he were a robot and to kiss her again. To convince her that what had happened last night hadn't been some crazy kind of dream that was fading by the second.

But he didn't. He seemed suddenly *distant*. As if he had retreated behind an invisible barrier she couldn't access. Instead of being her cajoling and vital lover, he had effortlessly morphed into his real role of lofty and exalted sheikh.

Like a scene from an adventure movie, she found herself following him across the dark and snowy grass towards the helicopter, beside which stood a couple of burly men who bowed deeply before the sheikh before speaking in a fast and foreign tongue. Briefly, she wondered how Saladin was explaining the presence of a pale-faced woman in a woolly hat who was accompanying him.

With the helicopter lights flickering they flew over the night-time countryside to an airstrip, where a private jet was waiting. Aware of the veiled glances of his advisors, Livvy boarded the sleek plane, whose sides were adorned with the royal crest, startled to discover that she and the sheikh would be sitting separately during the flight.

She wondered if he saw her look of surprise just before one of the stewards ushered her through a door at the rear, to a much smaller section of the plane—though, admittedly, one that contained its own bed. Pulling out her books and music from her holdall, she looked around. Actually, there was a TV screen—and a neat little bathroom offering a tempting display of soaps and perfume. But even so…

Moments later, Saladin came to find her—all quietly

brooding power as he stood in the doorway with his cool black eyes surveying her.

'You are satisfied with your seat, I hope?' he questioned.

She was trying hard not to show she was hurt—but suddenly it wasn't easy to bite back the feelings that were bubbling up inside her. 'I wasn't expecting us to be sitting apart. Not after...' She clamped her lips shut, aware of having said too much. Did expressing vulnerability count as tenderness? she wondered.

He glanced over his shoulder before lowering his voice. 'Not after having had sex with you—is that what you mean?'

'It doesn't matter,' she mumbled.

'It does,' he said, suddenly breaking into an angry torrent of Jazratian, which was directed at the hapless steward who had appeared at the doorway behind him, but who now beat a hasty retreat. 'It matters because I'm afraid this is how things are going to be from now on.'

She stared at him, not quite understanding what he meant until his stony expression told her more clearly than any words could have done. 'You mean—?'

'What happened in England must stay in England, for we cannot be intimate in Jazratan,' he said. 'The laws of my country are very strict on such matters—and it would offend my people deeply if it was discovered that I was having sex with an unmarried woman. Particularly an unmarried foreigner.' He shrugged, as if to take some of the heat from his words. 'For I am the sheikh and you are my employee, Livvy, and from now on we will not be stepping outside the boundaries of those roles.'

It was several moments before Livvy could trust herself to speak, and if the giant plane hadn't already been taxiing down the runway, she honestly thought she might have run up to the steward and demanded they let her out.

But she couldn't. She had agreed to take the job and she was going to have to behave like a professional. And anyway—mightn't this strategy be the best strategy for keeping her emotions protected? If she and Saladin were to be segregated, it would be very difficult to foster any kind of attachment to him. So even though his words hurt, somehow she found the strength to force a careless smile onto her lips.

'Well, that's a relief,' she said.

His black eyes narrowed. 'A relief?'

'Sure. I've got a lot of reading I want to get through before we land. I told you it was a long time since I'd worked with horses.' With a wave of her hand, she gestured towards the books she'd just unpacked. 'So I'd better have a browse through these. Reacquaint myself with the species, even if it's only theoretical—until I get to meet Burkaan. So please don't let me keep you,' she added. 'I'll be perfectly happy here on my own.'

His face was a picture—as if he'd just realised that in effect she was *dismissing* him—yet he could hardly object to her demand for privacy after what he'd just said.

But once he'd gone, and she was left with the opened but unread pages of *Healing Horses Naturally*, Livvy found herself staring out of the window at the black sky as England receded, unable to deny the sudden pain that clenched like a vice around her heart.

He'd made her sound…

Like a cliché.

An unmarried foreign woman he was forbidden to have sex with.

She closed her eyes. He had come to the house determined to employ her, and for a while she had resisted him. Had he looked at her and wondered whether seduction was a price he was prepared to pay in order to guarantee her services? She bit her lip.

Even when she'd told him that she was a virgin—and a twenty-nine-year-old virgin, to boot... A lot of men might have stopped at that point. But not Saladin. Had he guessed that sex would make her eager to do his bidding? Did he realise that she would find it very difficult to refuse to work for him after what had taken place between them?

Damn him.

So stop letting him take control, she thought. *Be grateful that he's shown you are capable of sexual pleasure but also be grateful that he has put this barrier between you, because there is no future with Saladin and there never can be.*

She picked up the cup of jasmine tea that had just been put on the table by a slightly nervous-looking steward.

She was going to have to start being rational. She was here on a life-changing salary to help his horse, and she would do her utmost to accomplish that. The sex she must forget. She *had to.*

She slept for almost six hours and, when she awoke, discovered that the little shower was much better than the one at home. Afterwards she felt a million times better and was just tucking into a bowl of delicious porridge topped with iced mango when the curtain between the two sections of the plane was drawn back, and she looked up to see Saladin standing there.

It was slightly disconcerting that he'd changed from his Western clothes into an outfit more befitting a desert sheikh, because it only seemed to emphasise the vast gulf between them. Gone were the trousers, sweater and cashmere coat, and in their place were flowing robes of pure silk that completely covered him, yet hinted at the hard body beneath. His ebony hair was now hidden by a headdress, held in place by a circlet of knotted scarlet cord—and against the pale material his golden-dark features looked forbidding.

He looked like a fantasy.

Like a stranger.

And that was exactly what he was, Livvy reminded herself grimly.

His eyes fixed on her, he waited, and she was sure he expected her to scramble to her feet, but she simply finished her mouthful of porridge and gave him a faint smile.

'Morning,' she said.

He frowned before slowly inclining his head, as if forcing himself to respond civilly to her casual greeting. 'Good morning. Did you sleep well during the flight?'

'Like a dormouse, as they say in France.' Again, she smiled. 'Did you?'

Saladin felt the pounding of a pulse at his temple, her glib response only adding to his growing annoyance and frustration. No, he had not slept well, for the night had seemed endless. He had tossed and turned and eventually had drawn up one of the blinds to stare out at the jewelled and inky sky as the plane travelled through the night towards Jazratan. It had been a long time since he'd endured such restlessness. Not since...

But the realisation that he was comparing simple sexual frustration to the worst time of his life filled him with an angry guilt. Pushing aside the turmoil of his thoughts, he acknowledged the insolent way in which Livvy Miller was leaning back on her elbows, watching him. Her amber eyes were hooded and her lips gleamed from the mouthful of jasmine tea she had just drunk. How dared she continue to drink and eat in his presence?

He had told her there would be no more intimacy, but he certainly hadn't given her permission to abandon all protocol. Didn't she realise that there was an etiquette that needed to be adhered to whenever he entered the room? You did not greet the king of Jazratan with such blatant carelessness, and this was something she needed to be aware of before she arrived at the palace.

'You are supposed to stand when I enter the room,' he said coolly.

'Am I?' She fixed him with a deliberate look of challenge. 'As I recall, you seemed to prefer it when I was lying down.'

'Livvy!' He glanced behind him as he ground out his protest, feeling the instant rush of heat to his groin. 'You mustn't—'

'Mustn't what?' she interrupted in a low tone. 'Tell it like it is? Well, I'm sorry, Saladin, but I don't intend to be a hypocrite. I accept the intimacy ban you've imposed because, now I've had time to think about it, I can understand it and I think it's a good idea. But if you think I'm going to be sinking to the ground into a curtsy and lowering my eyes demurely whenever you appear, then you are very much mistaken.'

Her passionate insolence wasn't something Saladin was used to, and he was shocked into a momentary silence. He wanted to do a number of things—all of which seemed to contradict themselves. He wanted to kiss her and to simultaneously push her as far away from him as possible. He wanted never to see her again and yet he wanted to feast his eyes on her in a leisurely visual feast. Suddenly he realised that here was one person—one *woman*—who would not be moulded to his will, and with a shock it suddenly dawned on him why that was. *Because he needed her more than she needed him.*

He could not expel her for insubordination—well, he could, but his stallion would only suffer as a result. And even though he was paying way over the odds for an expertise she had warned him herself might not work, he suspected that the money didn't mean as much to her as it might to someone else.

Did it? Or had her initial reluctance to take the job simply been the work of a clever negotiator? Perhaps he should test her out.

'Surely a little civility wouldn't go amiss since I am rewarding you so handsomely for your work.'

'You're *paying* me, Saladin—not *rewarding* me,' she contradicted. 'You were the one who made the over-inflated offer in the first place, so please don't start reneging on it now. And if you want me to show you respect, I'm afraid you will have to earn it.'

'*Earn* it?' he echoed incredulously.

'Yes. Is that such an extraordinary proposition?'

He gave a short laugh. 'It is certainly one that has never been put to me before.'

She stood up then, clenching her hands into two small fists and sucking in an unsteady breath as she looked at him. 'I'm not a complete fool, Saladin,' she hissed. 'I'm fully aware that you seduced me for a purpose. And it worked.'

He looked into the amber eyes that blazed as brightly as her fiery hair. He thought how magnificent she looked when she was berating him, and suddenly he felt a lump rise in his throat. 'Believe me when I tell you this,' he said huskily. 'I seduced you because I wanted you.'

Livvy heard the sudden passion that had deepened his words and something inside her melted. Stupid how she'd almost forgotten what they'd just been arguing about. Stupid how her body was just *craving* for him to touch her.

Did he feel that, too? Was she imagining the slight move he made towards her, when suddenly the plaintive lament of what sounded like *bagpipes* broke into her thoughts and shattered the tense atmosphere. Disorientated, she met Saladin's gaze and it was as if the noise had brought him to his senses, too, because he stiffened and stepped away from her, and in his eyes flared something cold and bleak.

'What the hell is that?' she whispered.

Her question seemed to shake him out of his sombre reverie, though it took a moment before his eyes cleared and he answered. 'A hangover from my great-grandfather's holidays at your own royal family's Scottish residence,' he said. 'He was very impressed by the bagpipes that were used to wake everyone in the morning. After that he decided that they would become a permanent feature of Jazratian life. Thus a returning sheikh is always greeted on his arrival by the unmistakable sound of Scotland.'

'It's certainly very novel.'

'You will find much about my country that surprises you, Livvy,' he replied. 'In a moment I will leave the aircraft and one of the stewards will indicate when it is appropriate for you to do the same. There will be transport waiting to take you to my palace.'

She screwed up her eyes as she looked at him. 'So I won't even be travelling with you?'

He shook his head. 'No. My homecoming is always greeted with a certain amount of celebration. There will be crowds lining the route, and it would not sit well with my people were I to return to the palace in the company of a foreign female, no matter how skilled she might be in her particular field.'

'Right,' she said.

'You will be given your own very comfortable suite of rooms. Once you have settled in, I will send one of my advisors to take you to the stable complex, so that you can meet the vets and the grooms, and get to work on Burkaan straight away. You will, however, take meals with me.'

Without waiting for a response, he turned and walked away with a swish of his silken robes. And if Livvy felt momentarily frustrated by his sudden indifference, that wasn't what was currently occupying her thoughts. It was the way he had looked during those few moments when she'd thought he was going to reach out and touch her.

Because when the smoky passion had cleared from

his eyes, it had left behind a flicker of something haunting. The trace of an emotion that she wouldn't necessarily have associated with a man like Saladin.

Something that looked awfully like guilt.

CHAPTER TEN

LIVVY STOOD BENEATH the bright Jazratian sunshine and looked around her with a sense of awe and a slight sense of feeling displaced—as if she couldn't quite believe she was here in Saladin's homeland, and that it was Christmas Eve.

The Al Mektala stable complex was lavish, and no expense had been spared in providing for the needs and comfort of over a hundred horses. She'd read about places like this, in those long-ago days when an equestrian magazine had never been far from her hand—but had never imagined herself actually working in one.

Fine sand paddocks were edged with lines of palm trees, which provided welcome shade, but plenty of areas had been laid to grass and it was curiously restful—if a little bizarre—to see large patches of green set against the harsh backdrop of the desert landscape. There were plush air-conditioned boxes for the horses and even a dappled and cool pool in which they could swim. Grooms, physiotherapists and jockeys—all clad in the distinctive Al Mektala livery of indigo and silver—swarmed around the place as efficiently as ants working in harmony together.

After arriving at the palace Livvy had been shown

to a large suite of rooms, where she'd changed into jodhpurs and a shirt and then followed the servant who had been dispatched to take her to the stables. She hadn't been expecting to find Saladin waiting for her—and she certainly wasn't expecting to see him similarly attired in riding clothes, his fingers curving rather distractingly around a riding whip.

She had to force her thoughts away from how lusciously the jodhpurs were clinging to his narrow hips and hugging the powerful shafts of his long legs. It was difficult not to let her gaze linger on the way his billowing silk shirt gave definition to the rock-like torso beneath, making him resemble the kind of buccaneering hero you might find on some Sunday-night TV drama. She told herself that she wasn't going to remember the way he had held her when he'd been making love to her, or the way it had felt to have him deep inside her. She wasn't going to think about how good it had felt to be kissed by him—or the way she'd cried out as she had reached her climax, over and over again. She was here to see if she could help his horse—and that was the *only* reason she was here.

But it was hard to stand so close to him and to resist the desire to reach out and touch him, even though she was doing her best to keep her smile cool and professional.

'So what do you think of my stables, Livvy?'

She smiled. 'As you predicted—it's very interesting to see what you've done in such an extreme climate. And it's all very impressive—just as I would have expected,' she observed as she glanced around. 'Perhaps I could see Burkaan now?'

Once again Saladin felt that inexplicable conflict

within him. He was irritated by her lack of desire to make small talk with him—yet couldn't help but admire her cool professionalism. Just as he was irritated with himself for having almost reached out to her on the plane, when temptation had wrapped itself around his skin like a silken snare. But he had stopped himself just in time, and that was a good thing, although it hadn't felt particularly easy at the time. Because he'd forced himself to remember that he was back in Jazratan where expectations were different and where the memory of Alya was at its strongest. Here, his role was rigidly defined, and casual sex with foreigners simply was not on the agenda. He needed to put that delicious interlude out of his mind and to see whether or not she could live up to her reputation.

Raising his hand, he indicated to the waiting groom that his horse should be brought outside, and he felt his heart quicken in anticipation, as if hoping that some miracle had happened while he'd been away and that Burkaan would come trotting out into the yard with his former vitality.

But the reality shocked and saddened him. The sight of his beloved stallion being led from his stable, looking like a shadow of his former self, made Saladin's heart clench painfully in his chest. The magnificent racehorse's frame seemed even more diminished, and his normally glossy black coat looked lacklustre and dull. The stallion was usually happy, but he was not happy now. Saladin could almost read the anguish and the pain in his eyes as he bared his teeth at his master.

'Don't go near him yet,' he warned Livvy. 'He's been very vicious. Few people can get close to him. Even me.'

But to his annoyance and a concern he couldn't quite hide, she completely ignored his words, moving so quietly towards the horse that she could have been a ghost as she held out her hand in a gesture of peace.

'It's okay,' she said to the animal, in the softest, most musical voice he had ever heard. 'I'm not going to hurt you. It's okay, Burkaan. It's going to be fine.'

Burkaan was more used to being spoken to in Jazratian, and even before his accident had been known for his intolerance of strangers, but Saladin watched in amazement as Livvy moved closer to the powerful animal. There was a split second when he expected the horse to lash out at her and braced himself in readiness to snatch the stubborn woman out of harm's way. But the moment did not come. Instead, she slowly reached out and began to stroke his neck. And Burkaan let her!

'It's all right,' she was crooning quietly. 'I've come to help you. Do you know that, Burkaan? Do you?'

The horse gave a little whinny, and Saladin felt his throat constrict with something that felt uncomfortably like hope. But he knew better than anyone that misplaced hope was the most painful emotion of all, and he drove it from his heart with a ruthlessness he'd learned a long time ago. Just because the horse was prepared to allow the Englishwoman to approach and to touch him didn't mean a thing.

'I wonder, could you ask the groom to walk him around the yard a little?' she said. 'Just so I can see how badly he's injured?'

Saladin nodded and spoke to the groom, and the stricken stallion was led forward and began to hobble around the yard.

'You will note that he has injured his—'

'His near foreleg,' Livvy interrupted crisply, her gaze following the horse as it slowly made its way to the other side of the yard. 'Yes, I can see that. He's clearly in a lot of pain and he's hopping to try to compensate. Okay. I've seen everything I need to see. Please ask the groom to bring him back now, and put him in his box.'

Feeling like her tame linguist, Saladin relayed her instructions to the groom, and once Burkaan had been led back into his box, Livvy turned to face him. He thought her smile looked forced, and he wondered if she was aware that the bright Jazratian sunshine was making her hair look like liquid fire. And, oh, how he would love to feel the burn of it against his fingers again.

'I'm just going to try a few things out,' she said. 'So I'd prefer it if you and everyone else would leave now.'

Disbelief warred with a grudging admiration as she spoke to him, because Saladin realised that once again she was *dismissing* him. She really *was* fond of taking control, wasn't she? He had never been dominated by a woman before, and he was finding it more exciting than he could ever have anticipated—but he would not tolerate it. No way. Surely she must realise that this was *his* stable and *his* horse, and of course he would wish to observe her. He fixed her with a steady look. 'I'm not going anywhere, Livvy,' he said. 'I want to be here.'

She sucked in a deep breath. 'I'm sorry, but I prefer to work alone.'

'I don't care. I want to be here,' he repeated.

She narrowed her eyes as if trying to weigh up whether there was any point in further argument, before obviously coming to the most sensible conclusion.

'Very well,' she said. 'But I don't want any distractions. You must keep very quiet and not interfere. I want you to stand over there out of the way, to keep very still and not say a word. Do you understand?'

Saladin's mouth thinned into a grim smile as her cool words washed over him. One thing he *did* understand was that nobody else had ever spoken to him like this before, not even Alya—especially not Alya, who had been the most agreeable woman ever made.

Instinct made him want to march over to Livvy and pull rank and ask her who the hell she thought she was talking to. To remind her that he was the sheikh and he would damned well do as he pleased. Yet what alternative did he have but to accede to her demands, when the welfare of his beloved horse was of far greater importance than his own sense of pride and position?

'Yes, Livvy,' he said drily. 'I think I get the general idea.'

Afterwards he would try to work out exactly what she had done to Burkaan, but, apart from a vague impression of her laying her palms on the animal's injured foreleg, her time with the horse seemed to pass in a blur. Maybe it was because for once Saladin got the distinct impression that her words had been true. She really didn't want him there, and would have preferred it if he had gone back to the palace as she'd requested. It was certainly the first time in his life that he had been completely ignored.

Because sheikhs were never ignored and people were always conscious of his presence. No matter how large an official function or social gathering, everyone always knew exactly where he was situated, although they often pretended not to. Nobody ever left a room while he remained in it, and nobody ever turned their back on him.

But none of this seemed relevant as he watched Livvy whispering into Burkaan's ear and running feather-light fingertips over the horse's injured limb and then stroking their way over his back. To his surprise, the stallion seemed to tolerate almost every touch she made—only jerking back his head and showing his teeth on two occasions. Eventually, she straightened up and wiped the palms of her hands down over her jodhpurs, and he could see sweat beading her pale brow.

'I've finished now,' she said. 'I'll see him later. Make sure he gets some rest and is undisturbed until I do.'

He saw her glance at her watch and realised that he had effectively backed himself into a corner. He had told her—quite correctly—that they would be occupying separate sections of the palace. He had told her that their lives would cross only at mealtimes and when she was hands-on with Burkaan. Yet now the thought of that did not please him—on the contrary, it positively *rankled*. He had found it necessary to lay out his boundaries during the flight over, in order to emphasise to her that the sex had meant nothing—and he had been expecting a host of objections from her, or maybe even a petulant sulk. Because women always tried to cling on to him when he rejected them—as reject them he inevitably did.

But Livvy was showing no signs of clinging—or sulking. She had travelled separately to the palace without protest, and, on arriving at her suite of rooms, had apparently made some complimentary comment to one of the servants about the ancient tiled floors and the beauty of the palace gardens. And ironically, he had found himself curiously unsettled by her apparent acceptance of the situation in which she now found herself.

'We have plenty of time before lunch,' he said. 'Perhaps you would care to ride with me?'

For a moment, Livvy felt temptation wash over her as his suggestion brought back echoes of a life she had left far behind. She thought of being in the saddle again and the feeling of having all that impressive horse power beneath her. She thought of the warm, desert breeze against her skin and the incomparable sense of freedom that riding always gave her, but, resolutely, she shook her head. 'I don't ride anymore.'

'Why not?'

She met the question in his narrowed eyes. 'Because riding demands time and commitment and money—and I've been too busy running my business to have any of those things.'

'But you have time now,' he pointed out coolly. 'And money isn't a consideration.'

'It's out of the question,' she said. 'I'm completely out of practice.'

There was a pause. 'And maybe you're scared of getting back on a horse after so long away?'

His unexpected insight caught her off guard. Was that why she answered him so truthfully?

'Maybe a little,' she agreed. But it wasn't fear of the horse that frightened her. It was the thought of re-entering a world that had brought her pain and that now seemed so long ago it might have happened to another person.

'Then, why not get back in the saddle?' His voice

deepened. 'Kill your fear by confronting it. Don't they say that the more you practise, the better you get?'

And suddenly there was an undeniable sexual innuendo whispering in the air around them and whipping up an unspoken need inside her. She could feel sudden tension heating her skin, and the tips of her breasts had grown suddenly sensitive. She could feel it in the way her lips parted, as if silently inviting him to kiss them—and, oh, how she wanted him to kiss her.

Livvy stared at Saladin as she tried to dampen down the rising tide of desire. To remind herself of the way he'd treated her since she had agreed to treat his horse. He had kept her away from him during the flight and ordered separate journeys to the palace, where she had been allocated quarters in the staff section. She didn't have a problem with that—because she *was* staff. What she *did* have a problem with was his assumption that he could treat her like some kind of plaything. Act icy one minute and then flirt with her the next. Well, he had better learn that it didn't work like that. She didn't dare let it.

'I don't want it to come back,' she said.

'Why not?'

She glanced down at the tips of her riding boots, which were covered in fine dust, before lifting her gaze to meet the jet-dark gleam of his eyes. 'Because when I split with Rupert I walked away from riding. I bolted—and I shut the stable door behind me. I left my job, realising that I had no appetite to face the knowing looks and the knowledge that he'd been sleeping with my best friend.'

'You could have found different stables.'

'I could. But horse riding is a very small world,

and gossip always follows you around. I wanted to be known as more than the woman who'd been involved in a spicy scandal. I wanted a clean break and that's what I got. The old Livvy has gone and so has the world she lived in. I'm not looking to recapture something from the past—I'm here because I'm trying to take care of my future. So if you've finished with the interrogation, I'd like someone to show me back to my room because this palace is so big, I don't trust myself not to get lost.'

With a thoughtful look, he inclined his head. 'Certainly. I will show you to your suite myself.'

'There's really no need. A servant will do.'

'My servants don't speak English.'

'I'm quite happy to forego conversation.'

'I will show you to your room, Livvy,' he said, with silky insistence. 'And please don't oppose me just for the sake of it, or you will discover how quickly my tolerance limit can be reached.'

His reprimand was stern and maybe it was justified, but as Livvy fell into step beside him she realised that even *opposing* him was making her feel things she didn't want to feel. Desire was throbbing through her body and making her want to squirm with frustration. It was all she could do not to reach out and touch him—to whisper her fingers possessively over his riding shirt and feel the hard torso beneath. Was it because he'd been her only lover that she was feeling this way? Was she building it up in her head because he'd taken her virginity so that what had happened seemed powerful and significant?

Yet maybe that wasn't so surprising when sex with Saladin had seemed so *easy*. It had happened so naturally. It had felt as if she'd been waiting all her life for the desert sheikh to make love to her. As if she hadn't been complete until he had completed her.

And wasn't that the way it was supposed to feel?

Blocking out the disturbing thoughts that were threatening to overwhelm her, she focused her attention on the splendour of her surroundings instead. The temperature dropped as they passed through the shaded portico into the main palace, where the polished floors were deliciously cool and smooth.

They crossed a courtyard and, on the far side, Livvy saw a shining silver bower, festooned with tumbling roses of scarlet and orange and pink. Glittering brightly in the midday sun, it was topped with an intricate silver structure of filigree metal flowers and leaves and Livvy's footsteps came to a halt. 'Wow,' she said slowly. 'What is that place?'

By her side Saladin stiffened as he followed the direction of her eyes. 'That is the Faddi gate, leading to the palace rose garden,' he said abruptly.

'Oh, it's beautiful. Could we go that way?'

But suddenly he seemed to be having difficulty controlling his emotions and Livvy looked up to see a tiny nerve working frantically at his temple and that his mouth had hardened with an expression she couldn't quite fathom. He shook his head.

'The gardeners are working there,' he said abruptly. 'And they do not like to be observed. Come, I will take you a different way.'

He remained tense for a minute or two, but as they walked towards her rooms he began to recount some of the history of Jazratan and of the palace itself. And somehow the change of subject was enough to make him relax—and Livvy relaxed, too, so that after a while she found herself engrossed in the things he was telling her. He talked about battles that had been fought and won by his ancestors, of sheikhs whose lifeblood had seeped like rust onto the desert sands. He told her about the brave mount who had led one particular victorious battle—a forerunner to his own, beloved Burkaan.

She realised then why his horse was so important to him, and it had nothing to do with money, or even a close bond that transcended his royal status. Because Burkaan was a link between the past and the future. If the stallion was put out to stud, then his illustrious line would continue. And continuity was the lifeblood of a ruling monarch.

He's so different from you, Livvy thought. *So don't ever make the mistake of thinking it could be any other way than this.*

They had just reached her door when Saladin suddenly reached out to wrap his fingers around her wrist, and the unexpected gesture shocked Livvy into stillness. She wondered if he could feel the sudden hammering of her pulse. He must do. It sounded so thunderous to her own ears she was surprised it hadn't brought the servants running.

'Thank you for what you did today,' he said.

'I did very little.'

'On the contrary. You calmed a horse who has been nothing but vicious since his accident. It was the first time I've seen a fleeting moment of peace in his eyes.'

And Livvy found herself looking into *his* eyes, helplessly snared by their ebony light. She'd seen many emotions in them since that snowy afternoon when he had first walked into her life. She'd seen them harden with irritation and determination. She'd seen them soften with desire and lust. And she'd seen them cloud over with something that had looked very like sorrow as they had stared at the Faddi gate leading to the rose garden. Did Saladin have his own dark demons raging within him? she wondered.

Reluctantly, she pulled her hand away from his—even though deep down she wanted to curl her fingers into his palm, like a cat settling down for the evening. But that way lay danger. He'd already set out the boundaries and, even though her body wanted to push at those boundaries, she recognised that distance from Saladin made perfect sense.

'You really must excuse me,' she said, bringing a note of formality into her voice. 'I need to call England to check that Peppa is okay and that the snow hasn't caused any lasting damage.' She smiled. 'I'll see you at lunch—presumably you will send someone to collect me?'

And with that, she walked into her suite, quietly closing the door—not caring that he was still standing there looking darkly displeased by her dismissal. Not caring about anything other than a need to put some distance between them before she did something crazy like fling herself against that hard and virile body and beg him to make love to her again.

CHAPTER ELEVEN

IT WASN'T AS easy as he had thought it would be.

It wasn't easy at all.

With an impatient flick of his hand, Saladin waved the servant away and lowered his body into the deep tub of steaming water. How was it possible to feel exhausted when you had only just risen from your bed? Could it have anything to do with the fact that he'd spent yet another sleepless night frustratedly recalling that erotic fireside encounter when the innocent Livvy Miller had cried out her passion in his arms?

Maybe he'd been naive to think it would be easy to adhere to his self-imposed sex ban when she was living here at the palace. When thoughts of her kept drifting into his mind at the most inconvenient times—usually without warning or provocation. Sometimes he found himself sitting through meetings of state and thinking about her pale skin and fiery hair. About the way he had cupped her narrow hips and driven into that slender body. He would sit uncomfortably with a massive erection hidden by his flowing robes, and wonder why he had insisted that she remain totally off limits.

Because he could not trash his sacred memories of

the past by indulging in a casual fling, especially here in the palace.

For a while he lay in the cooling water and thought about the long days that had passed since Livvy's arrival. The Englishwoman had settled in well—better than he could ever have anticipated. She had worked diligently with Burkaan four times a day and, although she grudgingly permitted his presence at these sessions, she had made it clear that she expected total silence from him—and he had found himself complying!

At other times he had barely seen her. She hadn't seemed to mind missing any of the holiday celebrations she would have enjoyed back in England. He'd heard from the servants that she spent much of her time reading on the shaded terraces outside her suite. And it infuriated him to realise that it would be completely inappropriate to disturb her there, even though he was master of all he surveyed. He felt as if he was caught in a trap of his own making. Sometimes he caught a glimpse of her as she made her way out to the sprawling expanse of the palace gardens and watched as she peered through the Faddi gate. And wondered why it was no longer Alya's face he could see in his mind, but the face of the freckly Englishwoman.

Because she was off limits?

Because she wasn't coming on to him? That was something else he found it hard to get his head round. There had been no coy glances or lingering looks. She hadn't been flaunting her body in close-fitting clothes to torment him with memories of what lay beneath. No, she had acted with an admirable—if infuriating—decorum.

Only at mealtimes were the wretched rules relaxed—

and then he found himself eager to talk to her. He quizzed her about his horse's progress and gradually, once she had lost some of the new guarded expression she seemed to assume around him, she began to open up a little more. It was a unique situation, he realised, for rarely did he have the opportunity—or inclination—to get to know a woman. Women were there for his sexual pleasure, and once he had taken his fill he walked away. But with Livvy, there was no opportunity for sexual pleasure. And not only was he unable to walk away—bizarrely he found he didn't want to. This pale and stubborn Englishwoman was intriguing him more than he had expected to be intrigued.

She told him about getting on her first horse at the age of three, and her mother's love of riding. Of her own increasing skill on horseback and the way the two of them used to gallop across the dewy fields around Wightwick Manor. She spoke of frosty landscapes washed pink with the light from the rising sun. She told him about the first time she realised that she could understand horses in a way that most people couldn't and the 'awesome feeling of responsibility' it had given her. She described the day she'd brought home her first rosette, aged six, and then her first shiny silver trophy a year later.

It was after one such recollection after lunch one day that he heard her voice falter and Saladin found himself leaning back in his chair to study her.

'You must miss it,' he said. 'Riding.'

She gave a little shrug. 'Sometimes.'

'So what can I do to tempt you back into the saddle?'

'You can stop trying—I'm not interested.'

'Aren't you?'

She put down her golden goblet with a thud. 'No.'

And suddenly Saladin wanted to break all his own rules. He wanted to forget that he was a king and a widower and to behave like any other man. To seek pleasure and comfort when it was available. To try to rid himself of some of this obsession he had for the titian-haired Englishwoman. Because soon there would be no reason for her to remain. Burkaan was improving daily—everyone had commented on the fact. Soon she would be headed back to England and he would never see her again. Because deep down he suspected that, unlike other lovers, Livvy would not be interested in a brief relationship back in England, simply to burn their passion away. He suspected that she would disapprove of such a cold-blooded suggestion.

So couldn't it burn itself out here and now? Wasn't he the king of all he surveyed, who could change the unspoken rules of his land, just as long as he wasn't blatant about it?

'Ride with me today, Livvy,' he said suddenly. 'For mercy's sake—what harm can it do?'

Livvy looked at him, acknowledging the suddenly urgent note in his voice. She wanted to refuse. To tell him that it felt too poignant, too intimate, too...too *everything*. And yet...yet...

She looked into the gleam of his black eyes. The temptation was strong and her thoughts made it even stronger. What harm could one little ride do, on one of the sheikh's magnificent horses, as she had been longing to do for weeks? To be alone with the desert king—far away from the watchful eyes of the palace servants. 'I'll ride with you later,' she said. 'After Burkaan's final session of the day.'

The state of excitement inside her for the next few hours was disproportionate to the short ride that he'd undoubtedly scheduled. At least, that was what Livvy told herself. But no matter how much she tried to minimise the impact of some time alone with Saladin away from the palace, nothing could get rid of the fizz of excitement in her blood.

Her heart was pounding as she swung herself up into the saddle with Saladin watching her closely, his hand on the reins.

'Okay?' he questioned.

She nodded as she felt the first ripple of the animal's power beneath her. 'Okay,' she echoed softly.

The beautiful chestnut mare he'd given her was placid, and, with Saladin mounting a much bigger roan stallion, they trotted out of the stable complex side by side onto the hard desert sands. The rhythmic pounding of the horses' hooves was both soothing and exhilarating as they began to canter. The sun was low and the sky was an inverted bowl of deepest blue as Livvy breathed in the warm air. She felt...*alive*. The most alive she'd felt since...

Since Saladin had made love to her.

She turned to look at him, thinking that he resembled a figure from a fantasy tale. No jodhpurs today—instead, his white headdress billowed behind him and his silken robes clung to the hard contours of his body as he rode alongside her.

'How do you know your way around?' she questioned. 'Aren't you afraid of getting lost?'

He gave a brief smile. 'I grew up in this land,' he said. 'And it is as familiar to me as my own skin.'

'Really?' She thought using his skin as a comparison

probably wasn't the best idea, under the circumstances—but she kept her expression neutral. 'In what way?'

He shrugged as he slowed his horse down. 'You see nothing but sand, but I see ridges and undulations on the surface where the winds have blown—and I can read the wind by sight and sound as others can read music. I know where there are underground rivers and lakes, where vegetation can thrive and provide shelter. And I always make sure I'm carrying adequate supplies of water and a compass—as well as a cell phone.' He flicked her another brief smile. 'Would you like me to take you to an oasis?'

She thought at first that he must be joking, because it sounded so *corny*. She half remembered some pop song her mother used to love. Something about midnight at an oasis. Livvy gripped the reins a little tighter as she met the gleaming question in his black eyes and suddenly she wondered what the hell was making her hesitate. When else in her life was she ever going to get the opportunity to see an oasis?

'I'd love to,' she said.

'Then, come,' he urged, and when he saw the look of hesitation on her face he gave a quick smile. *'Come.'* Pressing his knees into his horse's flanks, he set off at a gallop and after a moment's hesitation Livvy started after him.

It came back within seconds—that raw exhilaration and sheer *joy*. She'd forgotten the speed and sense of power you got when you were riding a horse at full pelt, and any lingering reservations were melted away as she galloped after the sheikh.

Over hard and undulating sands they rode—with nothing but the heavy sound of hooves pounding. They rode until Saladin slowed down the pace so that they could mount a steep incline, and Livvy's breath died in her throat when she saw what was on the other side. For there was an unexpectedly wide gleam of water surrounded by grasses and a line of lush palm trees that provided acres of shade.

'Oh, wow,' she said softly. 'A real oasis.'

'Did you think it was a mirage?' he questioned drily.

The truthful answer would have been yes, because nothing felt quite real as Livvy's horse followed Saladin's down to the desert lake, and she jumped down to lead her mount towards the water. She could hear the strange squawking of a bird in one of the palm trees and the glugging splash as the two thirsty animals drank. Saladin gestured for her to tether her horse in the shade next to his, while he drew out a canister of water and offered it to her.

Rarely had any drink ever tasted as delicious as this, and Livvy gulped it down with gratitude and a strange sense of being at peace with herself. She was standing beneath the shade of a palm tree and Saladin was taking the container from her suddenly boneless fingers and drinking from it himself. And she wondered how sharing water with a man could seem so ridiculously *intimate*. Because they had shared so much more than this? She watched the swallowing movement of his neck and suddenly her mouth felt dry again—even though she'd just drunk about half a litre.

He didn't say a word as he put the empty container back and then took her by the hand, leading her towards the cool canopy provided by the palm trees—and she didn't ask him where he was taking her or what he was about to do when he got there, because she knew.

It was obvious from the sudden tension in the fingers that were firmly laced around her own. The way in which her heart had suddenly started to race in response. He came to a halt when their faces were shadowed by the cool fronds above their heads, and her face was grave as he removed the wide-brimmed hat from her head and placed it on the ground.

'Saladin,' she said breathlessly as he framed her face in the palms of his hands.

His voice was quiet, but insistent. 'I'm going to kiss you.'

'But you said—'

'I said that we couldn't have sex in the palace, but we aren't in the palace now. Are we?'

She shook her head, wishing he'd made it sound a little less *anatomical*, wishing he'd responded with a few romantic words in what was a very romantic setting. But maybe she would have to make do with this—along with the realisation that at least he wasn't making mirages of his own. He wasn't wooing her with empty promises—he was telling it the way it was. And anyway by then he was kissing her and all her objections were forgotten as she opened her lips beneath his, because hadn't she been missing this, more than she would have ever thought possible?

His hands were hot and urgent as they raked through her hair and over her body, and her own were equally hungry as they explored the hardness of his magnificent physique. Impatiently, he slithered off her jodhpurs and shirt before peeling off his own silken robes, and Livvy gasped to discover that he was completely naked beneath.

'It is another characteristic we share with the Scots,'

he murmured as he spread the robes onto the sand to make a silky bed for them. 'Who I believe wear nothing beneath their kilts?'

But Livvy didn't answer because by then she felt as if she were in the middle of a dream—the most amazing dream of her life—as he laid her down. His eyes were unreadable as he moved over her and made his first thrust, and she gasped out his name as he entered her.

'It's good?'

She bit her lip and moaned. 'It's terrible.'

He laughed, but then his voice changed to a note she'd never heard before as he began to move inside her. 'Oh, Livvy.'

She didn't answer. There were things she'd like to have known and questions that maybe she should have asked. But she didn't. She couldn't. She was powerless to do anything other than respond to the feel of Saladin deep inside her. Because by then she had started to come, and there wasn't a thing she could do to stop it.

They rode back after night had fallen, even though Livvy had initially been fearful of crossing the dark desert on horseback. But Saladin had run the tip of his tongue along the edge of her lips, and she had felt him smile as he answered her question.

'I told you that I know this desert as well as my own body,' he said softly. 'Don't you realise that there's a great big celestial map overhead?'

That had been the point when she'd looked up at the stars that she'd been too distracted to notice before. The brightest stars she'd ever seen—silver bright against the indigo backdrop of the sky. And there was the moon rising in splendour—a bright, gleaming curve above the palm trees where they'd spent the past two hours making love. Livvy felt a lump rise in her throat. It was like a fairy tale, she thought.

Except that it wasn't a fairy tale. It was nothing but a brief interlude, and Saladin had already warned her that real life would soon intrude.

He had pulled her against him after they'd dressed and brushed away stray grains of sand from their clothing. He had tilted up her chin so that she was caught in the dark gleam of his eyes and, in that moment, she'd felt very close to falling in love with him.

But his black eyes had been empty. The barrier was back, she realised, with a sinking heart.

'You know that when we return—'

'I'm to act as though nothing's happened.'

His eyes glittered in the starlight. 'How did you know that's what I was going to say?'

'Wasn't it?'

He seemed surprised by her calm response. Was that why he provided an explanation she hadn't asked for?

'This cannot happen within the walls of the palace,' he said. 'It would place you at a disadvantage were people to find out that we were having some sort of relationship.'

'Sweet of you to be concerned about my reputation, Saladin. Are you sure it isn't your own you're worried about?'

'I don't think you understand,' he said, his voice growing cool. 'It will impede your work if there is any suggestion that we are intimate. I will not have any negative fallout because we've just had sex.'

'Because soon I'll be gone and it will all be forgotten?' she questioned lightly.

There was a pause.

'Precisely,' he said.

His honesty should have pleased her, but right then Livvy could have done without it. She wanted him to tell her soft things. Tender things. She wanted the man who had made love to her so beautifully, not this cold-eyed stranger who had taken his place and was swinging his powerful body up onto his horse. But it was a timely wake-up call, she reminded herself. Just because something *felt* like magic—didn't mean it was. She mustn't ask the impossible of a man who had not promised her anything he was incapable of delivering. She must approach this…*affair* like any other woman of her age—with enjoyment and enthusiasm and a lack of expectation. She mustn't start to care for him more than was wise, but take what was on offer and not look beyond that.

She could choose to stay or to run away—and it seemed that she had chosen to stay.

The palace gleamed like a citadel in the distance as they rode in silence towards it. They brought the horses in and handed them over to two grooms, before entering the marbled splendour of Saladin's home. A servant appeared and the sheikh spoke to him in rapid Jazratian, before walking her to the door of her suite.

The corridor was empty, and she could feel the whisper of the warm, scented air that drifted in from the nearby courtyard.

'Sleep well,' he said, and with the briefest of smiles he was gone, leaving her staring at the swish of his silken robes and wondering if she'd dreamed the whole thing.

Livvy went into her suite and slipped into a robe, once she'd showered the desert dust from her body. Afterwards, a female servant knocked on the door with a tray containing iced pomegranate juice, along with a plate of sweet cake and juicy segments of peeled fruit—but although Livvy drank, she had little appetite.

She went to stare out at the night sky, thinking about what lay ahead—knowing that the X-ray that Burkaan had undergone yesterday had shown the 'miracle' to have happened. The stallion was responding to the gift she was terrified she'd lost, and soon her skills would be redundant. No longer would she have those proud and hawklike features to gaze on during mealtimes. There would be no more passionate interludes like the one she had experienced in the desert today. She would become the ordinary person she'd been before the sheikh had awoken her. And he had awoken her in so many ways—she must never forget that. He had introduced her to sex and helped her overcome her reservations about getting on a horse. He had injected colour into a world that seemed to have become monochrome. He'd made her feel vital—and desirable. He'd made her feel that she *mattered*.

And the thought of never seeing him again was like having a knife rammed straight into the centre of her heart.

As she got into bed she found herself wondering why he hadn't married—why some beautiful royal bride hadn't been found for such an eligible man, despite his occasionally irascible nature. Perhaps he was contented with his single status. Perhaps the demands of running a country were enough to satisfy him, or he might just be one of those men who didn't want marriage. She knew he'd had countless liaisons with gorgeous models and actresses, but even so it was confusing. Surely such an autocratic man longed for an heir to carry on his bloodline? She found herself wondering why he had become so emotional the first time she'd seen the Faddi gate, but she hadn't dared bring up the subject again, and none of the servants spoke enough English for her to ask.

She got into bed and the excitement of the day must have caught up on her because very quickly she fell asleep. She thought she must be dreaming when she felt the bed dip and a rough, muscular thigh slide over hers. Heart pounding, she turned over and reached out to find a naked Saladin in bed beside her, his hard body washed silver by the moonlight flooding in from the unshuttered windows.

Her lips swollen with sleep, she stumbled out the words—half-afraid that speaking would break the spell and make him disappear. She wanted him so badly, and yet wasn't there a part of herself that despised her eagerness to have him touch her again? 'Saladin,' she whispered.

'The very same.'

'What are you doing here?'

'No ideas?' he mocked as he reached out to curve his hand over her breast. 'Such a shocking lack of imagination, Livvy.'

And he bent his head to kiss her.

She started to speak but he shook his head.

'Don't say a word,' he warned softly. 'I feel that you and I have done enough talking to last a lifetime.'

'A lifetime? Well, that isn't something that is ever going to be relevant in our case, is it?'

Saladin heard the unmistakable sadness behind her defiance and wondered if she was hoping for reassurance. Perhaps thinking that because he was about to start making love to her in the palace, there was now the potential for longevity. His mouth hardened. But there wasn't, and hypocrisy and raising false hope would be an insult to a woman like Livvy. He wouldn't whisper sweet words that meant nothing, or tantalise her with glimpses of a future that could never be theirs. Nor would he torture himself with the certainty that this was *wrong*, and that he was tarnishing the memory of all that was honest and true.

Ruthlessly he blocked the voice of duty, which had been a constant sound in his head since he'd been old enough to comprehend its meaning. And concentrated on touching Livvy instead, wondering how her petite body could make him almost incoherent with lust.

The ragged moan he gave as he eased himself inside her sounded unfamiliar. Just as the feeling in his heart was unfamiliar—the sense of growing and explosive joy. He said something fervent in his native tongue and her eyes flew open in question.

'What was that you said?'

'I said that you feel as tight as one of the drums played by the Karsuruum tribe.'

Her pupils dilated still farther as she bit back a smile. 'And is that…?' There was a sudden intake of breath as he thrust deeper inside her. 'Is that supposed to be a compliment?'

'Yes,' he ground out. 'It is.'

He wanted to come immediately but he forced himself to wait. He teased her to a fever pitch—until she was whispering his name in something that sounded like a plea. And still he held back—until he felt her convulsing around him, her soft cries muffled by the pressure of his kiss as he cried out his own ragged pleasure.

Even afterwards, he didn't want to let her go. He didn't move from his position inside her, his palms possessively cupping her buttocks to maintain that sweet contact. He could feel her breath warm against his neck and the pinpoint thrust of her nipples and he thought he could have stayed like that all night.

Eventually she spoke, her voice muffled against his neck.

'I thought we weren't going to do this.'

'This?'

'Making love in the palace. That's what you said.'

'Did I?'

'You know you did.'

'Maybe when I had the chance to think about it, it seemed a little short-sighted.' He stroked her hair. 'It suddenly occurred to me that I have much experience while you have barely any at all. It seemed to make sense that while you are here you should learn from me. We are harming no one provided that we keep our liaison discreet—and I am very good at being discreet, *habibi*.'

She lifted her head and her amber eyes were suddenly serious. 'You mean, I'm to be your pupil? Like a novice rider who comes to the stables and needs to be taught everything about horses?'

'In a way, yes. But you are more to me than that.'

'I am?'

'Indeed you are. You are also a temptation I find myself unable to resist.' He saw the hope that died in her eyes as he took her hand and moved it down between his legs. 'See how you arouse me so instantly, Livvy?'

She looked down. *'Oh,'* she said, but her voice trembled a little.

'Yes, *oh*. Now stroke me,' he instructed softly. 'Whisper the tips of your fingers up and down my length. Like that. Yes. Only lighter. Oh, yes. Just like that.'

He came suddenly, his seed spilling over her fingers, and then he stroked her moist flesh until she was writhing beneath him and he had to muffle the cries of her orgasm with the pressure of his kiss.

And only when her eyelids had grown heavy and her breathing had slowed into the steady rhythm of sleep did Saladin slide from her bed and, after pulling on his robes, slip silently from the room.

CHAPTER TWELVE

BE CAREFUL WHAT you wish for.

Livvy stared up at the ceiling, aware of the minutes that were ticking away, knowing that soon Saladin would rise from her bed and leave her room—like a ghost who had never been there.

She'd told herself that she would be contented with what she had. That making love with Saladin was sublime—and she should make the most of the sexual pleasure they enjoyed, night after night.

But it was not enough—and she didn't know why.

During the day he treated her with a polite neutrality. He ate his meals with her and chatted to her, and came to the stables to watch her working with Burkaan whenever he had space in his schedule. It was hard to believe that this very *formal* sheikh was the same man whose touch always brought her to life in bed, leaving her sighing with pleasure as she snuggled up to him. But once the pleasure had worn off she was increasingly aware that he always kept something back. That there was a darkness at his core that he wouldn't share, something hidden from her and the rest of the world.

It left her feeling incomplete. As if she was getting only half the man. She knew that what they had couldn't last—but she couldn't bear to leave Jazratan without having known her lover as completely as possible. Surely that wasn't too much to ask.

So why act like his tame puppet who just accepted whatever he was prepared to dole out? Surely sexual relationships allowed for all kinds of discovery, other than the purely physical?

She rolled over on the bed and ran her fingertips along the rough rasp of his jawline.

'Saladin?'

There was a pause. 'Mmm?'

'Can I ask you something?'

Beneath the rumpled sheet, Saladin stretched his legs, and as he did so his thigh brushed against the softness of hers. She really did have the most beautiful thighs, he thought as he yawned.

As usual, he had come to her bed once darkness had fallen, driven by a fierce sexual hunger that showed no sign of abating. He knew it was a risk to his reputation—and hers—to persist in his nightly seduction, but it was a risk he was prepared to take. Because he was beginning to realise that the qualities that made her such a consummate horse whisperer were the same qualities that made her such a superb lover. She was intuitive and curious—gentle yet strong. He'd thought that the innocence that had stayed with her until a relatively late stage might have made her cautious, or wary. But he had been wrong. There had been no variation on the act of love that Olivia Miller hadn't embraced with an enthusiasm and sensuality that easily matched his own.

He tried not to react as her fingertips made dancing little movements across his chest, but he could feel the renewed throb of desire at his groin. 'You can ask me anything you wish, *habibi*—although whether or not I choose to answer it is quite another matter.'

Seemingly undeterred, a single fingertip now made a journey upwards to drift along his chin—its progress slow as it scraped against the new growth there.

'Why have you never married?'

The question came out of the blue and hit him like a slap to the face. He stilled and moved away from her. Had he been too quick to commend her? Too eager to think the best of her—his perfect lover—when deep down all she wanted to do was to probe into matters that did not concern her?

'It never ceases to amaze me,' he breathed, 'how you can be in bed with a woman and all she wants to do is talk about other women.'

He felt her stiffen beside him.

'Are you trying to change the subject?'

'What do you think?'

She clicked on a small lamp and stared at him. 'I think you are.'

'Well, then. Take the hint. Don't ask.'

'You're not the only one who doesn't *do* hints.' She tucked a strand of hair behind her ear and kept her gaze fixed steadily on him. 'I'm not asking you because I'm angling for some kind of permanent role in your life. I know what my limitations are. I know this is just sex—'

'*Just* sex?' he echoed, the taunt too much to resist as he reached for her breast.

She pushed his hand away. 'I'm only asking because I'm curious,' she said doggedly. 'Your single status doesn't seem to sit comfortably with a man who adores his country, but who seems to care more about the bloodline of his horse than his own. And I can't work out why that is.'

'Maybe you're not supposed to.'

'But I want to.'

Saladin didn't speak for a moment. This was intrusion, unwanted and unwarranted—a question she had no right to ask. Yet something tugged at him to tell her, and he couldn't work out what that something was. Was it an instinct she possessed—the same instinct that made angry and injured horses respond to her, which perhaps she extended to humans?

He hesitated, feeling the momentary sway of his defences as she surveyed him with that air of quiet stillness and determination. Was this why Burkaan had let her pet him, why his viciousness and pain had been temporarily forgotten in her company—because she exuded an air of healing reassurance, despite her occasional spikiness? He told himself not to confide in her, because keeping his own counsel wasn't just a matter of privacy, it was one of power. The unique and lonely power of a monarch who must always stand apart from other men.

But suddenly the weight of his guilt and his own dark secret felt heavy—too heavy a burden to carry on his own, and for the first time in his life he found himself sharing it.

'Because I have already been married,' he said.

She was shocked; he could tell. For all her bravado in saying this was just about sex, it wasn't that simple. It never was. Not where women were concerned. They always had an agenda; they were conditioned by nature to do so. They always wanted to bond with a man, no matter how much they tried to deny it. He watched as she tried to cultivate just the right blend of nonchalant interest, but he could see that her eyes had darkened.

'Married?' she said unsteadily. 'I had no idea.'

'Why should you? It happened a long time ago, when I was very young—in the days before these wretched twenty-four-hour news channels existed. Those distant days when Jazratan was a country without the world looking over its shoulder.'

'And your…wife?'

He could hear the tentative quiver in her voice. What did she expect him to say—that Alya was locked up in a tower somewhere, or that she was just one of a number of wives he kept hidden away in a harem while he entertained his foreign lover?

'Is dead.'

She didn't respond at first. If she'd come out with some meaningless platitude he probably would have got out of bed and left without saying another word, because nothing angered him more than people trying to trivialise the past. Instead, she just waited—the same way he'd seen her wait when Burkaan angrily stamped his hooves in his box before letting her approach.

'I'm so sorry,' she said at last, her voice washing like cool, clear balm over his skin.

'Yes,' he said flatly.

'She…she had something to do with the Faddi gate and the rose garden, didn't she?' she asked tentatively.

He nodded, but it was a moment before he spoke. 'She was designing it to celebrate our first wedding anniversary, only she never got to see its completion. I had landscape designers finish it, strictly adhering to her plans, but…'

'But you never go in there, do you?' she said, into

the silence that followed his words. 'Nobody does. It's always empty.'

'That's right,' he agreed.

Perhaps it was the fact that she said nothing more that made Saladin start telling her the story, and once he had started the words seemed to come of their own accord—pouring from his lips in a dark torrent. Maybe because it was so long since he'd allowed himself to think about it that he'd almost been able to forget it had ever happened. Except that it had. Oh, it had. He felt remorse pierce at his heart like tiny shards of glass, and following remorse came the guilt—always the guilt.

'Alya was a princess from Shamrastan, and we were betrothed when we were both very young,' he began. 'Our fathers wanted there to be an alliance between two traditionally warring countries and for a new peace to settle on the region.'

'So it was—' she hesitated '—an arranged marriage?'

His eyes narrowed and he felt a familiar impatience begin to bubble up inside him. 'Such an idea is anathema to Western sensibilities, is that what you're thinking, Livvy?' he demanded. 'But such unions are based on much firmer ground than the unrealistic expectations of the romantic love. And it was no hardship to be married to a woman like Alya, for she was kind and wise and my people loved her. She was beautiful, too—like a flower in its first flush. And I let her die,' he finished, the words almost choking him. *'I let her die.'*

She tried to touch him but he shook his head and rolled away from her, turning to stare at the flicker of shadows on the walls—as if it were a betrayal to even look at her while he was speaking of Alya.

'What happened?' she said, from behind him.

He could hear the thunder of his heart as he dragged his mind back to that terrible morning—and, despite his having locked it away in the darkness, the memory seemed as vivid and as painful as ever. 'I had to leave at dawn,' he said heavily. 'For I was due to ride to Qurhah to negotiate with the sultan there, and I wanted to get away before the sun was too high.' He swallowed. 'I could have flown—or even driven—but I wanted to visit some of the nomadic tribes along the way and it is better to take a camel or a horse into these regions, for they are still suspicious of modern transport. I remember Alya waking up just before I left, because she always liked to say goodbye to me. She was screwing up her eyes against the morning light, but we had been awake for some of the night and I thought she was just tired.' His voice cracked. 'So when she complained that her head ached, I told her to go back to sleep and to see how she felt when the maid came to wake her for breakfast.'

'Go on,' she said.

He stared straight ahead. 'I remember she smiled at me and nodded, looking at me with all the trust in the world as I bent over to kiss her. She told me to take care in the desert. And that was the last time I saw her alive.' His words ground down to a painful halt, because even now they were hard to say. 'Because when her maid came to rouse her, she found Alya lying dead.'

'Dead?'

He heard the shock in her voice and he turned over to see that same shock reflected on her face. 'Yes, dead. Cold and lifeless—her beautiful eyes staring sightlessly at the ceiling. Struck down by a subarachnoid haemorrhage at the age of nineteen,' he said, his voice shaking with loss and rage and guilt. 'Lost to us all and let down by the one man who should have saved her.'

'Who?' she questioned. 'Who could have saved her?'

He shook his head incredulously. 'Why, me, of course!'

'And how could you have done that, Saladin? How could you have possibly saved her?'

He clenched his fists together, so that the knuckles turned bone white as they lay against the sheet. 'If I'd thought about *her*, instead of being wrapped up in my own ambition. If I hadn't been so full of triumph about the impending agreement with Qurhah, I might have realised the severity of the situation. I should have delayed my trip and called the doctor, who would have been there by the time she started to vomit copiously. I might have been able to help her, instead of being halfway across the desert when news reached me.'

'You don't know that,' protested Livvy. 'That's pure conjecture.'

'It's fact,' he snapped. 'I could have taken her to hospital.'

'And all the intervention in the world still might not have helped,' she said. 'But you'll never know— because that's just the way life is sometimes. We have to accept that we have no control over it. You have to cherish all the beautiful memories you had with Alya and let go of the bitterness and the blame.'

'Oh, really?' He gave a bitter laugh. 'So suddenly you're an expert on relationships, are you, my little virgin horse whisperer?'

She flinched a little as if she had only just registered the harshness of his words. 'It's always easier to diagnose someone else's problems rather than your own,' she said stiffly. 'And presumably you told me all this because deep down you wanted my opinion.'

He wasn't sure *why* he had told her. He wondered what had possessed him to open up and let her see his dark heart. Was it to warn her off the tenderness that had started to creep into their nightly lovemaking, even though he had warned her against such tenderness at the very beginning? And now he regretted his impetuous disclosure. He wanted to rewind the clock. To take back his words—and his secrets—so that she would become just another anonymous woman in his bed. So what inner demon prompted him to voice his next question? 'And what is your opinion?'

Livvy sucked in a deep breath, knowing that what she wanted to say required courage, and she wasn't sure she had enough within her—not in the face of so much sudden hostility. Yet wasn't it better to live your life courageously? To face facts instead of hiding away from them? Saladin might be a sheikh who ruled this wealthy land, but in this moment he needed the words of someone who wasn't prepared to be intimidated by his position and his power. Who would tell it the way it was—not the way he wanted to hear it. She drew in a deep breath. 'You once accused me of allowing the fact that I'd been jilted to affect my life negatively— and you were right. But haven't you done exactly the same with Alya?'

His eyes narrowed. 'What are you talking about?'

She licked her lips. 'Aren't you in danger of using your wife's death as an excuse to stop you from living properly, in the here and now? She died when you were newlyweds…' Her voice faltered for a moment as she met the angry glint in his black eyes, but she'd started now. She'd started and she had to finish. 'She was young and beautiful and time hadn't tarnished your perfect relationship in any way—'

'And you're saying it would have done?' he demanded hotly. 'That all relationships are doomed to end in failure or misery? Is that your Western view of marriage?'

'That's not what I'm saying at all. Nobody knows what would have happened,' she said fiercely. 'Because nobody ever does. All I know is that you seem to be letting your unnecessary guilt hold you back.'

'And what if I don't think it's *unnecessary*?' he bit out. 'What if I feel it is the burden I must carry until the end of my days?'

'Then, that's your choice, because nobody can change your mind for you, Saladin. Only you.' She hesitated because this bit was harder. 'Though maybe you prefer it this way. Your lovely wife was cut off in her prime and nobody else is ever going to be able to live up to her, are they? She was perfect in every way, and she always will be because you've put her on a pedestal. And no living woman can ever compare to Alya.'

His eyes narrowed with sudden perception and slowly he nodded his head. 'Ah,' he said tightly. 'Now I understand.'

She was alerted to the dark note that had entered his voice, and her head jerked back. 'Understand what?'

He gave a short laugh. 'Self-regard disguised as advice. Isn't that what you're doing?'

'I'm afraid you've lost me now. I was never very good at riddles.'

His mouth hardened into a cynical line. 'Oh, come on, Livvy. You must know what I'm saying. You seem to have settled very well here in Jazratan. Even my advisors have commented on how well you have fit in. Unobtrusive, modest, yet supremely hard-working—you put to shame our enduring stereotype of the Western woman as a hard-living party animal. Of course, nobody but us knows that our nights have become a feast of sensual delights. And that under cover of darkness you become someone quite different—a creature of pure pleasure.' His black eyes became hooded as he looked at her. 'Perhaps you are reluctant to walk away from all that you have found here. Did you look around at my palace and like what you saw—is that it? Did my pure little virgin see herself as the future queen of Jazratan?'

Livvy stiffened as his words shot through her like tiny arrows. He had taken her well-meaning advice and twisted it, making it sound as if she'd been seeking her own happy-ever-after when all she'd been doing was trying to comfort him. He made her sound grabbing and self-serving and *cheap*.

'You dare to accuse me of something so cynical?' she demanded, hot breath clogging her throat.

'Yes, I dare!' he challenged. 'What's the matter, Livvy—have I touched a raw nerve?'

Pushing her hair away from her hot face, she noticed the tremble of her fingers. 'Actually, I find your arrogance and your assumption breathtaking, if you must know, but at least it's made me see things more clearly.' She drew in a deep breath as she wriggled away from him. 'And I'm going back to England.'

He shook his head. 'No, not yet.'

'It wasn't a suggestion, Saladin—it was a statement. I'm going and there isn't a thing you can do to stop me.'

He reached for her then, his hand moving underneath the sheet to slide around her waist, and Livvy despaired of how instantly her body reacted when he touched her. She bit her lip as he began to stroke her and wished he could carry on stroking her like that until the end of time.

'Look, maybe I shouldn't have said those things.' A note of something like contrition entered his voice as he continued with his seductive caress. 'Maybe I was lashing out because I'd told you so much. More than I've ever told anyone else.'

'It doesn't matter what you say to me now. My mind is made up and I'm going,' she repeated, pushing away his hand. 'Because there's no reason for me to stay. You're obviously suspicious of my motives, and that is your prerogative. But I don't want to be hidden away like a dirty secret anymore. Do you understand?'

His face darkened. 'And what about Burkaan?'

Livvy felt her heart plummet as his reaction confirmed what she already knew—that his racehorse meant more to him than anything. Of course it did. When would she ever learn that she was one of those women who fell for the kind of men who would never love her back?

'Burkaan will be fine,' she said. 'He doesn't need me anymore—we both know that. He's got his appetite back and he's no longer vicious with the grooms. The X-ray results are conclusive.' She paused, suddenly realising how much she was going to miss the feisty black stallion. But not nearly as much as she was going to miss his judgemental master. 'The vet told me this morning how pleased he is with his progress—and he'll continue making good progress, as long as you take it slowly. So don't rush him. A month walking, followed by a month trotting. After that, you can try cantering.'

'Livvy—'

'I mean, obviously there's no guarantee he'll ever race again,' she rushed on, desperate to cut him off before he tried another of those appeals, which this time she might not be able to withstand. 'But you should certainly be able to put him out to stud at some point in the future. And now I think it's best if you leave. No. Please don't try to touch me again, Saladin. It will only complicate things. We both know that.'

She saw the incredulity that had narrowed his dark eyes and wondered if anyone had ever ordered him from their bed before, or tried to oppose his wishes. Probably not. But she needed to do this. She needed to put distance between them and she needed to find an inner strength. Because, despite her furious denial that she was hoping for some kind of future with him, wasn't there a part of her that was doing exactly that? A part that had grown closer to this complex and compelling man and wanted to grow closer still, if only he would let her. A part that badly wanted to love him, as she suspected he needed to be loved.

And she couldn't afford to think that way. Because falling for a desert sheikh who was still in love with his dead wife was asking for trouble.

He sat up in bed, the sheet falling away from him. 'You're really asking me to leave?' he demanded.

'I really am.' She forced a smile. 'Think of it as character-building.'

Saladin felt a fury and a frustration racing through his blood as he stared into her stubborn face. Who the *hell* did she think she was, trying to take control like this? She would leave his employment when *he* was good and ready and not a moment before. Yet she enjoyed taking control, didn't she? She had laid down her rules right from the start—not seeming to realise what kind of man she was dealing with—and had expected him meekly to accept them. Well, maybe it was time she realised that he'd had enough of *her* rules and *her* control.

Yes, he had enjoyed her time here—who wouldn't have done? She had entranced and pleased him on so many levels and cared so beautifully for his beloved stallion. But that was all pretty much academic. Because where could this relationship go? Absolutely nowhere—no matter how much he liked her. And wouldn't her infernal refusal to be sublimated by his power and position irritate him after a while?

'You want to go?' he snapped, getting out of bed and picking up his discarded robe. 'Then, go!'

He saw the brief look of alarm in her eyes that she couldn't quite hide.

'Right,' she said uncertainly.

'I'll arrange transport for you tomorrow. You can leave first thing.'

With a sinking feeling of dread, Livvy watched as he pulled the robe on over his naked body and jammed his headdress into place and then stormed across the room. He didn't slam the door behind him, though he looked as if he would have liked to have done.

And she was left in the empty room with the dread growing heavier inside her and all she could think was, what had she done?

CHAPTER THIRTEEN

IT WAS ICY cold back in England after the seductive warmth of the Jazratian sun. Livvy returned to a stack of unopened mail, a cat determined to ignore her and the realisation that she didn't have a clue what she wanted to do with the rest of her life—except that deep down she knew it no longer involved making beds and cooking breakfasts.

She had left Jazratan with a heavy heart—without even a final kiss from Saladin—knowing she had only herself to blame. She had kicked him out of her bed and told him she was returning to England and he had retaliated by angrily telling her to go ahead. Had she really expected the proud sheikh to mount some sort of campaign to get her to change her mind? She kept telling herself that he'd been offering sex, not security or love. And anyone with half a brain could see it was better to get out now, while her heart was still intact.

Unless it was already too late. Hadn't her heart felt crushed when she'd left Jazratan on Saladin's private jet? When, earlier that same morning, she'd crept along to the stables to rub her cheek against Burkaan's thick mane and the stallion had stamped one of his hooves—almost as if he had shared her grief at parting and had known the reason why salty tears were flowing down her face.

Saladin had been courteous when she'd been granted an audience to say a formal farewell to him—in the throne room, where he was surrounded by his powerful advisors and bodyguards. Had he correctly interpreted the silent plea in her eyes that had asked for a moment alone with him—and simply chosen to ignore it? Or had his mind already been on other things?

Either way, he had given her nothing but a brief handshake and a flicker of a smile, accompanied by a few words of thanks—which had only added to her feelings of misery as one of his staff had presented her with a cheque. And she felt as if she'd sold *herself* somewhere along the way.

But she *hadn't*, she told herself fiercely. She wasn't a victim—not anymore. She'd been sexually awoken by a man who had turned out to be an amazing lover. She had been persuaded back onto a horse and had realised just how much she loved riding, and she must be grateful to him for that. If she had learned anything it was that you couldn't let yourself live in the past and be dominated by it. Not like Saladin and the beautiful young wife he was unable to forget. And that was the irony of it all—that he didn't follow the same advice he'd so eagerly given her. He could dish it out, but he couldn't take it.

And if she now believed herself to be in love with him, well—she would have to wait for it to pass.

At least Stella—her part-time help—had disposed of the Christmas tree, and the decorations had been returned to the loft. The snow was all melted and the holiday was nothing but a distant memory when Livvy arrived home. All that remained were a few stray mistletoe berries, which had rolled underneath a bureau in the hall and somehow escaped being swept up.

Livvy wrote an email to Alison Clark and her friends saying what a shame it was they'd had to cancel their visit and expressing her hope that they'd enjoyed their Christmas in the London hotel. Unenthusiastically, she looked down at the blank pages of her diary. Could she really face trying to drum up more business for the year ahead? To wipe out most of her summer by clearing up after people, when she'd been doing it for so long? All to maintain a house that just didn't feel the same any more. Her inherited home now seemed like nothing but a pile of bricks and mortar, not something she was tied to by blood. She found herself looking around the rooms with a critical eye. It was just a too-big house that needed redecoration and a family to bring it alive, not some aging spinster who rattled around in the rooms.

'So what was it like?' questioned Stella as they were cleaning one of the bedrooms a few days after Livvy had returned from Jazratan.

Livvy gave the bedspread another tug. 'What, specifically?'

Stella shrugged her generous shoulders. 'You know. Living in the desert.'

Livvy puffed out her cheeks and sighed as she straightened up. 'It was…different.' She hesitated, trying to be objective. Trying to forget the man who was the very heart of the place. The man who made her own heart ache whenever she thought about him. 'It was lovely, actually. Really lovely. The palace itself is unbelievable—and so are the gardens. There's a kind of beauty in all that heat and starkness, and the stars are the brightest I've ever seen.'

'And didn't they feed you?' asked Stella critically. 'You've lost weight.'

'Of course they did. It's just that—' Livvy gave a wan smile '—I didn't seem to have a lot of appetite. It was very...hot.'

No, not because it was hot. Because she'd been so obsessed with Saladin that she'd barely been able to think about anything else. She still couldn't and it was driving her crazy. There was her future to decide, and she was busy obsessing about a man with black eyes and a hard body, who had taken her to those bright stars and back.

And she would never see him again.

'Well, there's a pipe leaking in the red bathroom. Better get it seen to before it brings the roof down,' added Stella, with her customary love of domestic drama.

The plumbing problems distracted her for a while, and then Livvy burned off a load of frustration by picking up the leaves that had gathered in a sodden heap by the front door.

It was after lunch, when Peppa had finally decided to forgive Livvy for going away and had started winding her furry body around her legs at every opportunity, that the telephone rang. Stella bustled along the corridor to answer it, her eyes nearly popping out of her head as she listened to the voice at the other end.

'It's him,' she mouthed.

'Who?' Livvy mimed back.

'The *sheikh*.'

With a tight smile Livvy took the phone and carried

it through to her little study, trying to control her suddenly unsteady breathing as she gazed out at the garden where water was dripping from the bare branches of the trees and the grass resembled a sea of mud. As a reflection of the way she felt, it was perfect. *You need to stay calm*, she told herself. *You need to be strong.* For all she knew, Saladin might just be phoning for a chat to check she'd got home safely. This was probably normal for people who'd briefly been lovers. He might even be wanting to ask her advice about Burkaan. Yes, that was probably it. But she could do nothing about the wild thunder of her heart.

'Hello?' she said.

'Livvy?'

'Yes, it's me.' But as the silken caress of his voice washed over her, some of her forced calm began to trickle away and Livvy realised that she wasn't any good at playing games, or pretending to be friends. Not when she wanted to blurt out how much she missed him. Not when she wanted to feel his arms around her, holding her very tight. She heard the ping of an email entering her inbox. 'What can I do for you, Saladin?'

'Which isn't the friendliest greeting I've ever heard,' he observed drily.

'But I thought that's the way you wanted it. Formal and polite. I thought we'd concluded our business together. I thought we'd said everything that needed to be said. That was certainly the impression I got when I left.' She paused. 'Which makes me wonder why you're ringing?'

At the other end of the line, Saladin stared out at the sky. Why *was* he ringing? It was a question he hadn't wanted to confront and one that instinctively he shied away from answering. He wondered if he could persuade her to return to Jazratan by telling her that his horse was pining for her, which was true.

He suspected not. He sensed that financial inducements would no longer sway her, no matter how much more generous he made his offer. Just as he sensed that pride wouldn't allow her to accept something that could only ever be second best. He sighed. He realised that, for all her newly awoken sexual liberation, Livvy Miller remained a fiercely traditional woman who would not look kindly on the sort of relationship he usually offered his lovers. And the pain in his heart was very real, wasn't it? The question was how far he was prepared to go to be with her.

'I need to talk to you.'

'Talk away. I'm not stopping you.'

'I'm not having this conversation over the phone.'

'And I'm not offering you an alternative,' she answered coolly. 'What do you want, Saladin?'

'To see you.'

'Sorry. No can do.'

'Livvy,' he growled. 'I'm serious.'

'And so am I,' she said. 'You said some pretty tough things to me that last night. You were suspicious and hostile and accused me of all kinds of devious motivations—'

'For which I apologised.'

Only because you had to, thought Livvy. *Only because you had to.* 'Yes, you did. So surely we've said everything that needs to be said. It was a fantastic affair and I'm sorry it had to end that way—but the point is that it had to end some time.' She cleared her throat. 'How's Burkaan?'

'He's fine. Livvy—'

'Look, I've got to go,' she said desperately as she heard another email ping into her inbox. 'Someone's trying to contact me. Goodbye, Saladin, and...take care of yourself.'

She cut the call before she had the chance to change her mind, or to be lulled by a seductive voice into doing something that would only bring her pain.

After Livvy had put the phone down, she sat down at her desk. She wasn't going to make a fuss about it, she thought, even though her heart was crashing painfully against her ribcage, because the pain would go. It might take time, but it would definitely go. She would answer her emails and carry on as normal and rejoice that she'd had the strength to resist him. Her hand hovered over the mouse and her whole body stiffened as she clicked on the first email and began to read...

An hour must have passed before she realised that she hadn't moved and was sitting in total darkness and that Peppa was mewing plaintively by her feet and Stella had long gone. She ought to do something. She ought to feed the cat and...

And what?

Sit there for the rest of the evening thinking about what a *devious bastard* Saladin really was?

Her eyes skated down the rest of the emails. There were two tentative booking enquiries, plus one of those round-robin jokes that one of her school friends always insisted on sending and that she didn't find remotely funny. And a 'Singles Nite' being offered by the local pub. She screwed her eyes up as she looked at the date. Tonight's date.

Print out this voucher for free entry to the Five Bells 'Singles Nite'. Music, karaoke and so much more!

A sudden new resolution flooded through her as, impetuously, she pressed the print button, fed Peppa and then went upstairs to get ready.

She told herself that she was going to stop acting like a startled hermit and get out there and put everything Saladin had taught her into practice. No longer was she going to live like a nun. There was no reason why she couldn't have other relationships—in the same way that there was no reason she couldn't have another career. Defiantly, she applied more make-up than usual, fished out a sparkly top to wear with her jeans and piled her hair into an elaborate topknot so that it wouldn't get wrecked by the wind on the way out to the car.

When she drew up outside the pub, she almost turned around to go home because music was blaring out at a deafening pitch. Inside it was crowded, but at least the noise became less loud when a woman started swaying around on a small stage, tunelessly singing about her intention to survive. There were a few people Livvy recognised from the village, but not well enough to sit with—so she bought herself a tomato juice, told herself that she would drink it up and then go. *Baby steps*, she thought. *Baby steps. You've come out on your own and it hasn't killed you. And although it's pretty dire—next time might be better.*

She found a corner seat and sat there smiling as if her life depended on it. She tapped her feet to the music and tried to look as if she was having a good time and eventually a man about her age wandered over, with a half-drunk pint in his hand. He had thick hair and crinkly blue eyes and he asked if he might join her.

But before she could answer, a silky and authoritative answer came from behind him.

'I'm afraid not.'

Livvy didn't need to hear the deeply accented voice to know it was Saladin. She should have realised he'd walked in because the pub had suddenly gone quiet and even the woman doing the karaoke had stopped singing as she stared at him incredulously. But who could blame her? Powerful olive-skinned sheikhs wearing dark cashmere weren't exactly at a premium around these parts.

Livvy put her tomato juice down on the table with shaking fingers as the conversation all around them took on a sudden roar of interest.

'How did you get here?' she demanded, her heart starting to race. 'You're in Jazratan.'

'Obviously, I'm not. I flew in today and came here by helicopter,' he answered.

Her face remained unwelcoming, but she kept it that way. *Why* had he followed her and *why* was he here on *her* territory, when she was just starting out on a long journey to forget him? 'What do you want?'

'There are three things I want,' he said grimly. 'And the first involves having a conversation, which won't be possible with all this noise going on. So can we go outside, Livvy? Please?'

She opened her mouth to say that she didn't want to go anywhere with him, except that was a blatant lie and she suspected he would see right through it. And he was asking in the kind of voice she'd never heard him use before. But even so…

'It's raining,' she objected.

'You can sit in my car.'

'No, Saladin,' she said fiercely. 'You can sit in *my* car, and you can have precisely ten minutes.'

He didn't look overjoyed at the suggestion but he didn't object as he followed her into the blustery and rainy night. Outside an enormous limousine was parked with a burly bodyguard standing beside it, but Livvy marched straight past it towards her own little car, feeling inordinately pleased at the almost helpless shrug that Saladin directed at the guard.

But the moment he removed a sock from the passenger seat—what was *that* doing there?—and got in beside her, she regretted her decision. Because the limousine would have been better than this. It was bigger, for a start, and there wouldn't be this awful sense of the man she most wanted to touch being within touching range…and being completely off limits.

'So what's the second thing?' she questioned, in a voice that sounded miraculously calm. 'How did you know I was here?'

'I had someone watching your house who was instructed to follow you,' he said unapologetically. 'When I arrived, they told me you were still here. It was at that point that a ball of fur hurled itself out of nowhere and decided to start attacking my ankles.' He grimaced. 'Your cat doesn't like me.'

'Probably not. I got her from the rescue centre.' She shot him a defiant look. 'She was ill-treated by a man as a kitten and she's never forgotten it.'

There were plenty of parallels between the woman and the cat, Saladin thought. Livvy had been ill-treated by a man, too, and it had made her wary. And he hadn't exactly done a lot to try to repair her damaged image of the opposite sex, had he? He had treated her as if she was disposable. As if she could be replaced. And wasn't it time he addressed that?

He looked at her in the dim light of the scruffy little car, his gaze taking in an unremarkable raincoat and the fiery hair, which the wind had whipped into untidy strands that were falling around her face. She was wearing too much make-up. He'd never seen her in such bright lipstick before and it didn't suit her, and yet he couldn't ever remember feeling such a raw and urgent sense of desire as he did right now. Was that because she had shown the strength of character to reject him—to walk away from the half-hearted relationship he'd given her? Because by doing that she had earned his respect as well as making him realise that they were equals.

'I miss you, Livvy,' he said softly.

He saw a flicker of surprise in the depths of her eyes before her face resumed that stony expression.

'The *sex*, do you mean?' she questioned sharply. 'Surely you can get that with someone else?'

'Of course I miss the sex,' he bit out. 'And I don't want to *get it* with anyone else. There are other things I miss, too. Talking, for one.'

'I'm sure there are many people who would be only too happy to talk to you, Saladin. People who would hang on to your every word.'

'But that's the whole point. I don't want someone hanging on my every word. I want someone who will give back as good as she gets.'

'*I want* doesn't always get,' she responded, infuriatingly.

'I miss seeing the magic you worked on my horse,' he continued resolutely. *And on me*, he thought. *And on me*. 'I want you to come back to Jazratan with me.'

It was as if that single sentence had changed something. As if she'd removed the stony mask from her freckly face so that he could see the sudden glitter of anger in her amber eyes. 'And how far are you prepared to go to get what you want?' she demanded. 'How many people are you prepared to manipulate just so that Saladin Al Mektala can get his own way?'

His eyes narrowed. 'Excuse me?'

Angrily, she punched her fist on the steering wheel. 'I've just had an email from Alison Clark, who you probably don't even remember. She was the woman who was due to spend Christmas here with her polo friends, before you decided you needed me in Jazratan. The group who miraculously decided not to come at the last minute and to spend their Christmas in a fancy London hotel instead. A trip *financed by you*, as I've just discovered in an email written by the grateful Alison. So what did you do, Saladin—have your *people* track down these guests of mine and offer them something they couldn't resist, just so that you could whisk me away from Derbyshire?'

He met her accusing stare and gave a heavy sigh. 'They seemed perfectly happy with the arrangement.'

'I'm sure they were. All-expenses-paid trips to five-star hotels don't exactly grow on trees! But it was a sneaky thing to do and it was *manipulative*,' she accused. 'It was just you snapping your powerful fingers in order to get your own way, as usual.'

'Or a creative way of getting you to come to Jazratan, because already I was completely intrigued by you?' he retorted.

'You just wanted me to fix your horse!'

'Yes,' he admitted, in a voice that suddenly sounded close to breaking. 'And in the process, you somehow managed to fix me. You found a space in my heart that I didn't even realise was vacant. And you've filled it, Livvy. You've filled it completely.'

'Saladin,' she said shakily. 'Don't—'

'I must.' He reached out then and took one of the hands that was gripping the steering wheel and pressed it between the sensuous warmth of his leather gloves. 'Every word you spoke was true,' he said quietly. 'I was using my early marriage and my guilt as a block to forming a meaningful relationship with someone else. But I've realised that what I have with you transcends anything I have known before. That we have a truly adult relationship and we are equals. Yes, equals,' he affirmed as he saw her open her mouth to object. 'I'm not talking about the trappings of my kingdom, or the division of wealth. We are equals in the ways that matter. Or at least, I hope we are because I love you, Livvy Miller. And I'm hoping that you love me, too.'

His words were so unexpected that for a moment Livvy thought she must have imagined them and she tried to ignore the excited leap of her heart—shaking her head with a defiance that suddenly seemed as necessary to her as breathing. 'You're still in love with your dead wife,' she said.

'I will always love Alya,' he said simply. 'But what I had with her was so different from what I had with you. She was very young and in complete thrall to me. I was her king, not her equal. And you were right. She was taken at a time when she was perfect, and that's what her memory became to me. My single status became a kind of homage to her, as well as being a safety net behind which I could hide. When I spoke so disparagingly about romantic love, it was because I didn't believe in it, but now I do. I didn't think it could ever happen to me, but now it has.' His black eyes burned into her steadily. 'There are many different types of love, but believe me when I tell you that my heart is yours, Livvy. That I have found my equal in you. And that even though your stubbornness and refusal to do exactly as I say sometimes frustrates the hell out of me, I love you passionately and truly and steadfastly.'

And then Livvy *did* believe him, because it was too big an admission for a man like Saladin to make unless he really meant it. The passion that blazed from his eyes was genuine and the conviction that deepened his voice crept over her skin like a warm glow, but still something held her back.

'And I love you, too,' she said. 'Very, very much. But I'm not sure if I'm going to be able to be the kind of lover you need.'

'And what kind of lover is that?' he asked gently.

'I've pretty much decided that I'm going to sell up and use the money you gave me to start my own stables,' she said. 'I don't have a clue where that might be. And you'll want a mistress, I suppose. I thought I wouldn't be able to tolerate that kind of relationship, but now that I've seen you again I'm beginning to have second thoughts.' She shrugged her shoulders. 'But when I start imagining the reality—I don't know if I can see myself being set up in some kind of luxury apartment so that you can come and visit.'

He frowned. 'So that I can come and visit?' he repeated, in a perplexed voice.

'Whenever you're in the country. Isn't this how these things usually work?'

His answering laugh sounded like the low roar of a lion as he gathered her into his arms and tilted her chin very tenderly with the tip of his thumb. 'I was hoping you might return with me to Jazratan, as my queen. I was hoping you would marry me.'

Her cheeks burned as she met his eyes, remembering the accusations he had thrown at her.

'I know,' he said ruefully. 'But maybe I accused you of being matrimonially ambitious because already it was playing on *my* mind. Because I've realised there is no alternative scenario that I am prepared to tolerate.' He drew in a deep breath. 'So will you, Livvy? Will you marry me?'

And suddenly Livvy had run out of reasons to keep telling herself that this couldn't possibly be happening and that there must be a catch somewhere. Because there wasn't—and when it boiled down to it, Saladin's past didn't matter and neither did hers. Because right then he was just a man with so much love in his eyes, which matched the great big feeling that was swelling up inside her heart and making it feel as if it were about to burst with joy.

'Yes, Saladin,' she said, putting her arms around his neck and holding on to him as if she would never let him go. 'I'll marry you tomorrow if you want me to.'

EPILOGUE

THEY MARRIED TWICE. Once in the quiet stone chapel where Livvy's own mother and father had been wed, and once in a lavish ceremony in Jazratan, attended by world leaders and dignitaries—as well as a sizeable hunk of the horse-racing fraternity.

At first it felt weird for Livvy to see her photo plastered all over the papers, with Saladin holding tightly on to her hand, her filmy veil held in place by a crown of diamonds and rubies and her golden dress gleaming like the coat of a palomino horse.

She settled happily in the country she had quickly grown to love, determined to learn to speak the Jazratian language fluently and to see Burkaan winning the famous Oman Cup. And if people ever asked her how she had managed to adapt so comfortably from owning a B & B in Derbyshire to being the queen of Jazratan, she was able to answer quite honestly. She told them that the grandness of her husband's palace never intimidated her, because wherever Saladin was felt like home. He travelled less than before, and everywhere he went he took Livvy with him—for he was eager to show off his new bride to the world.

Livvy started working in the stables, whenever her

royal role permitted it, and quickly earned herself a reputation among the staff of being gifted and reliable and never pulling rank. She liked to go riding with Saladin when the sun had started to sink low and the sting of the heat had left the day. Sometimes they rode to 'their' oasis, where they made love beneath the shade of the palm trees.

After a gentle campaign she persuaded Saladin to have a ceremony declaring the beautiful rose gardens officially open—and invited Alya's parents, along with her two brothers and their wives, as guests of honour. It wasn't the easiest of meetings—not at first, for there were tears in Alya's mother's eyes as she tied a small posy of flowers to one of the intricate silver coils on the Faddi gates. And yes, Livvy saw tears in Saladin's eyes, too. But Alya's parents were persuaded to bring their grandsons to play there at any time, and afterwards they all sat beneath the shade of a tree, drinking jasmine tea and laughing as the two sturdy little boys toddled around among the scented bowers.

It would be several years before Burkaan would triumph in the Oman Cup and many more before he was put out to stud, and a new foal—the image of his father—was born. But Peppa the cat grew grudgingly to accept Saladin's presence in her mistress's life and found herself happily living in the royal palace, enjoying the way that the staff fussed around her. There was a bit of a shock when it was discovered that she had sneaked out and mated with a stray tom who had been seen lurking around the back of the stables—but she proved herself an exemplary mother of five kittens.

Wightwick Manor was never sold. Saladin decided that the house should be kept as a base for them whenever they wanted to escape the desert heat to enjoy a spell in the English countryside.

'And it is important that any children we may have will grow up knowing and loving their mother's inheritance, because your roots are just as important as mine, *habibi*,' he said, tenderly stroking Livvy's head, which was currently resting upon his bare chest. 'Don't you agree?'

Livvy wriggled a little, changing her position so that she could prop herself up onto her elbow and stare into the enticing gleam of her husband's black eyes. She trailed a thoughtful path over his chest with her finger, circling lightly over the hard muscle and bone covered by all that silken skin, and it thrilled her to feel him shiver. She liked making him shiver.

'I agree absolutely,' she said as he began to brush his hand against her inner thigh and now it was *her* turn to shiver. 'And in fact, that brings me very nicely to some news I have for you.'

His hand stilled and she knew he was holding his breath—just as she'd held hers when she'd surreptitiously done the test that morning. They hadn't actively been *trying*, but she knew that Saladin longed for a child of his own, and she'd been wanting to have his baby since the moment he'd slid that wedding ring on her finger.

'I'm pregnant,' she whispered. 'I'm going to have a baby.'

And suddenly he was laughing and kissing her and telling her how much he loved her, all at the same time. And it was only after a little time had passed that she noticed that his hand was no longer making its tantalising journey up her thigh.

She caught hold of his fingers and put them right back where they had started from. 'Don't stop,' she said.

'Is it safe?'

She danced her lips in front of his. 'Perfectly safe.'

And that was how she made him feel, Saladin realised dazedly. Safe. As if he'd found something he hadn't even realised he'd been looking for. As if she were his harbour, his refuge and his joy. As if the whole world suddenly made sense. He cradled her head in the palms of his hands and kissed her as deeply as he knew how. And thanked the heavens for that snowy Christmas night, which had given him the greatest gift of all.

The gift of love.

* * * * *

COMING SOON!

We really hope you enjoyed reading this book.
If you're looking for more romance
be sure to head to the shops when
new books are available on

Thursday 19th December

To see which titles are coming soon, please visit
millsandboon.co.uk/nextmonth

MILLS & BOON

LET'S TALK

Romance

For exclusive extracts, competitions and special offers, find us online:

f MillsandBoon

X @MillsandBoon

◯ @MillsandBoonUK

♩ @MillsandBoonUK

Get in touch on 01413 063 232

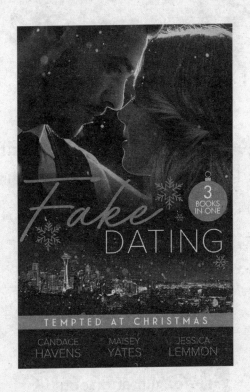

Epilogue

Dale Anderson, ex-correctional officer, now has a lifetime job as a prisoner. He lives on the other side of the bars that he once guarded. From prison, he continues to involve himself in murder investigations throughout the country. Anderson even claimed to have information about each case, many of which occurred after he was imprisoned.

His convincing nature brought detectives from all over the United States to visit him in Menard State Prison, only to leave angry when they realized that they had been a victim of a cruel game. Anderson was able to get the United States Secret Service to visit him, when he alleged that he had information on an assassination plot to kill President George Bush.

Six months into his life sentence, Anderson was attacked by an inmate and lost the sight in his left eye. He was relocated to Joiliet State Prison in the northern part of the State.

* * *

Linda Anderson started a new life, a new job, and remarried.

John Lanman met a woman through his church and later married her.

Carolyn Tuft visited Rodney Woidtke in prison in June of 1990, and wrote an article telling the drifter's side of the story.

Brian Trentman continued his struggle to win Woidtke a new trial.

Dee Heil resigned from the Illinois State Police to work full-time in his private detective agency. Heil has worked with Trentman on Woidtke's behalf.

Dennis Hatch ran for State's Attorney in Washington County, Illinois, and won the election.

Alva Busch started his sixteenth year with the Illinois State Police.